DARK DEEDS OF OLD LONDON

Edwin J. Brett
"Boys of England" Office
173 Fleet Street
E.C.

DARK DEEDS
OF OLD LONDON.

Complete in Two Volumes.

BEAUTIFULLY ILLUSTRATED.

VOL. I.

LONDON:
"BOYS OF ENGLAND" OFFICE, 173, FLEET STREET, E.C.,
AND ALL BOOKSELLERS,

"CLIFFORD PUSHED THROUGH THE SOLDIERS AND CONFRONTED COLONEL BLOOD."

"A TALL, BLACK FIGURE STOOD WITHIN TWO PACES OF HIM."

DARK DEEDS OF OLD LONDON.

Book the First—The Plague.

CHAPTER I.

IS OF THE ARRIVAL AT PENTONVILLE—OF THE WONDERFUL DISCOVERY—AND OF THE DARK DEED COMMITTED BY "THE MAN IN BLACK."

A DARK and boisterous night towards the close of the year 1664.

A really terrible night; the wind blowing considerably more than half a gale from the east.

A wild, howling wind which bent the tops of enormous trees like reeds—a wind which fiercely shook the tradesmen's signs, and sent many of them flying into the streets.

It was close upon the hour of ten, and scarcely a shop remained open.

Hardly a soul was to be seen abroad.

Shortly after the hour of ten had struck, a person suddenly turned into old Clerkenwell, and made his way towards Pentonville.

He was a man somewhat above the middle height, and, though his frame was concealed by a long and heavy cloak, nine persons out of ten would have been inclined to take him for a military man.

His cloak was richly and heavily furred, he was booted and spurred, wore a broad beaver hat, ornamented with a black feather, fastened by a gold and diamond buckle, and his face was entirely concealed by a mask.

Reaching Penton Fields, he struck across them, turned sharp off to the right, and hurried through a turning called Vargo Street.

This street was of the narrowest description, and it was crowded with houses four and five storeys in height, these dwellings—all wooden—leaning forward to such an extent that from some of the windows hands could be shaken across the street.

In about the centre of the street the masked traveller paused and looked around him.

"Ah! here we have it," he muttered, as he crossed the street and paused before a door, on which was engraved, in neat letters, the following—

DOCTOR JONAS JARDELL.

Beside the plate was a large brass handle.

The traveller pulled this, and a bell rang within the house.

In a few moments the door opened and an elderly woman, carrying a lamp, appeared.

"Your business?" she asked, in sharp, surly tones.

"Is with Doctor Jardell," was the reply.

"He is engaged."

"Indeed! With whom?"

"That is *his* business."

"No doubt. But look you, my good woman, take this ring to him, and tell him that the owner waits. And, here, see this gold piece, that is for yourself."

"I thank you," grunted the woman; "and I will take the ring to Master Jardell. Though," she muttered, as she turned away, "I know you well enough, though you have a mask upon your *pretty* face."

Presently the woman returned.

"Doctor Jardell will see you," she said, "and at once."

Closing the door, she added—
"Follow me, sir."

She led the way along the narrow passage, and ushered the traveller into a room at the further end.

It was a small apartment, used as a surgery, and filled with articles generally to be found in such a place.

The top shelf of all—a shelf which ran right round the room—was crowded with grinning skulls.

Beneath each was a label bearing a name and date.

In various parts of the room, crowded together, were a number of skeletons, perfect specimens, of which the doctor was mightily proud.

In a recess, near the huge fireplace, was Dr. Jardell's "masterpiece."

It was a skeleton, dressed in Court costume, and wearing a long furred cloak.

A long sword, with a jewelled hilt, depended from its side, it wore a black curled wig, surmounted with a broad beaver hat, in which was a black feather, and the grinning skull was concealed by a black mask.

The hollow sockets were filled with a pair of fierce-looking eyes, which could be moved in any direction by the touching of a spring.

Before this remarkable object the traveller paused.

He looked very closely at it, examining in the most attentive manner every point.

Then he turned to a mirror at the back and surveyed himself.

"By thunder!" he muttered. "I'm hanged if the likeness isn't remarkable! Ho, ho!"

"Well, well, what are you laughing at?" enquired a weak, squeaky voice.

And the speaker slowly entered the apartment.

He was a somewhat short, attenuated man, of about sixty years of age.

The top of his head was perfectly bald, but from the sides hung long, almost straight locks of snowy whiteness.

His face was clean shaven.

He was attired in a black mantle, wore black hose, and French shoes ornamented with Sheffield buckles.

About his neck hung a gold chain, and to the end of this—which was placed within his bosom—was attached a small case of surgical instruments—articles which he always carried about with him, and even wore in his bed, in case of being suddenly called up in the night.

This individual was Doctor Jonas Jardell, one of the most extraordinary men, and one of the most skilful physicians practising during the reign of Charles the Second.

"What are you laughing at?" repeated the doctor.

"One moment—one moment," was the reply, as the traveller held out his hand; "let me first say how glad I am to see you, doctor. I hope you are very well?"

"I am always well."

"Lucky man! I wish I could say the same."

"Probably you could if you would give up the drink and other evils in which you and your associates are in the habit of——"

"Hold — hold, I entreat! hold! Doctor, I congratulate you—most emphatically congratulate you. That figure yonder is unquestionably——"

Here the traveller broke off and indulged in a loud burst of laughter.

"I am glad you like it," replied Doctor Jardell, gravely; "but I almost regret having made the bargain with you."

"What? Regret the bargain? Why?"

"A lot of trouble may be the result of the perfecting of this model."

"Bah!" replied the traveller, in contemptuous tones. "No trouble whatever will ensue. And, besides, supposing any trouble *did* occur, would you have to suffer for it? No! Now, doctor, when will you send it me?"

"Whenever you like. I suppose, however, you do not require it to-night?"

"No."

"And now as to money matters?"

"To be sure; let us speak of money matters. The fact is, Doctor Jardell, I am particularly in want of money."

"Indeed!" replied the doctor, dryly, and his tones showed that he was very far from being pleased.

"Such is the case," said the traveller. "I don't know how it is, but lately my luck at the tables has completely changed. However, I have no doubt I shall be able to command the sum you require in the course of a few days."

"Good. Well, until then, of course, the model can remain. It is not in my way."

"You mean, doctor, that you will not let me have it until the money is paid?"

"Precisely," replied the doctor, coolly. "And I am sure you cannot blame me."

"Looking at my position," said the traveller, angrily, and so fiercely did his eyes glitter through the holes in the mask, that they now bore a most striking resemblance to those stuck in the grinning skull in the recess, "you decline to trust me?"

"Am I any exception to——"

"No matter," interrupted the traveller, impatiently, "you decline to trust me?"

"Suppose I said yes? In that case you would, no doubt, threaten me."

And as he asked this the doctor smiled.

"I can not only threaten, but I can also act," said the traveller, "and that you know; but, let me see, what sum remains?"

"Five hundred guineas."

"Ah! five hundred guineas. Eight hundred was the sum agreed upon, and of that I have already paid three hundred, so I fancy that after all the model is more mine than yours."

"How?"

"Well, what is the value of these bones, this cloak, this costume?" asked the traveller, indicating the various articles on the skeleton.

"When you have estimated the value of those articles," said the doctor, in severe tones, "perhaps you will estimate the value of the months of study and attention which I have given to bring that model to perfection. But you have not yet examined it. Look here!"

The doctor approached the model and touched it with his foot in a certain place.

Lo! the eyes opened to their fullest extent, and looked straight into those of the traveller.

"Wonderful!" he muttered.

"That is not all," said the doctor. "Observe!"

He now stood on one side, and again touched the figure.

An exclamation of astonishment escaped the traveller's lips as the skeleton moved its head, looked round, and then slowly walked forth.

Erect it came, without making the slightest sound.

It placed its feet upon the floor just like a human being, and walked towards the door, at which the doctor checked it.

"Ha!" cried the traveller, starting. "This is wonderful."

"You are right. See, I hold a wire. But it is so slight that it can scarcely be seen."

"With what particular part does the wire——"

"No matter. When the money is paid, the model and the secrets connected with it are yours."

"Good! Doctor, I again congratulate you. You have surpassed yourself. I don't believe there is another man in London—nay, in all England—who could do as you have done."

Doctor Jardell bowed.

"Then you will *not* trust me, doctor?"

"It is against my rules."

"*You* cannot be in want of money."

"What makes you say that?"

"Well, you never spend any, and yet, with your extensive practice—the most *valuable portion* of which was introduced by *me*—you must be receiving a very large income."

"I will not deny either that I have a large and valuable practice, or that I am receiving a large income. Yet I *am* in want of money."

"You astonish me."

"Perhaps so; but, nevertheless, I am in want of money. Had you brought with you the remainder of the sum agreed upon, the money would have enabled me to overcome a serious difficulty."

"I trust the difficulty is not one in which your daughter is concerned?"

This question was asked in an apparently off-hand fashion, but the doctor directed a swift, inquiring glance into the other's eyes, and replied—

"Whether my daughter is concerned in the difficulty or not is a matter of no moment to you. Some——"

"I should have thought," said the stranger, quickly—"and you will pardon me giving you the hint—that one of your wealthier patients would willingly advance you any sum you might name."

Doctor Jardell slowly shook his head.

"No," he replied, "I am not of your opinion. But supposing that one of my wealthier patients felt inclined to advance me any money, he would naturally enquire for what purpose it was required, and if I told him the purpose he would most likely laugh in my face."

"I don't know that. People are well acquainted with the fact that you are a man much given to scientific research."

"Perhaps if I told you for what purpose I require the money *you* would laugh."

The traveller shook his head.

"Well," whispered the doctor, advancing, and laying his hand on the traveller's arm, "I have been for months past engaged in the discovery of a cure for a terrible disease."

"A terrible disease?" faltered the traveller.

"Ay, it has not yet reached these shores, but it will come. My friend and fellow worker, the astrologer, Zodcaster, prophesied it months and months ago. He even fixed the time, and that time is rapidly approaching. It is coming, my friend," continued the doctor, solemnly, "and when it comes, heaven help us all."

"Doctor," cried the traveller, starting, "*you mean the plague!*"

"I do—the death plague. But you know nothing of it. As for myself, I have a secret about it."

"I know more than you think for of the plague, Doctor Jardell. But let us not talk of it."

"You know where it is at present raging in all its fury?"

"I do — at Hamburgh. But the astrologer and you, doctor, will find yourselves mistaken. We have sharp eyes on this side the water. Precautions have——"

"Despite every precaution," interrupted the doctor, "*the plague will come and death will follow!*"

"And you have discovered a cure?"

"I have not yet completely discovered the secret; but I feel confident that I am close upon it."

"I hope you will be entirely successful, for, in case of any danger, I will not fail to come to you."

At this moment a knock was heard upon the door.

"Enter," said the doctor.

The elderly woman appeared on the threshold.

"A gentleman desires to see you," croaked the woman.

"His name?"

"He gave none, but said that you would find his name written on this slip of paper."

The doctor took the paper, looked at what was written upon it, and then said—

"Ah, 'tis highly important. Show the gentleman to my private room; and," he whispered in the old woman's ear, "don't say who is with me, for I suppose you are aware of the name of my *patient?*"

The woman nodded, grinned, and retired, and in a few seconds she was heard passing up the passage and the staircase with the new arrival.

Turning to the traveller, the doctor said—

"You must now excuse me, for it is important that I should see the gentleman, a patient, who has just arrived. As soon as ever you get the money the model is yours; or, in fact, if you can get but a fair proportion of the sum due 'tis yours."

"Good. I will pay you another visit in the course of a day or two. Adieu, doctor."

Doctor Jardell walked to the door in order to open it for the traveller.

Now the doctor, after reading the name on the slip of paper, had placed it on a sideboard.

As the traveller passed it he bent rapidly over, and instantly made out the name.

"Once more adieu," said Doctor Jardell. "Jane, the door."

As the old woman came forward, the doctor passed rapidly up the stairs.

Swiftly the traveller traversed the passage, but at the door he paused.

Taking more money from his pocket, he pressed it into the woman's hand.

"Listen to me," he said, speaking in a rapid whisper, "here are two golden pieces for you.—do me a favour."

"What is it?"

"Show me into a room next to the one in which the doctor and his so-called patient are."

The old woman looked at him in amazement.

Then she said—

" Take back your gold pieces; what you ask is impossible. Besides, what can this visitor, who is only a patient, have to do with you, or you with him ?"

" The patient, as you call him," cried the other, fiercely, " is Sir Christopher Cullum, one of the king's private secretaries."

" How know you——"

" No matter how I know. Show me up."

" No."

" Look you, Jane Jeevers, by whose assistance did your beautiful son leave the jail of Newgate on the last occasion, eh ?"

The old woman turned as pale as death, and trembled so violently that the lamp she held seemed in imminent danger of falling to the floor.

Seeing the impression he had made, the traveller continued, in threatening tones—

" It would be far more easy to put a man into Newgate than bring him forth."

" Ah, you coward !" hissed the old woman, " you coward ! But if you want to know what is passing between those two, go up yourself. If you are discovered it may be death to you."

" I will chance what will follow."

*   *   *   *

The doctor's private room was not the least comfortable apartment in his house.

It, however, contained many hundreds of things not usually found in a person's private room—doctors not excepted.

Doctor Jardell, apparently, had a mania for collecting skulls, for there was a shelf right round the room completely crammed with these ghastly objects.

Entering the apartment, which was illumined by a lamp, the doctor shook hands with his fresh visitor.

He was a tall, finely-made man of about thirty, beautifully, though not grandly attired, as befitted his rank.

Sir Christopher was admitted to be one of the handsomest men at Court.

Though possessed of a fine face, which, though generally wearing a light smile, was capable of expressing the most intense passion, his principal attraction was, unquestionably, his hair and eyes.

The former hung gracefully down his shoulders in long ringlets, black as jet.

His eyes were of the same hue as his hair, and were extremely large and piercing.

" Glad to see you, Sir Christophei," said the doctor, as he warmly shook the knight by the hand. " And how fares it with you ?"

" But ill in one respect," replied Sir Christopher. " I can get no money from his majesty, who, as you know, is always swearing that he does not possess a crown in the whole world. But at last, doctor, I have found the key to wealth untold."

" I am very pleased to hear it, Sir Christopher, very pleased," replied Doctor Jardell, lightly passing one hand over the other. " I thought that before now you would have come to tell me that you had at last discovered the mystery of the Lincoln's Inn."

" That is now my errand," exclaimed Sir Christopher.

His tones were so exultant that no doubt as to his sincerity remained in the doctor's mind.

" You will let me know all about it ?" said Jardell.

" Certainly."

" You have hitherto been so full of mystery in reference to the matter that——"

" I will now explain it all," interrupted Sir Christopher, with a bright smile; " but before I commence, do you think——"

He paused abruptly, looking anxiously into the doctor's face.

" I know what you were about to say," said Doctor Jardell. " You were about to ask whether it would not be as well that Clarissa heard the story ?"

" Exactly."

" I will fetch her."

" Thanks—a thousand thanks, doctor," replied Sir Christopher.

The doctor left the room.

In a few moments he returned, leading a young girl by the hand.

This was Clarissa, his only child.

She was about nineteen, rather above the medium height, not too slender, but as graceful as a fawn.

She was the happy possessor of a face which was absolutely perfection as regards beauty.

As the reader has, no doubt, already guessed, Sir Christopher and Clarissa were lovers.

Sir Christopher had been paying court to this obscure beauty (for obscure she was at present) for many months.

They would have been married long ago had it not been for the fact that the want of money effectually checked the consummation of Sir Christopher's desires.

Having greeted each other in the most affectionate manner, Sir Christopher led Clarissa to a seat.

Doctor Jardell seated himself by his daughter's side, while Sir Christopher commenced his narrative.

"It is now many years ago," he said, "since I first made the acquaintance of David Driffield—I daresay it is twenty years ago. Then, as you know, doctor, he was known as the old miser of Lincoln's Inn. His history, I believe, was a strange and most terrible one. Like other people, I heard a little of it, but it was so little, that there was no connecting it. At one period of his life Master Driffield had been a successful lawyer, but he gave up his practice on the death of his wife. It was in his capacity of lawyer that my father made his acquaintance.

"I have heard my father say that he proved himself a very upright, honest man of business, and that he was a perfect gentleman.

"However, something terrible occurred in his family. Driffield disappeared for some time, but again he appeared at his chambers, and never more did he quit them.

"No one but myself ever visited the old man—indeed, he never would see anyone but me.

"That he was enormously rich was well known, but his riches were not in houses or lands, but in cash.

"Yet, where he banked, if he did bank at all, no one knew. He never once spoke of his wealth. And he had the appearance of a person wanting the bare necessities of life.

"Hence he got the name of the 'Miser of Lincoln's Inn.'"

"But," interrupted Clarissa, "you have not said whereabouts these chambers are situated."

"Your father knows them well enough, and no doubt, you yourself have fre-quently passed them. The chambers are in the old gateway which leads to Lincoln's Inn, and on one side of which is Chancery Lane.

"The chambers are situated on the right hand side, and are approached by a narrow flight of stairs. They are at the very top of the house.

"Five years ago the old man was taken seriously ill. For many, many long weeks I attended him, and I alone, for he would have no one else even enter his rooms. At last he became unconscious. I summoned a doctor. It was too late. Hardly had the doctor reached his bed-side, ere he breathed his last.

"Now the doctor found in his right hand a piece of paper, on which was written—

"'*To Christopher Cullum I leave all I am possessed of in this world. God send it does him more good than it has——*

"'DAVID DRIFFIELD.'

"'You are a lucky man,' the doctor said to me, 'for it is very well known that Master Driffield is possessed of enormous wealth. I am your witness that that paper was found in his hand on his deathbed.'

"Master Driffield was buried without a friend to mourn him but myself, and then I proceeded to examine his papers, of which there was an enormous quantity.

"Patiently for days and days did I wade through them, but to no purpose. Among all that vast mass of manuscripts I found not the slightest mention made of money matters.

"I gave up the search in despair.

"But I could not rest. Again and again I returned to the attack. Useless—useless task! I discovered nothing.

"Then I thought that perhaps there might be some secret door or trap in the apartments.

"I searched in vain for such a thing. At last I called on the bankers and the goldsmiths. All of them knew that Master Driffield had been a rich man, but only one had had any transactions with this strange, gloomy, and secret old man, and that was the celebrated Richard Reiner, of Eastcheap. At one time he said he held a very large amount of Master Driffield's money, but it was suddenly withdrawn, and since then he had never even set eyes upon the man.

"Well, the search proving fruitless, I had the chambers bolted and barred up. As I continued to pay the rent of the place, no one interfered with this arrangement. At last, nearly five years after the old man's death, I once more paid the place a visit. On this occasion I took with me my valet, a man named Lucas.

"I should think that Providence must have had some hand in causing me to take that man. Lucas was stricken with curiosity to look at the old man's bedstead, a strange-looking affair, the top of which reached almost to the ceiling.

"While my back was turned he got to the top, and, lo! he saw a long wooden box. He brought it to me, and I opened it. It contained a paper, on which was written—

"'All above, Chris—all above—every penny! Ha, ha! they tried to rob me, many and many a time; but it was of no use. Chris, just beneath the right fire-dog, you will see a steel button. Press that, and you will see what will follow. No secret doors, Chris. No, no. And all that great piece of work was *my* work. Aye, in the dead of the night I worked for *years*, and the grand secret was finished at last.'

"That was what the paper contained. You see I know every word by heart. It was evident that the old man intended to tell me where this box was before he died. So now——"

"And the button?" asked the doctor, who was now much excited. "Have you not tried it?"

"My dear sir," said Sir Christopher, with a smile, "you, who have so often laughed at me, should be present when the button is touched. At present I do not know myself what secret the touching of this button will reveal. All is ready, doctor, and my man, Lucas, awaits us at the chambers. It certainly is a wild night, but——"

"Were it a thousand times more wild," cried the doctor, "I would accompany you. But first let us partake of supper. At midnight I have a most important call to make; but after that I am at your service."

"Very well," replied Sir Christopher, who, though anxious to get to Lincoln's Inn, was just as anxious for a quiet *tête-a-tête* with the lovely Clarissa. "My man, Lucas, than whom a more faithful servant never lived, is quite used to waiting an hour or two after the time given, and therefore he will not be anxious."

* * * *

It was just at this moment that the masked traveller crept cautiously down the stairs.

Jane Jeevers, lamp in hand, was most anxiously awaiting his descent.

Rapidly she advanced and opened the street door.

"If you would not be seen," she whispered, "keep in the shadow of the houses until you reach the end of the street."

"I shall not forget; and mark, not one word, as you value your son's liberty."

"I shall say nothing; but beware! My son, in one of his many adventures, may lose his life. In that case I have nothing further to fear from *you*; then, *beware!*"

The traveller passed out, while the old woman, softly closing the door, descended to the kitchen.

Meantime the traveller walked rapidly on, returning as he had come.

There was no break in the storm; on the contrary, the wind had increased in force, and every now and then a shower of frozen rain rendered the streets more dangerous than ever.

At a tremendous pace the traveller went on, keeping well in the shadow of the houses.

Occasionally a low chuckle left his lips.

"Ha!" he muttered, "this is the most fruitful journey I ever made in my life. I have heard all that story long, long ago, and I have not the slightest doubt but that somewhere in those old chambers, old David Driffield hoarded away his great wealth. Sir Christopher Cullum—how I hate and detest the man!—has always been poor—at least, if he hasn't been poor, he has never been rich. Supposing he suddenly came into the possession of a huge fortune, what would be the result? First, his Most Gracious Majesty Charles would borrow *half*, giving him all sorts of wild promises as security; next, he would be created a peer of the realm, and then—ah, let me not think of it.

"There's that old woman," he mused, "and she alone knows that I overheard what passed between the doctor and Sir Christopher. If I succeed in the plan which has entered my head, she will know the thief to be myself. Still she dare not open her lips. She *would* speak, I know, but that her son bars the way, and I can buy the son, soul and body, for a bag of gold."

Turning into Gray's Inn Lane, the traveller made his way to the nearest hostelry, where he called for a jorum of wine.

This was served to him.

The host himself brought it in.

"Look you, my friend," said the traveller, "do you happen to have a couple of spare horses in your stables?"

"Oh, yes, I have half-a-dozen."

"Then pray saddle and bridle two."

"Excuse me, sir," answered the host, "but as you are a stranger to me, I cannot let you have a couple, or even one, of my horses, without you leave in my hands either their value, or something equivalent to the——"

The traveller interrupted him impatiently.

Leaning forward he seemed about to whisper something in his ear.

But apparently he thought better of it.

Drinking his wine, he said—

"I was about to tell you who I am, and——"

"You might have done so, your worship," interrupted the host, calmly and firmly, "but I should not have believed you."

"What?"

"I say that I should not have believed you. There is nothing like *hard cash.* In these days all sorts of knaves strut about and say they are this and that."

The traveller made no reply.

Taking his hat from his head he removed the gold and diamond buckle, and placed it in the hands of the host.

"There," he said, "you are such a clever man that you can have little difficulty in ascertaining whether that is or is not genuine. Take it as security, and at once get the horses ready."

"I will."

"And here; have you a couple of large leathern bags?"

"Leathern bags—leathern bags?" repeated the host, directing his eyes upon the well-smoked ceiling, as if he expected to see the desired articles suddenly drop through. "Well, I have a couple of heavy leathern corn bags."

"They will do admirably. Fasten them to one of the saddles. Now, my man, hurry up."

The host made his way to the stables, and proceeded to saddle and bridle the horses.

Having speedily accomplished this task, he took the animals to the front.

"Good!" said the traveller, as he sprang into one of the saddles. "I shall return the animals at my convenience."

"When do you expect, your worship——"

"No more need be said," interrupted the traveller, haughtily. "You have the security, I have the horses."

So saying, he dashed off along the dark road.

"Ha!" thought the landlord, gazing after his singular customer until he and the horses had disappeared in the darkness, "and I wonder who he thinks *he* is? Ho, ho! Two horses and two bags. I wonder what he wants the bags for? Strange times these are, and strange, dark deeds are done in this old city."

At a rapid rate the traveller rode across Holborn and turned down Chancery Lane.

Almost opposite the grand old gateway, which is still standing, stood a large building known as "Potter's Bar."

It was in the occupation of a locksmith of the name of Prichard Preston.

The house was of the most peculiar construction imaginable.

There was an entrance right and left, and in the centre was a huge arch, which led to a series of workshops at the back, for Prichard Preston was a man with a very large connection.

Apparently well acquainted with this archway, the traveller rode beneath it, and sprang from the saddle.

All around was extremely dark, and not a living soul was anywhere to be seen.

Satisfied that he was not observed, the traveller took the bags from the saddle, and placed them beneath his cloak, which he drew closer about his person, and pulled his hat further over his shaggy brows.

Then leaving the animals just where they were, he strode off.

But when he considered that he was not seen, he was most grievously mistaken.

He *was* seen, and his appearance and stealthy movements made such an impression on the person who had seen him that he was followed.

When within the old gateway of Lincoln's Inn, the traveller again paused, looked carefully on all sides of him, then producing a taper and a tinder box, he struck a light.

Having found the staircase he required, he at once extinguished the taper.

"Lights," he muttered, "are the very worst things to attract attention; and besides, I flatter myself that I am fairly well acquainted with these rotten old staircases."

Slowly up went the traveller, treading as lightly as possible, so as to avoid making the least noise—slowly, cautiously onwards, until the very top of the house was reached.

The staircases and landings were very dark, but when the top was reached, his eyes caught the faint glimmer of a light through a crack in a door almost immediately opposite him.

Over that door, though the traveller could not see it, was the name—

DAVID DRIFFIELD,

Attorney-at-Law.

Even in the broad daylight this name was scarcely distinguishable, for the devouring hand of Time had wrought havoc with the once beautifully-formed letters, and they were now well nigh obliterated.

Before giving to our expectant readers the details of the frightful tragedy which this night was consummated within those gloomy old chambers, before revealing the wondrous secret which David Driffield had kept locked within his own breast for so many years, we must enter in advance of the murderous traveller.

The chambers consisted of three rooms, one opening into the other.

The two first rooms were crammed with all sorts of the most extraordinary objects that a man could collect in a number of years.

How David Driffield ever came in possession of these things no one knew.

Passing through the two rooms, the bedroom was reached.

This was (or *had* been) unquestionably the most comfortable room of the three; but now there was a peculiar mouldy smell, which invariably emanates from a room which has been shut up and forsaken for any great length of time.

The strangest article in this bedroom was the bedstead, which was of unpolished oak, very massive, ornamented with beautifully-engraved brass work, and shaded with what at one time had been valuable Indian curtains.

The top of it was within a few inches of the ceiling.

Seated at a small table near the bedstead was a man.

He was a strongly-built fellow—an individual whose appearance denoted a great deal of coolness and determination.

This was Lucas, Sir Christopher Cullum's valet, a man in whom he trusted implicitly, for he knew him as an honest and a brave man.

He wore a pair of high boots, a fine warm cloak—Sir Christopher's gift—and in his belt was stuck a pistol, while at his side hung a long, straight, heavy sword.

It was quite evident that Lucas was on this night very uneasy.

Occasionally he rose, took the small lamp, and went through the rooms and on to the landing.

He was no believer in ghosts; but one might conjure up almost anything in a dark, gloomy, deserted old place such as this.

"Midnight has long since struck," muttered Lucas. "I hope nothing has happened to him. He might just as well have allowed me to go with him. Lord! what a place this is! How uncanny that old bedstead looks, with its clothes so nicely arranged.

"Why, one would almost fancy that if they waited a few moments the old boy would suddenly—but, pooh! Ha, ha! I must not think of such things. Heavens! how slow the time passes. Now, if there was such a thing as a bottle of sack of some sort, the time would pass quicker. If he doesn't soon come I shall no longer be able to resist the temptation to touch that button.

"Well, once *more* I'll have a look round and see if all's safe."

Rising, he slowly passed through the rooms.

The door leading to the landing was reached.

He opened it, and instantaneously a gasping cry of astonishment escaped his lips.

A tall, black figure stood within two paces of him, a pair of fierce eyes were fixed upon his face, and the rays of the lamp he held were reflected a thousand times in the glittering blade that black, mysterious figure held within its right hand.

For the space of a few seconds neither moved, and thus, perfectly motionless, they presented a most extraordinary picture.

In those few seconds Lucas recovered his presence of mind.

Suddenly drawing himself erect, he whipped his blade from its sheath.

"Who are you?" he asked. "And what seek ye here?"

"Put down that blade," was the reply, in haughty tones.

"Put down the blade, eh?" replied Lucas, never budging an inch from the spot whereon he stood. "Put down the blade? If you do not instantly tell me who you are, and for what purpose you are here, I will put this blade into your heart."

"Fool!"

"*Ha!*" replied Lucas. "You will find that——"

"Put down that blade, lacquey!" roared the traveller, as he took a step forward.

Lucas's reply was to cross swords with the stranger.

The act apparently somewhat astonished the traveller.

"Well," he growled, "since you decline to do my bidding—curse you!—I am obliged to compel you, so your death be on your own head."

Instantly the weapons went to work, and in such good earnest that the mouldy old chambers fairly rang again.

But though Lucas's bravery was unquestionable, he was certainly no match for this tall, masked, mysterious stranger, who in a few seconds had compelled him to retreat into the room.

There Lucas managed to put down the lamp.

"This wretch," he thought, "evidently has got to know the secret of what belongs only to my master, and he is here for murder and robbery. He is, by the look of him, a person of some consequence; but he is, at this moment, a common thief, and therefore I am entitled to put a ball through his brain."

Watching his opportunity, Lucas snatched his pistol from his belt, pointed it full at the traveller's face, and pulled the trigger.

The flint flashed, but that was all—the weapon had missed fire.

At the same instant, the traveller, throwing back his cloak, took a pistol from his belt, and presented it at Lucas, who, ducking his head, sprang upon the traveller, knocked up his arm, then seizing him by the throat, endeavoured to drag him to the ground.

So fierce was his grip that a yell of agony escaped the traveller.

He dropped both his weapons, and, with a fearful oath, gripped Lucas by the throat with both hands.

Thus, for the space of a few seconds, they fought.

Backwards and forwards they went, overturning everything which stood in their way, until at last the apartment presented the appearance of having been partially wrecked.

In the course of his career Lucas had taken part in many and many a terrible fight, but never before had he fought with such ferocity as on this occasion.

Presently the traveller forced Lucas back against the post beside the door leading to the next room.

In endeavouring to loosen himself, Lucas slipped, and in an instant was on the floor, the traveller on top of him.

But he never let go his hold.

With all his strength he endeavoured to throw the traveller off him.

He might have succeeded in his object, but, suddenly, the traveller, with a wild, savage yell, said—

"Now I have you! *Now!*"

Lucas looked; he saw a flashing blade raised on high. Frantically he attempted to stay the descending arm. He checked it, certainly, but only for a moment, for the traveller's knee was pressing so heavily on him that he could scarcely breathe. A few violent struggles and a long dagger was plunged into the neck of the faithful valet, and so deep that he was actually pinned to the floor.

The fearful blow killed him almost instantaneously.

Exhausted and bleeding in many places, the traveller rose to his feet.

"That was the longest fight I ever had," he gasped; "and by the thunder of Job! it looked shaky for me several times. Had that pistol gone off, I should no doubt have been lying in his place—an ounce of lead in my head! Hem! I never thought that Sir Chris-topher's servant, or anybody else's servant, was possessed of so much bull-dog pluck.

"Ah! and how hard he tried to get this mask off. He would have succeeded in that too, had the spring at the back given way. By the Virgin! I would give something for a small tumbler of the most fiery brandy ever distilled at this——But let me not delay. The button—the steel button, and then the treasure. The right firedog, eh!"

Taking the lamp he entered the bedroom, this being the only apartment containing firedogs.

CHAPTER II.

OF HOW THE MASKED TRAVELLER TOUCHED THE STEEL BUTTON—OF THE RESULT— AND OF HOW HE WAS CONFRONTED BY CLIFFORD HANSARD.

"HA!" muttered the masked man, as he set the lamp down, and critically surveyed the apartment, "and so this is the bedroom of the miser, old David Driffield. By the dragon of Naples! it is certain that the old man would never have gained a medal for cleanliness. But now for it, for by the shade of Satan! I am burning to learn the secret of this room."

Approaching the firedogs, he lifted the right one from its position.

A small steel button attached to a rod which was sunk into the hearth was revealed.

He took up the left firedog.

There was no button beneath that.

He placed his foot on the button, and slowly pressed it.

A loud and startling crash rang out.

It sounded like the falling of a tremendous weight of iron.

Moreover, it appeared to the traveller as if the apartment trembled and shook violently.

So startled was the traveller, that he jumped back, uttering as he did so a cry of surprise.

For some few seconds, he stood alternately looking at the fireplace, then at the bedstead and into the dark corners of the room.

At last a low laugh escaped his lips, and once again he stepped to the button and placed his foot upon it.

He, of course, fully expected to hear the extraordinary noise repeated.

But no! No sound was heard for some few seconds.

Presently, the traveller's foot being still on the button, a curious noise was heard; louder and louder it became, until it bore a most striking resemblance to the horrible noise made by the winding of an ungreased windlass.

It was evident that the pressure on the button had set some machinery in motion.

At first the noise appeared to proceed from beneath his feet, but gradually it worked round the room and seemed to travel overhead.

The excitement of the traveller was now greater than ever.

Suddenly another loud crack rang out. The traveller instantly turned his head, and was just in time to see the ceiling oscillate violently. Then it began to fall at the further end, but the action was so slow as to be barely perceptible.

Down it came, and at last it was lowered to a depth of several feet.

The traveller was about to take his foot off the button—indeed he had taken some of the pressure off—when he saw to his alarm the ceiling began to rise.

So again he placed the pressure on, and lower, and yet lower went the ceiling, until at last it stopped, making a noise as if locking itself.

The traveller took his foot off the button, seized the lamp, and rushed to the aperture.

He now saw that the inner part of this mysterious ceiling had pieces of wood across it, placed like a ladder, while beside it was a piece of thick rope.

Seizing the latter, the traveller was quickly up this extraordinary flap, and he found himself beneath the roof of the house.

To the right and left was the machinery used in the construction of this ingenious receptacle for treasure; but it was dreadfully rusty, this proving that it had not been used for many years.

And all this was the work of an old man—the work of many years.

But it was not the complicated series of bolts, bars, wheels, and chains which attracted the attention of the masked traveller.

No.

He was feasting his eyes on the row of shelves which were filled with small bags—bags of gold !

Each was carefully and boldly marked with the amount.

The traveller, trembling violently with excitement, held the lamp against them, and read the marks.

Every bag contained the very same amount—namely, five hundred guineas.

And there must have been five hundred of them !

A quarter of a million of money, and, therefore, an enormous fortune.

It was out of all question that the traveller could carry away a twentieth part of the amount.

"By the blessed Virgin !" he gasped, as he ran his eyes over the vast treasure. "No wonder that the goldsmiths have complained of the scarcity of gold pieces. Great heavens ! if I am here much longer, I may be caught by Sir Christopher Cullum and the doctor. Ha ! I have it. There must be vaults attached to this house—perhaps vaults which are never used. I will at once descend."

Down he went, and, descending the stairs with all speed, he reached the vaults.

There were several, and, judging from their appearance, they were never used.

Pushing the door of one open he

entered—his entry being followed by a rush of monstrous rats.

He found the vault partially filled with old timber, stones, and the like.

"The very place," he muttered, "here, right at the back, will I place the bags, and anon I will fetch them away. The rats can only gnaw the canvas, and I will come prepared for that."

Ascending the stairs again, and clambering into the loft, he commenced to throw down the bags.

This being done, he filled the two leathern bags, carried them down, and emptied them in the vault.

Again and again did he do this.

Eventually he had carried all the bags, with the exception of a dozen which he placed in the two large bags to take away, to the vault.

Then once more placing his foot on the button, the ceiling resumed its former position, and it did not bear the least indication of having been tampered with.

The traveller then tied the mouths of the two bags together, flung them over his shoulders, and descended the stairs.

He was about to cross the threshold of the door when a voice cried out—

"Hold, on your life !"

"Ah !" muttered the traveller, "I am caught. But, by the Virgin, I will cut my way through them if need be. Who says hold ?" he asked, as he drew his sword.

Further forward he went, and made out a tall, active-looking figure before him.

But only one.

"I say hold !" was the reply. "I have a question or two to ask you."

"Oh, indeed ! And pray who are you ?"

"As to my name, that's of little importance to you. You——"

"Why, if I mistake not, you are an apprentice ?"

"You have made no mistake. But what are you doing in this house, and at this hour ? And what is the meaning of the noise——"

"What noise, eh ?—what noise ? But stand aside, curse you ! Depart. How dare you attempt to bar a gentleman's way ?"

"Gentleman !" sneered the apprentice, for such he was. "Your proceedings for some time have not been very gentlemanly."

"Ah! you intend to insult me, you grinning cub, do you? Out of it! Out of it, or I'll cut you down!"

And his sword's point was placed threateningly against the breast of the apprentice.

The young fellow, however, moved not.

"Gentlemen," he said, "do not generally commit murder at a moment's notice. Look you, Master Masker. I have had my suspicions as to your movements ever since you placed your horses beneath 'Potter's Bar.'"

"You followed me, rascal?"

"Ay! I followed you, because I felt sure that you were a villain."

With a cry of rage, the traveller let the bags fall from his shoulder, and springing forward, he caught the apprentice by the throat, receiving, as he did so, however, a tremendous blow on the face from a short but heavy club the apprentice carried.

"Scoundrel, I will have your life!" yelled the traveller.

"Robber!" returned the apprentice, emphatically. "Robber! By Heaven, I will hold you until assistance arrives and this house is searched, to see what deed you have done."

"Let go your hold! Loose me, curse you, let go your hold, I say!"

"No!" replied the sturdy apprentice, who had seized the traveller's sword arm in such a manner that he could not raise the weapon. "I will hold you, I say, while I have strength and life."

Now thoroughly alarmed lest assistance should arrive, the traveller dragged the apprentice hither and thither, fiercely endeavouring to shake off his vice-like grip.

At last the entrance to the gateway was reached.

Here the traveller suddenly remembered his pistol.

Snatching it from his belt, he took hold of the muzzle and dealt the apprentice such fearful blows with it, that the brave young fellow was at last compelled to let go his hold.

The traveller then without the least hesitation cocked the weapon, levelled it at the apprentice, and fired.

At that moment the brave apprentice, though his face was bleeding freely, was rushing upon the traveller with upraised club.

The ball struck him, but though he dropped his club, he did not fall.

Springing upon the traveller, and with such impetuosity that the villain was almost knocked off his feet, he made a snatch at the mask, and tore it from the traveller's face.

"Ah!" he cried, "I know you. I know you—villain! Cowardly wretch, I know you!—*you are Colonel Blood!*"

"Ay," was the savage reply; "and you are Clifford Hansard, and I have punished you."

The apprentice, now weak, and suffering intense agony, staggered back, while the traveller, again raising his heavy pistol, dealt him another blow, and this time with such effect that it stretched the youth full length on the stones.

As he fell loud cries were heard from within the inn, and the colonel—for the notorious Colonel Blood it indeed was—saw lights rapidly advancing.

To pause he knew meant arrest.

Darting upon the bags, he flung them across his shoulder, and hurried through the archway.

Barely had he gone through, when an old man, partially dressed, and carrying a flaming link over his head, hurried up.

He was followed by a number of men and women, all of whom had been thrown into a state of terror by the shouts and the shot they had heard.

The light at once fell upon the prostrate body of the apprentice, and its rays were reflected in a pool of blood beside it.

"Murder!" shouted the old man. "Murder has been done!"

And "murder" was echoed from the throats of all present, and with such earnestness, that the cries were heard all over the neighbourhood.

In a few minutes the place was besieged by a tremendous crowd of citizens of both sexes, all eager to gaze upon the body of the murdered person.

Such was the scene which met the eyes of Sir Christopher Cullum and the doctor, who came up a few minutes after the old man had discovered the apprentice.

"Murder, say you?" asked the doctor

in horror-stricken tones. "Murder here in a public roadway, eh?"

"Make way, my friends," cried Sir Christopher. "Make way, this gentleman is a doctor, and will examine this unlucky person. Make way."

"Ay, ay," said the old man, "make way—make way."

The doctor pushed his way through the crowd, and knelt beside the apprentice.

He did not want to look twice to see what a terrible struggle had taken place.

Taking a kerchief from his pocket, he wiped the blood from the face.

The features were now distinctly seen.

Simultaneously a number of voices shouted—

"Clifford Hansard, Clifford Hansard."

"And who is Clifford Hansard?" asked the doctor.

"Why," replied the old man, "he is one of Pritchard Preston's apprentices."

"Pritchard Preston?"

"Ay, the locksmith at Potter's Bar in Chancery Lane yonder."

"Well, it is a good job for him that he is known, my friends," replied the doctor; "for though he is not actually murdered, he is not far from it. Summon his master, some of you, and let him be carried into the house. His wounds must be attended to. Tell his master that Doctor Jardell will attend upon him."

Traces of blood were seen at the doorway of the old chambers, Sir Christopher having borrowed a lamp from one of the bystanders, but it did not strike either of them that the struggle had first taken place there.

"I consider it strange," said the doctor, "that your man was not to the fore in the crowd."

"I have thought of it," answered Sir Christopher, "and I consider that, as he knows that there is a vast amount of money somewhere in those chambers, he has remained at his post. If that is not the case, then he has fallen asleep, and the cries have not attracted his attention."

"I should say that that is the more likely solution of the two reasons why he is not present," replied the doctor; "but now let us ascend."

The pair reached the top of the house, Sir Christopher being first.

The latter wore spurs, and as he ascended the stairs they made plenty of noise.

As Lucas came not to meet them, Sir Christopher was now convinced that his valet must be fast asleep, for he felt perfectly certain that he would never leave his post—no, not if his master were twenty or forty hours behind the appointed time.

Pushing open the door he entered.

The place was in darkness.

Sir Christopher raised the lamp he carried and looked round.

But Doctor Jardell was the first to catch sight of the body of the unfortunate valet.

"Merciful heaven!" he gasped, clutching Sir Christopher's arm with one hand, and pointing the other at the ghastly object. "Look, look! Murder has been done!"

"Gracious Providence!" cried Sir Christopher, drawing back and surveying the dreadful object almost at his feet. "Can I believe my eyes? This is *Lucas*. Heaven! yes, 'tis indeed he, and with a dagger plunged to the hilt in his throat."

"Ay," murmured Doctor Jardell, "pinned to the very floor, which proves with what terrible force that blow was delivered. And, behold!—look everywhere, and see the unmistakable evidences of a fearful struggle having taken place."

So overcome was Sir Christopher at the dreadful sight, that for some few seconds he seemed rooted to the spot.

At last he said, and his tones were hoarse and tremulous—

"Doctor, who in the name of mercy could have committed this foul deed?"

"I have no hesitation in saying that this deed has been done by some of the blackguardly assassins who are allowed to roam unchecked about London," replied the doctor, "and you can see how the brave fellow has tried to defend himself."

"My impression is that this foul murder, and the shocking outrage just within the gateway, have been committed by the same person."

"THE DOCTOR FOUND THAT THE AMOUNT WAS ALL RIGHT."

"Or persons," said the doctor, "for I can hardly believe that all this has been done by only one."

Hastily Sir Christopher entered the bed-chamber.

There was no evidence within that mouldy old place which would indicate that a struggle had taken place.

"Considering the dreadful tragedy which has transpired," said Sir Christopher, "I can scarcely bring myself to act in accordance with the recently discovered document."

"Since we are here," replied the doctor, "it would be as well to carry out our intentions. You need only try the effect of the button, and the money being revealed you will be satisfied. You can of course leave whatever you may be lucky enough to discover until a more fitting time occurs to take it away."

Sir Christopher advanced to the fire-dogs and removed the first, the button then being revealed.

We need not repeat what followed, nor need we describe the astonishment which rested on the faces of the pair as the ceiling slowly descended.

Sir Christopher took the lamp in his hand, and proceeding to the flap ascended it in precisely the same way as had the mysterious masked traveller—the brutal ruffian, whom we now know as Colonel Blood.

"What see you? What see you?" queried the doctor, in agitated tones, as Sir Christopher reached the curious place above, and waved his lamp around.

No answer.

"I say, Sir Christopher! what see you, eh?" repeated the doctor.

Now came the answer in low, hushed tones.

"*Nothing!*"

"Ah!" replied the doctor, starting back, "David Driffield then deceived you; and you, Sir Christopher—you who have lived so long in hopes—you who have fed yourselves, as it were, on——"

"Hold, doctor," interrupted Sir Christopher. "I implore you withhold for a few moments your denunciations. Catch hold of this rope and ascend."

Doctor Jardell did so.

His eyes opened to their fullest extent as he surveyed the complicated machinery on all sides.

He looked into Sir Christopher's face.

By this time the baronet had somewhat recovered from the effects of the dreadful sight in the other apartment, and the doctor saw that his features were now very calm.

"Doctor," said Sir Christopher, "not only has my faithful servant been slain, but a great robbery has been committed. For observe—look at these shelves. Can you not see these almost round clean patches, and that these same patches are surrounded with a thick accumulation of dust?"

"Ha!"

"Ay! look at the large number of them, Doctor Jardell, *where these clean patches are rested bags of gold!*"

The face of the doctor now wore an expression of blank dismay.

"I feel you are right, Sir Christopher," he replied. "Robbery hath been committed. But then—gracious Providence!—by whom? Who but yourself knew of the existence of this wonderful secret? You surely did not inform your man of——"

"I did, doctor—I did. Poor Lucas was entirely in my confidence. But do you think that, in a moment of weakness, he betrayed that secret? No! I would wager my very existence that he did not."

"Well, well, I believe you; but I know not what to say, or what to think. Ha!" suddenly exclaimed the doctor, as he pointed to the floor, "what is that there glittering close to your feet?"

Sir Christopher stooped, and picked up a small piece of chain.

Both examined it.

"This," said Sir Christopher, "may prove of the utmost importance. It is a piece of gold chain, you observe, and somewhat massive, which would make it appear as if one of the robbers, at least, was a person of some means. And see—the last link is broken."

"By that means it became detached from the wearer's cloak," replied the doctor—"for a cloak chain it certainly is. Put it in your pocket, and carefully guard it. And now let us hasten to the apprentice. Who knows what he can tell us."

"You are right," replied Sir Christopher.

Both descended, *leaving the ceiling down.*

"Poor Lucas!" murmured Sir Christopher, in broken tones, as he stood once more before the body of the faithful valet. "A more honest, generous-hearted servant than thou wert never lived. Though the loss of what money was in this mysterious old place is a dreadful blow to me—though its loss extinguishes all my hopes; yet it will not be in endeavouring to recover the property that I will try to hunt down the person or persons who came here. No; but I will never rest—never—until I have discovered the man who plunged that dagger in thy throat, and then thou shalt be avenged!"

"That speech," said Doctor Jardell, "does you infinite credit, Sir Christopher. We shall, of course, endeavour to recover the stolen property; but if that fails, why, then, you and Clarissa must come together *without* money."

"Thanks, doctor, thanks," exclaimed Sir Christopher.

Leaving the unfortunate valet, they descended the stairs and reached the gateway.

A large number of persons were assembled outside.

The doctor found that his instructions with respect to the apprentice had been carried out, and in a skilful fashion by the locksmith himself.

Ghastly pale did the poor youth look.

It seemed as if the grim Angel of Death were already hovering over the bed ready to swoop down on its victim.

"What is the age of this youth?" asked the doctor.

"Nearing his twentieth year, your worship," replied the locksmith, in tones of deep emotion.

Sir Christopher at once asked—

"Is he any relation of yours?"

"Oh, no, sir," was the reply; "but we are all so fond of him—he is both brave and good."

"How came he to be out at so late an hour?"

"Ha, that is indeed a mystery. He supped with us, gentlemen, at about ten of the clock, when we were all very happy together. When we parted we all went to our different bedrooms."

"Humph! I suppose that if he wished to go out, he need only have asked you?"

"That is all, sir. He is, and always has been welcome to come and go as it pleases him. But tell me, doctor, do you think he will recover?"

Doctor Jardell looked long and earnestly into the pale face, felt the feebly throbbing pulse, and timed its beat by his watch.

All eyes were eagerly fixed upon his face as if to ascertain what was passing in his mind.

At last Doctor Jardell said—

"There is no immediate danger. But the utmost care must be bestowed upon him. Keep the house quiet, and avoid causing him to become, in the slightest degree, excited. In a short time no doubt I shall be able to tell you whether he will live or die. And now let me tell you this, Master Locksmith," the doctor continued in solemn tones, "a most foul murder has been committed in the old chambers in the gateway."

"Murder?" gasped the locksmith, while cries of consternation were uttered by all present.

"Aye, and I believe that murder, and the attempted murder of this youth, sprang from the same cause. But listen."

Rapidly the doctor made them acquainted with all that had transpired.

All listened with deep attention.

When he had finished, the locksmith said—

"Then, gentlemen, what to me was always a profound mystery has now been made clear."

"What mean you?"

"That David Driffield obtained all his materials for the construction of the place you describe from me. I had not long taken my father's place in this business when he commenced to buy from me. Of course it was always a wonder to me what he could want with all these things, but knowing him as an eccentric character, I asked no questions. I used to allow him to go among my stock and collect what he wanted.

"Sometimes he would bring an article to be polished or cut, or what not, and as he paid liberally for what was done, he was asked no questions. But now, gentlemen, I wish one of my apprentices to tell you something. Here, Harry! Harry!"

"Here, sir," answered a young lad, as he entered the room.

"When you heard the cry of murder," said the locksmith, "you jumped from your bed and looked from the window?"

"Ay, master."

"Tell these gentlemen what you saw."

"I saw a tall man, clad all in black, riding one horse and leading another by the bridle, come from beneath the arch."

"What arch?"

"The arch beneath this house, sirs."

"Ay, ay; go on, my good lad," said Sir Christopher.

"I noticed," continued the lad, "that the horse he led carried two heavy leathern bags, which were slung across the saddle."

"Ha!"

"And he rode away towards Holborn as if the very fiend were at his heels, sirs."

"You are sure there was only one man?"

"Quite sure."

"Well," said the doctor, "at present all is buried in mystery. Heaven knows what this lad could say were he conscious. But now, Master Preston, I and my friend must away. In a few hours we will return."

Sorrowfully the doctor and Sir Christopher took their way towards Pentonville.

CHAPTER III.

SHOWS HOW SIR CHRISTOPHER CULLUM DENOUNCED COLONEL BLOOD—OF HOW THE WARRANT FOR HIS ARREST WAS SIGNED BY THE KING — AND OF WHAT STIRRING EVENTS FOLLOWED.

AT Pentonville Sir Christopher left the doctor.

After duly considering the matter the pair agreed that Clarissa should not at present know the whole of the particulars, as such knowledge might have a very depressing effect upon her.

Sir Christopher agreed to return to Pentonville in time to leave with the doctor for the house of the locksmith.

It was about ten of the clock in the morning when a coach drove down the narrow street in which the doctor resided, and stopped before his house.

A man of about fifty years of age, attired in a strange-looking suit, jumped from the coach and rang the bell.

So strange an object did the inhabitants of the street consider him, that the majority ventured to gaze from doors and windows.

Their curiosity did not escape the bloodshot eyes of the doctor's visitor, and more than one fierce oath escaped his lips.

A more depraved, dissipated-looking creature than this man surely never passed through the street.

The door having been opened by the elderly woman, Mistress Jeevers, the man handed her a note.

"Walk in," snapped Mistress Jeevers.

"I'd rather wait without," was the surly reply.

"Well, wait without," replied Mistress Jeevers, as she instantly slammed the door in his face.

This, however, did not appear to ruffle his temper.

In a few moments the doctor appeared.

"Bring it in," he said.

The man thereupon threw open the coach door, and took out a huge white canvas bag, which contained something bulky.

That it was very heavy anyone could see by the way the man handled it.

"Follow me, my man," said the doctor, "and——"

"Pardon me, sir," quickly exclaimed the man, "have you no man-servant?"

"I have not! Why do you ask?"

"Humph! Why do I ask, sir? Let me tell you, Doctor Jardell, that I am not in the habit of turning *myself* into a servant at a moment's notice."

The doctor looked curiously into the man's bloated and profusely pimpled face, then referring to the letter, he said——

"Colonel Blood says 'my man.'"

"Probably; but that might mean anything. Does he not mention my name?"

"He does not."

"Humph! Well, my name is Captain Drinkwater, and no doubt you have heard the name hundreds of times."

"I can't say I have."

"What?" thundered the captain, drawing himself to his full height.

"I repeat," answered the doctor, quietly, "that I have never before heard of you."

"Sir," cried the captain emphatically, "you completely astonish me. I feel ready to sink into my very boots, sir."

"Well," replied the doctor, still in his quiet tones, "I should say that your boots are quite good enough for the purpose. However, I am glad that I can now say I have actually beheld the redoubtable Captain Drinkwater. You are to be sincerely pitied, captain."

"Pitied, sir? Why?"

"Because your name is a libel upon yourself."

"Sir," thundered the captain, "I came not here to be insulted."

"I am aware of it, my friend. You came here to bring that bag, and you have duly brought it; and now follow me. I assure you, captain," and here the doctor bowed mockingly, "that I sincerely regret not being able to afford such a luxury as a man-servant. Had I been provided with one he should have been instantly placed at your disposal."

The dissipated-looking wretch believed that the doctor was sincere.

"I accept your apology, doctor," he said, "and with as much pleasure as I shall accept the bottle of canary which you will no doubt order to be placed before me."

So saying the captain took up the bag again, and followed the doctor into the surgery.

Owing to the little diamond-paned windows being draped with heavy curtains, the apartment was in a state of semi-darkness.

"Just wait within one moment," said Doctor Jardell, "and I will bring a lamp, and you a bottle of sack."

The doctor proceeded below, while the captain endeavoured to make out what the room contained.

He could not easily see the different articles, and as the doctor was a long time, on account of the gloom, he produced a tinder box and taper and quickly got a light.

After seeing that the wick burnt freely he looked up.

His eyes at once rested upon the marvellous automatic figure which so resembled Colonel Blood.

The captain darted back.

"A trick," he said. "Ha, ha, ha! A trick to see whether I should bring that money hither all right. Ha, ha! ho, ho! Well, well, I forgive you, colonel—I forgive you. But how did you reach here before me, eh?"

He was addressing himself to the black mysterious figure against the fireplace, under the impression that it was Colonel Blood.

Of course there was no answer.

"I say," commenced the captain, and now he advanced and stood beside the figure, "I——well I *am* a fool! But upon my soul I could have sworn that it was the colonel. It isn't a human being, is it? No! and yet, those eyes appear to look into my face like the orbs of a living being."

He reached up to lift the mask, when suddenly the figure stalked forward.

A wild, ear-piercing yell of horror did the captain utter, and turning he fled towards the door.

"Murder!" he shouted. "Murder! Save me! Murder—mur——"

"Ho! what is this?" interrupted the doctor, who at this moment, lamp in hand, entered the apartment. "What means this, eh? You have been tampering with that figure, sirrah."

"No, no; on my soul I have not."

"Stop."

The doctor took from the captain's cloak a small hook with a piece of wire attached.

In reaching forth his hand to lift the mask this hook had become fixed in the cloak.

The consequence was that the wire set the machinery in motion.

Directly the doctor seized and jerked it in a peculiar way the ghastly figure abruptly stopped, turned, and to the amazement of the captain, walked majestically back to its place.

"Never again attempt to meddle with

anything which concerns you not," said the doctor, gravely, "and more especially anything contained in a surgeon's apartment."

"Why, you see, doctor," replied the captain, continuing to gaze on the marvellously constructed automaton, "I could have sworn that that was the colonel."

"It is much like his figure, you think, eh?"

"Exact, doctor."

"Well," said the doctor, with a smile, "sit down, my friend Captain Drinkwater, and drink *wine*. Here is a bottle of good sack, and the drinking of that *sack* will, I doubt not, be more suitable to your taste than the carrying of that *bag*."

"You are right, doctor, but I must drink it up as rapidly as possible, my instructions being that I am to return with all speed."

"Well, you see, I must first count the gold."

"Count it? I trust, Master Jardell, that you do not suspect me of pilfering any——"

"Oh, no; but it is one of my rules always to count money offered in payment of any article."

"I suppose I have to take something back."

"You have to take that figure with you."

"That figure? Will it ride in the coach with me?"

"It will; but do not be alarmed. It cannot hurt you."

"I am not so sure of that," replied the captain, casting another suspicious glance at the black-looking object. "I had far rather deal with a live man than one of these things."

"It will be placed in a box."

"Oh, in a box. Well and good. I'll take precious good care to see that the lid is properly fastened," muttered Drinkwater.

"It is a most remarkable thing," thought the doctor, as he proceeded to count the mass of money which he had poured on the table, "that whereas last night the colonel had no money, he to-day has plenty. Can he have had—but no, no; 'tis impossible."

The doctor found that the amount—five hundred guineas—was all right, and he wrote out a receipt, and handed it to the captain.

Then he called Mother Jeevers, and directed her to bring up the box which she would find below.

This was done, and in a few minutes the model was within the box and the latter properly fastened.

It was found, however, that it would not go inside the coach, its length being quite six feet, and so it was placed on the driver's box; and when Captain Drinkwater had entered the coach, it rolled away.

Punctually at the appointed time Sir Christopher Cullum made his appearance, and he and the doctor set off to keep the appointment at Potter's Bar.

When the doctor and Sir Christopher entered the apprentice's bedroom they were agreeably surprised to find him sitting up in the bed propped up by pillows.

The locksmith at once advanced towards them, saying—

"Gentlemen, what I am sure will prove to be a startling revelation is about to be made. But, first, Clifford will give you the story."

"I see that you are greatly excited," answered the doctor, "but I am glad to observe that this young man is now well on the road to recovery. Do you feel fit to tell us the story, my young friend?"

"Oh, yes; and I am very anxious to do so."

And at once Clifford told the story.

"But," said Christopher in a breath, "you surely must be mistaken. From what we saw of the shelves there must have been hundreds of bags of money. All this could not have been contained in the two bags this man carried."

"I cannot tell you where the money is," replied Clifford, "but this can I swear to. I was looking from the window when the man came down the lane with the two horses, and I am positive that there was not a soul with him. I followed him, saw him enter the chambers, and continued to watch until he made his re-appearance. He was not joined by anyone."

"This is indeed marvellous!" ejaculated Sir Christopher.

"And at last you succeeded in snatching off the mask?" said the doctor. " And you saw the face of this man ? "

" I did."

" And you would recognise him again ? "

" Yes, I know his face well, and I know his name——"

" Ha! his name. Speak! " cried Sir Christopher.

" Colonel Blood! "

A cry of consternation left the lips of Sir Christopher and the doctor.

Both for some moments appeared perfectly speechless.

At last the doctor said in low, hoarse tones—

" Are you sure of this ? "

" Yes! " replied Clifford, in the most emphatic manner. " It is out of all question that I can be mistaken. I have been to Colonel Blood's house to repair his locks some dozens of times. On each occasion he took great notice of me. He knew my name well, and spoke it immediately after I uttered his."

" There can be *no* mistake about it," cried Sir Christopher, excitedly. " Colonel Blood is the thief—Colonel Blood is the assassin. By heaven! he shall suffer for his crime! "

" Calm yourself," said Doctor Jardell, who, however, was very far from being calm himself. " I am convinced that what the lad says is right. The treacherous villain! Heavens! that man is indeed most truly named! "

" I will to the king," commenced Sir Christopher, but the doctor interrupted him.

" No, no," he said, " not at present—not at present. Remember, you have no *witness*. In a week's time Clifford Hansard will have recovered sufficiently to be able to accompany you. *Then* and not *till* then, can you lay all the facts before his majesty.

" You speak most truly," replied Sir Christopher; " but, oh! it will be a hard trial to confine this secret within my bosom until Clifford is able to come with me."

" I know it; but, nevertheless, you *must* hold the secret."

" London is ringing with the 'Lincoln's Inn Murder,' as it is already called," observed the locksmith.

" Truly," said Sir Christopher, " and the Court is ringing with it. I have not seen his majesty to-day, but no doubt he is acquainted with some of the particulars. As soon as he knows that the murder was committed, and the robbery carried out in the chamber of old David Driffield he will speak to me on the subject."

" Tell him all then," replied the doctor, " except that the robber and the assassin is Colonel Blood."

Aside he muttered—

" And to think that the money I received from Colonel Blood this morning was (for there is no doubt of it) part of the proceeds of this most daring robbery! Ha! I would not have Sir Christopher know it for any amount."

" Master Preston," said Sir Christopher, addressing the locksmith, " you will be kind enough to summon all the members of your household and give them strict orders not to mention the name of Colonel Blood."

" None know it," answered the locksmith, " except my wife, daughter, and myself."

" Good! I can rely upon you? "

" You can."

" Every day," said the doctor, " I will visit Clifford. He shall be strong enough at the end of the week to pay a visit to King Charles."

As Clifford heard this his heart seemed to leap into his mouth.

" A visit to the king! " he muttered; " a visit to the king! Who knows? After all I may be something better than Clifford Hansard, the locksmith's apprentice! "

*　　*　　*　　*

Our readers must now accompany us to a totally different quarter of London— Whitehall.

A week had passed away—a week of great anxiety to Sir Christopher Cullum.

As secretary to the king, Sir Christopher always had ready access to his majesty, and as the young baronet was a great favourite of the erratic, pleasure-loving monarch, it may easily be supposed that Sir Christopher could always get him to listen to anything, more especially if what he had to say was of an amusing or sensational character.

Sir Christopher was provided at Whitehall Palace with a suite of apartments.

It was six o'clock in the evening, and Sir Christopher had attired himself in the most elegant manner, and had descended to his principal room.

Hardly had he taken his seat when an usher announced Doctor Jardell.

He was directed to show him in.

In a few moments the doctor appeared, followed by the hero of our romance, Clifford Hansard.

According to Sir Christopher's instructions, a new suit of clothes had been provided for him, and though they were of the class usually worn by apprentices when holiday making, they fitted him to a nicety, setting off his elegant figure to the best advantage.

Though still pale and weak, he certainly presented a striking appearance.

As Sir Christopher welcomed him he directed a keen, searching look upon him, and at once arrived at the conclusion that Clifford Hansard was one of the handsomest youths he had ever set eyes upon, and he considered it exceedingly likely that his majesty would take particular notice of him.

"I am indeed right glad that you have come in time," said Sir Christopher, "for as you have no doubt observed, guests are rapidly arriving."

"You are correct," replied the doctor, gravely, "and among them is a person you and I know very well."

"Ha! who is that?"

"While waiting in the lobby," replied the doctor, "two gentlemen elegantly attired and wearing a profusion of jewellery, brushed past us. Suddenly one turned and looked at me. He wore a heavy beard and moustache, but I at once recognised him. It was Colonel Blood!"

"By heavens!" exclaimed Sir Christopher. "Surely you must be mistaken."

"No, I am not mistaken. I recognised him, though Clifford did not, which, however, is not to be wondered at. But I recognised the walk, the savage glittering eyes, and I noted the expression of surprise as he looked upon me."

"Did he speak?"

"Not to me; he merely muttered to his companion something about having made a mistake, then he swung swiftly round and went on."

"I must see to this, he certainly has not received an invitation to be present to-night. He is here for some dark purpose."

"All the better for your plans. The warrant could be made out, and the colonel could be arrested before he could leave the palace."

"Yes, yes; he shall — but hush! voices! Silence! it is the king."

Several voices in animated conversation were heard within the next apartment, which was the king's private cabinet, and every now and then Charles's loud, boisterous laughter fell on the ears of our three friends.

"He is in a good humour to-night," whispered Sir Christopher. "I trust he has read the note I placed on his private table."

Presently the sound of voices died away, a door closed, a light footstep advanced, the heavy curtains which divided the two rooms were drawn aside, and the king entered.

"Ha!" he said, "whom have we here? Some of your friends, Sir Chris, eh?"

Sir Christopher bowed.

"Yes, sire," he said, "they are my friends. I mentioned them to your majesty in my note."

"Ah, so you did. Rise, doctor, for this I suppose is the doctor, eh? Yes! And this is——"

"Clifford Hansard, sire."

"Hansard, eh?" said his majesty, surveying our hero from head to foot; "and verily, Sir Chris, he is a fine young man. But proceed, Sir Chris, and let us know what it is you wish us to lend our ear to."

"No doubt your majesty has heard all about the atrocious murder at the chambers within Lincoln's Inn gateway?"

"Well, we certainly have heard something, but we were about to ask all about it, knowing that you, Sir Chris, could give us the true particulars."

"Alas, your majesty, I wish I could give you the true particulars."

"It was your man, Lucas, who was killed?"

"Yes, sire; no doubt your majesty remembers him. Poor Lucas was the man who some six months ago checked your majesty's maddened steed at Hampton Court."

"Ha!" cried Charles. "We have every reason to remember him, Sir Chris. We promised to reward him; but—but so many State affairs crop up to distract our attention that it is no wonder we forgot the circumstance. But I am anxious to hear all. Proceed; and let me tell you, Sir Chris, that that poor man's assassin shall swing from the highest gibbet ever erected!"

Sir Christopher, the doctor, and Clifford each told his story; but the doctor, wishing to wash his hands of Colonel Blood and his affairs, did not mention anything of having had business transactions with him.

To the stories the king listened most attentively.

The peculiar movement of his right foot, the occasional elevation of his eyebrows, and the restless crossing and recrossing of his hands, showed that he was powerfully agitated.

"Young man," said the king, addressing Clifford, "are you certain that the man whose face you saw was Colonel Blood?"

"I am positive I saw him, sire," replied our hero.

"I believe the man is quite capable of committing any atrocious act," said Charles; "but I think that you, Doctor Jardell, must be mistaken in so far as you say you saw him, disguised, enter this palace but a short time ago. I can hardly think that he has the brazen impudence to mingle with those who, if they discovered his identity, would at once arrest him—but we must see into it," he hastily added. "Let the warrant for his arrest be at once made out, Sir Chris, and I will sign it."

Sir Christopher immediately prepared the document, which the king signed, and the great seal having been attached, the warrant was read.

"Place the warrant in the hands of the officer on duty, Sir Chris," said the king, "and I will tarry here awhile, for I am anxious to know whether Colonel Blood is really within this building."

"It will be necessary that Doctor Jardell accompanies us," said Sir Christopher, "for otherwise the captain will not know his man."

"Ah, true! Let the doctor accom-pany you by all means. Clifford Hansard can remain here."

Sir Christopher and the doctor departed, while Clifford, drawing back to the further end of the room, watched the king, as, in the most agitated manner, he paced the apartment.

A quarter of an hour went by, then the sound of many voices, the hurried tramping of feet, and the clash of arms, showed that something of an exciting nature was taking place.

Sir Christopher was the first to reenter the apartment, Doctor Jardell following him closely.

"Well?" queried the king.

"Sire, the doctor was not mistaken—"

"Gad's blood!" shouted the king, "do you really say, then, that the scoundrel colonel has been taken?"

"No, sire, but the doctor was right when he said that he recognised the colonel in the lobby. He *did* enter the palace, being conducted through the lobby by a gentleman who I thought could not possibly have any dealings with such a man."

"And this gentleman?"

"Master Mattock, your majesty's principal jeweller."

"Ha! And we owe Master Mattock a large sum," muttered Charles.

After a few seconds' pause, during which he showed how uneasy he was, the king, turning to Sir Christopher, said—

"I trust you have not allowed Master Mattock to leave the palace?"

"Sire, I took upon myself to give Master Mattock into the custody of Captain Winter."

"You did quite right. Let him be shown in."

So saying the king resumed his seat.

In a few moments Captain Winter entered, followed by a file of soldiers.

Between them stood Master Mattock.

The old man looked fit to drop.

His white face, trembling lips, and staring eyes showed the mighty fear under which he laboured.

Being taken to within a few feet of the frowning king, Master Mattock prostrated himself.

"Sire!" he gasped, "I am innocent."

"Innocent, eh?—innocent? Of what? Listen to it, Master Mattock, thou hast proved thyself a vile traitor."

"Oh, sire!" gasped the jeweller, who really felt that his last moments of liberty at any rate had come to a conclusion, "it is true that Colonel Blood, disguised, was with me; but it was entirely against my wish. He suddenly confronted me at Charing Cross, and swore that if I did not pass him into the palace it would neither be well for me nor my family."

"By the Virgin!" roared the king, again starting to his feet, "he thus dared to threaten you?"

"He did, sire; and trembling for my family, I at last consented to escort him through."

"You have lost nothing by being thus outspoken, Master Mattock," said Charles; "and what did he do within the palace?"

"I know not, sire. He came to speak with someone, so he told me; but who the someone was I know not, for so soon as we got within the thick of the crowd in the reception-room, he slipped away."

"Well, Master Mattock, we believe your story. Rise, return to the reception-room, and should you be questioned —as no doubt you will—say that a mistake has been made."

Master Mattock rose, pouring forth a torrent of thanks, backed himself towards the door and departed.

Captain Winter was about to order his men to march, when Sir Christopher cried out—

"Hold! Here, Captain Winter, is your warrant. See that it is executed."

"By all means," said Charles. "If Colonel Blood was but a short time ago within this palace, it is quite certain that he cannot be far away at the present moment."

"As no doubt you know, Captain Winter," said Sir Christopher, "Colonel Blood is a desperate man."

"What! think you that he will offer resistance to our warrant?" asked the king.

"I do, sire."

"Ha!" cried Charles, now in a towering rage, "capture the villain! Capture him at any risk! Gad's blood! we'll see who is master."

"Sire," said Clifford, "I am well acquainted with Colonel Blood's house. I have been there on many occasions to repair his locks."

"Ha! what if this youth accompanies the captain, Sir Chris?"

"An excellent plan," replied Sir Christopher, eagerly.

"Good, then let it be so. Depart and return with the news that this audacious scoundrel is in safe custody. As soon as ever you lay hands on him, Captain Winter, let him be taken to Newgate, and let the governor know that he is to be placed in the strongest cell within the prison."

Captain Winter bowed, and with his men filed out.

Humphrey was about to cross the threshold of the door, when Sir Christopher whispered—

"Be guarded, my lad; remember that you have a commission from the king, and there is no telling what may follow it."

* * * *

There was not a more extraordinary man in London than Colonel Blood.

It was well known that he was the leader of a gang of ruffians of a more desperate and determined character than the depraved crew who made Alsatia their dwelling-place.

The colonel was the owner of that strange-looking, mysterious dwelling known as the "Black Priory," which at the period of our romance, stood on a portion of the ground which is now occupied by Leicester Square.

It was a tall building, constructed for the most part of stone.

It was to this house that Clifford Hansard had come to repair the locks.

Colonel Blood talked with Clifford, and "sounded" him as to his opinions.

In the result he found that Clifford was too honest for him, and so he had to abandon his idea of securing Clifford as his "helpmate."

Colonel Blood's visit to the Court had been to obtain an interview with one of the courtiers, and after he had transacted his business, he made a hurried exit.

"I have many appointments," he mused, as he reached Charing Cross. "Let me see, what shall I do? Ha! I must at once return to the Priory; then, afterwards—well, we shall see how things go."

Entering the grounds from the front, he passed round, and entered a private door in the house at the back.

Touching a bell which hung over the door on the inside, a hideous old crone made her appearance with a lamp, which she handed to the colonel.

"Who is within?" asked Colonel Blood.

"Captain Drinkwater, and two of his companions," was the reply.

"Where are they?"

"In the captain's room, smoking, drinking, and card-playing."

"Don't disturb them at present; I want to overhear some of their conversation," continued the colonel.

"Ay, ay," chuckled the old woman.

The colonel ascended to his bedroom, and proceeded to throw off his disguise.

When he descended, he was most beautifully attired, his costume being such as would be worn by the wealthiest noblemen.

Having listened for a few moments to the conversation of his rogue-in-chief, Captain Drinkwater, and his two companions, the colonel descended another flight of stairs.

Reaching the bottom the colonel took from his pocket a key, and opened a door directly in front of him.

A pair of heavy, gold-edged curtains hung just inside the door.

Passing through these the colonel was in his own private apartment (*an apartment which was something more than what it looked like*) as our readers will see anon.

It was beautifully furnished, the furniture, hangings, paintings, lamps, everything being of the richest and costliest description.

Looking from the doorway one would have considered that the room was divided, for on the right hung another pair of curtains.

They reached from the ceiling to the floor.

That those curtains concealed something of an important but secret character there was no doubt.

The colonel took his seat at a small table placed against the wall, and on which was a pile of documents, together with the materials for writing.

Having summoned the old woman and told her to send Captain Drinkwater and his men down, he commenced to write.

In a few moments Captain Drinkwater entered.

"Glad to see you, colonel," he said, with a grin, which showed to perfection the enormous width of his mouth, "for I want to have done with that matter."

"What matter?"

"The bony counterpart of yourself."

"Ha! just so. It is all right?"

"Every bit of it; and a very nice job I had with it. The successful carrying out of such a task as you gave me is worth—what shall I say?—the Crown Jewels."

"No doubt," replied Blood, dryly, "but you will be perfectly satisfied with whatsoever I choose to give you, which will prove that though you are a profane swearer, a drunken sot, a shocking liar, and a miserable coward, you are nevertheless in possession of an ordinary amount of common sense."

At this summary of Drinkwater's character—a very true summary by the way—his companions burst into a roar of laughter.

Drinkwater scowled fiercely, but well aware of the fact that his glances had no terror for the colonel, he forced a smile and said—

"I thank you, colonel, for your kind estimation of my character."

"I hope," observed Blood, "that you will not be disposed to question what I have said?"

"Certainly not, colonel."

"Now," said the colonel, arranging several papers before him, "to-night, captain, you will take from me most important instructions. How many men can you command?"

"As many as you care to pay for."

"Well, I will consider how many I shall want, for—Holy Mary! hark to that scream," he suddenly cried, starting to his feet with such violence that the table was overturned, and the papers scattered in all directions.

He had been interrupted by a wild, piercing, but most peculiar scream.

That sound he had often heard when danger threatened—the piercing scream of Mother Ellwood, his housekeeper.

Captain Drinkwater and his companions started up, plucked their swords from their scabbards, and stood in an attitude of defence.

In a few seconds loud voices were heard, then the tramping of feet, and presently Mother Ellwood rushed into the apartment.

"The trap, colonel! the trap!" she gasped; "they have come to capture you!"

"Come to take *me?*" said Blood, as he folded his arms across his chest. "Bah! this is a mistake. Who are they?"

"Quick, colonel!" pleaded the old woman; "quick, the trap!"

It was too late, even if the colonel had decided to escape by one of his secret exits, for the door was violently opened, and Captain Winter, sword in hand, and followed by his men, to the number of a dozen, crowded into the apartment.

"What means this?" asked Colonel Blood, haughtily.

"It means, Colonel Blood," replied Captain Winter, as he took the warrant from his pocket, "that I am here to arrest you and convey you to Newgate."

"Under what charge?" asked Blood.

"*Murder!*"

"Murder? Whom am I supposed to have murdered?"

"One Lucas, valet to Sir Christopher Cullum!"

Blood started, but it was very slightly.

It was, however, observed by Clifford, who stood at the back of the soldiers.

"And also," continued Captain Winter, "you are charged with the attempted murder of one Clifford Hansard."

"Ha! On whose information am I charged?"

"On the sworn information of three persons — namely, Doctor Jardell, Sir Christopher Cullum, and Clifford Hansard. And now, colonel, I trust you will surrender yourself."

"Ha!" thought Blood, "now I know the purpose for which Doctor Jardell and the youth were at the palace."

Aloud he said—

"All this is a great mistake, captain. I have only just reached London after a visit to——"

"'Tis false!" cried a loud, firm voice. "But your denial will avail you nothing. Captain Winter will arrest you, and you have the satisfaction of knowing that the king has signed that warrant with his own hand. Dastard—coward that you are! it will be my pleasure to see you swinging from the highest gibbet in London."

And Clifford, his hands tightly clenched, his fine figure drawn to its fullest height, his large eyes flashing forth his intense indignation, pushed through the soldiers, and confronted the colonel.

That the colonel was astonished we hardly need say, but he betrayed little surprise.

"Ha!" he growled, "*you* here—my locksmith's apprentice, Captain Winter," he said, coolly addressing the officer. "My locksmith's apprentice imagines that I have done him an injury in some manner."

"Well, colonel," cried Captain Winter, impatiently, "you can say what you have to say at the proper time and place. Your sword, sir."

"Captain Winter," said Blood, in fierce tones, "you do not know that it is a dangerous thing to enter my house and attempt to put a warrant into execution."

"*What*, man, would you speak treason? This is the king's warrant."

"Let me see it."

Captain Winter handed it over, and the colonel, without even glancing at the contents, tore it into shreds, and stamped his spurred boot upon the seal.

"That is as much as I care for the warrant, be it a king's or anyone else's. And now, captain, since there is *no* warrant, you cannot execute it. I therefore beg that you and your men, and this rascally apprentice will at once retire."

"Sir!" thundered Captain Winter, "the outrage which you have just committed will command the attention of those in higher authority than myself. I shall arrest you and take you before the king."

As he spoke he stepped forward.

Colonel Blood drew back, and instantly his blade flashed from its sheath.

He motioned to Captain Drinkwater and his companions, and they drew close to him.

Captain Winter saw that they held pistols in their hands, whereas neither he nor his men were so armed.

The men carried pikes, he himself a sword.

For a few moments the captain hesitated.

He looked straight into the colonel's

face, and read there the ruffian's determination to slay whosoever dared to advance.

On the face of Captain Drinkwater the word "Coward!" was most distinctly imprinted, and the same may be said of his two comrades; but there was no doubt that, at the colonel's word, they would draw the triggers of the weapons they held, and thus two or three of the soldiers—and, perhaps, the captain himself—would fall.

Colonel Blood's action with regard to the royal warrant, and his impertinent —nay rather, let us say insulting— conduct, had fired all the blood in Captain Winter's veins, and he felt eager to attempt to cut the wretch down.

Yet he knew well enough that he would find no joke in fighting with the notorious colonel, for he was unquestionably an expert swordsman.

Nevertheless he determined to capture Blood at any risk.

"Forward, men!" shouted Captain Winter, dashing upon the colonel.

Their blades met with a crash, and simultaneously three shots rang out, and one of the soldiers fell, a ball having pierced his heart.

And now in that splendidly-furnished apartment did a most determined battle proceed.

The effect of the pistols, besides the killing of one of the soldiers, was to fill the apartment with smoke.

So dense was it, that the combatants seemed like phantoms.

Clifford took the dead soldier's dagger from its sheath, and joined in the fray.

Quickly he became engaged with one of Drinkwater's companions.

The man defended himself furiously, but he was not proof against the remarkable agility of our hero, who, making a sudden spring, clutched the man by the throat, bore him to the floor, and plunged the dagger into his body.

Then taking the sword from the man's hand, he rushed towards the spot where stood the colonel and the captain hotly engaged.

Suddenly the colonel, who by degrees had worked himself round the apartment, shouted—

"*Now*, fool! what of the warrant?"

As he spoke a sharp clap rang out,

and as swiftly as the lightning's flash, Colonel Blood shot through the flooring!

He had worked himself to a part of the flooring fitted with a secret trap, which simply required the touching of a spring to accomplish the purpose for which it had been designed.

Captain Winter was petrified with astonishment.

Down on his knees went Clifford, for the flap with the carpet which covered it had resumed its position, and certainly it required very close looking at to see that it was a trap.

"We must capture him!" yelled Captain Winter, nearly frantic at the idea that after all Colonel Blood would succeed in making good his escape.

"Follow me, Clifford," Winter added, "and do not fear. Your courageous conduct shall be reported at the proper quarter."

"Yes, yes," shouted Clifford, taking care that his voice should be distinctly heard, "I follow!"

Aside he hurriedly whispered—

"I will wait in the room, for I feel sure that if you *descend* he will *ascend*."

Away with a rush went the men, one of them carrying the lamp with him.

In the course of the fight both of Drinkwater's companions had been slain, one by Clifford, and the other by one of the soldiers.

But the libidinous captain was comparatively unharmed.

Making certain that he should be cut down, if he stood up long enough, he flopped on his knees, yelled for mercy, and crawled away to the side of the room.

The craven-hearted villain, as soon as the soldiers rushed from the room, got upon his knees.

"Not dead yet," he chuckled, "yet I might have had my *nut* cracked before the *colonel* was caught. Lord! what a world this is. Ha! they have descended; and now, like a Jack-in-the-box, up comes the colonel. Capital trap that!"

"Silence, man!" said Clifford, as he clapped his hand over Captain Drinkwater's mouth, "and keep where you are—perfectly still. Move or utter a sound, and I will plunge this sword into your body."

Down again flopped the captain.

"Who are you?" he gasped.

"It matters not to you who I am," was Clifford's reply. "And I again tell you, keep silent for your life."

Loud voices, hurried trampings, Captain Winter's loud words of command, and the clashing of arms came from below, and continued for some few minutes.

Suddenly there was a noise such as would be made by the sudden and violent shooting of a bolt, the trap fell, a blaze of light came through, and up shot the colonel.

"Ha, ha! foiled them, by Jove!" he chuckled.

"Not so!" cried Clifford, "for I have foiled *you*, murderer!"

And placing his leg behind the colonel's, he flung him backwards to the floor.

CHAPTER IV.

IS OF THE MANNER IN WHICH COLONEL BLOOD WAS LODGED IN NEWGATE—OF THE DARING WAY IN WHICH HE ESCAPED—OF THE VIOLENT SCENE BETWEEN KING CHARLES AND MISTRESS CLARIBEL CAMERON—AND BY WHOM THE KING WAS SUDDENLY CONFRONTED.

CAPTAIN DRINKWATER held in his hand a discharged pistol, a heavy weapon with sufficient weight in it to stun an ox.

Clutching this by the muzzle, he crawled towards the spot where Clifford and the colonel were struggling, his intention being to deal our gallant young hero a deadly blow.

Ere he could use the pistol, however, the door was burst open, and the soldiers, with Captain Winter at their head, appeared.

He took in the situation at a glance.

Clifford was right on top of Blood, his hands fixed upon his throat.

Wildly, but unsuccessfully, the colonel struggled.

The bold lad had fairly pinioned the villain Blood to the floor.

"Seize upon him," cried Captain Winter, whose perspiring face showed plainly enough the exertion he had made to get at the colonel, "seize upon him, and fasten his hands securely behind his back."

The soldiers pounced upon Blood and dragged him to his feet.

Belts were taken off, and Colonel Blood's hands seized and dragged behind his back.

"Am I to suffer this indignity?" he asked, hoarsely.

"You deserve to suffer anything," the captain coldly replied.

"Now that I am really captured, I swear that I will quietly accompany you and make no further attempt at resistance."

"I do not believe you."

"What? Do you doubt my word?"

"Ay, I repose not the slightest trust in it."

"I shall not forget you, Captain Winter."

"Nay," replied the captain, shrugging his shoulders, "and I shall not forget you. If you mount the scaffold, colonel, as rapidly as you descended that flap, you will meet with the admiration of at least a portion of the audience."

Of this sarcastic remark the colonel took no notice.

His fierce eyes were now fixed upon the handsome face of Clifford Hansard.

Our hero returned his stare with very great interest.

That stare was so full of meaning that the colonel could not possibly be mistaken respecting it.

"Beware!" he growled, "beware! I am not likely to forget you. Remember, I shall not always be in Newgate."

"I sincerely hope not," replied Clifford, "for I trust it will be my good fortune soon to see a noose about your neck."

"Say no more," whispered the captain, "for I am anxious to depart from this house. Hillo, there! Who is this man, eh? Drag him to his feet," he said, pointing to the now cowering figure of Captain Drinkwater.

The man instantly darted upon him, and dragged him up.

"Who are you, sirrah?" asked Captain Winter.

"Keep your mouth shut," said Blood to Drinkwater.

Then to Winter he said—

"You hold no warrant for him."

"No," was the reply; "I wish I did."

"Then," continued Blood, "as you hold no warrant, you have no right either to touch him or ask him questions."

"Let the man go," said Captain Winter. "Show him the door."

The soldiers pushed him towards it.

The door being reached, Captain Winter cried—

"Kick him out."

And kick him the soldiers did, and most heartily, clean through the doorway.

In a few moments Colonel Blood was out of the house and in the public street.

The appearance of the soldiers, with the colonel in their midst, at once attracted a large crowd.

"Is it your intention to have me taken through the streets in this fashion?" said Blood.

"Why, yes; what other fashion would you have?"

"I should be taken in a coach."

"The warrant said nothing to that effect."

"Curse the warrant. I want a coach."

"You will have to want, colonel."

"But I will pay any sum for a coach."

"No doubt. But were a coach offered this moment for your conveyance I would not accept of it."

"Ha! you wish to see me insulted?"

Captain Winter made no reply.

Turning to Clifford he said—

"You, of course, will return to Whitehall and give the particulars."

"I will."

"Omit nothing."

"Never fear."

"You are a very gallant young man, Master Hansard," said Captain Winter, warmly shaking our hero by the hand, "and I wish you luck. Look to Sir Christopher Cullum; he can do you a lot of good."

So they parted, Clifford hurrying towards Whitehall, and the soldiers and their prisoner towards the gaol of Newgate.

No sooner was Blood's back turned than the crowd heartily hooted him.

Mad with rage, Blood wheeled, no doubt, to speak, but the soldiers roughly pushed him forward.

* * * *

At the period of which we write, the gaol of Newgate (soon to be razed to the ground by the great fire) was a most dreadful place.

The governor had purchased his office, and though by no means at all competent to have charge of the persons committed to his care, no one dared to complain of him.

At the time of our romance prisoners, no matter for what offence they were incarcerated, were allowed to have just whatever they could afford to buy.

As may be supposed, the principal thing bought was drink.

Nowhere else in the whole of the great city was Bacchus so blindly worshipped as within that filthy, fever-stricken prison.

Night and day the prisoners smoked and drank, played cards, and swore, and frequently fought desperately.

During the day friends were allowed to visit the prisoners, without having to procure a pass.

A visitor was also passed through at night, providing always that the hand of the governor was well weighted with gold.

Almost everything could be bought but freedom, and no amount of money would have the effect of causing the governor to let slip a prisoner, the reason being that a prisoner's escape meant the instant dismissal of the governor.

It was soon after ten of the clock when Blood and his guards reached the prisoners' entrance to the gaol.

Of course, since Blood had destroyed the warrant, the captain was unable to present it.

Consequently the warder at the wicket declined to open the door until he had communicated with the governor.

However, in a few moments the door was opened, and Blood was passed in.

He was hurried down a long, narrow passage, and passed into the governor's "office"—a small, dingy apartment.

The place was like an oven, owing to the presence of an enormous fire, the logs on which were piled half way up the chimney.

"THE KING TURNED TO FIND HIMSELF FACE TO FACE WITH COLONEL BLOOD!"

The lime-washed walls were hung with enormous chains, bolts, bars, and weapons, from a gigantic club to a lady's poignard.

Seated in one corner, a long German pipe in his mouth, and a tankard of mulled wine at his elbow, his shoeless feet perched on the back of a chair, was Master Hatchard Hammond, reputed to be the most "jovial" governor Newgate was ever "blessed with."

He was a short, stout man, with a puffed, red face, a decidedly "jolly nose," little blear eyes, and what is known as a "bullet head."

"Ha!" he said, as he surveyed Blood from head to foot; "and so you are the redoubted Colonel Blood, about whom we are hearing so much?"

"At your service," answered Blood, with a slight inclination of his head.

"Oh, I beg your pardon," replied the governor, "you are not at *my* service— I am at yours. You have no warrant, captain?"

"No, sir, Colonel Blood tore it to pieces, though it bore the king's own signature."

"Holy Virgin! that is a grave offence!"

"Suppose," said Blood, "that I denied there was a warrant at all?"

"My men can swear there *was*," said Winter.

"And I should believe there *was* a warrant," said the governor. "However, you would not be such a fool, colonel, as to deny there was a warrant?"

"No, I shall not deny it."

"Well, colonel, I am sorry—I am exceedingly sorry to have to tell you that I am full."

"You look it," replied Blood.

"I mean that my best cells are full."

"Oh, I beg you will not trouble yourself. I am quite ready to depart."

"Ho, ho! I see you will have your little joke. But let me explain. I have a number of *second* best empty. You shall be accommodated in one of them."

So saying the governor rang a bell.

It was answered by a pair of stalwart warders.

"Take charge of this gentleman," said the governor, pointing to the colonel, "and let him be placed in the cells beneath the first corridor."

"One moment," interrupted Blood, who knew considerably more of the interior of Newgate than the governor was aware of. "I can command any amount of money, and here is an earnest of it."

Thereupon the colonel threw a heavy purse upon the table.

The eyes of the governor twinkled greedily.

"Ah!" he said, "that puts quite a different complexion on affairs, for now that I come to think of it, I *have* one or two first-class cells vacant. Escort the noble colonel to number six."

So, between the warders, Blood was escorted to his new "apartments."

Captain Winter having received from the governor an acknowledgment to the effect that the prisoner was duly handed over to him, took his departure.

The apartment to which the colonel was taken was not *below* the first corridor (where were simply underground dungeons) but *above* it.

There was a row of these cells, admittance to each of which was gained by a low, narrow door of enormous thickness, well "ornamented" with huge bars, and secured by ponderous bolts, as well as a huge lock.

These doors were so secured, that it was utterly impossible that a prisoner could open them, no matter with what tools he might try.

There was no chance of the warder ever forgetting to lock these doors, for the simple reason that they closed and locked of themselves, and at the same time rang a bell over the entrance.

This was the reminder to the warder to see bolts and bars secured.

Colonel Blood found himself in a clean but scantily - furnished stone chamber.

At the end of it was a door.

This led into a smaller apartment, which contained a bed and a few et ceteras.

"I hope I shall have a fire," said the colonel.

"You will have it if you pay for it," was the reply.

"I *have* paid for it! Go to the governor and tell him my wants."

A fire was eventually lit, and a cold collation, together with wine, placed on the little wooden table.

The warder who brought this said—

"The governor desires me to tell you

that he will pay you a visit in the course of a few minutes."

"Good!" answered Blood.

When alone he rose and took a careful survey of the apartment.

The window—a very small aperture—was carefully secured by enormous iron bars.

The colonel saw that to endeavour to wrench them out would be worse than madness.

"There is only one way," muttered the colonel, grimly—"only one! By all the fiends! if I cannot succeed in escaping, to the gallows I shall certainly be doomed. That one way must be tried. Ha! voices. The governor comes."

Hurriedly Blood placed his hand within his doublet, and took out a phial.

That little bottle contained a few drops of the deadliest poison.

Its secret was known only to Doctor Jardell, for Colonel Blood had stolen that bottle from the doctor's case on the occasion of one of his visits.

Into the bottle of wine Colonel Blood poured every drop from the phial, and a mixture was made sufficient to kill a dozen men.

"Ha! my noble colonel," said the governor as he entered, "and how do you feel?"

Blood noticed that a tall, powerful warder walked behind the governor, but he remained on the threshold holding the door back.

"Fairly—fairly," replied the colonel, "considering the circumstances."

"Of course—of course. Glassbury," he said to the warder, "retire, and see that all is secured. When I am ready you will hear my bell."

The door went to with a crash, and Blood, to his astonishment and dismay, heard the warder fix the bolts and bars.

Affecting to smile, he said—

"Why, governor, do you mean to say that you allow yourself to be bolted in?"

"Ha, ha! Yes; it is one of my rules. A strange one, no doubt, but safe—very safe. My bell is instantly answered."

And he placed on the table a small handbell.

Taking a seat, he placed it near the fire, produced his pipe, lit it, and then from his pocket drew a pack of dirty cards.

Ostensibly he had come to amuse the prisoner, in reality to *sound* him as to what he was prepared to pay for *special* treatment.

"Do you smoke, colonel?" asked the governor.

"Rarely," replied Blood, whose mind was now considerably agitated as to how he was to deal with that stalwart warder.

"I have nothing with which to bribe him," he reflected, "and it is nine chances to one as to the governor having any money about his person. Thank heaven! he carries a dagger!"

"You seem dull, colonel. Come, cheer up; for though things may look black, no doubt——"

"Oh," interrupted Blood, with a forced laugh, "I've no doubt all will soon be set right. Come, drink."

And he poured out a tankard of the wine for the governor.

His own he had filled before poisoning the wine.

"I thank you," replied the governor, with a merry twinkle in his eyes; "here's your good health; and my other and best wish to you is that you will not have the ill-luck to be my guest for long."

"Thank you," answered Blood, raising his wine to his lips. "Here's prosperity to you."

The governor was a tremendous drinker, more especially at other persons' expense, and half the contents of the tankard immediately went down his capacious throat.

Instantaneously the powerful poison began to show its effects.

The pallor of death o'erspread the governor's face, and with a startled cry he started from his seat.

Trembling, as with the ague, he fixed his eyes upon the colonel's face.

He was about to speak, but his face suddenly became distorted in a most horrible manner.

He seized upon the chair to steady himself, then he opened his mouth.

But the fearful shriek he was about to utter never left his lips.

Blood started up, clutched him by the throat, and bore him to the floor.

But by this time the poison had rendered the governor insensible.

Blood snatched the dagger from the governor's girdle, then raising his hand, he deliberately brought it down on the bell.

After this he sprang to the side of the door.

He did not have long to wait.

"Hark!"

The warder's quick tramp was heard, and then the noise of the unfastening of bolts and bars.

The door was flung open, and the warder appeared.

With wonderful agility, Blood was upon him.

The poor fellow did not have the time even for the utterance of a cry of alarm.

The keen flashing blade Blood held in his hand was raised in an instant, the next it was buried in the man's heart.

So true was the aim, that the warder at once dropped at his feet lifeless.

Blood was determined to run any risk to escape. Murder was as nothing to him.

Now that he had commenced the attempt there was no retreating.

He plucked the reeking blade from the warder's breast, and hurried towards the governor's room.

He reached it, and, just as he got there, he heard voices at the outer gate.

"I tell you," said a voice, "I bear an order from the king's secretary. Behold it!"

"I say then," was the reply, "that the governor is engaged in Colonel Blood's apartment."

"Then I will wait."

"Enter then, your worship, and wait."

Bolts and bars were unfastened, and the massive gate drawn back.

Now was Blood's opportunity.

Gathering himself together, he rushed forward.

With the speed of a racehorse he went along that passage.

He reached the gate.

The startled warder placed his hand on his sword hilt.

Blood hurled him violently aside.

The next instant the visitor and the colonel were face to face.

"By heaven!" muttered Blood. "Doctor Jardell!"

Such indeed was the name of the visitor.

In an instant Blood had escaped.

The warder quickly recovered himself.

Rushing into the governor's room he seized the bell which acted as a fire alarm, and rang it violently.

Then the prison was filled with the most unearthly yells.

They proceeded from the prisoners, who, terrified at the ringing of the fire alarm, were raving and yelling to be released.

At this moment the chief warder made his appearance.

Blowing his whistle, he quickly brought together his men.

Then arose the cries—

"Where is the governor?"—"An escape! An escape!"—"Colonel Blood has escaped!"

Doctor Jardell hurried forward.

He had not taken half-a-dozen steps when loud cries of horror were heard.

Two or three of the warders had beheld the awful sight in "number six," for the dead warder's head prevented the door from becoming quite closed.

The chief warder, his men, and the doctor hurried forward.

The fearful cry of "Murder!" rang again and again through the long corridors.

Doctor Jardell rushed into the cell.

But just as he crossed the threshold an object on the floor met his eye.

He picked it up.

It was the phial which had held the poison.

The doctor at once recognised it as his property, owing to the peculiarity of the stopper, and immediately he understood what Blood had done.

"Half an hour has not yet elapsed since the poison was administered!" he cried. "Run, one of you, and get some salt and vinegar!"

Away rushed one of the warders, and he was back with what the doctor required in a few moments.

Taking up a basin which happened to be on the table, the doctor half filled it with vinegar, placed a large quantity of salt in it, and stirred it well.

"Hold up the governor's head," he cried.

The chief warder dropped on his knees and held up the governor's head, while Doctor Jardell forced open the mouth, and poured some of the stuff down his throat.

A series of rapid, convulsive movements agitated the body, and the head moved from side to side.

"Lift him up!" cried Jardell, "and hurry him round the cell."

The warders quickly did as desired.

One stalwart man took the governor by the right, and another by the left arm, and hurried him round the cell.

Doctor Jardell followed, slapping the governor soundly on the back.

Round and round they sped.

Gradually the stiffened legs began to show signs of the return of their functions, and suddenly a long-drawn sigh escaped the governor's lips.

"Stop!" cried Jardell, as with wonderful agility he caught the governor round the waist. "Stop!"

The governor opened his eyes and looked around.

"He is saved!" cried Jardell, "he is saved!"

A loud, ringing cheer left the warders' lips.

But their cheers died away into low, vengeful mutterings, as their eyes once more rested on the figure of their murdered comrade.

The governor was taken to his room, and Doctor Jardell advised that a skilled physician should be at once summoned, as he himself had important engagements to fulfil, and could not stay.

The governor was conscious, but unable to speak.

"I came here," said Jardell, "in order to interview Blood. Now I shall return to Whitehall, and place before Sir Christopher Cullum particulars of what has transpired."

"Sir," said the chief warder, "I hope it will not be long before Blood is again here. Though we shall not have the power of slaying him as he slew our comrade, he shall know what torture means within the goal of Newgate."

* * * *

In about the middle of Long Acre—which at the period of which we are writing was a country lane, and contained about a dozen houses—was a large residence, enclosed by high stone walls, called "The Convent."

As a convent it had been used many generations before our romance commences.

Now, however, it was put to a very different use, it being the residence of a lady called Claribel Cameron.

Mistress Claribel Cameron was a perfect mystery.

That she was a lady of fortune, was taken for granted, for she lived like one.

Whether she was married or a widow was not known, although it was a very well-known thing that at certain times she was visited by a gentleman who was called Master Rushton.

This gentleman was supposed to be the family attorney.

The servants stated that they understood so, though they never said whether they were paid to give this explanation.

Mistress Claribel Cameron was one of the most beautiful women a man ever beheld.

No one knew her history, and as Mistress Cameron never visited, and never invited visitors to her house, there was little chance of anyone learning anything about her.

It is just an hour after Colonel Blood made his daring escape from Newgate that we reach "The Convent."

Judging from the appearance of the exterior, one would have felt inclined to believe that every soul within that building had retired.

Not the faintest gleam of light was anywhere discernible.

In total darkness and in deep silence the whole house appeared to be wrapped.

Such, however, was not the case, at least so far as darkness is concerned.

"The Convent" boasted many large, lofty apartments, and all of them were furnished in princely fashion.

In the largest of these sat Mistress Claribel Cameron.

The apartment was illuminated with many lamps held by silver cherubs suspended from the richly-painted ceiling, but their light could not be seen from the road owing, firstly to the shutters, and secondly to the dark, massive curtains falling over them.

Mistress Cameron, superbly attired, was seated beside the table knitting.

Close beside her lay a slip of paper, on which were written the words—

"*To night before midnight.—Thine for ever and ever, R.R.*"

The initials meant Rupert Rushton.

Occasionally Mistress Cameron fixed

her eyes upon this paper, and more than once an expression of bitter scorn rested for a moment upon her face.

At last she laid her work aside, and walked to the window, as if to throw aside the curtains, open the window and look out.

But abruptly she checked herself.

"No," she muttered, "I must not do that—lest idle tongues should wag. Heavens! with what leaden feet does Old Father Time creep on this night! Will he come? Oh, if ever I desired the presence of Master Rushton, it is now—*now*. Yet, do I not try to keep calm?" she added, approaching the glass and eagerly surveying her features. "Yes, I am calm—very calm, considering that my bosom is torn with so much anxiety. Ha! that sound! The door closes! 'Tis he!"

Hastily Mistress Cameron resumed her seat and her knitting.

A light, quick tread was heard on the stairs, and a man hastily entered the room.

He was heavily cloaked and masked, and was well armed.

"Ha, ha!" he laughed, "at work, eh, my sweet Claribel?"

He snatched off his mask, threw back his cloak, and revealed the face and the figure of

Charles Stuart, King of England!

Mistress Claribel started up, but Charles, after embracing her, led her back to her seat.

"My dear Claribel," he said, "I most sincerely regret my inability to stay with you for any length of time. Matters of the utmost importance compel me to hurry away."

"Oh, Charles!"

"Don't cry now—don't cry! Odds fish! This will never do. What is the matter?—what ails you?"

"Charles, where are you going?"

"Ha! ha! What! jealous?"

"No, no, I am not jealous, but I should really like to know your destination."

"You would recoil in horror did I tell you, my sweet Claribel," replied Charles, his face assuming a gloomy expression.

"Not I. I have had to deal with so many horrors, that the horror which would shock me must be a horror indeed. Tell me where you are going?"

"Well, if you persist, I will tell you. *I am going to Newgate!*"

"Newgate!" cried Mistress Claribel, starting up.

"Ay, Newgate. I told you you would be shocked. I am going there to investigate. I suppose your servants have not heard the news, or they would have told you that that accursed Colonel Blood has escaped?"

A wild scream left the lips of Mistress Cameron.

She stepped back a pace and surveyed the king for a few seconds with an expression of incredulity.

"Impossible!" she said.

"No," was the stern reply, "it is *not* impossible, it is *true*. But what should cause you to utter that cry when I spoke the scoundrel's name?"

No reply.

"Speak, and tell me."

Still no reply.

"Mistress Cameron!" thundered Charles, "tell me what it was which caused you to utter such an exclamation of surprise? What is this Colonel Blood—this red-handed ruffian—this murderous villain who tears up our royal warrant and flings it in the face of our captain—what, in the name of Heaven, madam, can this man be to you?"

"Are you aware that this man is a wretch whose hands are deeply dyed with blood? Heaven's mercy on us!" he added, vehemently, "there is not a corner in the kingdom that shall not be scoured for him; and when he is caught, not one spark of mercy will I show him!"

With a low, gasping cry, Claribel Cameron sank upon her knees before the king.

With uplifted hands, with heaving bosom, with eyes streaming with tears, she said—

"Oh, sire, talk not thus. Spare him—for my sake, I conjure you, spare him!"

The king was appalled.

Stock still he stood, the expression on his face showing the conflicting emotions under which he laboured.

"Spare him!" he repeated in husky tones, "spare him! Did we ever hear the like? Madam, what is this man to you?"

"*He is my son!*" was the faltering reply.

For the space of a few moments Charles stood looking down upon that upturned tearful face like one dumfounded.

Then, without uttering a single word, he dropped into a chair, and buried his face in his hands.

"Oh, sire—Charles! Charles!" pleaded the beautiful woman, "you have often said how dearly you loved me—you know well enough how I love *you*—have I not—oh, so often—proved it? Charles—Charles, look at me; tell me that you will allow him to leave the country."

"No," cried Charles, starting up and pacing the room excitedly, "no, it cannot be. My people will demand his instant execution. The man has proved himself to be a villain of the deepest dye. I have no power to pardon a man who is guilty of a foul and brutal murder. Did I have the chance, I would capture the wretch with my own hands!"

"*Then capture him!*" cried a deep voice.

Aghast the king turned, to find himself face to face with Colonel Blood!

Yes, there stood the ruffian, apparently very calm, and looking but little the worse for what he had so recently passed through.

With an air of defiance he fixed his eyes upon the king.

No cry had left either the lips of the monarch or the beautiful woman at his side.

Both were absolutely dumb-stricken.

Charles quickly recovered himself.

"Murderous ruffian!" he said, "are you aware to whom you are addressing yourself?"

"Why, yes," sneered Blood, "the redoubtable Charles Stuart. But this is the very first occasion on which I have had the honour of seeing you in my mother's house. So, my dear mother, *this* is the celebrated Master Ralph Rushton! By the shades of Satan! I congratulate you both. Is it still your intention to attempt to arrest me, sire?"

"Cecil!" cried Mistress Cameron, in excited tones, as she stepped forward. "Cecil! I entreat—nay, I *command* you, cease!"

But Blood was not in the humour to listen to her.

He repeated his question.

"What if I *did* attempt to arrest you," asked Charles, "would you have the audacity to resist?"

"*Would* I? Why, look at me, sire, and judge for yourself. King of England you may be, but your power ceases at the threshold of this house. Therefore, if you attempted to lay a hand on me I would not treat you as a king, but as an impertinent intruder, and would thrust you forth. And if you happened to be injured you would be wise enough to keep the particulars as to *how* you got your injuries and *where* to yourself."

The king's rage now knew no bounds.

He was absolutely white with suppressed passion.

One look he directed upon Colonel Blood's face—a look the ruffian never forgot—then, turning, he walked swiftly towards the door.

But ere he reached it, Mistress Cameron rushed towards him.

"Charles!" she cried, frantically, "is *this*, then, to be the end of all? Oh, Charles, think how I have loved you; think of all the sacrifices I have made for you. This can be no surprise, for you knew that I had a son."

"Assuredly," replied Charles, halting and slowly turning, "I knew you had a son, but I had no idea that that son was the murderer—Blood."

"My mother is not responsible for *my* actions," said Blood, coldly, "any more than I am responsible for *hers*."

Charles well knew what was meant by this.

After a few moments the king said—

"For your sake, Claribel, I am willing to do many things a king should not do; but I cannot grant your son a free pardon. Why, this very night he has murdered one of the warders of the prison, and nearly murdered the governor. But I will permit him to at once leave the country on condition that he will never return. I will issue private instructions that he is not to be arrested."

"Good!" said Blood, with a chuckle of satisfaction. "And now, my dear mother, I am willing that you should advance *Master Rushton* the money you spoke of."

"Ha!" cried the king, with a sudden start; "what means he, Claribel?"

"You told me, Charles, the other night, when you were here," replied

Mistress Cameron, "that you did not know how to turn for want of money."

"Most true," replied Charles, with a deep sigh. "Little troubles me but money, and of that I have very little. I expected some money from France, but——"

"Rely not upon French promises," interrupted Mistress Cameron. "You are aware of my great experience with these people. They are avaricious, cunning, and treacherous."

"There is some truth in what you say," replied the king, moodily.

But suddenly brightening up, he said—

"Have you really the money I require?"

"I have, dear Charles, but it was necessary that my son should consent before I could give it you."

"I—I understand," replied the king, in agitated tones.

His own heart told him to turn and fly from that house.

But then the knowledge of the lowness of his treasury, that on all sides were clamouring creditors, that several of his "favoured ladies" were sadly in want of money, caused him to stay.

"I am afraid," he said, "that the little you could offer, Claribel, I must accept."

"*Little!*" replied Mistress Cameron, with a forced laugh. "Why, sire, I can within twelve hours place within your hands the whole of the money you want—and in *gold.*"

The king was more than startled.

"What!" he said. "Thirty thousand crowns?"

"Ay, thirty thousand! Will you accept it?"

"Most willingly. But I deal entirely with you, remember, Claribel."

"To be sure. Be seated, Charles; sign for the amount, and without fail it shall be delivered to you."

"Stay, stay! On second thoughts, Claribel, I will fetch it myself, little by little; thus no one but ourselves will be aware of the transaction."

To this Mistress Claribel agreed.

She rapidly and skilfully drew up the required document, and Charles signed it.

Then the king rose to go.

Mistress Cameron accompanied him to the door.

"Hurry off your son, Claribel," whispered Charles. "As you value a continuance of my favour, hurry him off."

"Yes, yes; he shall depart at *once.*"

"You promise?"

"I *swear* it."

Satisfied, the king departed.

Reaching the door, he replaced his mask, drew his hat over his brows, and his cloak closely about his person, and went off at a rapid pace.

But ere he had got far, he abruptly paused.

"Gad's life!" he muttered, "a strange suspicion has crossed my mind. It was Blood who murdered the man Lucas at the chambers in Lincoln's Inn. And he was also the man who stole the money which was concealed in the old place. Odds fish! I believe that they are about to lend me some of the stolen coin. It must be so, or where did Claribel so suddenly get the money she thus offers to lend?

"By heaven and earth! I must not have it. I will return to Claribel—but no," he added, after a moment's pause; "no; money I *must* have. But, gad's life; what would be said if it should ever become known that King Charles actually received stolen property. Ah," he sighed, "this is a dreadful thought —I must wash it down with a bottle of canary."

As soon as the king had taken his departure, Blood seated himself beside his mother.

The first words she asked were—

"The money is safe?"

"Every farthing."

"How did you manage it?"

"Easily enough," was the reply. "I thrice tried to remove it, but it was impossible. There were so many people about connected with those accursed attorneys. But as I never let anything master me I soon formed a plan. I engaged the services of one Hartlock."

"Hartlock?"

"Ay, the sexton at St. Andrew's Church at Holborn."

"Yes, yes; I remember him."

"Well, I gave him fifty guineas to do what I directed him. I watched the opportunity, and smuggled him —pickaxe, shovel and all—into the vault where the money was, and having entered myself, I barricaded the door.

"Until midnight we waited, and then we—or, I should say, Hartlock—commenced. But he was very slow digging up the earth, for the sight of the enormous amount of gold had, apparently, nearly paralyzed him.

"The top stones being removed, the rest was easy, as the earth was soft.

"Suddenly Hartlock paused. His shovel had come in contact with stones. Still I ordered him to dig, for the hole was not large enough to contain the treasure. He removed stone after stone, until quite a pile stood beside the hole.

"Hartlock jumped into the hole the better to throw up the earth and stones, when with a loud cry he shot right through.

"Holding the lantern over, what do you think I found?"

Mistress Cameron shook her head.

"Well, then, I found that there was *another* vault beneath the one in which I stood, and into this Hartlock had fallen.

"He had not hurt himself. I lowered him the lantern, and then flung every bag of gold to him.

"Having accomplished this task, I descended and looked round. I saw that it was a small brick vault.

"There was a door on the right, and that, after some little difficulty, I forced open with the pick-axe. Imagine my intense astonishment when I found myself in the strong room of an attorney's office.

"I decided to get a new lock of the same pattern as the broken one, and with the key in my possession, I could always get at the store of gold."

"Which way?"

"By the attorney's office. That must, of course, always be done at night. Well, I got a new lock, fixed it to the door, and I have the key. As to the upper vault, that looks as though it had never been touched."

"But you have forgotten one most important matter, my son," said Mistress Cameron.

"Indeed! What is that?"

"That man, Hartlock, holds your secret."

"Ay, he does, but he will never reveal it."

"What mean you?"

"It is locked within his breast for ever," said Blood, grimly, "*for in the hole where I intended to have placed the gold, lies the dead body of Hartlock!*"

"Just Heaven!" gasped Mistress Cameron, starting from her chair, and fixing her horror-stricken eyes upon the unmoved face of her son; "do you really mean to tell me, Cecil, that you murdered him."

"Hold!" interrupted Blood, sternly; "hold! lest I withdraw my consent as to that money, and thus render your contract with Charles Stuart useless, and cause the king's *favour* to be withdrawn from you."

"Oh, Cecil! Cecil——"

"Hist! hist! Remember our bargain, my dear mother; you were to go *your* road, and *I* was to go mine."

With these words Blood rose, and proceeded to pace the room.

Again sinking into her seat, the beautiful lady placed her arms upon the table, and buried her face in them.

"I am punished! justly punished!" she moaned.

CHAPTER V.

IS OF WHAT PASSED BETWEEN CLIFFORD HANSARD AND BLAKE BARRELL—OF THE FIGHT, AND HOW OLIVIA PRESTON SEPARATED THE COMBATANTS.

ONCE more we return to the strange-looking residence of Prichard Preston.

It was the night of the third day after Blood effected his escape in such a daring fashion from the gaol of Newgate.

By this time all London rang with the startling news.

It was freely circulated that Blood was being hunted for; but, as a matter of fact, the authorities had received a private hint—and from a very *high quarter indeed*—that Blood was not to be arrested.

Then it was rumoured that Blood had succeeded in evading the law, and had embarked for Calais.

It was a source of the deepest regret to Sir Christopher Cullum and our hero that he had escaped.

Of course our hero had not the faintest suspicion that, instead of his escape being prevented, it was assisted, and if Sir Christopher Cullum suspected anything, he was wise enough to keep it to himself.

Sir Christopher had assured our hero that he would ever find him his firm friend, and also that he would take the earliest opportunity of endeavouring to forward his prospects in life.

"It will not be long," he said, "ere you rise in the world; for, fortunately, you are a most excellent scholar."

It is hardly necessary to say that our young hero wanted to rise in the world; but then he considered that if he did so rise, he would have to leave "Potter's Bar," and there were many reasons why he should cling to the old house—the house of his childhood.

The principal of these was his consideration for those who had befriended him—those who had brought him up as their own—Master and Mistress Preston.

The next consideration was Olivia, the locksmith's daughter, a beautiful maiden of seventeen.

Thrown together from their earliest infancy, it is hardly to be wondered at that these two should learn to love each other with all the passion of their young hearts.

Master Preston, having a large and lucrative business, was compelled to keep a good staff of workmen and apprentices, the latter, as was the custom in the days of which we are writing, living and sleeping on the premises.

Everyone of those youths looked upon our hero as superior to them in every respect.

But stay! We have said "everyone" —whereas we should have said *all but one.*

Yes; there was one who looked upon Clifford Hansard with jealous feelings, who hated him—from the bottom of his heart—one who sincerely wished that if he plunged a knife into Clifford's heart, the crime could never be brought home to him.

The name of this young man was Blake Barrell; his age about twenty.

In height he was nearly as tall as our hero; but his figure was awkward—out of all proper proportions in fact.

He was neither good-looking nor ugly, but what is generally known as "passable."

But his features were spoiled by the expression which generally rested upon them.

A curious expression was this! A strange, savage expression!

It was the expression of one who allows his feelings to get the upper hand of him—who imagines that someone has done him a most grievous injury, and who goes about, day by day, filled with but one thought—the desire for vengeance.

This young man loved Olivia Preston —after his own fashion—but the young girl could never like him.

She regarded him much after the fashion that a fawn would regard a tiger. She feared him—distrusted him—suspected him, and avoided him on every possible occasion.

Clifford tried hard to be friends with him, but Blake would not have it.

Clifford was successful with the beautiful Olivia—he was not; and he therefore considered that he had every reason to hate Clifford, and he considered also that it would be to his interests to do our gallant young hero all the harm he possibly could.

It was, we repeat, on the night of the third day, after the unparalleled escape of Colonel Blood from Newgate that we return to Potter's Bar.

Master and Mistress Preston, together with several apprentices, had gone to a special service at St. Andrew's.

Olivia was dressing, while Blake was in his bedroom, and Clifford in the sitting-room.

Our hero was engaged in arranging Master Preston's accounts, for the worthy locksmith was no scholar.

Presently a low knock came upon the door.

Instantly Clifford rose and went to open it, for he thought that it might be Olivia — whose appearance he was anxiously awaiting.

Instead of it being our heroine, however, Clifford found himself face to face with Blake Barrell.

"Well?" asked Clifford.

"Aye, I daresay all may be well by-and-by, Clifford Hansard, but now all is *not* well."

"What has happened then?"

"Why, I've actually been and spoiled that beautiful lock which was ordered by Chief Justice Steer."

"Spoilt it—that can hardly be."

"I came to ask you if you would just come and look at it. For you, being so clever with locks of delicate workmanship, can, perhaps, give me a hint as to what should be done with it under the circumstances."

"To be sure," Clifford instantly replied; I will come down."

Not the slightest suspicion had he that Blake had any secret design upon him.

Blake descended to the workshop below, and thither he was soon followed by Clifford.

This workshop was the principal one of all, and was generally used by Master Preston and our hero.

There were two doors—one at the end of the stairs, and another at the further end of the workshop which communicated with a flight of stairs—seldom used, however—which led to Master Preston's bedchamber.

"Where is the lock?" asked Clifford.

"Sent home long ago," was the reply.

"Sent home?"

"Ay."

"Then what do you mean by telling me such a deliberate lie?" demanded Clifford, in indignant tones.

"What do I mean? I will tell you, and quickly, too. But first, I do not wish to be interrupted."

So saying, he turned, banged the door to, locked it, and placed the key in his pocket.

Then folding his arms defiantly across his breast, he strode up to Clifford, and said—

"To-night, Clifford Hansard, is *settling up night* between us."

Clifford was not at all troubled by these totally unexpected proceedings.

"I really don't understand you," he said, "but I shall begin to think that you have taken leave of your senses."

"Not so. I am perfectly sane—perfectly cool and collected. Clifford Hansard, to-night I leave this house for ever."

"Indeed? This is a very sudden resolve on your part, is it not?"

"No; it is the result of long deliberation. I am going to leave this house, I repeat. But before I go, I want to tell you this—that though you have gained the love of Olivia Preston, she shall never marry you."

"What wild raving is this?"

"For a long time past," continued Blake, his eyes now glittering furiously, "I have been treated by Olivia Preston, and by you as dirt."

"Blake Barrell," replied Clifford, in solemn tones, "I do assure you that you are mistaken. But you were ever full of strange fancies. Calm yourself—open the door, and let no more be said on the subject."

"No. I repeat that this is settling night. I have a deal to say to you ere I take my departure."

"Then I shall refuse to listen to you."

"I have locked the door, and so you will be *compelled* to listen to what I have to say."

"I trust, Blake Barrell," said Clifford, in calm, but firm tones, "that you will not compel me to *make* you open that door."

"That you cannot do."

"Well, I can take the key away from you."

"You dare not make the attempt."

"You will find that I *will* make the attempt."

"Attempt to *touch* me!" hissed Blake, "and I will plunge this into your heart!"

And as he spoke, he drew from beneath his jacket a large knife.

Clifford was absolutely horror-stricken.

"Good heavens!" he said, "is it really possible? Until this moment, Blake Barrell, I never knew your true character. Remember that if such a threat, as you have just now uttered, were heard and followed up, imprisonment would be your certain punishment."

"At a future time I shall have an opportunity of having my revenge."

"What childish prattle!" exclaimed Clifford, contemptuously.

" You will find that it is no childish prattle," growled Blake. " I mean what I say. There is only one thing which could cause me to renounce my determination."

" And that ? "

" Is, that you at once resign the hand of Olivia Preston to me."

" You must, indeed, be a perfect fool ! " replied Clifford, scornfully.

" You then decline ? "

" Do not talk such nonsense ! Open that door at once."

And Clifford strode towards him.

But Blake, clutching the knife dagger-wise, cried—

" Beware ! Attempt to take that key from me, and I will plunge this knife into your heart ! "

Clifford rushed towards Blake, intending to disarm him.

But, unfortunately, he slipped on a piece of steel plate, and fell headlong to the floor.

Instantly Blake was upon him.

Raising his knife high in the air, he said—

" Swear to do as I have asked you or you die ! "

Clifford spoke not a word.

With a sudden wrench he turned himself round, and seized the descending arm—for descending it most assuredly was.

The savage, vengeful look on Blake's face showed that he was determined to take our hero's life if he did not agree to his preposterous proposals.

With one hand Clifford clutched Blake by the doublet, and they struggled violently on the floor.

Clifford was certainly the stronger; and, moreover, while Blake raved, Clifford remained cool, but then he had the great disadvantage of being beneath Blake.

This position was, however, speedily altered, for Clifford, by an almost superhuman effort, flung him off, and then sprang to his feet.

Blake was quickly up, and, starting back with a fearful oath, he raised the knife, and, with all his force, hurled it at Clifford's head.

The aim was nearly true.

It went within an inch of Clifford's head, and buried itself, quivering like an aspen, in the wall.

" Dastard ! " cried Clifford. " Cowardly wretch ! But we are now on equal terms. Stand forward, and fight fairly with your fists. If you don't, I swear that I will thrash you within an inch of your life ! "

Blake, with upraised fists, dashed forward, and Clifford met him.

The sparring was of the very briefest duration.

Clifford launched out with his left, and dealt Blake a tremendous blow on the face.

He staggered back, then stopped, hesitated, and then seizing a hammer that lay on the floor, he rushed forward.

But at that moment the private door, which we have mentioned, opened, and the beauteous figure of Olivia Preston stood upon the threshold.

Stood, with wide-open, terror-stricken eyes, gazing upon the extraordinary scene.

" Hold ! " she cried. " Hold ! what means this dreadful scene ? Blake Barrell attacking with a hammer one who is unarmed ? Put it down, coward ! "

Blake slunk back, and let the hammer fall from his grasp.

" Coward ? " said Clifford, bitterly. " You are indeed right in calling him coward, Olivia ; for he is the greatest coward that ever I had to deal with. Olivia, 'tis a wonder that I stand before you alive. Behold ! " and he pointed to the knife in the wall.

" Holy Mary ! " ejaculated Olivia " Blake threw that at you ? "

" He did, and very close to me did it pass."

" Shame on you ! Shame on you, Blake Barrel ! " cried Olivia. " When my father returns, I shall lay before him your base conduct."

" Stay," interrupted Blake, " you may save yourself the trouble, for it is my intention to leave the house at once, and never to return. I will go now ; but before I leave, I wish to tell you, Olivia Preston, that your scornful neglect of me I will repay a thousand-fold ! "

" Scornful neglect ! What mean you ? "

" I love you."

" Ay, so you have said dozens of times. But I do not return that love, and I have often told you that I *never could* love you. Then and there the subject should have ended."

Blake shook his head.

"It will never end with me," he said, "until—but no matter, time will show."

"Listen to what I say, Master Blake," said Olivia. "You say you are going to leave my father's house for good. Well, I for one am not surprised, for on more than one occasion I have noticed how restless you were. The occupation of a locksmith does not suit you, Blake, and you know it. But beware! let me most earnestly warn you—ha!" she cried, starting in alarm, "what is that?"

A knocking on the window was heard.

They looked up, and were startled to behold a strange-looking face pressed against the glass.

Olivia clung to Clifford, but our hero expressed no surprise.

"This is one of Blake's companions," he muttered.

Blake looked up at the window, nodded, and the face disappeared.

"Remember!" cried Blake, seizing his cap—"remember, my time will certainly come."

"When you will be thrust into prison, eh?" replied Clifford, in sarcastic tones. "You are right — it *will* come."

Blake, without another word, opened the door and strode out.

"Do you think he has really gone for good, dear Clifford?" asked Olivia.

"I do, sweetheart! Olivia, he has, for some time past, been mixed up with bad companions. I recognised that face at the window."

"Ah?"

"Yes; *it was the face of John Jeevers*, the young villain that the notorious Colonel Blood engaged so many counsels for when on his trial at Newgate."

"Great heaven! you must be mistaken."

Clifford shook his head.

"No," he said, "I am quite certain of it."

Both went to the sitting-room, and on the arrival of the locksmith, he was made acquainted with what had transpired.

Calmly enough he listened until he was told of the face at the window. Then, with a loud cry, he rushed up the stairs to his bed-room.

He returned in less than a minute, the expression on his face showing that something alarming had occurred.

"'Tis as I suspected!" he groaned, as he sank into a chair and buried his face in his hands.

"What? What? Speak!" said Clifford.

"He has forced open my cabinet, and every gold piece has gone."

"Lord, Lord!" moaned poor Mistress Preston. "Olivia's dowry, and the savings of years all—all gone."

"The scoundrel long ago made up his mind to this," said Clifford; "but I will at once give information to the authorities."

"Do so—do so, good Clifford," replied the locksmith. "Delay not an instant, but return as quickly as possible."

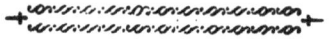

CHAPTER VI.

IS OF THE LETTER TO CLIFFORD HANSARD—OF WHAT TRANSPIRED BETWEEN BLOOD, JOHN JEEVERS AND BLAKE BARREL— AND OF THE PARTICULARS OF ONE OF THE DARK DEEDS OF OLD LONDON.

IT was a week after the incidents we have recorded in the foregoing chapter, that a letter was sent by one of the Court pages to Clifford Hansard.

Clifford was from home at the time, and the page was told that he might either leave the letter or return with it at nine of the clock, at which hour the locksmith expected Clifford would return.

The hour then was seven.

After some little consideration, the page replied that he would take the letter with him and return at nine.

It was not often that he found himself in this part of London, and he determined to stroll about the neighbourhood.

Master Preston did not know of his intention, otherwise he would have warned him that it was highly dangerous, in the then state of London, for a stranger to wander about, unless accompanied by two or three friends well armed, and well able to defend themselves.

Now this page, by name Henri Hadden, was a young fellow of about Clifford's age, and was admitted to be the handsomest page in the palace.

His figure was marvellously graceful and erect, and his features, though somewhat feminine in the delicate tracing of their outlines, would have won the heart of anyone.

His magnificent head of chestnut hair fell down his shoulders in massive ringlets, and waved gracefully with every movement of his form.

Surely there was not a happier lad in the whole realm than this youth.

There was always a merry twinkle in his bright blue eyes, and his musical laughter was catching in the highest degree.

After leaving Potter's Bar, Henri wandered up Chancery Lane and into Holborn.

Not the slightest suspicion had he that he was followed.

But as soon as he had emerged from the archway beneath Potter's Bar, a figure had glided after him.

It was John Jeevers, whose mother, as our readers will remember, was in the service of Doctor Jardell.

Jeevers did not follow the young page in anything like a secret fashion.

He sauntered leisurely after him, but taking particular care not to lose sight of him for a single instant.

Reaching Holborn the page glanced round him.

"I will ask someone the way to Cheapside," he thought. "I have heard a deal of talk about the thoroughfare, and should like to see it. Moreover, I have a guinea in my pocket—a few ribbons from Cheapside among the girls I know, will go a long way. Hi! I say, my friend."

"Ay; ay?"

And John Jeevers sauntered slowly to his side.

"Will you kindly direct me to Cheapside?"

"To be sure, young sir. Are you a stranger hereabouts?"

"Yes."

"I thought so."

"You, I suppose, are familiar with this part of London?"

"Oh, quite, young sir—quite."

"You are an apprentice, I presume?"

"Yes, a goldsmith's apprentice," replied John Jeevers, with all the coolness in the world. "And I presume that you—from your rich dress, the pretty dagger at your side, and the like—are a person of some importance?"

"Oh, no!" replied Henri, with a merry laugh. "I am not a person of importance, being simply one of his majesty's pages."

"Well, I always thought that that *was* an important position. But you want Cheapside. Now, if you will take my advice, young man, you will be careful how you proceed," and here Jeevers placed his hand on the young page's arm, and spoke in what he intended to be confidential tones.

"Careful how I proceed?" repeated the page, looking somewhat curiously into Jeevers' strange face.

"Ay; and for why? London abounds with bad characters. There are men who will lead you astray in no time, my friend. Now, I happen to be going to Bartholomew Close, which is not far from Cheapside. I have a little business to transact there, and it will take but a few minutes. After that I am at your disposal."

"Will you show me safely the way?" asked the page, eagerly.

"I will."

"I thank you most heartily, my friend, and will willingly accept of your kind offer," replied Henri; "I have a guinea in my pocket, and one half of it shall be yours to spend as ye may think fit."

Jeevers thanked him, but the unsuspecting page did not hear the low chuckle of satisfaction which left his lips.

"Follow me," said Jeevers, "and we will hasten off to Bartholomew Close."

This quarter being reached, Jeevers led him through many extraordinary maze-like passages, and descended a flight of stone steps into a sort of court.

This place was almost as dark as pitch, and now, for the first time, Henri began to feel somewhat alarmed.

Jeevers noticed it, and instantly he said with a laugh—

"Ha! ha! This quarter of London is very different indeed from the West, eh? But we shall not be here longer than a few minutes. You will find Cheapside quite a different thoroughfare. Plenty of light there, and plenty of noise the apprentices make with their ever-lasting, ' What d'ye lack?'"

Henri was reassured; he felt easier, and he felt easier still when Jeevers stopped before a huge wooden building bearing a goldsmith's sign.

As a matter of fact, this house had not been used as a goldsmith's for many, many years.

Empty it had remained for a length of time; but by-and-bye a "gentleman," whom, however, the neighbours seldom saw, took it, and occasionally stayed there.

Who he was, what he was, no one could ever ascertain.

It was quite certain that the individual who had taken it transacted no business of a commercial nature there, and it was equally certain that when he visited the dirty old house it was at night.

"This," said Jeevers, "is my master's workshop; but there are none of the apprentices here now. Will you enter or stay here until I return? I shall not be long. Perhaps you had better enter with me. There is a little sitting-room just inside, and you can wait there. My master would not say anything even if he knew of it."

"Your master is not here now?"

"Oh, no, only the manager of the business."

Thereupon Jeevers knocked upon the door.

The page never noticed it, but that knock was of a most peculiar character.

No one came to the door.

But a sharp click was heard, and the door opened, this having been accomplished by some person within by the simple pulling of a wire.

Jeevers entered, the page following him.

A taper burned in the hall, and taking it up, Jeevers conducted Henri into a small room on the left.

"There you are," he said, as he placed the taper on the table. "This is a pretty little apartment, is it not? Well, I shall not be a minute."

Along the passage he went, rapidly ascended the first flight of stairs, and knocked upon a door immediately opposite him.

He was directed to enter.

He opened the door and was in the presence of—Colonel Blood!

Seated near the crime-stained villain was Blake Barrell!

The colonel rose as Jeevers entered, and at once noticing that the young gaol-bird was somewhat excited, he said—

"Ha! you have succeeded in something? Who is that with you?"

"Colonel," replied Jeevers in low, hurried tones, "I waited and watched as you told me."

"Ay, how long?"

"More than an hour."

"Proceed."

"Nothing could I see of Clifford Hansard; but by-and-bye a page passed beneath the arch."

"A page? What sort of page?"

"A Court page."

"Ha! Go on. Whom did he seek?"

"Why it struck me that he might bear a message from this Sir Christopher Cullum—the gentleman of whom you are so much afraid—"

"Afraid!" thundered the colonel; "I am afraid of no man."

"Oh, pardon me," grinned Jeevers; "but to proceed. I crept as closely as I possibly could, and listened. He produced a letter, and asked for Clifford Hansard. Master Preston made some reply, but what it was I know not. Still, there can be no doubt that it was something about Clifford Hansard being then from home. I heard him ask the page whether he would leave the letter. He would not, but said he would return later on. Thinking that this letter would be of importance to you, I have inveigled the youth here."

"Ha!" exclaimed the colonel, "a sudden idea strikes me. Blake Barrel, your longing for revenge is about to be satisfied. The time has come!"

"'LOOK! A HUMAN FACE!' CRIED CLIFFORD, EXCITEDLY."

Another Beautiful Coloured Picture will be Given next week.

"You will demand the letter, colonel?" queried Jeevers.

"No; *you* will."

"Yes; and then he may go?"

"No!" thundered Blood. "He must never again cross the threshold of this house, except as a corpse."

Barely had these fearful words left his lips ere a cry of terror was heard, and footsteps hurriedly descended the stairs.

The curiosity of the page had prompted him to ascend those stairs, and he had thus overheard nearly all that was said.

At once he saw the fashion in which he had been trapped.

He was no coward; but he saw that to offer resistance to three persons, and one of those the notorious Colonel Blood —the very mention of whose deeds had frequently caused his flesh to creep —was useless, and he considered that flight was his only chance of safety.

He dashed to the door—he seized the catch—he pulled violently at it.

But no—it stirred not; and the reason of that was that before Jeevers ascended the stairs, he had drawn down a secret catch at the top of the door.

It was hidden by the woodwork, and thus it escaped the page's notice.

Oh, what heartrending cries the poor unfortunate lad uttered.

"To you, Jeevers, I leave him!" exclaimed Blood; "and for the work— a hundred crowns shall be yours."

Jeevers hesitated a few moments only.

Then he descended the stairs.

The page at once turned towards him, with a startled face.

Jeevers spoke not a word; but from beneath his doublet he took a huge broad-bladed knife.

At the same moment the page remembered his dagger.

He instantly snatched it from its sheath, and firmly grasping it, he stood boldly facing his foe.

"Villain!" he said. "Wretch that you must be to decoy me to this place."

Jeevers made no reply.

With the terrible-looking knife clutched firmly in his hand, he crept towards the lad.

But there was a certain way in which he thus crept.

Had the page not been full of the dreadful words he had heard above, he must have noticed that Jeevers was working him into the little sitting-room, and towards the back window—a window which, however, was most securely shuttered and bolted.

Suddenly Jeevers rushed to the fireplace, and placed his hand upon what looked like a bell.

Instantly the unfortunate page uttered a pitiful cry, for he felt the floor giving way beneath him.

He tried to jump from off it, but it was too late.

The portion of the flooring on which he stood went down with a bang, and Henri shot through with the speed of lightning.

Seizing the taper, Jeevers held it over the trap.

At this moment the colonel strode into the room, Blake at his side.

"He's down," grinned Jeevers; "but I can see that he's twisting about."

"Descend then, and despatch him!"

Seizing the taper from him, the colonel sank upon his knees, and held the light so that Jeevers could see to descend.

Hanging from the top of the trap was a thick rope ladder.

Down this, the knife placed between his teeth, went Jeevers.

The distance from the mouth of the trap to the ground below was *twenty-five feet.*

Upon the ground, horizontally, and at a height of about two feet, three steel bars were placed.

So the unlucky individual falling through this trap would certainly break either his neck, his back, or some of his limbs.

Before Jeevers reached the bottom he heard the poor lad groaning.

"Lower the taper," cried Jeevers.

Blood handed the taper to Blake, directing him to descend the ladder.

Jeevers had sufficient light in a few seconds.

Right across the bars lay poor Henri, unconscious, but groaning fearfully.

"Take his clothing from him first!" shouted Blood. "Down with you, Blake, and help him."

Blake required not to be twice told.

Down he went, and the two set to

work and stripped the page of almost every article of attire.

"What now?" asked Blake.

"This!" replied Jeevers.

And raising the knife, he deliberately plunged it into the heart of the unfortunate lad.

Reader, do not imagine that such a terrible tragedy as this is a deed emanating only from the brain of a romancer.

This deed is only one of many hundreds which occurred every year in London, when the crown of England was worn by Charles Stuart, and only one out of many which we shall have to record.

The villain Blake did not shudder. He stood looking on without remorse.

His disposition was savage in the extreme, and our readers will see, in the course of this narrative, that he actually delighted in deeds which would turn cold the blood of an ordinary mortal.

"Well?" shouted Blood.

"All right now, colonel," replied Jeevers, "he's dead. The only thing now is where he's to be put?"

"You know where he is to be put well enough."

"I don't, until you tell me."

"Fool! *The river!*"

"Ha! The river—good!"

"He was a fine-looking lad, eh?" asked Blood.

"Ay, ay! Court pages always are, so they say," replied Jeevers, with a hoarse laugh; "though, for my part, I never could see it."

"Of course you couldn't. You are too ugly to see anything of the kind."

"Ha, ha!" chuckled Jeevers; "too ugly. Well, I think we are much about the same, you and I, Blake, eh?"

"So they have said."

"They? Who?"

"Olivia for one."

"Well, if she said so, Blake, you may take it for granted there is some truth in her assertion——"

"Peace!" cried Blood. "Here, Blake, up with those clothes."

Blake made them into a bundle, and carried them up.

A rope was then lowered, and, by Jeevers, placed round the horribly mutilated body of Henri Hadden.

This having been done, Blood and Blake pulled it up.

At last it was landed in the apartment, and the trap door was replaced.

"I recognise the youth," said Blood, as he gazed upon the now ghastly features; "I have passed him frequently. Unless I am much mistaken, this is Henri Hadden, a favourite page of his majesty."

"Ha!" grunted Jeevers, "there's plenty more of them."

"Now, Blake," said the colonel, "search the clothes for the letter."

It was soon found and handed to the colonel, who at once opened it.

It read as follows—

"To MASTER CLIFFORD HANSARD.

"At last I am able to fulfil my promise to you. By the permission of his majesty, I am to have an assistant in my duties, and that assistant is yourself. At first the salary will be small; but by strict attention to your duties, you are most certain to rise.

"To-night I have some important business of a private nature at Whitehall, and I wish to be assisted by a person in whom I can place every reliance for attention and secrecy. Do you meet me at twelve of the clock this night at the landing-stage beside Whitehall steps. Fail not, my lad, to keep this appointment, and accept the best wishes of your faithful friend,

"CHRISTOPHER CULLUM."

Having read this document to himself, Colonel Blood, after a pause of a few moments, during which he was buried in profound thought, read it aloud.

"So you see," he said, "unless checked, this apprentice will be a person of some importance at last. Blake Barrel, this night you shall have the revenge you seek."

"Show me how—show me how!" exclaimed Blake, excitedly, "and I am your slave for ever."

"I will show you *how*," chuckled Blood; "and Jeevers, in consideration of the share you gave him of the locksmith's money, will assist you."

"I will," said Jeevers, "and most willingly. So now, colonel, let us know how we are to proceed."

"Well, then listen to this: You, Jeevers, will attire yourself in the page's clothes—but halt. Do you fancy there is any chance of your being recognised?"

"No, I think not. At any rate, I will take care not to stand in the full light."

"Do so; for if, by any chance, either of the apprentices recognise you, the whole plan at once falls to the ground, and I cannot say what may happen to you."

"You may depend upon it, I will be well on my guard."

"Upstairs with you, and don the clothes at once. And you, Blake, come with me. I will show you how we get rid of any objectionable person."

Thereupon he led the way upstairs to his own apartment.

Since he left the house of Pritchard Preston, the locksmith, Blake Barrel had frequently been in this apartment.

But though he had seen much, he was by no means acquainted with all its mysteries and its secrets.

Every place with which Colonel Blood was associated appeared to be full of mysteries.

The colonel took from his pocket a small key—so small, indeed, that one might have fancied it was a watch key.

"Now," he said, "you would hardly fancy that this wall"—and he advanced to that part near the fireplace—"is nothing but the door of a cupboard. Such is the fact, however—behold!"

Inserting the key in a little hole, he turned it three times.

The door of the cupboard did not come open in the usual way with cupboard doors.

No, right into the floor it shot.

"Whatever locks old Preston ever made," chuckled Blood, "he never made a thing like that."

"No," replied Blake. "I have heard him say he does not care to dabble in the manufacture of secret locks, springs, and the like. But Clifford Hansard, I have heard the apprentices say, is rather clever at that sort of thing."

"Yes, he is a clever youth, for, of course, you know he has been to the 'Black Priory' on many occasions, and though he had some difficult things to do, he never let any of them master him. Now, look here."

Blake approached the cupboard and looked within.

He was astonished at the size of it—

it being as large as a medium-sized room.

On the sides and the back hung weapons of all shapes and sizes; but daggers, swords, and pistols predominated.

There was a goodly collection of oils and candles, while links in dozens hung here and there, curiously intermixed with masks and wigs.

But what principally attracted the attention of the ex-apprentice was a pile of what looked like black cloths.

Colonel Blood picked up one and shook it out.

It was a black bag, in length rather over six feet, in breadth two.

"Observe this," said Blood, grimly, as he turned the bag over and laid it on the floor. "What see you?"

Blood looked and saw in the very centre of the bag this mark—

It had been painted there in white, the mark being large and distinct.

And now indeed Blake was completely startled.

"Ah!" chuckled Blood, "you have heard of these bags before, eh?"

"I have," murmured Blake. "Several like them have been found in the Thames."

"Not *empty*?"

"No; with bodies in them."

"You are right; and the bodies are those of persons who have made themselves obnoxious either to me or my associates," said Blood, the expression now upon his face being one of savage brutality; "and you will do well to serve me faithfully, Blake, and thus all chance of *you* ever finding your way into one of these bags will be——but, ho, ho! don't tremble! I am only joking, my lad! ha! ha!—only joking! I am given to joking at times. But here, take this bag—it is for the page—and wrap this about him; I shall not use it again. There, be quick, lad—be quick, I say."

So saying he took up a black cloak and flung it to Blake, who placed it with the bag.

"Now," continued Blood, "here is another cloak you see; take that for yourself, and select what weapons you may think proper. But if you will take my advice you will have a sword and dagger only, for pistols in inexperienced hands are extremely dangerous. This hat too—which is the property of that fool, Captain Drinkwater—(he is as drunk as a fiddler in the cellar below) will serve to conceal your features, being broad of brim. So now that you have got all, let us descend."

In the sitting-room below they found Jeevers awaiting them.

He had donned the whole of the page's clothes.

They entirely altered his appearance, and if he could but keep his face concealed from curious eyes, the plot might succeed.

"Now then," said Blood, "wrap the old cloak about the youth, and then place him within the bag."

Blake and Jeevers did this between them, and shortly, all that remained of the handsome but unlucky page was hidden within that black bag, the bag on which was that glaring white mark—the mark that was, up to the present, very well known, but as to what secret society it belonged was shrouded in mystery.

"Now, Jeevers," said Blood, "in the first place, you will go to the *usual place* at Blackfriars. Blake, with the sack, will accompany you. Go the usual way, through Alsatia, and with the password I gave you, you will not be questioned. When the body is safely in the river, Jeevers will take the letter to the house of the locksmith, and will wait until he receives *positive* assurance that

Clifford Hansard will keep the appointment mentioned in the letter. You, Blake, will conceal yourself beside the landing-stage, and as soon as ever Clifford Hansard sets foot on it, dash upon him."

Blake rubbed his hands gleefully together, and his eyes shone with a fierce light as he thought of how near he was to his contemplated vengeance.

"Jeevers," continued Blood, "will be near you, so you have nothing to fear."

"But supposing that Sir Christopher Cullum should be at the landing-stage first?"

"Ha! Well, say that it would be well if Clifford hurried along, as it is likely Sir Christopher will be there before the time. After you have settled this apprentice, come to me, both of you, at Leicester Fields."

In a short time both Jeevers and Blake had left the house.

Unquestioned they passed through the streets and reached Whitefriars, where Blood's password had to be given.

The river at Blackfriars was at last reached, and Jeevers stood aside, while Blake was glad to get rid of the unfortunate king's page.

As soon as his two assistants had gone, Colonel Blood once more returned to his private room.

"So far, good," he chuckled, as he placed a bottle of wine on the table. "Ha, this very night, Clifford Hansard will certainly be removed from my path. As to Sir Christopher Cullum, I will deal with *him* myself."

CHAPTER VII.

IS OF WHAT TRANSPIRED AT THE WHITEHALL LANDING-STAGE, AND ON THE "RED STEPS"—OF A SUDDEN AND TIMELY APPEARANCE, AND OF THE GHOSTLY OBJECT FLOATING IN THE THAMES.

THE finish having been put to the Bartholomew Close tragedy, Blake proceeded to Whitehall, and Jeevers to deliver the letter, which Blood had taken the precaution to see securely fastened up, and in so careful a fashion that no suspicion was likely to be entertained as to its having been tampered with.

It was now a long way past nine of

the clock, Clifford had long since returned, and becoming uneasy as the page did not put in an appearance, he sallied out in search of him.

During his absence Jeevers appeared with the letter.

Olivia and her mother had retired, as also had the apprentices, and Pritchard Preston himself answered the door.

"So you have returned, master page," he said. "We were beginning to fear that some calamity had befallen you. Clifford Hansard has gone off in search of you."

"Indeed, sir?" was the reply.

Pritchard Preston started—and that start was observed by Jeevers, who instantly resolved what to do—he would sham being the worse for drink.

"A most remarkable alteration in the voice," thought the worthy locksmith; "for I remarked on the sweetness of the lad's tones, as also on the almost feminine beauty of his features. Alas! how sad —how very sad! I see how it is."

Aloud he said—

"Young man, I am, indeed, most sorry to observe that, during the comparatively short time which has elapsed since you first came here, you have been drinking, and I fancy pretty freely. I was about to ask you to step within my house, and while awaiting the return of my apprentice, to partake of supper. That, however, is now out of all question. I should strongly recommend you to hasten back to your quarters."

"I will, master locksmith," replied Jeevers, in hoarse tones.

And leaving the letter and the message Blood had told him, he staggered away.

Master Pritchard watched him until he passed through the arch, watched him with a puzzled expression on his kindly face.

"He suspects me," muttered Jeevers; "and that being so, I will hasten to put a good distance between us."

Plunging into the narrowest and the very darkest thoroughfares, Jeevers hastened towards Whitehall.

In less than an hour Clifford returned.

"The page?" he asked.

"It is all right, my son," replied the locksmith; "at least, the letter is all right."

"I trust no harm has befallen the page?" asked Clifford, anxiously.

"No harm has happened to him," replied the locksmith, gravely; "but my heart was saddened indeed when I saw that he had been drinking pretty freely."

"Drinking?"

"Ay, and what he had drank had most strangely altered him."

"He will be punished at the proper place. But now let me read the letter."

He did so aloud.

"I like not the hour nor the place for the appointment," said the locksmith, "but it will not do to disappoint Sir Christopher. And so, after all—after all these years, Clifford, you are going to leave me."

And as the locksmith uttered these words tears gathered in his eyes.

"Oh! my kind master," cried Clifford, as he seized both Master Pritchard's hands, "nay—my more than master— my father, if you do but say the word I will renounce all thoughts of aspiring to honour and position."

"No, no, my son," cried the locksmith, hastily, "no, no! Not for anything would I bid you stay with me! You shall be the assistant secretary to Sir Christopher Cullum, Clifford. It is a proud position. It is the first rung in the ladder of fame, and now that you have seized it let it not go."

"And, Master Preston," said Clifford, in eager tones, "you will, ere I leave you, tell me of my parents?"

"My son, as I have often hinted, there is scarcely anything to tell you. Your father, Hawksley Hansard, was a very, very poor man. But he was very talented; yet his talents never got him a living."

"What was his trade or profession, Master Preston?"

"His profession was a military one, or it *had* been," replied Master Preston, in slow and uneasy tones, "but there can be no doubt that he is now dead. It is many—many years since I saw him, quite eighteen, I should think. I will not tell you under what circumstances you came under my charge."

"Why will you not tell me?"

"Because, Clifford," answered the old man, in deeply solemn tones, "if I did so I should only darken that future, which will, no doubt, otherwise be a bright one for you. Though I am not bound by any promise to preserve the secret—if it is a secret—you would not wish me to re-open a wound which old Father Time has partially healed?"

"You are right; I would not. Yet my heart yearns to know my parents' history."

"Their history, Clifford, was not a

romantic one. Your mother, like your father, was very poor. She died a few months after your birth, abroad. Some said she died of fever, others of a broken heart."

"What do you believe?"

"The latter, Clifford; the latter. I fancy that your father was a source of great distress to your poor mother, who was a very delicate, timid, young creature."

"And have you not formed some idea as to *why* he was a source of distress to her?"

"I know this much, that Hawksley Hansard was a man of mystery. More I do *not* know, for I never sought to pry into his secrets. He was a brilliant scholar, a most accomplished swordsman, a man who was never known to flinch in the midst of the greatest danger; but as I have said, he was poor."

"Do I resemble him in features?"

"You resemble him strongly. But I repeat, Clifford, that I cannot doubt he is dead. If he were not, I should have heard from him, for he and I were old friends—very old and tried friends."

"You were very good, Master Preston, to my poor parents, I am sure," faltered Clifford.

"I have every reason to be glad that I did what I could. And I thank Heaven that I took charge of Hawksley Hansard's son, for he has ever proved himself an upright, honest, and conscientious young man. But now, Clifford, attire yourself in becoming garments, for you *may* see the king himself. And if you will take my advice, you will go to the place of meeting well-armed, for though I sincerely trust you will not have occasion to use dangerous weapons, it is as well to be prepared."

The worthy locksmith proceeded to his own bedroom, and took from a cabinet two articles. One was a sword, the other a cloak.

Clifford, attired in his best, soon made his appearance, and the addition of the sword and the cloak was a great improvement, for he certainly looked remarkably well in them.

"Adieu, my son," said the locksmith, as he accompanied Clifford to the door. "Adieu, take good care of thyself."

"Fear not," replied Clifford. "I will be well on my guard, and I promise you I'll render a good account of myself if I am attacked."

"And you will hasten home as soon as possible?"

"I will. Adieu."

So master and apprentice parted, and *for ever*.

Never again would Clifford look upon that kind face; never again would he press the hand of him who had ever been as a father towards him.

The iron hand of Fate willed it that this night was the last they should look upon each other in this world.

* * * *

Deeming it to be the safest plan, Clifford took the broadest and most frequented thoroughfares.

But he found that, at this hour of the night, the streets were almost deserted.

It was the first time that our hero had been in the streets at so late an hour; but so far from wishing himself at home, he was delighted to be out, for he was charmed with the strangeness of the scene.

The Strand presented a most striking sight, the noble mansions lining the riverside being lit up with the silvery light of the moon.

Every now and then he caught a glimpse of the Thames.

At the Savoy, from which a beautiful view of the river was obtained, he paused a few moments in order to take a good look.

Little did he think of the horrible secrets that river held within its broad bosom.

Little did he think of what terrible sight would presently meet his eyes.

The steps beside the palace were reached at last, and, in a moment, he stood on the landing-stage.

By the side of this was a long flight of narrow steps, built of red brick, and called the "Red Steps."

They were dangerously steep.

These steps led to a broad pavement, which communicated with a flight of steps leading to Whitehall Gardens.

Clifford glanced around him.

No one was visible.

Save for the sighing of the wind along the river bank, and the murmurings of the river profound silence reigned.

Folding his arms, Clifford gave way to reflection.

Suddenly there was a slight rustle behind him, and then a voice cried—

"Die! Perdition on you, die!"

Instantly Clifford sprang aside, and by so doing he saved his life.

Had he turned, instead of jumping aside, he would have received in his breast the long, glittering blade which was wielded by Blake Barrell.

As it was the dagger plunged into his cloak, which it slit to the bottom.

"Murderer," cried Clifford, "murderer! would you slay me in cold blood? Ah! vile wretch, I recognise you— Blake Barrell!"

The words had not left his lips, ere he sprang forward, and seized Blake by the throat.

Blake, in his turn, seized him, and frantically endeavoured to use the terrible weapon he held firmly in his hand.

They clung tenaciously to each other, each putting forth all his strength.

A few moments they rocked and swayed—and dangerously near to the edge of the landing-stage—and then Clifford hurled Blake to the ground with a thundering crash.

Clifford fell upon him with all his weight.

So terrific was the fall that one would have thought that Blake was rendered unconscious.

Such, however, was not the case.

Frantically he struggled to release himself from the iron-like grip of our hero, but it was of no use. Clifford pressed his throat with one hand until he was black in the face.

It was evident that Blake was endeavouring to shout.

"I would not be at all surprised," thought Clifford, "if that villain, Colonel Blood, is somewhere hereabouts."

At last Blake managed to cry out—

"Release me! Let me go! let me go!"

"No," thundered Clifford, "not until you tell me the name of the person who sent you hither. Tell me how you got to know I should be here? If you do not keep still, and tell me what I ask, so sure as I am now on this landing-stage, so sure will I drag you to the river and hurl you into it."

"Let me get up."

"And give you a chance of making another attempt to assassinate me? No, no, vile wretch, I will not permit you to rise—at least, not until you answer my questions."

"Suppose I won't answer them?"

"Then I will drag you to the river and throw you in."

Blake once again struggled desperately to get up, and this time he succeeded.

But Clifford did not release his hold —either of his throat or the hand holding the murderous weapon.

Once more backwards and forwards they went, and it frequently seemed as if both would go headlong into the river.

Suddenly a vivid flash lit up the scene, a loud report echoed over the river, and a bullet whizzed dangerously near our hero's head.

The smoke was too dense for him to see who had fired that shot, but thinking that it was the villain Blood, he at once released his hold of Blake and turned.

He caught sight of a dark figure speeding across the landing-stage towards the Red Steps.

Clifford did not hesitate.

Snatching his blade from its sheath, he dashed after the flying figure.

"If that is Colonel Blood," he thought, "I will either slay him or he shall slay me!"

Up the stairs rushed the fugitive, Clifford in hot pursuit.

"Hold, coward!" cried Clifford. "Hold!"

But the addressed paused not.

Clifford increased his speed, and when close to the top of the steps he caught the fugitive by the cloak.

Another instant and he had swung him round, and the point of his weapon was at his throat.

"By heaven!" muttered Clifford, "then it is not Blood after all. It is John Jeevers."

"What have I done that you should thus pursue me?" cried Jeevers.

"Silence, villain!" interrupted Clifford, sternly. "Silence, or I will send this sword through your heart. No longer do I remain in ignorance as to who sent Blake Barrell to waylay and

and murder me. It was Colonel Blood. Ah, the king shall know that he has *not* left the country."

As he spoke, Clifford noticed Jeevers' hand glide to his belt.

He at once seized it and found that it held a dagger.

Forcing him back he wrenched it from his grasp, and then, catching him by the waist, he hurled him from the top of the stairs to the bottom.

There the villain remained, groaning fearfully, and apparently quite unable to move.

And now, sword in hand, and ready to defend himself in case he was again attacked, for, of course, he was unable to tell whether or not some more of Blood's murderous assistants, and, perhaps, the colonel himself, were not at hand, Clifford descended the steps.

Barely had he reached the bottom when yet another figure stood before him.

Instantly our hero was on the defensive.

"Stay your hand, young sir," said the newcomer. "I am not here to injure you. You are Clifford Hansard?"

"I am—and you?"

"I am a Court messenger sent hither by Sir Christopher Cullum, who, being engaged on an urgent matter with the king, was unable to meet you. But you have been attacked?"

"I have."

"By whom?"

"By this person here, and by one Blake Barrell—both of whom are the myrmidoms of Colonel Blood."

"Ha! Then I suppose it was Barrell who, as soon as I made my appearance, dashed by me, nearly sending me into the river."

"No doubt it was he," replied Clifford, grimly, "for I do not suppose that he would await my reappearance."

"This person—is he dead?"

And the messenger stooped and examined Jeevers.

"Nay, he is not dead," responded Clifford; "but unless I am much mistaken, he has received such injuries that he is not likely to get rid of them for some time. It is certainly a wonder, master messenger, that you find me here alive."

"Had I known that the wretch who tried to slip past me had actually attempted to assassinate you, he would not have proceeded far, I warrant you. But we all have to be very careful, Master Hansard—very careful in these days—when assassins stalk unquestioned through the streets. Yonder river is the place most used by the assassins to hide the evidences of their crimes. No doubt you have heard of the number of sacks which, during the past few months, have been discovered in it?"

"Sacks?"

"Ay, with the fatal mark—a white circle."

"I *have* heard of them—I have heard Blake Barrell talking of them to the apprentices—Blake Barrell having been in the same workshop as myself—but it is not known from what secret society these bags emanate?"

"Unfortunately it is not. Hundreds of crowns have the government expended in the employment of secret agents to attempt to penetrate the mystery. On the last occasion ten of these secret agents were employed, and of these, after a month, but one returned."

"And the remainder?"

"Seven have as yet been found in the Thames, and all enclosed in the sacks with the white circle, which goes to prove that they must have been murdered and hurled into the river soon after they set off to penetrate the mystery."

"Great heavens!" exclaimed Clifford, with a shudder. "And this is what people are pleased to term the most enlightened city in the world! Surely it is the *wickedest* city in the world, and heaven will cause a fearful punishment to fall upon it."

"Clifford Hansard," replied the messenger, gravely, "a terrible punishment is *already* descending upon it."

"Ah, you mean the plague?"

"I do. It is already raging most furiously in a house in Long Acre."

"So close?"

"Ay, so close! It is to discuss this matter that the king and Sir Christopher Cullum, with a number of lords and gentlemen, are assembled within the palace. But what shall be done with this youth? Great heaven!" cried the messenger, "what is this I see? This youth wears the Court livery."

"Impossible!"

"Nay. What I say is only too correct. He wears the attire of a king's page."

"I had not noticed it."

"Because his cloak concealed the principal portion of his attire. But, in the name of the Virgin, how *came* he with these clothes?"

"He may have borrowed them from a costumier."

The messenger shook his head.

"No," he said, "though perhaps a costumier could provide such attire, he would never dare to have upon it the royal badge."

"Let us endeavour to arouse him," said Clifford, a terrible suspicion suddenly flashing through his brain.

He fell upon his knees and shouted into Jeevers' ears.

He took him by the arm and shook him gently at first and then violently.

No sign of life did Jeevers show, however.

The principal injury he had received was in the head, from which the blood was slowly oozing.

"It is vain to attempt to arouse him," said Clifford. "Let us leave him here, and as he is. If he recovers, well and good; if he does not, let the watch find him, and do with him as they think fit."

So saying, Clifford took away what weapons Jeevers had.

He advanced to the river to throw them in, when suddenly he paused.

"Look!" he cried. "Look at yonder black object. What can it be? See, 'tis floating towards us."

The messenger looked in the direction in which our hero pointed.

A cry of horror left his lips.

"Look!" he said. "Look! the *fatal white circle!*"

Erect at the edge of the stage stood Clifford, straining his eyes towards the black object.

In a moment he made out what the messenger saw—the black bag, on which was painted that fatal white circle.

On it came—slowly—very slowly.

"Lord!" said Clifford, in hushed tones, "this is indeed appalling. What is to be done? No boat is handy."

"Let us do *nothing* in the matter," said the messenger, in accents of alarm. "You would surely not permit yourself to come in contact with that body; for that there *is* a body within that sack there can be not the slightest doubt."

"My friend," replied Clifford, unfastening his cloak, and throwing it from his shoulders, "it is my intention to have a good look at that sack and its contents."

"Then Heaven help you! You may catch the plague."

"I do not think so. Do you remain here while I bring it ashore. Look! it floats nearer—nearer—ha! holy Virgin! see—*a human face!*"

Sure enough this was the fact.

The mouth of the sack had become unfastened, and the face of the unhappy wretch, who had been murdered, and then consigned to the river, appeared.

The moon's rays played full upon it, and so truly awful was the picture that Clifford felt, in the manner of speaking, paralysed.

But quickly recovering himself, he flung off nearly all his clothes, and plunged boldly into the river.

Clifford was a powerful swimmer, and but a few strokes were necessary to reach the object before him.

He soon towed the bag and the contents to the landing-stage.

The whole of the time the face remained turned to the sky.

Again did the messenger give utterance to a cry of terror; but though he shrank back a few paces some strange irresistible impulse urged him to creep forward again, and he approached the very edge of the landing-stage.

He fixed a startled, but eager look upon the white face—upon the large, wide-open eyes—which were fixed with a stony stare upon the heavens as if mutely pleading for vengeance, and then afar over the river was heard a wild cry of horror—a cry which issued from the ashen lips of the terror-stricken messenger.

"Oh, holy Mother! Oh, terrible sight!" cried the messenger, sinking upon his knees.

"Tell me! Tell me, I conjure you!" cried Clifford. "What is it? *Who* is it that you recognise?"

"Oh, Clifford Hansard, *this is the body of Henri Hadden*, the king's page, who was sent by Sir Christopher Cullum with the letter to you."

"Great heaven! It *cannot* be. You must be mistaken!"

"No—no—no! I can no more mistake this dear face than I could mistake the face of my mother. We have been friends for years and years."

"But," replied Clifford, springing up on the landing-stage, "only two or three hours have elapsed since he was at my home with Sir Christopher Cullum's letter."

"I see—I see," interrupted the messenger, excitedly, "he has been way-laid and his clothes have been taken from him."

"You are right! you are right!" said Clifford, "and the clothes Jeevers is wearing are no doubt the ones."

As he spoke he rushed to the spot, where, bleeding and insensible, he had left Jeevers.

He had disappeared.

A deep sigh left our hero's lips.

He began to see through the foul plot now.

But did Blood have a share in the matter? Or was it planned, and carried out by Jeevers and Blake alone?

He had no means of telling—probably he never would know.

"The villain has gone!" he said, returning to the landing-stage, "and that shows that he was either feigning unconsciousness, or he had some of his associates close at hand. Oh, what a terrible—*terrible* sight is this! Let us lift the murdered youth on to the stage. I feel bewildered, and know not what to think, or what to suggest."

"The king will leave no stone unturned in endeavouring to find the inhuman wretch who slew the page," said the messenger.

"Something has been learned from this atrocious deed," said Clifford, "and that is this—Blake Barrell and John Jeevers are acquainted with the secret society, which adopts this white circle as the mark by which it is recognised."

"You are right."

"What I propose is this—let us carry the murdered page to the palace. Let us place him before the king."

"Impossible!"

"Why so?"

"The king is within his own cabinet."

"That may be so; but all the better. Look you, master messenger, when King Charles has placed before him the particulars of anything of a character calling for instant investigation, he, at the moment, declares that what is required shall be done. Soon afterwards his intense passion for pleasure drives out of his head all thoughts of the matter."

"You are right, Master Hansard. But a crime like this—the victim, a youth, whom the king really loved, will never be driven out of his head."

"Well, my friend, little harm can there be in doing as I have said. On my shoulders let any blame fall. You see if the murdered youth is placed before his majesty, it is hardly likely that he will forget that the assassin is to be sought for."

"Well, then, we will do as you suggest."

"Do you know of any secret passage by which we may, unobserved, reach Sir Christopher Cullum's apartment?"

"Yes; I know of one; but to reach that passage, we shall have to descend to the vaults."

Clifford at once donned his garments, with the exception of the cloak, which was placed round the sack.

Then they took hold of the murdered page, and slowly and reverently they proceeded to bear him to the palace.

Clifford's heart felt ready to burst with the desire which filled it for speedy vengeance.

But the messenger was otherwise affected. Knowing the poor page for so many years, he was shocked, beyond the power of description, at his fearful end, and more than once, on the short journey to the palace, he broke down, and sobbed like a child.

*   *   *   *

Once more the reader is conducted to the handsome room occupied by Sir Christopher Cullum.

Seated at the table were several noblemen and gentlemen, among them being Rochester and the Duke of York.

At one end of the table, which was covered with documents, sat Sir Christopher Cullum; at the other the king.

The faces of those assembled persons were grave in the extreme.

The king having been flush of ready-money lately, had allowed himself to dash headlong into the whirlpool of dissipation; and he had squandered *every penny* which he had received from Mistress Claribel Cameron.

Dissipation had given his dissolute majesty a haggard, careworn appearance, and he now looked like a man suffering from extreme nervousness.

The matter under discussion was the disease which had broken out in Long Acre, and which several doctors had declared to be the plague.

The matter was of the highest importance to his majesty, owing to the fact that the residence of Mistress Cameron was close to the house—a clothier's shop—in which the plague was stated to have broken out.

Presently a page announced—

"Doctor Jardell."

"Let him be at once shown in," said Charles.

And the doctor was accordingly shown in.

"Well?" was the query, which simultaneously broke from the lips of all.

"I am truly sorry," replied the doctor, "to have to inform your majesty that the disease, which has broken out in Long Acre, is *unquestionably* the plague; and though I have seen many severe cases abroad, I can truly say that the cases in Long Acre are a dozen times *worse.*"

"Heaven help us all," exclaimed the king, shifting uneasily in his chair.

"Sire," said Jardell, "London has often been warned."

"Say you so? By whom?"

"By the clergy, and by those skilled in the science of astrology."

"Tush, tush, man! Don't preach a sermon to us, but think of what is to be done under the circumstances."

"Sire," persisted Doctor Jardell, in most respectful, but firm tones, "Zodcaster, the famed astrologer, has more than once foretold that London would be visited with a plague, the like of which has never been seen in the whole world—that thousands and thousands would perish miserably."

"Well, that is a nice thing for a man to prophecy. 'Sdeath, my lords, this Zodcaster should be placed in Newgate. But you, Doctor Jardell, can laugh at this prophecy, for Sir Christopher tells us that you have invented a draught that will prevent the plague taking hold of a person."

"Not prevent it, sire. Cure it."

"You have discovered a cure?"

"For *some* cases."

"Why not *all*?" asked his unreasonable majesty, impatiently.

"People are differently afflicted, sire; for instance, your majesty might be afflicted with the terrible disease."

A fearful cry left the king's lips.

White as a ghost, and trembling in every limb, he started from his chair.

"We might have this?" he gasped, "Holy Mary! Say no such thing again, doctor, as you value our patronage. Now how many cases are there at this clothier's shop?"

"Three, sire; and just as I came away, the second breathed his last."

"Three cases! In the name of all the saints, how did the plague get there?"

"No one can tell," said Rochester.

"For my part," said the king, "I believe that the Thames is responsible for the plague, for of late it has been the receptacle for scores of dead bodies."

"The bodies of *murdered* persons," said Sir Christopher, gravely.

"Nothing as yet has been discovered respecting this terrible society, which has as its sign a white circle?" asked the king, in uneasy tones.

"Nothing!" said Rochester, but in such an abrupt, peculiar fashion, that it attracted the notice of Sir Christopher.

"It is a strange affair," said Charles. "I wish I could get at the bottom of it. I don't like these mysteries. And I hear, my lords," and here his voice sunk into a whisper, "that wherever this strange sign appears, death follows in its wake."

"That is so," said Rochester.

"I should not be at all surprised, your majesty," observed Sir Christopher, "if the head and chief of this society is Colonel Blood."

"I don't think it," replied Charles, who, however, was becoming more uneasy than ever. "He has left the country."

Rochester gave a significant look at the nobleman beside him, the look not escaping the observant eyes of Sir Christopher, who immediately said—

"I am afraid your majesty is deceiving yourself. Colonel Blood has not left the country. He is in London. Of that I feel perfectly certain, otherwise how comes it that so many of those who were put on the track of this most atrocious ruffian have lost their lives?"

Sir Christopher was interrupted by the sudden opening of the door, and the appearance of the page.

"Has the messenger returned?" asked Sir Christopher.

"He has, sir, and brings with him one Clifford Hansard."

"Bid both await me in the ante-room."

"Clifford Hansard?" repeated the king. "Let me see—oh! I remember. He is about to become your assistant, Sir Christopher?"

"Yes, sire."

"Well, let him enter."

The page withdrew.

In a few moments the door again opened, and the messenger hastily entered.

His terrified appearance was instantly noted by all present.

Everyone leapt to their feet, wondering what was about to happen.

Close behind the messenger came our hero, carrying in his arms the murdered page.

Without a word Clifford bore him to the table and reverently placed him thereon.

"Great heaven!" exclaimed Charles, who looked as if about to dart through the curtains into his own cabinet. "What —what have you there? Some plague-stricken wretch?"

"Your majesty has no occasion to be alarmed," said Clifford, in firm, clear, yet saddened tones. "This is not anything to do with the plague. Sire, look at this."

And he snatched his cloak from the murdered page, and there was revealed the ominous white circle.

Terrified beyond description for a few moments, the king then burst into a terrific rage.

But ere he could give orders, Clifford said—

"I know that this act, for which I alone am to blame, is sufficient to get me cast into the Tower. But, oh, sire! you yourself, as well as all your subjects, from the highest to the lowest, will call for speedy vengeance. Here is one whom your majesty well knows."

So saying he gently drew back the top of the dreadful sack and revealed the well-known features of Henri Hadden.

Startled, horror-stricken cries left the lips of the king and those about him.

Even "Hardened Rochester" started and recoiled.

"Vengeance, say you?" cried Charles. "Ay, vengeance, indeed. And speedy enough shall it be! The white circle again!"

"Tell your story, Clifford," said Sir Christopher. "Tell us everything."

Clifford did so, rapidly and as briefly as possible.

"More than ever am I convinced that this is the work of Colonel Blood," said Sir Christopher.

"What makes you say so?" asked Rochester.

"Is it not evident that this Blake Barrell and John Jeevers are in the employ of Blood?"

"Not quite. We must have further proof."

"Behold it!" cried Sir Christopher, suddenly seizing upon the cloak which was wrapped around the murdered page. "Behold it!"

Placing his hand upon the collar, he tore off a piece of chain, and held it before the eyes of those present.

"What does that prove?" asked Rochester.

"His majesty will remember as well as I do," answered Sir Christopher. "This piece of chain—as I saw at a single glance—fits this piece," and he took another piece of chain from his pocket, "and this part was found at the chambers at Lincoln's Inn on the night that Blood murdered my man Lucas, and stole the property which was lawfully mine."

It was a remarkable piece of evidence; but the king had many reasons for throwing dust in the eyes of those who denounced Blood.

"Yes, yes," he said, "it looks black against Blood, to be sure. But—but— we will talk over this matter anon, Sir Christopher. At present our hands are absolutely full of more important matters. Poor Henri!" he added, lowering his voice and fixing his eyes upon the features of the murdered page. "Poor Henri! They could have robbed him of his letter, but they might have spared his life. The dastardly assassins shall be discovered and shall die. I swear it!"

"Clifford," said Sir Christopher, "what conclusion have you arrived at?"

"That Colonel Blood either did the foul deed with his own hand or he was an accessory to the fact."

"I warn you to be careful what you say of Colonel Blood," said Rochester. "That terrible white circle should be a warning to you to keep a guard upon your tongue."

"My lord," said Clifford, who knew Rochester well enough by sight, "I do not fear Colonel Blood. And the White Circle will have no terrors for me."

Rochester fixed a scornful glance on our hero's face.

"Well," he queried, "and who on earth do you think yourself?"

"My lord!" cried Charles, "desist, I pray you! This sort of conversation in the presence of the king!"

"It is evident that to speak to this young man in such a manner," said Doctor Jardell, "is a great mistake. He has proved himself a youth of undoubted courage."

"Yes, yes," replied Charles, "that is true, my lords. But not another word at present, I command ye. Let assistance be instantly summoned, and the body of poor Henri taken away. Let it be conveyed to one of the small apartments, the room locked, and do you take charge of the key, Sir Christopher. Anon we will discuss the matter."

So the murdered page was taken away by a number of domestics, among whom a perfect panic prevailed.

Clifford was shown into one of Sir Christopher's private apartments, and there, in a few moments, Sir Christopher joined him.

"Clifford," he said, "can you stay with me for the night?"

"Oh, yes; there can be no difficulty about that. But I should not like to stay unless Master Preston were informed of my intention."

"To be sure. A messenger shall ride to the house at once. Perhaps the worthy locksmith may not yet have retired."

"No doubt he will be up and awaiting my return."

"Good. The messenger shall be sent off at once. Do you stay here, Clifford. As soon as the council is dissolved, I will rejoin you."

"I await your instructions."

"Whatever you do, Clifford," said Sir Christopher, gravely, "do not ruffle the temper of that headstrong Rochester. It is my opinion that he knows considerably more of the business and the movements of Colonel Blood than anyone is aware of. Do not make him your enemy, for he is a most dangerous man. He is easily offended, and never forgives."

"I will take your advice," replied Clifford.

At once the messenger was despatched, and, within an hour, Sir Christopher joined Clifford.

He was accompanied by Doctor Jardell, who warmly eulogised our hero's conduct in plunging into the Thames, and bringing ashore the murdered Henri Hadden.

The three, after refreshments, seated themselves at the table.

The subject discussed was not only the plague, but Colonel Blood and the money, which there was no longer any doubt he had stolen from the chambers in Lincoln's Inn Fields.

Sir Christopher proceeded to draw up a plan for the *private* capture of the ferocious colonel, and he was promised the hearty assistance of the doctor and our hero, who begged that the taking of the villain should be left to him.

Not the slightest suspicion had Sir Christopher that there was a listener outside his door.

But there was.

That listener was Lord Rochester.

CHAPTER VIII.

IS OF THE MEETING BETWEEN BLOOD AND LORD ROCHESTER—OF WHAT PASSED
BETWEEN THEM, AND OF WHAT DARING EVENT HAPPENED AT WHITEHALL PALACE.

IT must have been close on the hour of two in the morning when Lord Rochester left the palace, and proceeded at a rapid pace in the direction of Charing Cross.

The streets appeared to be completely deserted; but presently his lordship observed a man staggering towards him.

Evidently he was a jovial fellow, and a staunch advocate of Bacchus; for while he staggered along he sang in a deep, hoarse voice, one of the ribald songs of the day.

Something, either in the man's appearance or voice, caused Rochester to march straight up to him.

"I am not mistaken," he muttered. "It is that fool Drinkwater."

Yes, it was Captain Drinkwater sure enough, and he was considerably more than half "gone," yet he was not so drunk as not to recognise Rochester.

He endeavoured to pull himself together, and to straighten himself by means of the shutters of a house beside him; but it was a failure, and so amused was he at that failure, that he burst into a roar of laughter.

So indignant did his lordship become at this daring piece of impudence that, raising his gloved hand, he delivered upon the captain's face such a smack, that Drinkwater was placed *hors-de-combat*.

"Lord!" he moaned, "what a world this is."

"You scoundrel," growled Rochester.

"Ah!" replied the captain, with a deep sigh, "not dead yet."

"I, for one, should be very glad to hear of your death," replied Rochester; "but there can be hardly a doubt that ere long you will meet with your deserts. Most likely you will be afflicted with the plague."

"The plague!" gasped Captain Drinkwater, as he turned over, got upon his knees, and then staggered to his feet; "is it already so bad as that?"

"It is. And first of all it seizes upon drunkards."

"I've heard to the contrary."

"No matter what you have heard. What I say is true."

"Well, well," cried Drinkwater, "if London became the scene of a fearful plague, Colonel Blood, myself, Lord Rochester——"

"Villain!" cried Rochester, clapping his hand on his sword-hilt, "beware how you mention my name."

"'Sdeath, what a world this is! I was only about to say that all of us are certain to profit by it. But your lordship is very late, or, rather, very early this morning."

"That is my business. Listen to me, sirrah. Where is your master?"

"My *master!* I have *no* master!"

"You haven't, eh? Then who pays you?"

"No one."

"How do you live?"

"By eating and drinking."

"Fool! How do you get your money?"

"By taking it whenever I have the chance."

"Where is Colonel Blood?"

"That is better," grinned Drinkwater. "Well, your lordship, my *friend* Blood is at his residence—at least, as far as I am aware."

"Which residence?"

"The Black Priory."

"Good. I am about to go there. And mark you, sirrah. Your conduct shall be reported to the colonel."

"Alas! how uncharitable some people are," muttered Drinkwater, staggering away.

His lordship, drawing his hat over his brows, and his long cloak closely about his person, strode off towards Leicester Fields.

He soon reached the colonel's house, and going to the door at the back, he whistled.

The signal was quickly answered by Mother Elwood, Blood's housekeeper.

She at once recognised the visitor, and opened the door to him.

"'I AM MORE MYSTIFIED THAN EVER!' CRIED SIR CHRISTOPHER."

A Coloured Picture is Given Away with this Number.

No word was spoken until the door was closed, when Rochester said—

"Your master?"

"Below, in his chamber."

Rochester descended, and reaching the door of the apartment in which Blood was, he knocked.

"Who is there?" asked the voice of the colonel.

"A friend," replied Rochester.

"Ay, ay; and what do you bring friend?"

"A ' *White Circle!* '" was the reply.

The door flew open, and his lordship entered.

He now stood in the apartment in which Captain Winter, assisted by Clifford, had captured the colonel.

The pair having shaken hands, Rochester took a chair, and placed it beside Blood's.

"I expected," he said, "that I would find you asleep."

"I sleep but little," replied Blood, "and the same may be said of your lordship."

"True. When we *do* snatch a few hours it is in the daytime. Night is too precious to waste in sleep."

"Most true. And I presume, judging from the hour, that you have news of importance for me?"

"You are right."

"Pardon me," said Blood. "Was it not to-night that a council was held at the palace?"

"It was," answered Rochester, with surprise. "How on earth did *you* get to know?"

Blood smiled.

"I generally manage to know matters of any importance," he said.

"Yes, you do. But let me proceed. Colonel Blood, do you not think that you are pushing matters too far as regards the White Circle?"

"I do not. But why do you ask?"

"I am acquainted with the last deed done, and certainly it is the most terrible yet committed."

"You surprise me. To what deed do you refer?"

"The murder of one of the king's pages—Henri Hadden."

Blood started from his seat.

"How do you know this?" he asked.

"The Thames refused to hold such a secret, colonel, and threw it under the very eyes of one who had the courage to plunge into the water, drag the murdered page out, and place him before his majesty!"

"You astonish me!" exclaimed Blood. "And who did this?"

"One who, unless he is at once put out of the way, will track you down, colonel, and will expose the mystic circle, and all connected with it."

"Ah, you mean Sir Christopher Cullum?"

"Nay; he certainly would be a guiding star in the matter; but it is not him that I refer to. It is one Clifford Hansard."

At the mention of that name all the colour left the colonel's cheeks; he became pale as death.

This was noticed by Rochester, who said—

"I see that you fully appreciate my remarks, colonel?"

"My plan has failed, then?" said Blood, in low tones. "You knew nothing of my plan, my lord?"

"Not from your own lips. But Clifford Hansard was allowed to tell his story to the king, and, from what he said, I gathered what your plans had been. Yes; they have failed—miserably. But where are those whom you commissioned to carry them out?"

"I know not. Neither has returned. By heaven, I swear that, on the next occasion, my plans will be of such a character, that failure will be impossible."

"Failure *would* be impossible with my assistance. Single-handed, colonel, many of your plans fail."

"Your lordship does me an injustice."

"Not so. If you wish me to enumerate several, which have most miserably failed, I will willingly do so."

"No, no. Not now—not now."

"You have under you, colonel, a large number of men, but not many among them can be trusted. Many of them are arrant cowards, and what are not cowards, are drunkards. I have but just now come across that knavish Captain Drinkwater."

"Where?"

"At Charing Cross. I trust he has no papers of yours in his possession?"

"I take good care of that."

"My great wonder is that you do not get rid of such a man."

"He may become a greater nuisance than he is at present," replied Blood, "and then I will soon dispose of him. When he is sober, however, I find him a most excellent assistant. When he is drunk I have little fear of him, for he never opens his mouth respecting my affairs."

"So far as you know."

"If he did, my lord, you may rely upon it that the fact would soon reach my ears."

"It may be so. But now listen to this. After the council was dissolved, Sir Christopher Cullum, Doctor Jardell, and Clifford Hansard, all repaired to Sir Christopher's room. Suspecting that their conversation would be in reference to yourself, I watched my opportunity, and acted the part of eavesdropper. I overheard much relating to you. But the principal matter spoken of was the murder at Lincoln's Inn Gateway, and the money stolen by you."

"*Supposed* to have been stolen, my lord. *Supposed* to have been stolen."

"There should be no secrets between us, Blood."

"Neither are there," was the calm reply.

"Share and share alike, was the agreement."

"I know it," answered Blood, "and I repeat that the money is only supposed to have been stolen by me."

"It is a matter of no importance," interrupted Rochester, haughtily; "you need say no more in reference to it. My impression is that you *had* the money, and it is also my impression that I *won some of this very money* last evening of his majesty!"

Had a thunderbolt fallen at the colonel's feet he could not have been more startled.

But quickly recovering himself, he said—

"Really, my lord, you make a very great mistake."

Rochester shook his head.

"Are you short of money?" asked Blood.

"Not at present."

"Well, when your lordship is short I can advance you a fair sum, no doubt. But we will talk of money matters at a more convenient time. I would now like to learn what these three propose to do towards effecting my capture."

"I don't know how they will set about it exactly," was the reply; "but I heard Sir Christopher Cullum say that he would leave no stone unturned to track you down. They know that it was either by your hand or by your instructions that the page was murdered. Proof was there."

"Where?"

"On the body. A certain cloak was wrapped about the murdered page."

"What of that? There are thousands of other cloaks exactly like it."

"No doubt. But attached to this cloak was a piece of chain. In nearly the centre it had been broken, and to the astonishment of everyone present, Sir Christopher Cullum produced from his pocket *another* piece of chain. This, beyond the shadow of a doubt, belonged to the other. Now, as Sir Christopher says that he found the piece he took from his pocket in the false ceiling at the chambers, I would like to know how you get out of the fact that you, and you only, took the money?"

"Again I say, my lord, we will, at a more convenient time, talk of money matters."

Rochester burst into a fit of laughter.

Blood surveyed him frowningly for the space of a few seconds, and then proceeded to pace the apartment.

"I will wait until your merriment has subsided," he said, angrily. "It is not often I am insulted."

"Insulted? Why, you do not call that being insulted, do you? But I tell you what it is. You regret the bargain —'share and share alike.' Still, colonel, we will, as you say, talk of this matter at a future time. Enemies are cropping up on all sides, and it will be necessary to make short work of some of them. The first must be Clifford Hansard."

"I would not slay him at present," replied Blood, fiercely.

"What would you then?"

"I would like to get him into my power."

"'Sdeath, man! For what reason?"

"I want to take some of the courage out of him. I would like to get him into my power, and put him behind— *yonder.*"

And he indicated the curtains which were drawn across the room, and evidently concealed something of a startling nature.

"Well, I would not willingly spoil your amusement," laughed Rochester. "Certain it is that if he gets there, he can never get out."

"You are correct. But from what you said, it seemed to me that you knew *how* we could get hold of him."

"Not *we—you*. I must not be seen in the matter."

"Neither must I," replied Blood, grimly.

"Whom can you trust?"

"I have two of my most trusted men now in the house. They are asleep at the top."

"Good. Then you had better disguise yourself in a most thorough manner, and take the command of the two men yourself. This proud young apprentice, whom by-the-bye I came very near knocking down, so insolent was he towards myself——"

"Which proves," grinned Blood, "that he does not yet know Rochester."

"True—true. Well, this young apprentice will, no doubt, be lodged in the apartment which is beside the bed-room occupied by Sir Christopher. Now I am well acquainted with that apartment, and know that there is a trap-door connected with it—a trap-door which is, no doubt, constructed much after the same fashion as yours yonder."

"Ha!" exclaimed Blood, "I see the drift of your remarks. With what passage is the trap-door connected?"

"The trap-door is reached from the treasurer's room, in the lower part of the building, and the treasurer's room is approached from the terrace. I will lead you and your men to the treasurer's room, and then I must leave you to yourselves."

"Ay, ay," replied Blood, thoughtfully, and it seemed somewhat uneasily; "but how is an entrance to be gained to the treasurer's room? I suppose we shall have to force it?"

"Certainly not," chuckled Rochester. "Behold!"

And plunging his hand into his pocket, he brought forth a key.

Blood eagerly took it.

"This, then," he said, "is the key of the apartment?"

"Ay, and it fits a door *within* the room. That door you will find at the further end. You will open it, and find yourself in a long vault, which is used as a receptacle for old arms, and the like. I need hardly caution you to be careful. In about the centre of the vault you will see a large hole in the roof. That is the position of the trap-door, which is easily reached by means of a ladder, which you will see close to your hand, and easily opened."

"There will be no difficulty in the matter," replied Blood, now greatly excited. "Your information is most valuable."

Rochester had little idea that Blood meant that it would be useful for *other* purposes at a *future* time.

Summoning Mother Ellwood, Blood told her to arouse the two men at the top of the house, and bid them descend with all speed.

The men were soon standing before Blood.

A couple of most ruffianly-looking fellows were these two.

That they had partially recovered from the effects of a "glorious" carouse was evident at a glance.

Colonel Blood poured out the contents of a bottle of the strongest wine he had, and told them to drink it.

They did not need twice telling.

Bidding them pull themselves together, and prepare to set out with him, Blood now ascended to his bed-room, accompanied by Rochester.

When he reappeared his whole appearance was completely altered, so much so that his own men would not have recognised him, had they not been aware of what their "master" was about to do.

All being in readiness the four set off.

"Look here, Mother Elwood," said Blood, "don't retire. Keep close to the door, and when you hear my signal, open it with all speed."

"Ay, ay," grunted the hag, who had no difficulty in guessing what Blood was about to do, "is it to be a man or a woman?"

"Neither."

"*That's* false, colonel."

"Ho, ho!" chuckled Blood. "I tell you it is neither. It's a youth."

"Come," whispered Rochester; "delay will be dangerous."

    *   *   *   *

The conversation between our three friends continued until the hands of the splendid clock over the mantel-piece pointed to the hour of three.

"I have already selected a room for you, doctor," said Sir Christopher, "and one of the pages will show it you. We will all assemble in the morning before the business of the Court commands my attention, and the discussion of this highly important matter will be continued. You, Clifford, will sleep in a chamber which adjoins mine."

In this apartment our hero, in a short time, found himself.

Clifford was soon undressed, and blowing out his taper got into bed.

Within a quarter of an hour he was sound asleep.

The palace at Whitehall was always well guarded, and when the king was present the guard was doubled.

Whoever, therefore, that slept in the palace would not imagine danger lurked within the very heart of the building.

Yet, despite the guard, danger was always present, owing to the many secret doors and passages which existed in this palace.

The king himself, though acquainted with many, was by no means familiar with half the passages.

Sir Christopher Cullum's acquaintance with the palace was extensive, and he knew of the existence of many secret sliding panels, traps, and the like, but not one quarter was he familiar with.

His own bed-room had been searched and sounded by practical men, and declared to be free from trap, sliding panel, or, in fact, anything of the kind.

As the reader will presently see, those "practical men" were mistaken.

If there was any person who knew all that we may call the Hidden Secrets of Whitehall Palace, that person was the Lord of Rochester.

His knowledge was most extensive, and many a time that knowledge had been used—much to the advantage of himself, and the disadvantage of others.

Profound silence reigned within and without the palace, save for the steady and monotonous tramp of the sentries.

Clifford might have been asleep nearly an hour, when a gentle tap was heard.

That tap was on the floor, and in nearly the centre of the room.

A pause ensued.

Then another tap was given, and again a pause ensued.

Blood and his rascally associates were in the vault below, and that tapping was on the trap-door.

The object was obvious.

To see whether Clifford would utter a cry of alarm.

If no cry was heard it was to be concluded that he slept, or that he was not within that apartment.

The knocking did not arouse our hero.

Had it done so, what misery—what suffering would he have saved him!

In a few more moments a portion of the flooring was slowly raised a few inches, and a ray of light shone through.

Once more there was a pause, and then the portion of the flooring slid noiselessly aside.

Then a hand, holding a lantern, protruded through the aperture, and the light was directed round the room, until it rested upon the bed.

Once again there was a pause, some conversation being carried on in whispers.

After this the lantern was again lifted, and placed upon the floor.

Then a head appeared, then a body, and presently a man—closely masked—stood in the apartment.

That man was Colonel Blood.

One after the other his two men, who were also masked, clambered up, and at a signal, they drew their daggers.

Blood motioned to one of the men to pick up the lantern.

He then took from beneath his cloak a small bottle.

Taking the cork out, he cautiously advanced to the bedside.

At the end of the bed stood the man with the lantern, which he was holding in such a position, that Blood was well able to see what he was about.

The colonel held the phial to our hero's nostrils for a few seconds.

The effect was extraordinary; for, in a short time, it seemed as if Clifford were being smothered.

He struggled as violently as a man would struggle to get his head from beneath the water; but the struggles ceased as suddenly as they began.

"Now," whispered Blood, "out with the bag."

One of the men, with a hideous leer, opened his cloak and took from beneath it a black bag.

It had no white circle on it, being quite plain, but at the top were several ventilation holes.

While the men held the bag open, Colonel Blood seized upon our now insensible hero and thrust him into it.

"Below with you," whispered Blood, "and be ready to catch the bag when I push it down. When I do so, tie it up the best way you can, and remove it to the further end of the vault. I will join you directly I have settled the other business. I wish I could get right into this other room," he muttered, fiercely. "I would plunge my dagger into the heart of Sir Christopher Cullum. However, he will be *warned*."

Both men descended, and stood aside while Blood, taking hold of one end of the sack, pushed Clifford down the hole.

Down he shot and fell, with a dull thud, on the flags wherewith the vault was paved.

Blood then took the lantern and proceeded to sound the wall behind the bedstead.

Having discovered what he wanted, he took the lantern to the trap and lowered it to the men.

"Keep the ladder ready," he whispered, "and hold your blades in your hands; though I don't think there will be any necessity to use them."

*　　*　　*　　*

Though our hero slept so soundly, sleep visited not the eyes of Sir Christopher Cullum.

Since that terrible affair at the old chambers in Lincoln's Inn Fields, refreshing sleep seemed to have almost entirely deserted him.

It was not only of the lost money that he was continually thinking.

In the silence of the night the face of his murdered servant seemed to peer at him through the darkness; his voice seemed to remind him, in tones of awful solemnity, of the vow he had taken.

He had left his taper alight, but it quickly dwindled to a mere spark, leaving the room in a state of semi-darkness.

He was only just able to make out the outlines of the heavy pictures and the massive furniture.

Suddenly a peculiar noise fell upon his ears.

It sounded to him like the noise which would be caused by a human hand being drawn across the wainscoting.

Considerably startled, he sat up and listened.

The noise was repeated, and now more curious than alarmed, Sir Christopher threw the bedclothes off him, and was in the act of leaping upon the floor, when a panel in the wall just behind the table on which stood the taper slid noiselessly upward.

Sir Christopher gazed at the dark aperture with wonder-stricken eyes. He seemed rooted to the spot.

A gloved hand was thrust through the opening, and something was placed upon the table. Then there appeared another hand, clasping a long glittering dagger.

Sir Christopher felt his blood run cold as the dagger was raised high up for an instant, and then plunged into the something which had been placed on the table.

At this moment, Sir Christopher, with a suppressed cry, started forward.

But ere he could reach the table, the panel descended; the draught it caused extinguished the taper, and the apartment was in total darkness.

Sir Christopher listened intently, but not the faintest noise fell upon his ears.

He now sought the tinder box, and having kindled a light, approached the table.

His astonishment was great, indeed, when he saw the dagger buried deep in the table, after having passed through a thin brass plate.

The surface of the plate bore the *White Circle*, and round it the word—

"BEWARE!"

For some little time Sir Christopher continued to look upon this startling evidence of consummate daring, then a sudden thought striking him, he seized the taper, and dashed out of his room.

Clifford had left his door unfastened, deeming the precaution of locking it unnecessary in a palace supposed to be guarded at every point.

Close by the staircase stood one of the guard.

That he was wideawake and on the alert was evident, for as soon as Sir Christopher swung his door violently open, he brought his weapon to the "ready."

Sir Christopher opened the door of Clifford's apartment, rushed into the room, and advanced to the bed.

It was enough.

His worst fears were realised.

Sir Christopher groaned aloud.

"Gone!" he gasped. "Gone! Blood's work again, I swear! He means to slay poor Clifford."

Rushing out of the room, he confronted the astonished sentry.

"Where have you been all the time, sirrah?" he asked.

"Where have I been, Sir Christopher? Why here."

"It is false?"

The man was thunder-stricken.

"Sir," he said, "I repeat that I have been here ever since I was placed on duty at midnight."

"Do you mean to say, then, that you heard no noise?"

"Where, sir?"

"In yonder room? And do you mean to tell me that two or three men entered that room without your seeing them?"

"Heaven help us!" ejaculated the man, more confounded than ever. "Why, your worship, no man ever crossed that landing from midnight until now."

"My man," replied Sir Christopher, speaking very rapidly and excitedly, "you remember who entered that room?"

"A youth."

"True; and that youth is now *missing!*"

"Missing?"

"Ay. He had gone to bed, and was evidently asleep, when his room was entered by some men, who have carried him off."

"Sir, you startle me! Shall I summon Captain Winter?"

"Do so with all speed."

Captain Winter, with half-a-dozen men, soon made his appearance.

"What on earth is all this I hear, Sir Christopher?" he asked.

"Clifford Hansard, captain, who was placed in this room, as no doubt you remember, has disappeared."

"Great heavens! Gone! It is marvellous. Come here, my man."

This was addressed to the sentry who had been on duty.

Captain Winter questioned him closely.

Then all the sentries within the palace, and the men from the terrace facing the river were summoned and questioned.

All stoutly denied that any person not connected with the palace had passed them.

Suddenly Captain Winter said—

"Ha! I thought one of my men was absent. Bring in Thomas Grant. He was placed outside the treasurer's room."

While one of the men went off, Sir Christopher informed the captain of the wonderful circumstance which had occurred in his own room.

While engaged in the discussion of this, the man who had been sent to fetch Thomas Grant was seen rushing towards them.

The expression on his face showed that something of an alarming nature had happened.

"Well?" queried Captain Winter.

"Lord save us!" gasped the man, his teeth chattering so violently that he could hardly get his words out. "A foul deed has been committed, captain. Thomas Grant is lying beside the door of the treasurer's room with a dagger buried to the very haft in his breast."

"Murdered?" cried Winter.

"Murdered!" yelled the men.

"The way those who kidnapped Clifford Hansard came," said Winter, "is now explained. They must have forced the treasurer's room; and yet—no, they could not have come that way. Had they passed through that room they would only have reached the vault which is used as a store-place for old arms."

"Captain," said the man, "the door has not been forced. I looked at it and tried it. It is locked."

"Mystery upon mystery!" said Sir Christopher; "but the disappearance of Clifford Hansard is the greatest. Who will fathom it? Captain Winter, Colonel Blood is at the bottom of it all."

"I have not the *least* doubt of it,"

replied Captain Winter, gravely. "The report as to his having left the country is entirely false. He makes his presence too well felt to leave any doubt as to whether he is in London or not. Yes, my opinion is that Blood is at the bottom of it. Whether it was his own hand, or his wretched followers, who laid Thomas Grant low, I know not. But this I *do* know, vengeance shall pursue him."

"You are right," replied Sir Christopher. "He shall be discovered. No stone shall be left unturned to bring him to justice."

Captain Winter ordered his men to take the body of their comrade to the guard-room, then to at once return.

Search was made in Sir Christopher's room, and in that lately occupied by Clifford, in order to discover the way by which the murderers had entered.

The walls were sounded, the floor was sounded, and, strange to say, both appeared to be perfectly solid.

Sir Christopher could, of course, point out the exact spot where the hand had appeared, and he ordered the men to bring chisels and hammers, and hack away the woodwork.

So the wainscot was torn away, and to the astonishment of all beholders, there was a solid wall behind it.

"What do you think now?" asked Winter.

"I know not what to think," answered Sir Christopher. "I am more mystified than ever. But I don't want to *think* about this, as I know it for certain, and you and your men can see in that dagger positive proof that a panel opened, and a hand was thrust through."

"Sir Christopher," replied Winter, "if, as you and I imagine, Colonel Blood is at the bottom of this, he must have assistants in this palace."

"I should be sorry to say that he had; but, certainly, it *looks* like it. The whole matter shall be investigated, and I have little doubt but that the king himself will lead the investigation."

"He may," thought Captain Winter; "but I am afraid he would not be *sincere*."

CHAPTER IX.

OF THE FEARFUL SPREAD OF THE PLAGUE—OF THE TERRIBLE CONDITION OF CLIFFORD HANSARD, AND OF THE COMPACT BETWEEN ROCHESTER AND BLOOD.

IT now becomes necessary for us to skip a month, and for this reason: Rochester, having most important business at Oxford, of a somewhat risky nature, he persuaded Blood to accompany him, and this the murderous scoundrel, after arranging his business in London, did, accompanied by three or four of his men, with Captain Drinkwater at their head.

Blood seldom went anywhere without his men, who, if they were not within sight, were usually within call.

During that month the plague, which had broken out in Long Acre, assumed extraordinary proportions.

Despite the greatest precautions, the fearful disease spread with most alarming rapidity.

So fearful were its ravages that the wealthier classes, becoming panic-stricken, began to close their houses and fly into the country.

Many of these Blood and Rochester saw on their journey, and the former chuckled with glee as he thought that when he got back to London he would be the head of a band who, taking advantage of the absence of the owners of the wealthier houses, would plunder them right and left.

King Charles, and in fact everybody connected with him were now in a state of feverish anxiety

Every hour almost, reports as to the progress of this awful visitation were being brought in to his majesty.

There were only two at Court who, in the midst of terror, remained calm and unruffled.

These two were Sir Christopher Cullum and Doctor Jardell.

So implicitly did the king believe in the skill of Jardell, and so taken was he with the compound manufactured by the doctor, and which was said to cure most attacks, that he was anxious to keep the worthy doctor continually at his side.

And yet, despite the fact that the plague was furiously raging in and about Long Acre, the king, disguised of course, had paid more than one visit to the house of Mistress Claribel Cameron.

That the plague would eventually attack that mysterious but beautiful woman, his majesty had not the slightest doubt, for on the door of every house within sight of her residence was placed the cross and the words—words which served as an appeal to heaven; and as a warning—

"𝕷𝖔𝖗𝖉 𝖍𝖆𝖛𝖊 𝖒𝖊𝖗𝖈𝖞 𝖚𝖕𝖔𝖓 𝖚𝖘!"

But as to the plague, more anon, for we must return to Clifford Hansard.

He was conveyed to the strange-looking house in Leicester Fields—the Black Priory.

By the time the house was reached he had shown no signs of returning consciousness.

On the contrary, when by Blood's orders he was thrown out of the sack, he presented more the appearance of a dead than a living creature.

So difficult was his breathing, so ghastly pale were his features, that Blood began to fancy he had administered too much of the powerful drug.

Mother Elwood, who was somewhat skilled in the art of bleeding and the use of herbs, and who had nursed the depraved colonel through more than one dangerous illness, was summoned to attend upon our hero, and soon afterwards she succeeded in restoring him to partial consciousness.

He was then placed in a small vaulted chamber, which had been converted into a prison cell.

As Blood had to accompany Rochester to Oxford, he was not able to see how far Clifford progressed towards complete recovery.

But before leaving the house he said—

"Look you, Mother Elwood, into the hands of yourself and your daughter I place that youth. I have not the least doubt but that in a few hours the house will be searched from top to bottom. But within the cage he is safe. Let them search till doomsday, they will not discover him."

"If he does not *shout*," grunted the old crone.

"See to it that he does *not* shout," was the fierce rejoinder.

Blood was quite right.

Within twelve hours the house was searched from top to bottom.

Sir Christopher Cullum accompanied the guard and assisted them in their search, but it was without result.

Just as he and the guard were quitting the house Blake Barrell made his appearance, but of course Sir Christopher knew him not, and put no questions to him.

Mother Elwood's daughter, Ann, was a young woman of thirty, and quite as ugly as her mother.

She was a woman of most ungovernable passions; indeed, she was a very fiend in the shape of a woman.

This creature conceived a liking for Clifford, and on many occasions thrust herself under his notice.

Our hero paying not the slightest attention to her, and plainly showing his intense disgust, the young woman resolved to be revenged, and she had her revenge, too, in more ways than one, and it is scarcely necessary to say that she was assisted by her mother.

The principal punishment they inflicted on our unlucky hero was—starvation.

Sometimes they kept him without food for two and three days.

At last our hero presented a really deplorable sight.

Fever seized upon him, and then Mother Elwood and her daughter, fearing that death would ensue, and that consequently they would have to answer for it to the ferocious colonel, summoned medical assistance.

But delirium in its worst form attacked Clifford, and kept him pinioned to his miserable pallet within that gloomy cell for days.

Mother Elwood bribed the surgeon who attended our hero to keep his mouth closed, and though, had he given information, he would certainly have received a very handsome reward from

Sir Christopher, he *did* keep his mouth closed.

A month had elapsed, and it is on the day that Blood and his men reached London that we return to the house in Leicester Fields.

Captain Drinkwater and the men under him ascended to the top of the house, where refreshments were quickly placed before them by Mother Elwood and her daughter.

Blood, who seemed somewhat care-worn, and who looked pale and anxious, went to his bedroom, where he attired himself in a Court suit.

After this he descended to his private apartment.

One of the tables had been drawn into the centre of the room, and had been spread with a goodly array of meats and wines, all of the very choicest and most costly description.

Beside the table stood Mother Elwood.

"How is the prisoner?" asked Blood, seating himself and pouring out a tumbler of wine.

"Poorly."

"Poorly!" grinned Blood. "Ha, ha! What, then, have you been doing with him?"

"Nothing."

"What has your daughter been doing with him?"

"Nothing. But what else can you expect? I should like to know who would be in that cell a month and look *well*?"

"You are right. How has he be-haved?"

"Like a caged lion."

"Indeed!" smiled Blood. "And how did you cure him?"

"Much after your own style. He has had the fever."

"What!" roared Blood, starting from his chair, "the fever? Do you mean the *plague*?"

"No, no; don't be frightened. He has not had the plague, though he is likely to get it, as we all are. It is close handy."

"Where?"

"Opposite. Two houses have been attacked, and the whole of the occupants carried off. The red cross is on the doors. I suppose you have heard that scores have been stricken down in Long Acre?"

"I have; but what of *her*?"

"Mistress Cameron? She is alive, I believe."

"Good. I will visit her soon."

"More fool you, then. You are almost certain to be attacked."

"I must risk it. Now—but hark! the signal! Quick, quick; Rochester is at hand, and we have important business to transact."

In a few moments Rochester en-tered.

He was beautifully attired in a Court costume—a costume which resembled very much the one Blood was wearing, and jewels of great value adorned his person.

"Now for further business," he said, "and this time business which better suits me than the last. But what of the youth? Is he dead?"

"Dead! No; but he has been near death's door."

"I don't wonder at that. And when I think of Mother Elwood and her daughter, I am compelled to arrive at the conclusion that his keepers have been none of the best."

"How dare you insinuate any such thing?" yelled Mother Elwood, who happened to be entering the chamber at the moment these words, uttered in con-temptuous tones, were spoken.

"How *dare* I?" replied Rochester, leaning back in his chair and surveying the old crone with an insolent stare. "Why, easily enough."

"How do *you* know what sort of keepers we make?"

"Well, I suppose you only want once looking at? I am under the impression that neither you nor your daughter, *clever* though you consider yourselves, are able to put on and take off your ugly faces at your pleasure. Ha, ha!"

At these words the face of the old woman became perfectly diabolical.

"Laugh, my lord," she hissed, shaking her bony fist in Rochester's face, "laugh, but look you—*you* who fatten on the crumbs which fall from the royal table —what would you say, did I tell you that at *one* time, years and years gone by, I was very, very beautiful?"

"I would say that you were speaking falsely," replied Rochester, coolly.

"Peace!" cried Blood. "Depart—depart."

Mother Elwood, with a bitter exclamation, turned and left the apartment.

"We have little time to waste," observed Blood, pushing a bottle of wine and a tumbler towards Rochester.

"Truly. Now, before we depart on our journey," said Rochester, "let us have a look at the youth. Have you seen him yet?"

"No."

"I suppose the place was searched from top to bottom?"

"Ay, Mother Elwood tells me the flooring and the walls in every room were sounded, but nothing was discovered."

Blood took hold of a cord hanging from the wall and pulled it.

Instantly the heavy curtains, which seemed to screen another apartment, divided, and there was revealed—

Nothing!

Nothing but what looked like a solid wall.

Blood now opened a tiny trap in the floor, and caught hold of a handle.

But here for a moment we must pause and return to Clifford.

* * * *

Two sides of the dreadful hole into which our hero had been cast were of stone, and the other two were rows of iron bars, and behind one row was a brick wall.

In the course of the month which had elapsed, when he had felt himself able to drag himself about the place, Clifford had searched the cell in the hope of finding some weak spot—some place where, if fortune favoured him, he could make an attempt to free himself.

But he found no such place.

The walls were as firm as rocks, the iron bars sunk deeply and securely into the solid stone.

In that cage many a dark and terrible deed had been perpetrated.

Many and many a time had it rung with the agonised shrieks of tortured victims—victims who were afterwards placed in the dreadful sacks and hurled into the Thames.

What food Clifford was allowed to have, was handed to him either by Mother Elwood or her hideous daughter through the iron bars.

On this particular evening, Clifford was seated on the pallet, his face buried in his hands.

His whole figure had wasted away in a truly shocking manner.

So altered were his features by the fever and the state of semi-starvation in which he had been kept, that it is very doubtful if the locksmith, Master Preston, would have recognised him.

Terrible indeed had been his sufferings!

Of how long he had been in this dungeon he knew not, though he was perfectly well aware who had placed him there.

But from the conversation of Mother Elwood and her daughter, scraps of which he occasionally caught if they were speaking in the passage, he knew that several weeks must have passed since he was taken away from the palace in that (to him) most unaccountable fashion.

But where was Blood?

Ah! that to Clifford was indeed a mystery.

Racked with pain, half starved as he was, this was not all his sufferings.

No, his mental sufferings were even greater than his physical ones, for he had caught enough from the old woman and her daughter to learn that the plague was raging furiously in several parts of London, and that it was spreading in every direction.

"Alas!" he thought, "should the plague attack the locksmith's, all—all may be seized and die. I may never again set eyes upon any of them in this world. Oh, Olivia! Olivia! May heaven have mercy upon us all."

The only light which reached the cell was through a small, circular, strongly-barred window.

But at night he was never provided with a light of any description.

Darkness, the most profound, always reigned then.

As we have said, our unfortunate hero was seated upon his pallet.

Suddenly men's voices fell upon his ears.

These voices seemed very near to him, and so surprised was he that he started up.

There was a pause, during which he listened intently.

Again the voices were heard.

Where could they be? Outside that window, in the passage? Or where?

Round and round the cell he went, placing his ear here and there, in the hopes of making out what was said.

That was useless.

Though he was certain that the voices were the voices of men, and though he was equally certain that they were very close to him, he could not tell exactly where the speakers could be.

Suddenly he heard a loud burst of laughter.

Instantly he stood bolt upright, quivering in every limb.

"Great heaven!" he muttered. "Surely I cannot be mistaken! That laugh! When did I last hear it? Ha! the night on which I placed the murdered page before the king and his lords. I cannot be mistaken. That fiendish laugh I recognise; it was uttered by Rochester."

Such indeed was the case.

Again there was a pause, lasting, this time, for some few minutes.

Suddenly Clifford, who had hold of the iron bars at the back of the cell, felt them vibrate.

Then there was a low, rumbling noise at his feet, the stone flooring shook—the whole of the chamber, in fact, shook slightly at first, and then violently.

Presently a brilliant light appeared above.

At first it seemed like a crack, extending from one end of the chamber to the other.

Clifford watched it eagerly.

He was not terrified, but his astonishment was profound when he saw that the brick wall behind the bars was sinking into the earth.

He knew at once that it was some mechanical contrivance, and erect and firm he watched for the result.

Lower, lower sank the wall, and at last a startled cry left Clifford's lips as he saw before him the very apartment wherein Blood had been captured by himself and Captain Winter.

There, at the table, sat the villainous colonel and his confederate—for he was nothing better—Lord Rochester.

Weak though he was, he would, had he had the opportunity, have rushed upon the pair, and he would willingly have lost his life in slaying either of them.

But he was powerless.

The iron bars divided him from the two wretches.

Blood and Rochester looked hard at him, as though thunderstricken at the alteration which had taken place in him; then both burst into a loud roar of laughter.

"Well," said Rochester, crossing his legs, and leisurely surveying our hero, "he presents an interesting sight, does he not, Blood?"

"Yes," rejoined Blood, "I must say that the alteration is absolutely startling."

"One would think, to look at him," pursued Rochester, "that he had been down with the plague."

"Ah, scoundrels!" cried Clifford. "Black-hearted wretches that you are! For the fearful treatment that I have received a most terrible vengeance will surely fall upon you."

Again Rochester's sardonic laugh rang out.

"As to *you*, vile murderer," continued Clifford, directing a look of bitter contempt at Blood, "*you* shall yet receive the reward your crimes have merited."

"Silence!" interrupted Blood, in his most freezing tones. "You will do well to keep a still tongue in your head, or I will quickly compel you to."

"Here is John Jeevers and Blake Barrell," exclaimed the cracked voice of Mother Elwood.

"The very two we require," said Blood, with a significant glance at Rochester. "Admit them, Mother Elwood."

In a few seconds in walked Jeevers and Barrell.

The change which had taken place in both these young ruffians since last we saw them was startling.

But the alteration in *their* appearance was not caused by inhuman treatment or severe illness.

It had been caused by drink.

During Blood's absence in the country they had been sober scarcely a single day.

Now their clothes were torn in many places, and their faces wore that hang-dog, depraved expression usually to be seen on the faces of men after a long bout of dissipation.

No sooner did they behold Clifford than they burst into a savage yell.

Blake, without the slightest warning, rushed forward, and, before our hero could draw back, dealt him a heavy blow on the mouth.

"You might have waited until you were told to do that," growled the colonel. "Stand aside, and don't take liberties."

"I owe him that and more," hissed Blake. "I would like to put a dagger into his heart now."

"Now?" queried Rochester, with a sneer—"*now?* Why, don't you see he is, in the first place, unable to defend himself; and, in the second, he is unable, owing to the bars, to return your blow?"

"I see all that," replied Blake; "but were it otherwise, I would not care. It would not be the first time that I have thrashed him."

"When he has been unable to defend himself?"

"No; when well able to defend himself."

"I doubt it. However, he is deserving of no sympathy."

"You are right," growled Blood, savagely, as if suddenly remembering the night at Chancery Lane, when our hero so nearly succeeded in checking him, "and no sympathy will he get. I wonder what the locksmith and the pretty—er—what is her name, Blake?"

Blake failed to detect the significant look Blood directed at Rochester, though it was observed by Clifford.

"Her name," replied Blake, "is Olivia."

"The prettiest girl in the city?" asked Rochester, with another sneer.

"She is," replied Blake, emphatically.

"According to whose idea? Yours and those who where your comrades?"

"Acording to the idea of everyone who has seen her."

"Ah! Well, let us ask yonder young man about her. She is a pretty maiden, Clifford Hansard, is she not?"

"Depraved wretch," replied Clifford, "address your queries to your dastardly companions."

"Ha, ha! Why, you see, Blood, that the confinement here has not taken the edge off his temper."

"So it seems. But now, my lord, no more nonsense; we are wasting most valuable time. You, Blake, and you, Jeevers, are to transact a little business matter. Go up to the top of the house, and you will find Captain Drinkwater. You are to place yourselves under his charge. Do as he tells you——"

"And he will make you as drunk as fiddlers!" interrupted Rochester, with a loud laugh. "He and his men are already well on the road. Can you not hear their sweet voices, Blood?"

"Aye; but they have had a bad time of it for the past month, and deserve a carouse. Now up you go."

Blake and Jeevers ascended the stairs to join the wretches above, while Colonel Blood, after a brief pause, said—

"Clifford Hansard, you would, no doubt, like to get out of that cage?"

"Aye, even if it were for only a few moments," replied Clifford. "Weak though you have now made me, I would yet summon sufficient strength to strangle you."

Blood smiled mockingly.

"Clifford Hansard," he continued, "his lordship, here, has taken a fancy to Olivia Preston, purely from the elaborate descriptions given of her, and we are about to pay her a visit."

He paused abruptly.

Clifford's face, now distorted by the dreadful mental agony he was undergoing, was fearful to behold.

His eyes were fixed upon Blood, like the eyes of a wretched prisoner fastened upon the judge about to pronounce sentence of a fearful death.

"Go on," said Rochester, with a brutal laugh, "you see you are only keeping him in suspense. Why do you not tell him that if the girl is as beautiful as I am led to believe, I will make her my companion."

A wild, heartrending cry left Clifford's lips.

Now worked up into a state of frenzy he seemed hardly to know what he was doing.

"Oh that I had the power of forcing out these bars!" he cried, as he tugged frantically at them.

"What!" cried Rochester, feigning the greatest astonishment. "Do you mean to tell me that this sweet city maiden would not prefer the attentions of a peer to those of a poverty-stricken apprentice? And, besides, the plague is now raging furiously; it is running towards the very middle of the city with appalling velocity; and in order to escape a terrible death, this young maiden would be only too glad to fly into the arms of one who would bear her into the country—far away from the touch of the loathsome plague."

"Enough, enough!" cried Clifford. "Loathsome you say the plague is. It is loathsome, indeed, but not one twentieth part so loathsome as you!"

Suddenly starting up and giving utterance to a savage cry, Rochester laid hold of a heavy bottle and flung it at Clifford with all his force.

The bottle struck one of the bars and was shattered into a hundred pieces, some of them striking our hero on the face.

"I cannot stand too much," cried Rochester.

"Enough of this," cried Colonel Blood. "We have let him know where we are bound; that, my lord, will cause him more agony than any physical torture. Presently we shall have more to say to him."

Once more Clifford advanced to the rails, but ere he could speak the wall was set in motion, and quickly resumed its original position, leaving our hero once more alone and in darkness.

Both Rochester and Blood now prepared to set out.

"Whom shall we take with us?" asked Rochester.

"I have been thinking that it would be far better did we go alone," replied Blood.

"Please yourself. But I should say, take John Jeevers," said Rochester.

"Why not Blake?"

"Blake? Ho, ho!" laughed Rochester. "What, take that young man to the very house from which we are about to abduct the girl he covets? Certainly the idea is a strange one. Ha, ha! But where will the coaches meet us?"

"At Lincoln's Inn. Each is provided with four horses and two postilions. These men, when well bribed, I have found ready and willing to do anything."

"That is also my experience," replied Rochester! "and so, after all, we shall have quite enough aid. The compact between us, Blood, is this: you are to help me to obtain possession of Olivia Preston, and I am to assist you in getting Clarissa Jardell."

"That is so."

"And whatever happens we are to help each other?"

"Precisely."

And now, having seen that their pistols were properly loaded, and their swords ready for instant use, they left the apartment.

"One moment," said Blood, pausing abruptly on the stairs, "I must return for an instant. I had forgotten the *skeleton*."

"What are you about to do with it?"

"Listen. That will occupy my place during my absence. I will join you in a few moments."

CHAPTER X.

IS OF CLIFFORD'S DARING COURAGE—OF WHAT BEFELL MOTHER ELWOOD'S DAUGHTER AND ALL WITHIN THE BLACK PRIORY.

IT was our intention to follow Lord Rochester and Colonel Blood at once, but before we describe their movements and the deeds which followed, we will return to those left at the Black Priory.

The whole of this extraordinary place was well furnished, and even the rooms at the top bore some traces of what would be called "luxurious" furnishing, though they were generally used by

Captain Drinkwater and those beneath him—if any man in London *could* be classed as beneath this drink-soddened, heartless ruffian.

Two or three of the rooms were used as bed-rooms, and the principal one, the largest of all, was the assembly room.

When Colonel Blood and Rochester had left, Mother Elwood ascended.

She was anxious to participate in the

liquor with which the men had been supplied by Blood's orders.

She found her daughter—now far on the road towards a state of beastly drunkenness—sitting on Captain Drinkwater's knee.

Her right arm was about his short, thick neck, while her left, raised high over her head, held a brimming tankard.

Her hair was disordered, and the expression on her face was almost beyond the power of description.

The two men with Blake and Jeevers were playing cards.

Occasionally, when Captain Drinkwater commenced to howl forth one of the ribald songs of the day—and he was acquainted with a round dozen or two—they would leave off and join in the chorus.

From a distance it sounded as if a dozen raving maniacs were howling forth horrible imprecations on their imaginary enemies.

But all this was a thing which old Mother Elwood relished with great gusto.

"Thank the Virgin," she growled, "they have gone."

"Gone!" cried Drinkwater. "Where?"

"Somewhere in the city. And may Rochester catch the plague."

"So say I!" cried Ann, Mother Elwood's daughter. "So say I! Ha, I owe him a grudge, and I'll pay him yet!"

"And what do *you* owe him a grudge for, my beauty?" asked Drinkwater.

"He called me a vixen."

"That's nothing."

"And said that I was about the most ugly lump of humanity he had ever seen."

"There he lied," replied Drinkwater, warmly, "for you are as pretty a creature as—as I've seen hereabouts. What say you, lads?"

"The same!" was the reply.

"And what say *you*, Mother Elwood ---what say you. Don't *you* think your daughter a fine wench?"

"Ay, marry do I. She *is* a fine wench. Why, man alive, I've seen her crack a skull as clean and as quickly as a heavy man could crack one. She would make a most excellent wife, because, if her husband didn't happen to have any manners, she could quickly knock them into him."

"To be sure—to be sure she could," mumbled Drinkwater. "But sit down, mother, and make yourself comfortable. Here is plenty to drink, though we have nothing left in the shape of eatables, and as to that——"

"Well," interrupted Mother Elwood, "I had forgotten. Ah, we will soon have something grand to eat. There's all those dainties from the colonel's special cupboard."

"Where?" cried Drinkwater. "Where, Mother Elwood?"

"Why, down below."

"Below, eh? Humph! I thought that the colonel and his lordship had eaten the dainties."

"Nothing of the sort. All they have tasted is the wine. Do you think Rochester would partake of any of the eatables? No! Blood pushed them towards him, and Rochester simply turned up his haughty nose and pushed them back."

"Which shows that he is a fool," said Drinkwater, "and that he don't know what is good for himself. Oh, and so those dainties are below? By the shades of Olympus! bring them up, mother—bring them up, I say; and I for one will show you that my paunch appreciates most thoroughly any dainties with which it has the good fortune to be supplied."

"Same here," said Jeevers.

"And here," hiccoughed Blake, who had been drinking very freely; "but what if the colonel should know?"

"What if he did?" replied Drinkwater, in contemptuous tones. "So up with them, mother. But, I say, what of the prisoner?"

"Clifford Hansard? Why, he is in the place he has been ever since he was brought here."

"Ay, ay! But I mean has not the colonel changed his diet yet?"

"Changed it? Just as if such a thing is likely!"

"Then he has had nothing but bread and water since he has been here?"

"No; and he deserves nothing better, does he?"

"You are right. It is the colonel's intention to poison him, eh?"

"Yes," said Blake, "and I hope to have the task of giving him the poison."

"'ONE CRY, AND I WILL PLUNGE THIS KNIFE INTO YOUR HEART!' CRIED CLIFFORD."

"Ay," grinned Jeevers, "while I hold him down."

"Now that Blood has gone," said Blake, savagely, "I don't see why I should not have my revenge on him. Jeevers, let us descend and torture him a bit."

"No, no," interrupted Drinkwater; "you must do nothing of the kind. I am in charge of the house, remember, and Colonel Blood will look to me for the safety of the youth. Besides, my friend, Blake Barrell, you might fatally injure him. He might die before Blood wishes it."

"What of it?"

"Well, well; you would see what of it."

"What would follow?"

"What would follow? Why, my young friend, Colonel Blood would, without the slightest warning, send a ball through your brain."

"For killing this dastard Hansard?"

"No, not for killing *him*. But for disobedience to his orders."

"Remain where you are, my dear," whispered Ann, going over to Blake, and placing her arm about his neck. "Remain where you are. *I* owe him a grudge, for he slighted me—ay, scorned me—treated me with contempt—me, the idol of every man———"

"Except Rochester," chuckled Jeevers.

But Ann took no notice of this.

"I will descend anon," she continued, in a whisper, "and you shall hear his wild shrieks even up here."

"What will you do?"

"Blind him!"

This terrible threat was uttered in the coolest tones imaginable.

It was a threat which would have caused any ordinary mortal to shudder with horror; but it had not this effect on Blake.

Hard his heart had always been; but of late his connections had caused it to become harder than ever.

He bade fair to become one of the most brutal ruffians in all London.

"Ha!" he said, "that would, indeed, be a splendid punishment. "Lord! how I would dance and yell before him."

"But the blindness would be only temporary."

"How do you mean?"

"Brandy, my dear, is good taken inwardly," replied Ann, with a hideous grin; "but it is terrible stuff taken *outwardly*—in other words, I shall presently descend, and under pretence of offering him a noggen of brandy, I will throw it in his eyes."

"And you will let me see him afterwards?"

"To be sure—to be sure!"

"Now, Mother Elwood, are you going down for those dainties, or am I to fetch them myself?" shouted Drinkwater."

"Yes, yes; I go—I go," replied the old woman.

Picking up a lantern she descended.

Having reached the bottom of the stairs a sudden thought struck her, and she turned up the passage which led to the chamber in which our hero was confined.

Approaching the bars she held up the lantern.

Its rays fell upon a ghastly, pale, haggard face and a pair of sunken eyes, fixed with a stony stare upon the ground.

"How do you feel *now*?" grinned Mother Elwood, who hated our hero with all her soul.

No answer was returned.

Clifford did not even raise his eyes.

Mother Elwood repeated her question; but getting no reply, she shook her bony fist through the bars, and uttered threats.

But they moved not our hero.

Apparently the blow, not long since delivered by Blood—the declaration that Olivia would soon be in the power of Rochester—had been a crushing one.

Blood was right when he said that it would have more effect than any bodily torture.

Mother Elwood placed her lantern on the ground, and went off, muttering—

"I know what to do—ay, I know what to do!"

It was the first time that Clifford had seen a lantern left near the bars.

Wondering what it meant he roused himself, and moved nearer the bars.

Presently Mother Elwood reappeared, having in her arms a large tray.

On it were the articles left by the colonel and Rochester.

There were tempting dainties of all sorts upon it—dainties calculated to drive a starving man mad.

Approaching close to the bars, she said—

"There! there! What do you think of all this, eh? Look! look! Feast your eyes on it—feast your eyes on it! You shall not take it!"

Before she could say anything more, Clifford seized hold of the edge of the tray, and jerked it violently from the bars.

The result was that everything on it went flying in all directions.

Some of the goblets—of gold and of silver—rolled towards Clifford's feet, and he kicked them contemptuously from him.

The old woman, fearing that some of the articles might become dented, was now in a terrible state.

Falling on her hands and knees, she commenced to scramble up the articles.

Suddenly a glittering object met our hero's eyes.

There it lay, not very far from his pallet.

He advanced to kick it out of the chamber.

But he saw that it was neither a goblet nor a plate.

No, it was a goodly-sized *knife*.

He dared not stoop to pick it up; but instantly sinking upon the pallet, he held his legs in such a position that the knife was completely hidden.

Three or four knives had been on the tray, though the old woman knew not exactly how many had been there.

But, as a matter of fact, she did not think of the knives.

Having picked all up, as she thought, she once more took the tray in her arms, then picked up the lantern.

"You shall rue it for that!" she hissed, showing what remained of her tusk-like teeth. "You shall rue it. Ha! terribly rue it! Wait—wait!"

"A knife!" muttered Clifford, gloomily, as he listened to the old woman's retreating footsteps. "A knife! Ah! it might be of immense service to me *outside* those bars, but 'tis useless within. A file would—but no, it would take hours to saw through those bars; and, besides, someone is always on the alert. Oh, heaven!" he moaned aloud,

"what have I done that I should suffer so? Would that I could get to know how long I have been here! And how long—ha! how long shall I remain ere death puts an end to my sufferings? That Blake is here—here in this house," he added, as he picked up the knife, and clutched the handle firmly in his thin hand. "Ay! he is here! Oh, if I could get at him—but no, no. Here I am, and here—*here* shall I remain until the end!"

The time wore on.

An hour must have passed ere the old woman had appeared at the bars, and those above had been enjoying themselves in their own peculiar fashion.

Their shouting had been fearful, but by-and-bye they became quieter.

On two or three the effects of the drink had been such as to send them to sleep.

But on Ann Elwood and Blake the effect had been different.

Mother Elwood's daughter had drunk until in a state bordering on frenzy.

Clifford had listened to the ravings of those above solely because he could not help it.

But when the cries had died down, he threw himself on his pallet.

He had not lain there many minutes ere he heard heavy footsteps descending the stairs.

He started up and listened.

The footsteps were decidedly unsteady.

Whoever was descending those stairs was in a state of intoxication.

That much he could tell, but whether the person descending was a man or a woman he was unable to make out.

But could it be Blake?

As he thought that it *might* be him, he leapt to his feet.

"But no," he thought, "I will lay on the pallet and feign sleep. If it is Blake he might be tempted to open the bars if he knows where the key is. Then when he enters—ah! when he enters—I will have no mercy upon him! No, no!"

Down on the pallet he lay, the knife clutched ready in his hand.

At this moment Clifford felt as if all his old strength had suddenly returned to him.

He felt ready to make a bold dash for

freedom and revenge if the opportunity offered.

But it was not Blake who was descending the stairs.

It was Ann.

In her right hand she carried a goblet half filled with powerful, undiluted brandy, and in her left the lantern previously brought down by her mother.

The rays of that lantern fell full upon her face—a face perfectly demoniacal in its expression.

No trace of the sex to which she belonged did it bear—it was the face of a fiend.

She approached the bars, and directed the light of the lantern into the chamber.

"He sleeps!" she muttered; "and that being so, there can be no danger in opening the bars. Blood will never know I did so. Yes, I will open the bars, approach him, and shake him violently. Then when he starts up I will dash the brandy in his eyes. Ha! that will make him smart, that will make him howl. He from whom no cry has yet been wrung, will scream with pain at this."

Thereupon she turned and entered the passage.

Here, high up on the wall, hung a small and most peculiar-shaped key.

This fitted a tiny lock in one of the bars, where was the only means of entrance.

As the reader has more than once been told, Clifford had frequently attended to the many locks in this house, but it is hardly necessary to say that he had never had anything to do with this one.

Reaching down the key, Ann returned to the chamber, placed the key in the lock, turned it, and the bars opened.

Oh, what a thrill of joy ran through our hero's veins as the harsh noise, caused by the moving bars, fell upon his ears.

Entering the chamber, Ann crept to the pallet, bent over the prostrate figure and listened—

"He sleeps soundly enough," she thought; "but it will be a long time ere he *again* sleeps soundly."

Cautiously she stooped to place the lantern on the floor.

Now was Clifford's time.

He did not lose the opportunity.

Just as Ann rose and stretched out her hand, Clifford darted from off the pallet with the rapidity of lightning.

Back a pace or two went Ann.

A great cry rose to her lips, but it was never uttered.

Clifford seized the wretch by the throat with such a grip, that she began to turn black in the face.

The danger she was in seemed to sober her, and wildly she attempted to shake off our hero's grip.

She was, as we have more than once observed, a powerful woman, and, considering Clifford's weak state, she would eventually have succeeded in throwing him off.

But something she had never expected suddenly put an effectual damper on her.

That something was the knife.

High up before her starting eyes that glittering blade was raised, menacing her with certain death.

"One cry!" hissed Clifford, "and it is your last; for I will plunge this knife deep into your heart! Ah, you—*you* who have tortured me for so long, quail —shrink at the sight of this blade. Fiend—fiend in the garb of woman— you deserve a thousand deaths, and I can scarcely stay my hand!"

"Spare me—spare me!" gurgled Ann.

"Spare you! Would you have spared me? Have you ever spared me? No; you gloried in my sufferings. In my illness I suppose it was—for that I *have* been ill and near death's door I know— I must have uttered the name of her who is all the world to me. And you have mocked me. Wretch, I can scarcely stay this blade from descending! *My* hour has now come. It shall now be death or liberty!"

So saying, he exerted all his strength, and flung Ann from him.

Had she been perfectly sober, she might easily have saved herself; but being unsteady on her legs, she could not recover her balance, and fell, her head striking the iron bars with terrific force.

The blow did not render her unconscious, however, but it rendered her powerless.

She lay where she fell, unable to utter a cry.

Her eyes, open to their fullest extent, and filled with an indescribable expression of terror, were fixed upon the knife Clifford held in his hand.

Our hero could easily have taken her life, and justly would she have merited a terrible death.

"I warn you," said Clifford, sternly, "not to make any outcry. Now, tell me. Have Colonel Blood and Rochester left the house?"

Ann nodded as well as she was able.

"Very well. And his villains are upstairs, including Blake Barrell and John Jeevers?"

Again Ann nodded.

"Keep where you are. Move not on your life," said Clifford.

And he picked up the lantern.

Ann's eyes eagerly followed him, and watched his movements as he left the chamber—that terrible chamber which, for so long, had been his prison, and a chamber of torture—a chamber which he certainly thought he would never leave alive. And as her eyes followed him, her soul was filled with horror as she thought that he might lock the bars.

Supposing he did, and closed the door above the stairs, and Blood did not return—perhaps for a few days—perhaps *never*—which was a very likely thing, considering the risk he ran, and and considering also that the plague was as likely to seize upon him as any-one else.

As Clifford got outside the bars she slightly raised her bleeding head, and tried to speak—tried to implore him not to lock her in.

But she found herself totally unable to utter a word.

The noise above had somewhat diminished.

But directly Clifford put his foot on the first stair, the noise broke out afresh.

Most distinctly Clifford made out the cracked voice of Mother Elwood.

She was shrieking out the chorus of some "song" in the manner peculiar to habitual drunkards.

Softly our hero ascended the stairs, taking care to conceal the light of the lantern as much as possible, and to keep the precious knife clutched firmly in his hand ready for any emergency.

He reached the second landing.

There was now one flight only to ascend ere the assembly room was reached.

From where he stood he had a good view of the door of that room.

He saw that it was a small one, but ponderous, and well supplied with bolts and bars.

While making this examination the door was suddenly pulled open, and out stalked Blake Barrell.

Becoming impatient at the continued absence of Mother Elwood's daughter, and burning also with a desire to wreak some terrible injury on Clifford, he was descending the stairs to the chamber.

A dagger hung at his waist, but, beyond that, he carried no arms.

Clifford, completely shading the rays from his lantern, slipped back into a recess.

"What shall I do?" he muttered. "He is now at my mercy, for easily enough could I rush forward and plunge this knife into his heart. But I should be a coward to slay him outright, especially in his present state, for he is more than half drunk. But I will render him powerless to assist those above—that is, supposing they offer to dash upon me."

Down the stairs came Blake, mumbling sentences which one would have thought could only emanate from the brain of a lunatic.

He reached the landing at last.

Hardly had his feet touched it ere Clifford sprang forward and dealt Blake such a crashing blow between the eyes, that he fell as suddenly as an ox falls beneath the deadly poleaxe.

Not a sound escaped his lips.

He fell, completely doubled up, as it were, beside the banisters.

The loud noise had, of course, attracted the attention of those above.

Captain Drinkwater, being under the impression that Blake had fallen down the stairs, burst into a loud laugh.

But it was checked as soon as Clifford appeared before the door.

Instantly a loud cry left the lips of the captain, and it was followed by one from Mother Elwood, who, in the sudden appearance of Clifford, saw that something had happened to her daughter.

Their cries aroused the two men, but not Jeevers.

He lay beneath the table sound asleep.

"Cut him down!" roared Drinkwater, drawing his heavy sword. "Slay him! or all of us will have to answer for it!"

One of the men sprang forward, drawing his blade as he did so.

As he reached the threshold Clifford stepped back a pace, and hurled the lighted lantern in the man's face.

Then springing forward he raised the knife, and plunged it into the fellow's body.

And there it remained, for Clifford did not withdraw it.

Captain Drinkwater, and the other man, had loaded pistols in their belts; but they seemed so appalled at what Clifford had done, that they neither offered to use their weapons, nor move from where they stood.

Another instant, and Clifford had drawn the door to with a crash, and shot one of the huge bolts into its socket.

Then it was that Drinkwater and the others within the room found the use of their limbs.

They rushed to the door, and tugged frantically at it.

But it was useless.

That one bolt would defy their united efforts was evident.

But Clifford shot *all* the bolts, and there were six.

"Stand back!" yelled Drinkwater to his companions.

Another instant, and the loud report of a pistol was heard.

Captain Drinkwater had tried the effect of a shot through the door.

That also was quite useless, for so thick was the door, that no bullet would pass completely through it.

Clifford quickly descended the stairs.

He was in darkness now, and therefore had to proceed with extreme caution lest an unexpected fall should bring to an abrupt termination the escape now so nearly consummated.

His foot came in contact with Blake's body.

He stopped and passed his hands over him.

So far as he could feel, it seemed as if the young ruffian had not moved from the spot where he had been stricken down.

As Clifford felt him, his hands came in contact with the dagger Blake wore at his side.

Quickly he plucked the blade from its sheath, and once more resumed the descent of the stairs.

Heaven help the person who would have attempted to bar the passage of Clifford Hansard at that moment.

But no one was left to interrupt him.

The street door was reached, and now Clifford paused and considered a few moments.

Then he descended still lower.

Blood's chamber was reached.

The door was ajar.

Could anyone be within that mysterious apartment? thought Clifford.

For he was enabled to see that a faint light burned within.

He listened intently, but no sound fell upon his ears.

Silence—profound silence reigned.

With the dagger in his grasp, ready to pounce upon whomsoever was in that room, he pushed the door open.

A cry nearly left his lips as, like a ghost, he glided into the chamber, for there at the table sat a masked figure.

"Blood!" thought Clifford. "Blood fast asleep! Then they lied—they lied! Ah, the monster is in my power! I will show the villain no mercy!"

Rushing forward, he raised the dagger aloft, and bringing it down with all his force, cried—

"Die, atrocious ruffian! thus do I take thy life as thou hast assassinated many!"

The weapon passed through the cloak, but it appeared to strike nothing else.

No sooner was the blow struck than the figure, our hero had taken to be Blood, started bolt upright, and turned swiftly.

The horrible, grinning face of a skeleton was revealed.

Full of desperate courage, as our hero now was—the courage of despair in fact—the sight was too awful even for him.

He drew back, and the skeleton, its eyes moving in their sockets, commenced to walk towards where our hero stood.

Had this been a human being, Clifford

would have stood his ground, and fought while the breath remained in his body.

But the object which now stood before him filled him with a horror such as he had never in all his life experienced.

He turned, pulled the door open, and dashed through it.

He found no difficulty in getting the street door open, and, in a few moments more, he was in the streets—free—free!

CHAPTER XI.

IS OF THE MOVEMENTS OF BLOOD AND ROCHESTER--OF THE HOUSE IN CHANCERY LANE—OF THE DEATH OF PRITCHARD PRESTON, AND OF WHAT HAPPENED TO OLIVIA.

COLONEL BLOOD and Rochester, during their journeys, had resolved on their future operations, and a part of those operations, as we have seen, had reference to Clarissa Jardell, and Olivia Preston.

Blood was to possess Clarissa, and Rochester, Olivia.

Blood had long been a secret admirer of Clarissa.

He had conceived a strong passion for her, and, moreover, he, as we know, hated Sir Christopher Cullum, and would be glad at the slightest opportunity to do him an injury.

What greater injury could he do him than carry off Sir Christopher's intended bride—the beautiful creature who was far dearer than life itself to Sir Christopher?

Blood saw that the old man, Doctor Jardell, had turned entirely against him; and while he did not wonder at this, he yet resolved to make him repent it.

At Kennington Cross they had hired a couple of coaches, each to have four powerful horses, and two postilions.

The proprietor of these coaches knowing Blood well, and guessing that he was bent upon some wicked errand, and would require men who would do exactly what they were told, selected four of the most ruffianly men in his establishment.

Rochester and Blood walked to Lincoln's Inn, and as they trod the streets they were horror-stricken at what they beheld.

The plague had already made fearful havoc, and instead of decreasing in fury, it was increasing at an appalling rate.

In some streets every house bore upon its door the ominous red cross, and the piteous words—

"Lord have mercy upon us!"

Some of which, but a short time before, had been the busiest streets, now wore an air of utter desolation, and in many places the grass was growing between the stones.

Moreover, almost every street had the peculiar smell of a charnel house.

They crossed Covent Garden, and close beside the house where his mother resided Blood paused.

"Why do you tarry?" asked Rochester.

"See," replied Blood, "a man approaches."

"You are right, and as you see, others are behind him," replied Rochester; "and what is it they have with them?"

"It looks like a cart. But my attention is directed to the individual in front, and who is hastening towards us. He looks like a priest."

"Well, and what do *you* require of a priest?"

"Wait—wait."

The individual continued to advance, and so did the men with the cart.

Presently the loud clanging of a bell broke the deep silence, and immediately afterwards a loud, harsh, melancholy voice cried—

"Bring out your dead! Bring out your dead!"

"Bring out your dead!" whispered Rochester; "has it come to that? By the saints! let us hurry on."

"One moment," said Blood. "Stand back, my lord, here comes the priest."

"What do you want of the priest?" asked Rochester.

"Do you not remember?"

And Blood directed his eyes at his mother's house.

"Ah!" exclaimed Rochester, "I do

now remember. Good heavens! I had almost forgotten."

"Hush, hush!" interrupted Blood, as the individual he had taken to be a priest came up with them.

"Pardon me," said Blood, assuming the most respectful tones of which he was capable, "may I ask you to correct me if I am mistaken in supposing you to be a Roman Catholic priest?"

"You are not mistaken, my son," replied the priest. "I am as you suppose: my name Father Lynn. What would you?"

"I would ask, father, whether you—"

"Come aside if you are about to speak of anyone near here. It does not do for *three* persons to be together."

"Indeed! Well," continued Blood, as he drew some little distance from Rochester, "I was about to ask you, father, whether you have had anything to do with those within this house?"

"*This* house—the Convent?"

"Ay."

"I have."

"I trust none are afflicted with this awful disease — this terrible scourge which an offended heaven has inflicted upon us?"

"Hish!" interrupted the priest; "let me assure you that, at *present*, none are afflicted with the plague in this house."

"Here, father, is a heavy purse to enable you to contribute, to a little extent, in the alleviation of the awful sufferings of the afflicted poor."

The priest eagerly took the purse, and, having pocketed it, he laid his hand on Blood's arm, saying—

"Bend down thine ear."

Blood did so.

"Colonel Blood," whispered the priest, "*you are an infernal hypocrite.* Odd's fish! I never came near such a one."

"By the shades of Satan!" exclaimed Blood, ready to drop with amazement and consternation, "it is the king!"

"Silence! Silence, fool! Yes, I am the king. Now listen to this—if you take my advice, you will hurry out of the country with all speed. I promised Mistress Cameron that I would spare your life, but only on condition that you left the country at once. Gad's life! you are a defiant scoundrel. Remember, if you are caught, I will not save you."

"I shall not forget, sire."

"What is Rochester doing with you?"

"Sire, we are only taking a walk to note the effects of the plague."

"No, no; that will not do. However, do not say that you recognised me."

"Certainly not, sire. But as your majesty is not a priest, you will do me the favour of returning my purse."

"I will see you *hanged* first!" replied the king. "A gift is a gift all the world over. But don't forget, colonel—don't forget—clear out of the country at once. Odd's fish! I shall feel much easier when you have gone."

Blood was about to reply, when Charles abruptly quitted his side, and walked rapidly away.

"You have had a lot to say," observed Rochester, as the journey was resumed.

"You are right," was the calm reply. "He is a learned man, and a favourite with the people, no doubt. I have commissioned him to pray for my mother."

"Lord save us!" chuckled Rochester. "And why did you not tell him not to forget yourself?"

"He will not forget since he has had a heavy purse for his trouble. But now let us hurry along."

Lincoln's Inn Fields being reached, they found the coaches already in waiting."

Addressing the principal man, Blood told him to wait where he was, and not take the coaches to Chancery Lane as originally arranged.

"Why this new arrangement?" asked Rochester.

"Because a link not formed cannot be traced."

"I don't understand you."

"Well, I will make my words plain. If we take the coaches to Chancery Lane, they will at once become objects of attraction. Our movements will be watched, and afterwards, the fact that Olivia Preston was taken away in a coach——"

"I see what you mean. Yes, yes; I see now. The arrangement is a wise one."

"Be ready, my men," whispered Blood, "to dash off at a moment's notice. Directly we have entered the coach with our burden, you will dash off to Pentonville as though the Evil One were at your heels."

"Don't mention it," grinned the postilion.

But that grin was forced, for neither this man nor his companions could forget that, wherever they were, they ran the risk of catching the deadly plague which was raging on all sides of them.

Even in this aristocratic neighbourhood—for, at the period of our romance, Lincoln's Inn Fields was the residence of the highest in the land—they occasionally heard the dismal death bell, and the mournful cry of the men with the plague cart—

"Bring out your dead!"

*   *   *   *

Since last we were at the residence of Pritchard Preston, the locksmith, great and awful changes had taken place in his establishment.

Three weeks after Clifford's extraordinary disappearance, one of the younger apprentices was stricken with the plague.

Medical assistance was at once summoned, but it was useless.

The poor lad died the same day.

He was taken ill, died, and was buried within eighteen hours!

But, apparently, no one else within the dwelling was afflicted, and when the worthy locksmith was about to return thanks to heaven for so mercifully sparing him and those with him, lo! no less than *four* more of the apprentices were stricken down.

This happened in the morning, and in the evening, four horrible-looking bodies lay on the beds which had been placed for them in the workshop—the very place where that memorable scene had occurred between Clifford and Blake.

The locksmith and his family were so stricken with grief that they knew not what to do.

Master Preston had no time to make arrangements for a decent funeral.

In one hour after the deaths, the red cross was upon his door, and four youths who, but a few short hours before, had been strong, healthy lads, were being carried off to their last resting-place by the plague cart!

When Colonel Blood and Rochester reached the house they were surprised, yet not astonished, to see the fatal red cross on the door.

"It spares no one, you see!" said Blood.

"Nay," replied Rochester, "and here they have also been attacked. But to what extent?"

"We can get no information hereabouts. The whole city is becoming one vast charnel-house, just as Zodcastor prophesied some time ago."

"Were I king," said Rochester, fiercely, "I would string up *any* man who so prophesied."

"What! are you superstitious?"

"No; but I don't believe in the black arts, or those who follow them. But look around. So far as I can make out, every house seems to have the red cross on its door."

"You are right."

"I wonder whether — but, verily, Blood, I think it would be the wiser course to depart."

"What! run away? For what reason?"

"Why, we might catch the plague."

"Bah! 'Tis only those who fear it who catch it."

"But this girl might be down with the plague, or she might be dead."

"That is true. Well, if such prove to be the case, there is then plenty of time to retreat. Yet, remember, if such *should* be the case, you will keep to your bargain, and assist me in getting possession of Clarissa Jardell?"

"Certainly. I do not shuffle out of a bargain. But let me know, how are you going to obtain admission?"

"I will see. Let us get beneath this archway. Soh! Now, do you hold this lantern while I kindle a light."

So saying, Blood took from beneath his cloak a dark lantern, and while Rochester held it, Blood quickly kindled a light and lit it.

An examination was now made of the door beneath the archway.

It was locked.

Turning off the rays of the lantern, Blood proceeded further up the archway.

A little way from the door was a small window.

This was one of the windows of the workshop.

"See," whispered Rochester, "a faint light burns within that room. What apartment is it?"

"I know not. But I will raise you, and if you clutch hold of the bars above you will no doubt be able to make an examination of the room."

So Blood raised Rochester, who, getting hold of the bars, had a good look into the apartment.

And what he saw filled him with astonishment.

The workshop was in a state of the direst confusion.

Hammers, files, chisels, springs, locks, everything used by the master and his men in their trade was mixed up with bottles of medicine, ointments, wines, spirits, and so on, and on all sides were scattered beds, bolsters, and blankets.

A dirty oil lamp, suspended from the ceiling, shed a miserable light over this apartment—this once busy room, which for some time now had been nothing better than an hospital on a small scale.

But it was not on the apartment itself that the eyes of Rochester became rivetted.

No, his eyes became fixed upon the figures of two youths lying dead on the floor.

From their position it would appear as if they had been in the act of leaving the apartment when the merciless hand of Death swooped upon them.

Their distorted features and limbs showed, alas! only too plainly, the nature of the disease which had laid them low.

The sight was a dreadful one—sickening beyond description.

Even this hard-hearted, profligate lord shuddered as he looked on the dead youths.

"Blood," he whispered, "the sight within the room is a terrible one."

"Indeed!"

"Yes; awful."

"What see you?"

"Two youths who have died with the plague."

"Bah! What of that? If you continue to look at them you will grow faint-hearted."

"Blood, I feel inclined to give up the affair—at least, for the present. I feel unable to enter this house, which, apparently, is nothing more nor less than a pest-house."

"Well, well," growled Blood, impatient and displeased, "do as you like; but I swear that I will go to Pentonville."

"Wait! wait! Don't lower me yet," whispered Rochester, excitedly. "A door in the room has opened—a young girl, clad in white, and as beautiful as an angel enters."

"'Tis Olivia Preston," replied Blood.

"She looks around the room," continued Rochester, "her eyes fall on the two bodies. She kneels and prays; and now she weeps. By all the saints, she *is* lovely!"

"Ay, ay. Does she look as if she had the plague?"

"No, no."

"Of course not, or she would not be in that room. Now, my lord, down you come, and let us find an entrance."

They went onward, and at last reached a small smithy.

This they entered, and prepared to make an examination of it.

The first things which met their eyes were half-a-dozen *coffins* piled one on top of the other.

Directly Rochester saw them he recoiled.

But not so Blood.

He turned on the lantern, and, jumping on an anvil, looked into the topmost coffin.

"It is all right, my lord," he said; "they are empty. Master Preston's undertaker, whoever he is, got a fairly good order at one time I should say."

"On my soul!" replied Rochester, "I never saw grim death so well anticipated before. But now look round. Do you see any door?"

"Yes. Ha, 'tis locked!"

"Well, there may be hammers about. Let us smash the lock."

"No, no; such a task would be dangerous; for it would attract attention. Perhaps some window—but hish! what is that?"

The noise which fell upon their ears was the unmistakable ringing of the plague bell.

It was close beside them; or at least, it so appeared.

"Bring out your dead!" growled a short, thin individual, clad in a long, black mantle, as he presently paused beneath the archway. "Bring out your dead!"

Then, as the dreadful cart, which was almost full of dead bodies, some stark naked, others nearly so, and evidently thrown in anyhow, came up, he addressed himself to the two men in charge of it.

"This is Preston's," he said. "Now let me see, there were two this morning. Wonder if there is any more? Bring out your dead!" he cried, as once more he rang his bell—"bring out your dead, and be sharp about it, for there's hundreds more wants moving, and there's no time to spare."

A window in front of the house was opened, and a sweet, sad voice, the voice of Olivia Preston, said—

"Master Mollbury, two more of the apprentices—the last two, alas! are lying dead in the workroom! I pray you remove them, and here is gold for your trouble."

And at the feet of Master Mollbury dropped a purse.

"Thanks, my dear," replied Mollbury, swooping down on it. "I'll see that all is right. Where is the key?"

"I am lowering it to you. Detach it from the string, and when you have done your duty, return it to me."

"Ay, ay, don't fear—don't fear."

"Master Mollbury," continued poor Olivia, in broken tones, "did you give my message to the rector of St. Andrew's?"

"Why, to be *sure*, my dear. And he promised to remember you and your parents in *all* his prayers."

"What of the plague now? Is it decreasing?"

"Lord save you—no! It is *increasing* at a fearful rate. A month ago there were but six carts, and now there are *twenty*-six."

"Lord have mercy on us!" cried Olivia, in horror-stricken tones.

"And the plague pits seem to get full as soon as they are made," continued Mollbury; "but, as yet, you are all right, Mistress Olivia?"

"At present—yes."

"And how fares your parents?"

At this question there was a pause of a few moments.

Olivia was evidently endeavouring to stifle the emotion which threatened to overpower her.

"They are but poorly," she said, in low tones.

"Not *touched* yet?"

"Not yet."

"Well, well, that is good. And they and you have much to be thankful for. Well, I'll return the key in a moment. Keep the string lowered. Come on," he said to his men; "let us finish here, and then straight off to Finsbury Fields; for when we have taken these two apprentices, our load will be complete. Hillo! whom have we here?"

As he was speaking, he and the two men had proceeded up the archway.

When just by the door, Blood, who had overheard all that had passed, placed his hand on his shoulder.

Both Blood and Rochester had placed masks over their faces; but it seemed as if the mask was of but little use in concealing the identity of the murderous scoundrel, Blood.

At any rate, Mollbury instantly recognised him, though this was not the case with respect to Rochester.

"Don't be frightened, my friend," said Blood.

"Frightened!" grinned Mollbury. "A likely thing, Colonel Blood."

"Ha! you recognise me?"

"Yes; just as I should recognise the evil one himself, even if he wore top-boots. But what do you want, colonel? Have you lost a friend, and do you want to search the plague pits for gold."

"No, no; nothing of the sort. I want you to do me a favour."

"Ah, I see. You want me to save you a coffin for one of your victims."

"Perdition on your foolery!"

"Ah! *that's* more like you, colonel," chuckled Mollbury; "but go on, what is the favour?"

"Simply this—when you have taken the dead apprentices out you will leave one door unlocked."

"No, no. Such a thing would be a deed—"

"Worthy of remuneration," whispered Blood, "and my friend here has a heavy purse ready in his hand."

So saying, Blood turned on the lantern and showed Rochester's hand, in which lay a well-filled purse.

Mollbury hesitated.

As the reader may have already guessed, this man was a most unprincipled wretch.

He could rant like a "hedge parson,"

or rave like a bully, just as it suited him and his pocket.

While he hesitated his men urged him to accept the offer by sundry nudges and gentle kicks on the heels.

"Well, I presume either you or your friend have been smitten with the locksmith's daughter," said Mollbury, with a sigh. "I suppose I must accept your offer."

The next instant the purse was in his pocket.

Blood and Rochester now drew aside.

Mollbury inserted the key in the door and opened it.

The men entered, and after a delay of but a few seconds reappeared, each dragging one of the dead apprentices by the heels.

None of these men had the least respect for those dead with the plague, no matter whether they were men, women, or children.

"Why not place them in the coffins, a number of which are within the smithy?" asked Rochester.

"Can't spare the time," replied Mollbury; "and, besides, when all are dead here I shall want the coffins."

"Did you make them?"

"Nay, but my men did."

"Well, and have you not been paid for them?"

"To be sure. But what of that?"

"Well, you certainly *are* a thieving rascal!"

Mollbury seemed about to burst into a loud laugh.

Approaching Rochester, and leering into his face, he asked—

"Well, master, if I am a *rascal*, what are *you?* It seems as if you have your designs upon the defenceless *living*, while I only fatten on the *dead!* Who is the bigger rascal of the *two!* Ha, ha!"

"Say no more," said Blood in warning, yet fierce tones, as he saw Rochester's hand glide to his blade; "say no more, lest you die of *sword fever* instead of the plague."

The two bodies having been thrown into the cart, and in such a disgraceful fashion that the head of one of the poor lads hung over the side until it nearly touched the wheel, Mollbury pulled the door to with a crash.

Then he gently unlocked it again and took the key out.

"Adieu, colonel," he said, "and adieu to your friend here, and whenever you think you are *near* death, pray send for me."

"Be off, or my sword shall put an end to your wretched life!" growled Blood.

Mollbury, with a laugh, went off.

Olivia, who had been awaiting the return of the key, had heard voices, but she was under the impression that they were the voices of Mollbury and the two men.

But that laugh of Mollbury's!

Who, she thought, would be so hard-hearted, so callous, as to laugh in the midst of the dead and the dying?

"Mollbury," she said, reproachfully, "who uttered that laugh?"

"Laugh?" cried Mollbury; "you are mistaken. No one laughed."

"I thought I heard someone laugh."

"No, no, Mistress Olivia; you are mistaken. Woe betide the man who would laugh in the midst of these terrible scenes. But I have placed the key on the string."

"You are sure the door is fast?"

"Quite. Fare thee well, miss."

And the scoundrel gave the word, and once more the black, death-laden cart moved slowly off up Chancery Lane.

Olivia, for some few moments, stood at the window, breathing, for a brief space, a little fresh air.

Alas! but little of that was there in the plague-stricken city.

Presently she stepped back, closed the window, and crossing the room, entered another.

Hardly had she crossed the threshold ere her ears were assailed with deep groans—groans proceeding from a man lying on a couch in a corner of the room.

That man was the kind-hearted, honest locksmith.

One glance was sufficient to see what terrible trials the poor man had passed through.

On the bed, just before the door, lay another body—a dead body—that of Olivia's mother!

"Is that you, Olivia?" asked the locksmith.

"It is, father."

"Have they taken them?"

"Yes, yes."

"Oh! why did you not persuade them to place your dear mother's body in one of the coffins, and bear it hence?"

"Oh, father!" cried Olivia, advancing and throwing herself on her knees beside the couch, "I tried to frame the words, but I could not—I could not. I felt that I must have my dear mother with me for a little—just a little while longer."

"Away, child!" cried the locksmith, sitting up and waving his hands wildly over his head. "Away, lest you take the infection. Oh, Olivia! I can no longer conceal from you the bitter truth. I—I am smitten with the loathsome disease!"

"You?" shrieked Olivia; "*you*, father? Oh, no, no!"

"Go—go—touch me not—touch me not!"

"Father! dear father!" cried Olivia, passionately, "I alone am spared. I alone at present. But I prefer death with you."

"Child! tempt not an already deeply offended heaven. Alas! I feel that, like all of us, your time will come, my poor child. It seems as if none will be spared. The innocent are suffering for the misdeeds of the guilty. But yet heaven may spare you for some good purpose. What is that? Hark!"

A noise as of the moving of some article of furniture was heard in the next apartment.

Olivia went to the door and listened.

But the noise was not repeated.

Deep silence reigned.

"'Tis naught," said Olivia.

"I thought I heard something move, my child."

"Nay, father, you are mistaken. Nothing moved."

"There it is again, Olivia," cried the locksmith. "Gracious powers, what can it be? Run and see."

Out of the room ran Olivia, and into the next apartment, which was the sitting-room.

The apartment was in total darkness.

Olivia looked and listened.

And as she looked, a bright light suddenly appeared, and shone full upon her.

A wild, piercing shriek escaped her lips, as, behind that light, she beheld two dark forms.

She turned to dash from the apartment, when one of the figures—it was Rochester—rushed forward, and caught her by the wrist.

Once again a shriek, this time, far louder than the other, left her lips.

It reached the ears of Master Preston, and the poor man managed to scramble off the bed, and staggered to the next room.

What he saw filled him with horror.

His daughter in the clutches of a pair of the human vultures with which London was now well stocked.

As he rushed into the room, Blood directed the rays of the lantern upon him.

"By the shades of Satan!" he said, "it is the old man."

Master Preston recognised his voice.

"Holy Mary!" he exclaimed, placing his hands wildly on his throbbing brow, "it is the monster—Blood!"

"Colonel Blood?" echoed Olivia. "Blood! who is responsible for the life of Clifford Hansard? Oh, father, father," she shrieked, as Rochester dragged her roughly back, "save me! save me!"

"My child," gasped Preston. "Monsters, let her go—let her go!"

"Keep back, old man, or you die," cried Blood.

Preston was unarmed, and there was no weapon within his reach.

Rochester, despite Olivia's frantic struggles, was gradually dragging her towards the opposite door.

In vain did the locksmith attempt to get to her.

Most effectually Blood barred his way.

The old man, now in a state of frenzy, knew not what to do.

But suddenly a thought struck him.

He drew back a few paces.

Blood saw his intention, but too late to draw his sword.

Uttering a loud cry, Master Preston bounded forward, and springing like a ferocious tiger on the colonel, he passed his arms about his neck, and held him in a vice-like grip.

"Ha!" he shrieked. "Take the foul disease with which I am afflicted. Take from me your death."

"Rochester, Rochester," yelled Blood,

"'KEEP BACK, OLD MAN, OR YOU DIE!' CRIED BLOOD."

"save me — save me. He has the plague!"

"Ay, ay," hissed Preston, "the plague —the plague."

Rochester was almost paralyzed for a few seconds.

But suddenly leaving go of Olivia's wrist, he drew his dagger, and, rushing behind the locksmith, buried the blade deep in the old man's back.

The unhappy old man, whose death must certainly have ensued in but a very few hours from the dreadful plague, loosed his hold, and with a wild appeal to heaven for vengeance, he expired.

Olivia had not seen that blow struck, for as soon as Rochester released her wrist, she dashed down the stairs, thinking to summon assistance,

She reached the door; but before she could open it, Rochester was upon her again.

Seizing her by the waist, he dragged her back.

"Loose me," cried poor Olivia, piteously. "Let me go, as you value your life, for I have the plague."

The shot was delivered at a venture, but it did not have the desired effect.

"Don't believe her," said Blood. "But hasten, Rochester—hasten, or in a few hours I may be a dead man. Let us hurry to Pentonville. If Doctor Jardell is at home he will give me some of this wonderful compound of his."

Olivia continued to struggle, but her efforts were in vain, for Rochester held her firmly.

"Why struggle, girl?" he said. "Why struggle when your efforts, as you see, are useless?"

"Let me go to my father."

"He is dead."

"I will not believe it. Oh, let me go! Let me go!"

. "Silence her!" cried Blood, fiercely.

As he spoke, he took a small bottle from his pocket— it was the one which he had used to render Clifford unconscious—poured some on a kerchief; and while Rochester held her hands, Blood forced the kerchief against her nostrils.

The stuff quickly had the desired effect, and, unconscious, she fell into Rochester's arms.

"Come along," growled Blood, "or a stop may be put to our movements. Take her in your arms, and I will arrange your cloak about her in such a position, that there will be no chance of her being seen."

Rochester took the lovely girl in his arms, and Blood, having arranged the cloak so that she could not be seen, they left the house.

Blood closed the door, and they went off with all speed towards Lincoln's Inn.

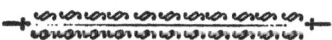

CHAPTER XII.

OF HOW CLIFFORD REACHED CHANCERY LANE—OF WHAT WAS CONTAINED IN A BLUE ENVELOPE—AND OF HOW CLIFFORD SET OUT FOR PENTONVILLE.

No pause must be made in this history —a history which the reader will bear in mind is by no means all fiction.

The greater part of it is fact—hard fact—as English history shows.

For some considerable distance Clifford met not a living person.

But he passed by more than one dead one.

Yes, his eyes fell upon more than one lifeless body lying in the open streets.

As he passed up the pathway which led to St. Martin's Fields, a window of a large house opposite him suddenly opened, and a white face was thrust forth.

It was the face of a woman.

Seeing Clifford, she cried out—

"Sir, sir! another dead — another dead!"

"Heaven help you, my poor woman," replied Clifford, feeling ready to burst into tears. "May heaven have mercy on us all!"

And now, for the first time, he saw the red cross and the piteous words above it.

"Oh, sir," cried the wretched woman, as she wildly wrung her hands, "remember us — remember us in your prayers."

"Ay, that I will—that I will!"

"And, sir, if you see the plague cart, pray send it here."

"I will—I will!" answered Clifford, hurrying on.

"Has it come to this?" thought Clifford. "Oh, that I can drag myself to Chancery Lane! What may have happened there?"

In a few moments he passed another house.

Before he could get quite past, the door suddenly opened—a body, almost naked, was thrown into the street, and again the door was closed with a bang.

Clifford paused.

He felt ready to sink to the ground at this dreadful sight.

"Young and old I see are going off rapidly," he gasped. "That body is that of a mere youth."

Soon he reached the first row of hedges, which lined the meadows of St. Martin's Fields.

On a large stone he sat, and, for a few moments, gave way to profound reflection.

He knew it was not right to pause; he knew only too well how precious every minute was.

But he was worn-out now. He was in want of nourishment and rest.

He walked rapidly on, however, determined to halt for a few moments only at the nearest hostelry and partake of a little refreshment.

At the other end of St. Martin's Fields Clifford entered a small hostelry.

Composing himself as well as he was able, he called for some hot wine, and this was quickly supplied.

The effect of the wine on Clifford, was to put fresh life and courage into him, and quitting the hostelry he, at a good pace, went on towards Chancery Lane.

It was reached at last.

Ah! what were Clifford's feelings as once more he trod the well-known ground.

At last "Potter's Bar" was reached, and Clifford's heart beat rapidly as he realised that in a very few moments now he would know whether those he loved so dearly were safe.

Clifford looked up at the house.

Not a light was to be seen.

Up the archway he went.

He heard no sound. A deathlike silence prevailed.

And now he knocked upon the door.

Getting no answer he knocked again, and yet again—louder, louder each time.

It now seemed to him that something terrible had occurred.

While he paused he heard the plague bell; then he heard the rumble of wheels.

Getting further up the archway so that he should not be seen, he waited until the cart should go by.

"Shall I ask the men?" he thought; "shall I ask whether—oh, Olivia, my beloved sweetheart, you in whom I centred all my hopes, can the plague have swept *thee* away?"

Slowly up the lane came the cart.

Before it walked a man with a lantern, the rays of which as they passed the archway were, for an instant, thrown upon the doorway.

Instantly a deep groan left Clifford's lips, for he had seen upon the door the fatal cross.

What was he to infer from that, and the fact that his repeated knocks elicited no response?

Did it not seem as if death had stricken down all within that house?

Again at the door did Clifford knock, and getting no response, he went to the smithy.

But there, like the archway, everything was buried in profound darkness.

He had no tinder box, and therefore could not get a light.

But he suddenly remembered the man at the head of the plague cart.

He rushed from the archway, and hurried up Chancery Lane after the cart, which he reached just as it was turning the corner.

"My man," he said, "will you sell me your lantern?"

"Eh! Lantern! And pray what do you want of a lantern?"

"No matter what I want it for. Will you dispose of it at a fair price?"

"Well, you see, it all depends upon what you *call* a fair price. A month ago a lantern, such as this, was worth half-a-crown. Now——"

"Now it is worth exactly what it will fetch," interrupted Clifford, impatiently. "I offer you a crown."

"'ATTEMPT TO TOUCH ME,' CRIED CLARISSA, AND I WILL HURL THIS TO THE FLOOR!"

"Oh, oh! a crown? What for a lantern like this? A lantern, the like of which could not be made at *any* price?"

"And why?"

"Why, my young friend? Because every blessed lantern-maker is dead of the plague."

"Here is a guinea for it. Will that do?"

"Ha! that is better. At a guinea it is yours—take it; but, whoa! Hold a moment, young sir. Let us see whether this is a good guinea. Yes," he added, after a moment's examination, "it *is* a good one. And, on my soul, it is brand new. It may bring me luck."

And thereupon he pocketed it with much satisfaction.

We may mention that this man soon supplied himself with another lantern, for he presently came to a couple of them slung across a street on a rope—then the mode of "illuminating" the streets—and taking both off, he extinguished one, hung it beside his cart, and taking the lighted one in his hand, prepared to resume his ghastly occupation.

"Someone else may want to buy a lantern," he said with a chuckle, his grim visage beaming with cunning satisfaction.

In those terrible times, and notwithstanding the sickening and ghastly spectacles which met the view on every hand and at all hours of the day and night, this sordid "despoiler of the dead" had a keen eye to business, and did not hesitate to appropriate not one simply, but *both* the lanterns.

Clifford hurriedly returned to the house.

Going straight to the smithy, he held the lantern on high.

A deep sigh left his lips as he saw the pile of coffins.

Then seeing that they were empty, he began to reflect as to why they had been placed there.

He arrived at the conclusion that six bodies were within the house waiting interment.

Placing the lantern on the floor, he began to remove them.

Soon he had shifted the whole some few feet further back.

There was now revealed a small door.

Clifford pushed it. It opened, and Clifford passed through.

This door led to a small lumber room beside the kitchen, and which was used as a store room for spare iron, tools, and the like.

Passing through it, Clifford presently stood in the kitchen, and then ascended the stairs to the workshop.

The latter was soon reached.

On the threshold Clifford paused in an irresolute manner.

Then he hurried on to the landing and called—

"Olivia! Olivia!"

This beloved name, in a voice of deep emotion, he several times repeated.

Now for a few seconds he paused.

He was about to enter the room before him.

What horrible sights would meet his eyes, he thought.

Fully did he expect to behold the lifeless forms of the locksmith, his wife, Olivia—all! all!

But then again, he thought, they might have died some time ago—might, at that very moment, be in the horrid plague pits with hundreds more.

Twice did poor Clifford place his hand on the door opposite him—the locksmith's bedroom—and twice did his hand fall to his side.

At last he summoned sufficient courage to enter.

Pushing open the door he advanced to the bedside.

He raised the lantern and looked.

The sight he saw was awful, but he was partly prepared for it, and so no cry escaped him.

There on the bed lay the body of the locksmith's wife—the kind, gentle lady who, for so many years, had been to him as a dear mother.

No cry escaped poor Clifford's lips; but, as he looked, more than one bitter, scalding tear rolled down his wasted cheeks.

Clifford searched the apartment, but found no other body.

He entered the next room, and now, indeed, a terrible cry left his parched lips, for there, stretched at full length on the floor, lay the locksmith.

Clifford instantly saw that he lay in a pool of blood.

Appalled at the dreadful sight, he

stood as if fascinated, looking down on the murdered man; for that he had been *murdered* was beyond all doubt.

He stooped, and tearing open his jerkin, placed his hand on his breast.

The body was hardly cold.

It was evident that the murder had been committed but a short time previously.

Also, it was evident that the villainous colonel, and the equally villainous Rochester, had forestalled him.

But, then, had they succeeded in their intentions?

Had they forced Olivia away, or had Death forestalled *them?*

In other words was Olivia alive and well when they arrived, or had she some time before been stricken down with the plague?

Of whom was he to inquire? Ah! of whom?

Re-entering the bedroom, and with slow, uncertain footsteps, for he was overwhelmed with what he had seen, he advanced to the little cabinet which stood beside the bed, and which the locksmith had used for his private papers.

It was unlocked.

Opening the first drawer, a blue envelope met his eyes.

Picking it up he read these words— words written with an unsteady hand, and evidently while the writer was undergoing great mental and bodily agony.

"*To whomsover may be spared to read.*"

Slowly Clifford opened the envelope, and took out a piece of parchment.

On it was written—

"Reader, you are at present spared! I conjure you, in God's name, to pray for the salvation of our souls! Under the greatest difficulties I pen these few words. It is now the fourteenth of February——"

"The fourteenth of February," muttered Clifford. "I will not forget that."

He continued reading.

"The fourteenth of February, and nearly all of us are swept away. The first to suffer were the poor apprentices. One by one they died, and so quickly, that I began to fancy my house the most grievously afflicted in the whole city. Some were taken away in coffins, others by the plague cart. This morning my dear wife died. This evening I find that I am afflicted with the terrible scourge. I cannot get a doctor for love nor money. And I know that die I shall within a very few hours. God's will be done. I am ready to go whenever HE may call me. One is left. One—my beautiful—my only child, Olivia. Oh, with what courage—with what patience—has my noble-hearted girl waited upon those smitten with this dreadful disease. Night and day she has attended them. Worn out, weary, sick unto death has she been, but not one word of complaint has passed her lips. For weeks she has been in the very midst of death, but she quailed not. Yes, God hath so far spared her.

"Reader, if my child is *spared,* all my property is to become hers.

"Before the plague seized upon this house, one of my apprentices, by name Clifford Hansard, who was on a visit to Whitehall Palace, mysteriously disappeared. They say he is dead. That may be so; but even at this moment I cling to the belief that he still lives. If such should turn out to be the case, and Olivia is spared—my brain is on fire; I must rest. I cannot write more."

This was all.

Once more Clifford perused the document. Then, abruptly dropping it, he hastily left the room, descended the stairs, and made his way into the street.

To the right and the left he looked, but not a soul could he see.

Away, as hard as he was able, he ran up Chancery Lane, and turned into Holborn.

Two men were hurrying towards him. Who, or what they were, he knew not.

Rushing up to them he said, in breathless tones—

"Gentlemen, tell me the date of the month."

"The fourteenth!" replied one, evidently much astonished.

"Yes," said the other, "the fourteenth of February."

With this they passed on.

Like one suddenly turned into stone, Clifford stood for some moments.

At last he muttered—

"Too late! Oh, heaven, too late! The fourteenth of February. *This very day* that document was written by poor Master Preston; and when he wrote Olivia was alive and well. Ah, it is all too true. She has been taken away by Blood and Rochester. And it was the hand of one of them which struck down that already dying man. Oh, Holy Mary, was ever such a dark deed committed?"

These words he continued to mutter as he returned, with breathless speed, to "Potter's Bar."

Once more he entered the sitting-room.

Regardless of the fact that he was almost certain to catch the plague, he lifted the body of the locksmith, carried it into the bedroom and laid it on the couch.

Clifford then gave way to profound reflection.

"Where," he thought, "could they have taken poor Olivia?"

Of course, he had not the slightest idea that they had gone on to Pentonville.

"Rochester," Clifford considered, "has two or three country seats, and there is no doubt that he will take Olivia to one of them. But *which* one? Oh," he groaned, "heaven grant that I may come across him, and quickly. Oh, Olivia, Olivia! the plague has spared thee, but for a worst fate."

Presently he rose, and going once more to the cabinet, opened every drawer, as if in search of something.

He soon found what he wanted.

In one of the little drawers lay a number of gold pieces.

A long drawer at the bottom contained two or three swords, a pair of heavy pistols, and a flask of powder and shot.

In another was an assortment of clothes.

"It can be no sin to take what I want," thought Clifford. "If poor Master Preston were alive I could have whatsoever I wanted. I will take these gold pieces, they may be useful in my search for poor Olivia. And I will don what clothes will suit me. With one of the swords, the longest and strongest, and these pistols, loaded, in my belt, will I set out in search of Olivia."

Quickly throwing off the filthy rags—for they were little better—he was then wearing, he proceeded to select what articles of apparel were best suited to him.

Then he buckled on the sword, and having carefully loaded the pistols, thrust them in his belt.

He was just arranging these when there came three tremendous knocks upon the street door, and immediately afterwards a loud, harsh voice shouted—

"Bring out your dead!"

Down the stairs like lightning ran Clifford, and, opening the door, he found himself face to face with a man our readers already know—Mollbury.

Of this wretch he had no personal knowledge, though he was aware of the fact that he carried on the business of an undertaker in Gray's-Inn-Lane.

Mollbury was astounded to behold our hero.

Not at once recognising him, he said—

"Eh? Ha! And who are you, I should like to know? What are you doing in this house like a thief?"

"You do not appear to recognise me," cried Clifford. "Well, well, I am looking ill, and must admit that a great alteration has taken place in me. I am Clifford Hansard."

"*What!*" exclaimed Mollbury, recoiling a few paces.

"Well, if that is so, you are *not* dead, eh?"

"It does not look like it. No, no, I am not yet dead; but I have been near death's door. Master Mollbury, upstairs in the bedroom—Master Preston's bedroom—lie the bodies of my poor master and his wife. Oh, sir, you will see that they are decently attended to their graves?"

"Well, well—ah!—you see, young man, times have changed of late. Separate graves can't be had for love nor money. The sextons can't dig them fast enough, and so all bodies have to be carted to the plague pit."

"Horrible! horrible! But you have known Master Preston for so many years——"

"That is true enough," grunted the hard-hearted undertaker, "but then I have known many other people many years."

"Master Mollbury, I have but little

money about me, but if you will swear that you will lay the bodies of the locksmith and his wife decently in St. Andrew's Churchyard I will, in less than a week from now, call and pay you the sum of one hundred guineas."

"You *will?*"

"I will."

"Ah!—but stay. How will you get one hundred guineas?"

"Borrow them."

"From whom?"

"Sir Christopher Cullum."

"Well, I will trust you. They shall be decently interred, and when you come to me and hand over the money, I will furnish you with the number of their graves."

"Agreed. And now Master Mollbury, let me ask you a few questions."

"He cannot know of what occurred a short time ago," thought Mollbury. "No, no; all was over in quick time, I'll warrant. Proceed, young man," he said, aloud.

"You have taken away the bodies of the apprentices."

"True," replied Mollbury. "I believe I took away every one that died—that is, I and my men."

"When were you last here for that purpose?"

"Last night!" replied Mollbury, telling this falsehood with all the coolness in the world.

"Last night! Are you sure?"

"Why, yes."

"Whom did you see?"

"Why, Olivia—pretty Olivia. I trust she is quite well."

Apparently the tones were so sincere, that Clifford could not possibly have thought the man knew anything of what had occurred.

He thereupon told him all.

Again and again did this human vulture—this despoiler of the dead—express his intense astonishment, which was echoed by the two men who, of course, took their cue from their leader.

"It's monstrous!" cried Mollbury. "It's—it's, why, it's frightful! And what do you intend to do in the matter?"

"Find out where she has been taken."

"I should! By all the saints, I'd never rest until I found out where she has been taken! And you *may* meet this precious pair, for the streets are not so crowded that you would miss them. And if you happen to meet them, or either of them?"

"It is my intention to hurl into eternity both, or either of them I chance to come across."

"Holy Mary! But that would be murder!"

"No; you are wrong. It would be but justice. But now attend to the bodies, Master Mollbury. I will keep my agreement, fear it not."

"Will you wait until we fetch the bodies down?"

"I will; for I want to see the house properly secured."

And Clifford walked to the end of the archway, where stood the black cart.

"Well, I *did* think," said Mollbury to the men when they reached the bedroom, "that we should have had a *picking* here when they were all gone. But you see we shan't."

"Not at present," replied one of the men; "but we will keep our eyes open, for, by the look of that youth, *he* won't live long!"

The locksmith and his wife having been placed in the coffins and then on the cart, Mollbury gave the word, and the vehicle moved on.

When it was out of sight, Clifford closed the door.

"A sudden thought has struck me," he muttered. "Doctor Jardell will be able to give me much information. I long to look once more on his kind face. At once will I hasten to him. Yet it is a long way. Ha! I have money enough in my pocket. Yes; I will hire a horse."

But Clifford found that this was a most difficult matter.

At the first hostelry, at which he called, the host said—

"You may go miles, my young friend, and not be able to hire an animal of any description. And this is how it is—the wealthier families, in all parts of London, are flying into the country as fast as possible, and they get horses from wherever they can. They do no hire them. No; they buy them right out, and I ave known th m e x gant prices to be asked, and given for animals not worth a snap of the fingers."

Substantially this was the reply given at many hostelries.

At last our young hero, despairing of hiring a horse, prepared to walk to Pentonville.

But passing the "Old Barley Mow" at the further end of Hatton Garden, he once more stopped.

"A flask of the finest wine," he considered, "might be of use to me. I will purchase it, and, at the same time, make one more inquiry as to a horse."

"Well, it so happens, young sir," replied the host, in reply to Clifford's question, "that I have a horse, and it is a good one. Letting out animals is not in my line, but a horse has come into my possession in the following manner. Yesterday morning a gentleman stopped here and partook of some refreshment. After that he was about to remount his horse, when he suddenly said, 'On second thoughts, host, I will not take my horse. I will leave it in your charge; and if I do not come for the animal, my groom will.' Now, last night my ostler happened to be in Holborn just as a plague cart went by, and, lo! he saw on the very top, the body of this gentleman!"

"Great heaven!" cried Clifford, much horrified, "how swift death overtook him!"

"You are right."

"But was your ostler certain?"

"Oh, yes. He has since been most fully corroborated. So you see, my young friend, the horse is mine. For since, no doubt, the groom knows not where the animal is, it is hardly likely that he will claim it."

"You are right. And you will lend this animal to me?"

"On security."

"I am sorry to say I have but little ready money with me. But what I have, with the exception of a few pieces, I will deposit with you."

"Good. I have no doubt about your honesty; but——"

"Business is business," interrupted Clifford, taking out his money, "in these times one can scarcely tell whether he is dealing with an honest man or a rogue."

It was only a small amount that he could deposit, but the host was perfectly satisfied, and he ordered his ostler to saddle and bridle and bring the horse round.

It was possessed of enormous strength Clifford could see at a glance.

Our hero gave the ostler a piece of money, and the man procured a pair of spurs and affixed them to Clifford's boots.

Then he assisted him into the saddle.

"One moment, my young friend," said the host, as he hastily came to the door, "one moment. You will, I am sure, pardon me for what I am about to say; but, as you just now said, 'business is business,' I am about to say this— if it should happen that the plague seizes you, you will place the horse in charge of someone so that it will be brought safely back?"

"If the plague seizes me, host," replied Clifford, gravely, and without a quiver in his voice, "I will see that your horse is brought safely back."

So saying, he rode off.

CHAPTER XIII.

OF WHAT OCCURRED AT DOCTOR JARDELL'S—OF HOW CLARISSA IS CARRIED AWAY— OF CLIFFORD'S ARRIVAL—AND OF HOW HE SHOT DEAD THE TWO POSTILLIONS AND DESTROYED THE COACH.

So that the reader will fully understand the stirring scenes in this chapter, we must return to the dastardly ruffians, Rochester and Blood.

When they reached Lincoln's Inn they were observed by the leading postillion, who, hastily dismounting, opened the coach door.

"One moment," said Rochester; "I had better have the strongest horses, Blood, because I shall have the longest journey."

"These are the best horses then," said the postillion; "and you will pardon me, gentlemen, if I take the liberty of urging you to be quick. We have been the objects of much attention."

"Ha!" exclaimed Blood. You mean you have been watched?"

"Precisely."

"By whom?"

"Two men. But they have now disappeared."

"Did you make no effort to discover who they were, sirrah?" asked Blood, in haughty tones.

"No," was the reply; "it is our business to look after the horses and coaches, and not to watch strangers."

"I would they reappeared," said Blood. "I warrant I would find out who they were, and their business."

By this time Rochester had placed poor Olivia within the first coach, and covered her with a couple of rugs.

The poor girl had not recovered from the effects of the drug administered by Blood.

Thus Rochester had no difficulty with her.

Our readers know, for they remember the affair at Whitehall, that the drug was a very powerful one, and it was not likely that Olivia would recover from its effects for some considerable time.

The two ruffians having entered the coach, the word was given, and away rolled both vehicles.

There were dark shutters to the windows of these coaches, and suspended from the roof of each was an oil lamp.

The two "comrades" were well able to see each other; also Rochester was enabled to feast his eyes on his new prize.

Rochester took off his mask, and his action was followed by Blood.

"Great heaven!" exclaimed Rochester, "what ails you? You are as pale as death;"

"Am I?" replied Blood, in agitated tones. "Well, well, don't alarm me. The fact is—I shall be glad to get to the doctor's, and have a draught of his mixture."

"What! you don't think you have actually caught the infection?"

"No, no; but I naturally feel anxious. It is no joke to have the arms of a plague-stricken man placed about one's

neck. But we are going along at a tremendous pace. We shall soon reach our destination."

"My opinion is, considering how frequently Doctor Jardell is with the king, that he will not be at home."

"It may be so."

"On the other hand, someone else may be there."

"Whom do you mean?"

"Sir Christopher Cullum."

"No; I caused inquiries to be made just before you came to my house, and I learned that he was at Whitehall."

On went the coach at a tremendous pace, but suddenly they came to a standstill.

"Have we arrived?" asked Rochester.

"I suppose so," replied Blood. "I told the man to stop at the top of Pentonville Hill."

* * * *

Seated before an enormous fire in the sitting-room of his dwelling was the doctor and his beautiful daughter, Clarissa.

That their conversation was respecting the awful scourge raging in London was evident at a glance, for their faces were grave indeed.

"And you father," said Clarissa, "have saved the lives of how many?"

"I have not counted, my child," was the reply; "but certainly scores."

"Of the wealthier classes?"

"Nay, nay, not only of the wealthier classes, for the very poorest have had a share of my attention. The want of money is no crime in my eyes."

"I know it, my dear father. Your heart is indeed in the right place. And Christopher you say——"

"Sir Christopher, my child, has behaved like a perfect hero. Into the very jaws of death has he walked in the endeavour to alleviate the sufferings of the afflicted."

"God bless him!" exclaimed Clarissa, fervently clasping her hands.

"Ha! my child, God will indeed bless him. During the past few weeks I have had great opportunities of closely observing him, and of reading his true character. Ah! no wonder old David Driffield left Sir Christopher all his money, for he is the most noble, tenderhearted man I ever had to deal with.

Proud indeed shall I be to call him my son-in-law."

"Oh, father, your words cause my heart to leap with delight!" cried Clarissa, a joyous ring in her tones.

Then she sighed.

"Poor Chris! how sad that the fortune for which he had waited so long should have so suddenly been swept away!"

"He does not feel the loss of it so much for himself as for you," said the doctor.

"Ah, my dear father, I should love him as well without a coin as with a fortune."

"I know it—*he* knows it. And then it is not only the loss of this money which troubles him."

"Nay, he has much to think of. There is the mysterious disappearance of that poor lad, Clifford Hansard."

"Ay," replied Jardell, in hushed tones. "Mysterious, indeed — mysterious is hardly the word. Great heaven! it was most marvellous!"

"Christopher has not again been threatened by the members of the White Circle?"

"He has not."

"I suppose, father, that you have arrived at the conclusion that the poor lad is dead?"

"No; on the contrary, my impression is that he lives.

"You, however, think that Blood had to do with his disappearance?"

"Assuredly. But what has become of that villain I know not."

"He may have fallen a victim to the plague."

"It may be so, certainly."

"Or he might have been slain in some drunken brawl."

"That also is likely. But it is his habit to lay quiet for awhile. Then all of a sudden he reappears——"

The door was suddenly pushed open, and the evil face of Mother Jeevers appeared.

"*Colonel Blood!*" she snapped.

Instantly the doctor started to his feet.

"What does he want?" he asked.

"I didn't ask him. He said, 'Is the doctor within?' I replied, 'Yes.' 'Well, then,' says he, 'I want to see him,' and he strode into the passage. 'Get out,' he growled, 'and go and tell the doctor I want him.'"

Nervously Clarissa clasped her hands, looking anxiously into her father's face.

"Stay where you are, my child," he said. "And you, Jane, I can trust you for *her* sake."

"Ha!" replied Mother Jeevers, "you can indeed trust me. Do you go to Blood, and I'll watch here."

"Has he anyone with him?" asked the doctor.

"Not a soul."

"No horse?"

"None."

"Strange," muttered Jardell, as he left the room, and descended the stairs.

He found Blood awaiting him in the surgery.

With a stern expression on his face, he waited for the colonel to speak.

"I am glad you are at home, doctor," began Blood, fixing his fierce eyes on the doctor as if to read what was passing in his mind.

"Colonel," cried Jardell, "let me know your business."

"You don't seem very pleased to see me," sneered Blood.

"Is there any person breathing who would be glad to see you? Quick, let me know why you are here," cried Jardell.

Haughtily waving his hand, Blood said—

"Doctor, examine me, and let me know whether you think I have the plague."

"There is no occasion to examine you. You have not the plague."

"You have perfected your discovery?"

"I have."

"And it will cure the disease?"

"Only light attacks."

"I should like a bottle. That is why I have paid you this visit."

Doctor Jardell breathed a sigh of relief.

"You shall have it at once," he said.

Thereupon he took a medium-sized bottle from a shelf, and placed it in Blood's hands.

The colonel put it in a pocket inside his cloak.

"And now," he said, "I am in want of something else. It is a drug bearing the name of 'Tarkaline.'"

"Ah! villain!" cried Jardell, excitedly, "you shall not have it!

Scoundrel! a bottle of that you stole from this surgery, and used it on the Governor of Newgate."

"Gently, gently," interrupted Blood, in low, but fierce and threatening tones. "Gently, doctor. You say I *stole* a bottle of this stuff from this surgery."

"Yes, yes," replied the doctor; "it was here—here—in this box."

And turning to a sideboard, he opened a small case.

His back was towards Blood, and the wretch at once proceeded to carry out the deed he had already determined upon.

With extraordinary rapidity Blood took a phial from his pocket, and then, creeping behind the unsuspecting old man, he placed his arms about his neck, and so tightly that the doctor was unable to utter the faintest cry.

Struggle frantically the old man did, but what was his strength compared with Blood's?

Blood, holding him firmly, held the phial to the doctor's nostrils.

Its effect was swift.

A few wild struggles and the doctor became insensible.

Blood then laid him on the floor, calmly recorked the phial, replaced it in his pocket, and then went to the street door and opened it.

Mother Jeevers had, as she stated, opened the door and looked without, but she saw not a soul.

When Blood opened it Rochester was there.

He admitted him and reclosed the door.

All this had been done rapidly and noiselessly—so noiselessly, indeed, that the two above never heard a sound.

But when within the passage, Rochester spoke to Blood in a loud voice.

Mother Jeevers heard his voice, and becoming suspicious, she descended a few stairs and leaned over the banisters, anxious to ascertain what was going on.

She saw the Colonel and Rochester.

But she did not alarm Clarissa.

"I will be ready for them," muttered the old woman, grimly, "and if I get the chance I will release my son from the power of Colonel Blood. Yes, yes, if I get the chance I'll kill him, as sure as my name is Jane Jeevers. But, in the name of all the saints, what has he done to the doctor? The villain! I always thought he had his eyes on Clarissa, and now I am sure of it. But I'll foil him!—ho! ho!—I'll foil him!"

Rochester entered the surgery with Blood.

"Ah!" he said, "I see that you have managed it. Is he a subject for the White Circle?"

"No; I have no intention of killing him. I have a strong belief in his skill as a doctor, and also I believe in the stuff he has invented. He may be useful by and by, and therefore I spare his life."

"What of the girl?"

"I have not yet seen her."

"But she is in the house, eh?"

"No doubt of that."

"Who admitted you?"

"Mother Jeevers; the mother of that drunken young brute, John Jeevers."

"Well, and where is she now?"

"I know not. However, we can do very well without *her* assistance. Do you take this lamp—soh! Now come with me."

"We had better be cautious."

"Cautious! Why, man alive, we have no need to be cautious. The only obstacle to our movements was the doctor, and he has been removed. Now come."

Blood thereupon commenced to ascend the stairs, Rochester being close behind him.

Barely had Blood's foot touched the landing when there was a sudden rush across it, and a voice hissed—

"Accursed wretch, take that!"

Before the Colonel's eyes there flashed a gleaming blade.

But ere it could descend a tremendous report rang out, and Mother Jeevers, dropping the knife, clapped her hands upon her breast, and fell in a heap to the floor.

"Thank me for your life, Blood," said Rochester, replacing his pistol in his belt."

"I do! I do! By the shade of Satan! It was as near a fatal plunge as ever I experienced. Cursed hag," he growled, as he raised his heavy boot and dealt the old woman a tremendous kick in the side. "A lot of good you have done for yourself."

"Is she dead think you?" asked Rochester.

"Dead or not," replied Blood, "it is quite evident that she will not again interfere with us!"

"And now, let us hasten," said Rochester. "The streets as you know, are full of skulking scoundrels——"

"No, no," grinned Blood, "not now —not now. The plague keeps the principal part of them in Alsatia. Now!"

With this he pushed open the door in front, and the two scoundrels found themselves face to face with Clarissa Jardell.

The beautiful girl did not scream out.

No. She did not move even.

Erect and apparently firm she stood, and had thus for some time been standing, waiting what was to follow.

The tremendous report of Rochester's pistol had caused her to start and tremble certainly; but she never moved from the spot whereon she had stationed herself.

Now that danger was *there*—there before her eyes — she was ready to meet it.

So entrancingly beautiful did she look as she stood thus that a murmur of admiration left Blood's lips— a murmur echoed by Rochester.

The young profligate was wondering which of the two, Clarissa Jardell or Olivia Preston, was the more beautiful.

A few seconds' contemplation, and he arrived at the conclusion that they were about equally matched.

"Your business?" asked Clarissa, and in such stern, cold tones, that Blood, for an instant, actually quailed before the large eyes looking so earnestly into his face.

"My business—*our* business rather," replied Blood, "can easily be guessed."

"Ah! Would you have me guess it?"

"If it so pleases you."

"Murder! or, more probably, robbery and murder! Oh, infamous ruffian! what dreadful deeds have you perpetrated?"

"Are you under the impression," replied Blood, "that we are here to answer whatsoever questions you think proper to put to us? If so allow me to inform you that you are mistaken."

"I heard the report of a shot," interrupted Clarissa, "and a heavy fall."

"You are right, lady," said Rochester, coolly. "An old woman attempted to to bar our passage, and so I saved her from being attacked by the plague!"

"In other words," said Blood, with a brutal laugh, "we shot her!"

"Monsters! Oh, when will heaven take vengeance upon you and those with whom you associate?"

"It is of no use addressing such questions to us," cried Rochester, "for we do not feel inclined to answer you. And also we do not feel inclined to waste any more time; therefore, mistress, prepare to accompany us."

"Accompany you? Whither?"

"That is my business," said Rochester.

"Nay," interrupted Blood, "it is *my* business."

"To be sure," laughed Rochester, "*your* business—my hands being already full. Ha, ha."

"What have you done to my father?" asked Clarissa, with just a perceptible quiver in her voice.

Neither Blood nor Rochester replying, she said, in a voice, choking with emotion—

"You have slain him—slain him. Murderer! my father's death shall be avenged!"

"Hold!" interrupted Blood. "Prepare to depart with us. Get yourself ready or go as your are. I will lose no more time."

And he advanced towards Clarissa.

The young girl started back, and seized upon a small black box.

Knowing the wonderful contrivances which it was the doctor's delight to invent, Blood recoiled.

"Attempt to touch me," cried Clarissa, holding the box high above her head, "and I will hurl this to the floor."

There was a pause of a few moments.

At length Rochester asked—

"And what would be the result?"

"The result would be," replied Clarissa, "that both of you would be stricken dead. At the same moment I should fall; but I had rather, ten thousand times, meet with a sudden and violent death than be, for any period, in your power."

"You are indeed a wonderful girl," sneered Rochester; "you are quite a heroine."

"Clarissa Jardell," said Blood, "take my advice and put down that box. I believe what you say—namely, that the contents might explode and slay us where now we stand; but, on the other hand, it might *not* explode. If you flung it down and it did *not* explode, what would be the result? I should instantly put your father to death."

"Ah!" almost screamed Clarissa, at once lowering the box, "he lives?"

"Ay," replied Blood, rushing forward and snatching the box from her hands, "he does—for the present. His life will depend on the way you conduct yourself."

"Villain! I am to place myself in your hands?"

"Yes."

"For what purpose?"

"That is my business."

"Whither am I to be taken?"

"That is *also* my business. But no further delay must there be," he cried, seizing Clarissa savagely by the wrist. "Come—at once."

Rochester at once pounced upon the girl; once more the phial was produced, and despite her struggles, Clarissa was forced to inhale the deadly odour.

Its effect was, if anything, more swift than in the doctor's case.

"Now," cried Blood, "place yonder tablecover about her."

Rochester quickly did this, and soon Clarissa was enveloped from head to foot.

Blood then took the insensible figure in his arms.

Taking the lamp, Rochester led the way.

Reaching the door, he unsheathed his sword.

"Better be ready for any emergency," he said.

"Ay," answered Blood, "for there is no telling whether the shot has attracted attention."

"Do you think the old woman is dead?" asked Rochester, and thereupon he struck her with the point of his blade.

The point entered her flesh, but it elicited neither cry nor movement.

"She's dead enough," replied Blood, impatiently. "Come, let us delay no longer."

Quickly the pair were in the street, and hurrying to where the coaches were left.

Rochester jumped into the first, and the word being given, away it dashed.

But Blood, having to shift his burden somewhat, was not ready for some few moments.

At last he got in, and the word being given, the coach moved on.

All might have been well, and both ruffians with their prizes might have got safe away, but for the fact that Blood neglected to close the coach window.

It had not proceeded many yards before a loud voice cried—

"Hold! Hold, rascals! Hold! on your lives!"

Dashing to the window, Blood looked out.

There, right before him on a powerful horse, was the very youth he had placed safe in the cage at the Black Priory.

The Colonel's eyes opened to their fullest extent in astonishment. He knew well the voice of Clifford Hansard!

Could he be mistaken? No, there was no mistake about it; the horseman before him was Clifford Hansard!

Our hero had risen in his stirrups and had presented a pistol point-blank at Blood's head.

The coach had come to a standstill, but it only remained so for a moment.

The postillions, fearing that something alarming was about to follow, laid their whips on their horses flanks in a most merciless fashion, and the startled animals dashed forward at tremendous speed.

Swiftly Clifford turned, took aim, and fired at the foremost postillion.

But the shot struck the second man —struck him dead from his horse.

He fell between the two he was driving, and instantly the ponderous wheels of the coach passed over his body.

The colonel, quickly recovering from the consternation into which he had been thrown, drew a pistol, and, leaning out of the coach window, fired.

The shot missed, and he tried a second.

That also missed, no doubt on account of the swaying motion of the coach.

On dashed Clifford after the vehicle.

"Thank heaven! thank heaven," he cried. "I have already discovered the villain. I saw the figure in the coach. That muffled figure of *my Olivia!*"

Suddenly the postillion uttered a loud cry, and in a moment the front horses rose high on their haunches.

Another minute and the coach swung violently round.

The postillion, in his excitement, had taken the wrong turning, and did not notice it until near *the very edge of a deep cutting in the road!*

The mistake cost him his life.

As he wheeled his horses round, Clifford again fired.

He was too near to miss his man.

The postillion received the ball in his breast, and he fell dead.

Clifford leaped from his saddle, plucked his blade from its sheath, and rushing to the coach door, wrenched it open.

"Vile murderer!" he roared, "come forth. If there is a spark of courage in you come forth."

He stopped, for the open door revealed the startling fact that Blood had vanished, and the wide-open opposite door accounted for his disappearance.

Round the coach ran Clifford—ay, and many yards to the right and left—but he could see nothing of him.

Returning to the coach, he entered it.

"Olivia, Olivia!" he cried, in rapturous tones. "Olivia, my beloved, awake! Look up! look up! look up! 'Tis I—Clifford—Clifford! returned to life."

As he spoke he tore off the table cover.

A startling cry left his lips as he saw before him—*not* his Olivia, but the insensible figure of a lady he had never before seen!

His astonishment, his agony was so intense, that for some few moments he remained as he was, his eyes fixed upon the lovely, but to him, unknown face.

What could it mean?

"Great heaven!" he muttered, "what strange mystery is this? Has the wretch carried her off, too? But where is Olivia? Ha! and where is Rochester? Holy Mary! Where can Olivia be? Perhaps this poor girl could explain. Who can she be? How beautiful, yet how deathly pale she is. I will take her to the doctor's. She wants instant attention."

Clifford now raised poor Clarissa in his arms, and then, taking his horse by the bridle, he proceeded towards the doctor's residence.

This he soon reached, and his astonishment may be imagined when he saw the door wide open.

And yet the house appeared to be in profound darkness.

"Good heavens!" thought Clifford, "what can this mean? Has yet another dark deed been committed?"

He knocked loudly on the door, and, at the same time, shouted—

"Doctor, doctor! Doctor Jardell!"

No answer was returned.

He went across the road, and looked at the houses.

Almost everyone of them had the dreadful red cross upon the doors.

With a deep sigh Clifford was about to recross the road, when the window of one of the houses suddenly opened, and a weak female voice asked—

"Sir, sir, what seek ye?"

"I seek Doctor Jardell," was Clifford's reply. "I found his door wide open."

"Ay, ay."

"And though I have knocked and shouted loudly enough, I have received no reply. So I thought someone might tell me——"

"My friend," interrupted the female in solemn tones, "there is no one left to tell you anything. Once this street was a busy hive, now it is even as silent as the grave. I am the only one left on this side of the way."

"Holy Mother! can it be possible?"

"It is true. Some little time ago I heard the report of a shot. It appeared to proceed from Doctor Jardell's house. I listened, but no cries reached my ears. I watched from this window, and saw two men leave the house. One of them carried in his arms—but by the blessed saints! I now see that *you* carry a bundle.

"You are right. But just listen to me for a moment."

And Clifford informed the female as to how he had come by Clarissa.

"Wait but a moment," replied the person, "and I will bring a light to the door—that is, if your are not afraid of taking the disease."

"Nay, mistress," replied Clifford; "I am not afriad."

"Ha! my son, you are really not afraid of this dreadful disease, and if you can only keep up your courage, you will be spared."

"Do you think so?"

"I am *certain* of it. I have not been afraid of taking it, and I have lived where dozens have been taken away on those fearful death cars—ha! as I speak, I hear it."

"What?"

"The plague bell."

"Hasten, madam, I conjure you hasten, for you may recognise the face of the unfortunate lady I hold in my arms."

In a few seconds the female opened the street door.

She held a lamp in her hand, and as soon as the rays fell upon the beautiful face before her, she started back.

"Heavens!" she exclaimed, "that is the doctor's daughter. Yes, yes; it is Clarissa Jardell. And she—why, I swear that she is attacked."

"Attacked! What with the plague?" Ay, with the plague?"

Clifford shook his head.

"You are mistaken," he said. "I am sure of it. The condition in which she is in, according to my thinking, has been caused by some noxious drug."

"Well, well, you may be right. Do you take this lamp. It will be of service to you across the way."

"Thanks," said Clifford, taking the lamp. "I return you my heartfelt thanks, madam, for you have greatly assisted me. May God watch over you."

"And may He stay His hand, my son," cried the woman, in fervent, tremulous tones, "lest London be made one vast charnel house."

Clifford now recrossed the road, and entered the doctor's house.

Once more Clifford shouted, this time far louder than he had done before.

On this occasion he was *answered*.

"Who calls?" asked a voice above.

The voice was low, and it seemed as if the speaker was in pain.

"One Clifford Hansard calls," replied our hero, "and I have with me Clarissa Jardell, who, but a short time back, was forcibly taken from this house."

"Ascend! ascend! was the reply.

Thereupon Clifford ascended.

Arrived at the landing, the lamp's rays fell upon the figure of a woman.

It was, of course, Mother Jeevers.

Huddled up in the corner, she was groaning dismally.

"What ails thee?" asked Clifford.

"Oh," was the reply, "put the girl down in one of the chairs, and I will tell ye. Oh, the Lord be thanked she is back safe and sound."

Clifford deposited Clarissa in one of the chairs, and then hastened to the old woman.

"Blood did it all," she howled. "Blood and Rochester. I know him. Ay, only too well.

"Where is the doctor?" asked Clifford.

"In the surgery—murdered—murdered!"

"Murdered?"

"Ay, ay, Blood did it."

Clifford was horror-stricken.

"Quick!" he exclaimed. "If you have the strength, tell me all that has happened in this house. But first tell me what ails yourself."

"I'm murdered—murdered," groaned Mother Jeevers, placing her hands on her breast, and violently rocking herself to and fro. "It struck me *here*—here."

"What struck you?"

"The shot. It was Rochester who fired."

"Are you sure the shot struck you?"

"Oh, yes, yes."

"In the breast you say?"

"Ay, here, here."

Clifford bent down, and placed his hand on the part pointed out by Mother Jeevers.

"The shot has never penetrated your *breast* far," he cried. "Why, as I live, you have been saved by the wood within your corset. The shot has broken it, but has not passed far through. Let me help you to rise—quickly. No time is to be lost. If she does not have instant attention, that poor girl may die."

Mother Jeevers was more terrified than hurt, for when Clifford assisted her she quickly got upon her feet, groaning the while.

The corset she wore, one of those old-fashioned things, and constructed for the most part of sycamore wood and canvas, had unquestionably saved her wretched life.

The shot had broken one of the front pieces of wood completely in twain.

Still the effect of the shot had been to completely double her up and to keep her for some time in that position.

Mother Jeevers, continually urged to be quick by Clifford, told her story.

At its conclusion, Clifford was more mystified than ever.

Rochester and Blood both at the house at the same time, yet Olivia was not with either of them!

It was most remarkable!

From this fact our hero began to consider that Olivia could not be far off.

Telling Mother Jeevers to light a lamp and at once wait upon Clarissa, Clifford descended the stairs.

As may be supposed, he expected to find the doctor dead on the floor.

But no. Just as he entered the room lo! the apparently dead body began to move.

"Doctor — Doctor Jardell!" cried Clifford, raising the lamp high over his head so that the light penetrated almost every part of the room.

"Yes, yes," groaned the doctor; who speaks? Heaven help us all. Who speaks?"

"Clifford Hansard."

"You here?"

"Yes, Doctor Jardell, it is Clifford Hansard who bends over you. You are not mortally injured, I trust."

"I am not mortally injured, my son, but it is no fault of Blood's. The loathsome villain forced me to inhale a deadly drug—and then— Ah! what followed" what followed? My poor daughter, Clarissa!"

"Your daughter, Doctor Jardell, is *safe*."

"Safe—safe, say you? Then she is not in Blood's power?"

"She is not."

"I see! I see! cried the old man in exultant tones; "Jane Jeevers foiled him."

"No; but she tried to. You say *him*, doctor. There were two of them."

"Two—two?"

"Ay. Blood and Rochester."

"Heavens! is this indeed so? Ah! within a few hours the king shall know. But assist me, my young friend, assist me to rise. Upstairs I have the antidote for the drug administered."

Clifford assisted him as desired, and the old man, having taken a draught from a certain phial, he took Clifford by the shoulders and looked full into his face."

"Clifford Hansard," he said slowly, "Clifford Hansard. And thou art indeed that ill-fated lad? They said you were dead; the victim of that secret society which marks its movements with the White Circle. But I always have clung to the belief that you lived. And the same may be said of Sir Christopher Cullum."

"How fares he?" asked Clifford in husky tones.

"Fairly well, my son, considering."

"I understand you, doctor. But your eyes are fixed in wonder upon my face. You are looking at the alteration which has taken place in me."

"Truly, truly. You look years older than when last I saw you. Poor lad, I can see that your sufferings have indeed been terrible. And the man who is responsible for all this is——"

"Colonel Blood! On whom may heaven's vengeance descend."

"I am compelled to echo your wish with all my heart," said Jardell.

"Doctor, I pray you ascend with the bottle you have just used. Your daughter, like yourself, has been drugged."

It took some little time to bring Clarissa to her senses, and still further time was required to enable her to remember all the dreadful circumstances which had occurred.

Presently, with her soft, white arms wound tenderly about the old man's neck, she said—

"Safe, father, safe! both of us safe!"

"Thanks to this youth here, my child—the very Clifford Hansard of whom, some little time before Blood made his appearance, we were speaking. He it was who brought you back to me."

"I seem as though I have just awakened from some hideous dream."

"I have no doubt of it. But listen, Clarissa, for it is important to all of us that Clifford Hansard tells us something of his adventures."

When Clifford had concluded, the doctor said—

"It is indeed most terrible. Poor Master Preston!"

"And not one has been left, say you?" said Clarissa, in hushed tones.

"Not one," replied Clifford, solemnly. "I saw the locksmith and his wife taken away, and then the house was empty."

"It is my opinion," said the doctor, who, for a few moments, had been lost in profound reflection—"it is my opinion that Rochester is the man to answer for the whereabouts of Olivia."

"Yes, yes," cried Clarissa; "there can be not the slightest doubt about it. Poor girl! Oh, how I long to clasp her in my arms. Father, if she is recovered, she shall be my sister."

"She shall indeed. Clifford can have no objection to that. But now, Clarissa, I must leave you in charge of Jane Jeevers."

"Father, you surely do not intend to leave me?"

"For a short time, child. But you will be safe enough this time, depend upon it. Jane, as soon as we have gone, bolt and bar up the house, and answer the door to no one."

"Fear it not," replied Mother Jeevers, grimly. "I will take care that the door is properly barricaded."

Refreshments were hastily provided and partaken of, after which Clifford reloaded his pistols, and he and the doctor set off.

"We will to Whitehall," said Jardell; "I can see the king at a moment's notice now—all owing to the plague, of which his majesty has the greatest dread."

Clifford persisted in making the doctor mount his horse, and he himself walked beside it.

Reaching Pentonville Hill, they stopped, and Clifford looked about for the coach horses.

They had disappeared.

But this was not the case with the two postillions, who were still lying where they had fallen.

Clifford made a brief examination of the first.

"This man, by the look of him," he said, "has been robbed. Even his spurs have gone."

"And, no doubt, you will find that the same thing has occurred to the other," replied the doctor, "though the streets seem so deserted. The human vultures are ever ready to pounce upon their prey. These men have but met with their deserts. It is such—hark! voices."

"It is the men with the plague cart,' replied Clifford.

Such was the fact.

Each of these men seemed possessed of the same peculiar voice.

The melancholy howl of—

"Bring out your dead! Bring out your dead!" And the monotonous clanging of a cracked bell was perfectly fearful to hear.

The cart was some little distance off, but it soon got so near, that the lantern, carried at the side, was seen.

"I have thought of something," said Clifford, "and you will see what it is directly the men, belonging to the cart, get near enough."

This was in a few seconds.

"I say, my man," said Clifford, "to the man evidently in charge of the cart, "here are two men."

"Eh?" interrupted the man, detaching the lantern from the cart, and holding it over the first postillion. "Two men, eh? Why I only see one.'

"There is another just a little further on."

"This one is a postillion, eh? Why what is this? Look! he has not died of the plague. He has been shot."

"No doubt of it."

"Ha. Well, sir," cried the man, poking his face into Clifford's, "and what do you know of this matter?"

"A great deal more than I choose to tell you!" replied Clifford, boldly.

"Oh, indeed. Then I'll bid you good-night," said the man, not at all relishing the look Clifford gave him.

"One moment, my friend. It would be just as well to remove these two bodies."

"'THAT WRETCH HAS SIGNED A FALSE NAME!' CRIED CLIFFORD."

"I am paid by the Lord Mayor to take away the bodies of those afflicted with the plague, and not those who get killed."

"Look!" interrupted Clifford. "Look at this. What is it?"

The man directed the rays of his lantern on Clifford's open palm.

"Why," he grunted, "it is a guinea."

"To be sure. And it is yours if you will let your men put these bodies in the cart."

"Why to be *sure!*" replied the man, with a grin. "To be *sure!* You are a very *civil* young man *indeed.* A guinea's a *guinea* all the world over, and times are *bad.*"

"Well," said Clifford, "you will find the guinea *good.* And I say, my man, you need not tell the Lord Mayor that you received a guinea from a stranger."

"Don't *mention* it, young master," leered the man.

Within the space of one minute the two postillions were placed in the cart.

"I would not be at all surprised if the plague ends the life of Colonel Blood—ay, and of Rochester too," said the doctor.

"And now let us on," said Clifford, "for I am most anxious to see Sir Christopher, and save Olivia."

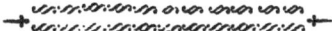

CHAPTER XIV.

OF THE VISIT TO THE ASTROLOGER—OF WHOM CLIFFORD SAW THERE, AND OF THE JOURNEY TO, AND WHAT TRANSPIRED AT HERTFORD.

WE need not say how warm was Sir Christopher's welcome to Clifford.

With open arms he received him.

"Ever since your disappearance," said Sir Christopher, "I have hoped and hoped that you would reappear. You are wonderfully altered. But I am most anxious to hear how you rescued my intended bride from the hands of Blood."

After Clifford had informed him of his adventure, he said—

"I must admit that things look black indeed for you, but I am almost certain where the poor girl has been taken."

"Do you know where Rochester's country mansions are situated?" asked Clifford.

"Yes. But my firm impression is that he will not take Olivia to either of his country residences. It is my belief that he will take her to a strange place. What is your opinion, doctor?"

"I am of the same opinion as yourself," replied Doctor Jardell. "I advise you to wait and watch, Clifford."

"Yes," sighed Clifford, "there is reason in what you say. I must wait—wait and hope."

"The principal thing to be done," said Sir Christopher, "is to watch Blood's house in Leicester Fields."

"And, in the meantime," said Clifford,

"I beg that you will lay the particulars before the king."

"I will do so," answered Sir Christopher. "And now, Clifford, I will pen a letter to a friend of mine in Pall Mall. He will accommodate you at his house for as long as you feel proper to stay. To-morrow morning you will assume your duties here, for———"

"Alas!" replied Clifford. "I do not feel able to undertake anything of the sort. My whole thoughts are centred upon Olivia, and I can think of nothing but her rescue, and my revenge on Blood and Rochester!"

"Be it so then," replied Sir Christopher, "and trust to me, Clifford, to have Blood's house thoroughly watched."

"I also will watch," said the doctor, "and I will instruct others to do the same."

The following hour Clifford was safe within the fine residence of Sir Richard Wemyss in Pall Mall, while a messenger was returning to Hatton Garden with the horse.

* * * *

Clifford found sincere sympathisers and friends in Sir Richard Wemyss and his beautiful wife, once the actress, Lottie Champyus.

It was about eight of the clock on the following evening, and Clifford, who had been well provided for in the shape of clothing by Sir Christopher, was seated opposite the charming Lady Wemyss, answering many questions, when they were interrupted by the sudden appearance of the footman.

"A letter, your ladyship," he said, "for Master Hansard."

"For me?" replied Clifford, rising and taking the letter. "Does the messenger wait?"

"No, sir. He simply handed in the letter and took his departure."

"What sort of a person was it who delivered this note?" asked Lady Wemyss, who, remembering Sir Christopher's warnings, was at once suspicious.

"I cannot describe him, your ladyship," replied the footman, "for he disappeared in the darkness with great swiftness."

"Ha!" exclaimed Clifford, who, by this time, had opened the letter, "it is from Doctor Jardell, and there is another letter enclosed."

When the footman had withdrawn he read the contents aloud.

"To my young friend, Clifford Hansard.

"Greeting.

"Important information has reached me. I am most sorry I cannot call upon you personally; but, the fact is, I am attending a dear friend down with the plague.

"Clifford, without fail, you will take the enclosed letter to the astrologer, Zodcastor——"

"Zodcastor!" exclaimed Lady Wemyss, turning quite pale, "Zodcastor! That is the man who predicted this dreadful plague."

"I understand," replied Clifford, "that this astrologer and Doctor Jardell are, and have been for many years, great friends."

"I don't wonder at that. Men of science generally fraternise. But I am curious," smiled her ladyship, "and I should like you to continue the reading of the letter."

Clifford continued—

"Zodcastor will read the enclosed, and will tell you what you are to do. Bear this in mind, he is a strange man, and will answer few and sometimes no questions at all. Simply do as he tells

you. Adieu for the present. May success attend you.

"Thy faithful friend,
"JONAS JARDELL."

Beneath the signature were the words—

"Remember, go alone."

"It is a most singular communication," observed her ladyship, thoughtfully, "and if the letter had come from anyone else, I should have advised you to have simply thrown it on the fire. Are you familiar with the doctor's handwriting?"

"I am not. I have seen it, but I am not sufficiently acquainted with it to say this is his."

At this instant Sir Richard entered.

He was quickly made acquainted with the contents of the letter.

"I have several letters in the doctor's handwriting in my possession," he said, "I will bring the last."

On the two being compared, there appeared to be no doubt that both were written by the same hand.

"Go at once," said Sir Richard, "and go well armed. I will give instructions for a horse to be got ready for you."

A fine steed was soon saddled, bridled and brought round.

Sir Richard's last words to Clifford were—

"Do exactly as the doctor has said in his letter. Rely upon it, that the important information mentioned by him is relating to that poor girl, Olivia."

So, once again, our hero rode through the streets of London.

He felt in every way better for the rest he had had, and the doctor's mysterious letter—for at present it certainly *was* mysterious—had put fresh life and hope into his breast.

The streets of London now presented a most terrible appearance.

Almost every house had upon it the terrible red cross, and in all directions the bell and the awful voices of the men in attendance on the plague could be heard, while against the doors of some of the houses, and even in the gutters, the distorted bodies of men, women, and children had been placed ready for consignment to the horrible plague pits.

The address on the letter, which had been enclosed, was—

" ZODCASTOR,
"HOCKLEY MANOR,
"ISLINGTON."

It was a place Clifford had never before visited ; but, before he inquired, he decided to go as far as the pretty rustic church of St. John's.

This was reached just as the clock chimed half-past nine.

Clifford paused beneath the old grey walls of the church, and looked around him.

Not a soul could he see.

Drawing nearer to the little churchyard, he heard sounds as of a person in deep grief.

Raising himself in his stirrups he looked over the wall, and saw, at some little distance from him, the figure of a young woman.

She was lying across a newly-made grave—one of scores—and sobbing as though her heart would break.

No doubt, in that little churchyard, all her friends, stricken down with the plague, were laid.

Nearer St. Paul's, those who died, would be taken away in the plague carts, and cast into the foul pit, for there were neither graves to spare in the churchyard, nor willing hands to make them.

Clifford decided not to disturb her, but wait until some person should pass.

Fully a quarter of an hour had he to wait until he saw some persons approaching.

They proved to be a man, his wife, and four little children.

Each was carrying a bundle or two, and Clifford saw from this that they were flying into the country.

Riding up to the man, Clifford asked him for the place he required.

"Ay, master," replied the man, "turn down yonder lane, and at the end you will find a stone building; that is Hockley Manor—God help us all—that is Hockley Manor. It is the residence of Zodcastor, the astrologer, as we doubt not you know. Ah, sir, that we had paid heed to his repeated warnings! Had we done so, I should not have lost six pretty children, my father, my mother, my wife's parents—all—all ! And more

than this, sir, my property was stolen by one Captain Drinkwater and his companions."

"Captain Drinkwater!" muttered Clifford, "I will not forget him for that."

Aloud he said—

"My good man, be assured that I sympathise most deeply with you. Look—here are two guineas. Take them, for they may be useful to you."

The man eagerly took the coins, and loud were his, and his wife's expressions of gratitude.

They continued their sad journey.

"*Luck,* wife!" muttered the man. "*Luck!* our luck is changing! God bless him whoever he is !"

"And keep the plague from him !" added the wife, bitterly, for as she spoke, she thought of her little children.

Slowly down the lane rode Clifford, and at last he halted before a huge stone mansion.

At one time this place had been known as the "Islington Monastery," and it required not a second glance at the grey walls to see that it was of great age.

It was surrounded with a low wall, but there was no gate attached to it.

An archway leading to the avenue, however, showed where once the gate had stood.

Clifford proceeded up the narrow avenue—an avenue several inches thick with dead leaves.

The rustling Clifford's horse made attracted attention, for, as our hero reached the door, a voice cried out—

"Who comes ?"

"A person on business," replied Clifford.

"You can have no business *here,*" was the gruff reply.

"What makes you say so ?"

"Your appearance tells me——"

"Come forth, my friend," interrupted Clifford, "and let me judge of *your* appearance."

"Depart !" was the stern reply.

Clifford, instead of doing anything of the kind, leaped from the saddle, and, taking the letter from his doublet, ascended the steps.

There was a little grating let in the door, and it was through this that the individual had spoken.

"Behold!" said Clifford, "here is a letter for the astrologer."

"Ha!" was the sulky reply; "and pray whom do you take me for?"

"His servant," replied Clifford.

The man behind the grating laughed softly.

Then he said—

"Push your letter through the grating, young man, and if you wait you will get a reply."

Clifford thrust the letter through the bars, and it was seized upon by the man behind.

Clifford could not see his face, owing to the fact that the hall or passage was pitch dark.

But in a few moments the man was heard returning.

This time he carried a lantern.

Advancing, without a word, to an iron rod, which was inserted in the flooring, and which acted as a lever, he pulled it, and the door moved noiselessly back.

"Enter," said the man, a tall, gaunt old fellow, clad in a long black mantle, "enter, and ascend to the first floor. I will give orders for the removal of your horse. As, however, you will not be long here, its harness shall not be removed."

"A pair of pistols are in the holsters," said Clifford; "will they be safe?"

"Heaven help the man who tampers with *anything* in or about these premises," answered the man, grimly.

Clifford strode along the hall, and loudly did his spurs clank on the stone, for the flooring was *all* stone, of various colours and patterns, and no attempt whatever had been made to cover them with anything.

At the end of the hall was the staircase.

Without hesitation Clifford ascended.

Arrived at the landing, a low, deep voice said—

"Enter!"

Clifford pushed open the door exactly before him, and found himself in an apartment, the like of which he had never even heard of.

It was about one hundred feet long by eighty in breadth, and was proportionately lofty.

Despite its size, there was hardly room to move, for nearly every inch of space was occupied by scientific instruments of all sizes and shapes.

Clifford was lost in astonishment at the most remarkable display before him; but he was quickly called to attention, for there presently stood before him a tall, grey-bearded old man, neatly, but plainly attired in black.

Our hero had *heard* much of Zodcastor, and had imagined him to be a man of most forbidding aspect, haughty and commanding, as befitted a man gifted with powers superior to the generality of men.

But the individual before him did not in any way approach the being he had, in imagination, framed.

On the contrary, the old man who thus so suddenly appeared before him was possessed of a kindly, though grave face, and his voice, though low and deliberate, was very far from inspiring anyone with awe.

"Your name," he said, "is Clifford Hansard; mine, Zodcastor."

Clifford bowed.

"The letter you bring from my friend, Jardell," continued Zodcastor, glancing at the missive he held in his hand, "is a singular one; I will obey it to the best of my ability. Are you able, my young friend, to control yourself?"

"I am, sir," answered Clifford.

"I ask the question solely on account of what is contained in this letter. And, now, bear in mind that I know nothing of the actual business of a person who will shortly be here, and whom you will see. Neither do I know why it is that Jardell requests me to do him the favour he has asked in this letter. And now, Master Hansard, pray follow me."

If Clifford felt mystified when he entered this room, how did he feel *now?*

Remembering what Jardell had said in the letter to himself he refrained from putting any question to this wonderful old man.

In about the centre of this enormous room stood desk and cabinet.

Close beside the desk was a tremendous globe, mounted on a huge stand.

Going up to it, the old man pulled back a small spring and opened a door.

"There," he said, "get in here, and I will so arrange it that your eyes will be brought opposite two tiny holes, so that you will see who my next visitor is; and, also, you will be able to overhear all that is said. I may tell you that I should not do as *I* am now doing for no other man living than Doctor Jardell."

Clifford entered the singular hiding-place.

"One moment," said Zodcastor. "You will most solemnly swear that all this you will keep secret."

"I swear it, solemnly. But one question, sir," interrupted Clifford. "Will you tell me the name of your visitor?"

"I cannot, because I do not at present know it."

"I am satisfied," answered Clifford.

The next moment the door was closed, and our hero felt the globe revolve on its pivot.

"Can you see?" asked Zodcastor.

"Most distinctly."

"'Tis well."

Zodcastor disappeared.

Half-an-hour passed, and then Clifford heard voices.

Shortly afterwards Zodcastor reappeared, and took his seat at the desk.

Most anxiously did Clifford listen.

Presently he distinctly heard the sound of spurs on the hall and the stairs.

"Something tells me," he thought, "that this visitor has something to do with *Rochester!*"

"Come this way, sir," said Zodcastor.

The visitor approached.

Through the tiny holes peered Clifford, and he saw before him a magnificently attired, well-armed man.

But he could not see his face, for he wore a black mask.

Before the visitor could speak, Zodcastor rose.

"Sir," he said, in stern tones, "I never, under any circumstances, permit myself to speak to a masked man."

"In that case," was the reply, "I will unmask."

Clifford saw before him Blake Barrell.

"Now, sir," said Zodcastor, "the information you seek is the whereabouts of Lord Rochester."

"It is," was the reply.

"And you require a pass to the house in which his lordship is at present staying?"

"That is so. You are acquainted with the whereabouts of Lord Rochester?"

"I am. But no one can enter his gates without the proper pass. This pass, as you may imagine, is only used by Rochester's bosom friends. Among the number is Colonel Blood. Behold! here is the pass."

And Zodcastor opened a drawer, and took out a small gold brooch.

Round it, in small diamonds, was the well-known white circle.

But, besides this, it has Rochester's private mark.

"This is Blood's pass," said Zodcastor. "How and when he lost it matters not. Now tell me for what purpose you seek admission to Rochester's mansion."

"Sir," replied Blake, "this villain has forcibly taken from her home my dear sister, Olivia."

"Your *sister?*"

"Ay, sir, my only sister."

"Good heavens!" thought Clifford, "does a more monstrous liar exist on the face of the earth?"

"If Rochester has taken your sister," said Zodcastor, gravely, "you may depend upon it she is lost—utterly lost. However, the mansion, at which he is at this moment staying, is Lorne Castle, Hertford. And you must remember, that this pass must not be presented until after midnight has struck."

"I shall not forget," replied Blake.

"And now, ere you go," said Zodcastor, "you will write your name, and the name of your sister in this book."

Blake at once did so, and then his trembling fingers seized upon the pass.

"When you have done with the pass," said Zodcastor, "you will take it to the person with whom you, in the first place, communicated."

"I will."

Zodcastor rang a bell, the attendant appeared, and Blake was conducted down the stairs.

After some few minutes had elapsed, Zodcastor opened the little door in the globe.

"Come forth, young man," he said.

Clifford came out, and the next moment stood before him.

His face was white, his limbs trembled violently.

"What ails you?" asked Zodcastor.

"Sir," replied Clifford, "I would that

you had only known the name of your visitor, that I could have come out of that globe, and seized upon the throat of that lying wretch——"

"Hush! hush!"

"Oh!" groaned Clifford, "you have indeed committed a fatal mistake. 'Tis I who should have had that pass. That wretch," he added, as his eyes rested upon the open book, "has signed a false name."

"It is 'Mark Attwood'—that is, the son of Justice Attwood."

"Yes; but that was not Mark Attwood. The name of that person was Blake Barrell, one of Colonel Blood's assistants."

"It is strange, but I will tell you the name of the person who knew I was in possession of that pass if you will keep the secret."

"I *will* keep the secret."

"Well, the name of the person is Claribel Cameron; and she, if what you say is true, has been as much deceived as myself. I am compelled to obey a message received from Mistress Claribel Cameron, and which really comes through a person who shall be nameless. Now, listen. This is Doctor Jardell's letter: 'By a mere accident I have learned that you are about to receive a visit from a person to whom you will give Rochester's present whereabouts, and also a pass admitting the holder to the mansion. You will, I am sure, allow the bearer, Clifford Hansard, a dear young friend, to overhear what is said."

"You have done the favour," replied Clifford, "and I thank you. Though the pass would have been of great service to me, I have, nevertheless, gained information of vast importance."

Zodcastor rang the bell, and Clifford was quickly conducted from the house, finding his horse awaiting him.

Quickly mounting it he rode slowly away.

"I see how it is now," he thought. "Blake has learned that Rochester has got possession of Olivia, and, mad with jealousy, he is determined to recover her. No doubt he is already on the road to Hertford. By heaven! he shall find that I am not far away. He will gain admission, certainly; but what may happen? He may be cut to pieces directly his intentions are known.

Rochester knows him well enough. On the other hand, if he obtains possession of Olivia he is bound to put up at some hostelry for the time being. *Then my opportunity will come!*

*　　*　　*　　*

Clifford had considered that Rochester would recognise Barrell.

Blake had already thought of this, and he had provided himself with a thick beard and moustache.

These articles he, on quitting the astrologer's house, at once donned, and he chuckled heartily as he thought what a fine gallant he must now look.

The beard and moustache, added to the rich clothing he wore, completely altered him.

There is no doubt that had Colonel Blood or Rochester now looked at him, neither would have recognised him; for it must be remembered that their acquaintance of him had only been for a short time.

At the first hostelry he came to, Blake dismounted, entered, and called for some refreshment.

Soon after he had left the hostelry, Clifford rode up.

The ostler at once came forward to take charge of the horse.

"I say, my friend," whispered Clifford, slipping a crown into the ready palm, "has a horseman just obtained refreshment here?"

"Several," was the reply.

Clifford described Blake's attire.

The ostler recognised it.

"But," he said, "you make a mistake when you say he is clean shaven, for the horseman wearing the garments you describe, was also wearing a black beard and moustache."

"An additional disguise," thought Clifford. "Very good. I am not likely to forget. Ah! little does the villain know who is so close upon his track."

Clifford considered whether it would be advisable to also procure some disguise.

He soon arrived at the conclusion that it was not necessary, and he recommenced the journey.

*　　*　　*　　*

The reader is now, of course, very anxious to learn the fate of poor Olivia.

The drivers of the coach had their instructions as to where they were to go, and as soon as Blood got into his coach with Clarissa, off they went.

Proceeding slowly at first, they gradually increased their speed, until they were presently flying along the dark roads at a fearful rate.

Ever and anon Rochester looked out of the window, but he could see nothing of Blood's coach.

Once or twice he felt inclined to stop the coach and see what had become of the other, but eventually he thought—

"Why should I do anything of the kind? I have fulfilled the contract. I have my prize and he has his. If he is not satisfied, I am—ho, ho! Still I should like to know why he has not followed. Can he have been intercepted? And, if so, by whom? Who but Sir Christopher Cullum?"

At such a tremendous pace did the horses go, that Hertford was reached in two hours.

Here the postillions, for the first time, halted, in order to get instructions from Rochester.

His lordship gave them the necessary directions, and once more the coach proceeded on its journey.

But little further was it now to go.

Lorne Wood was entered and quickly traversed, and at the further end the grey walls of Lorne Castle came in sight.

Here Rochester alighted, and proceeding to the gate, spoke a few words, the result of which was that the gates were instantly opened.

In a few moments the coach rolled up, and the housekeeper, Mistress Voldeck, a German woman, came forth, followed by several servants, male and female.

"Voldeck," said Rochester, pointing within the coach, "you see that girl?"

"I see a bundle."

"Well, there is a girl inside."

"Not very big, eh?"

"That is nothing to you. You are to take her to the room which, by special messenger, I ordered."

"Yes, yes, your lordship," said Mistress Voldeck, "it is all quite right. The room has been ready these several hours. I am to take her there, and——"

"Wait my further commands," replied Rochester, haughtily.

Mistress Voldeck entered the coach, and taking up poor Olivia, proceeded to enter the castle.

"Remember, she has not yet recovered consciousness," said Rochester, placing his hand on Voldeck's shoulder and whispering in her ear. "Some powerful stuff was given her by Colonel Blood. Make it your business to bring her to."

Voldeck nodded, and passed on.

Rochester next took some gold pieces from his pocket, and addressing the leading postillion, said—

"Your master has already been paid for the loan of the coaches, but here is money for yourself and your man. Now depart as quickly as you can."

Rochester now gave directions for a splendid repast to be prepared.

"And," he said to Voldeck, "the girl shall join me."

"Impossible, impossible, your lordship," was the reply.

"Why impossible?"

"She is too ill, your lordship."

"Have you administered anything to her?"

"I am just about to do so; but whatever is administered to her must be administered with the utmost caution. She is a delicate girl, and, from the look of her, has suffered——"

"No matter what she has suffered," thundered Rochester, "she is to be brought at once to consciousness. I will wait one hour."

Wishing to impress Olivia with a grand display of his wealth, Rochester had gold and silver articles placed upon the table.

But it was destined that his lordship should not partake of that meal.

Before an hour had passed, a special messenger arrived from Whitehall.

He bore a letter from the king, and to Rochester's consternation and annoyance, it directed him to at once for his life make his appearance before his majesty.

Rochester, at first, felt inclined to instruct the messenger to say that he was not at Lorne Castle; but then he thought of the fact that he had broken the royal seal.

He was, therefore, compelled to set out for London again.

Before his departure he paid Olivia a visit, and was much struck with her appearance.

Voldeck and two of the female servants were in attendance upon her, and it was evident that they had been trying every means to bring the unhappy girl to consciousness, but without effect—a fact which appeared to puzzle Voldeck considerably.

After some reflection, Rochester said—

"If, after a reasonable time, you do not succeed in bringing her round, you had better summon Master Mallins from the village. He's clever at this sort of thing. Tell him that there will be fifty guineas beyond his fee to keep his mouth shut."

"Business" at the Court kept Rochester longer from the castle than he thought for, and it was only on the night when Blake started upon his journey, with Clifford close at his heels, that he returned.

He did not return alone.

No, on this occasion he brought with him one of his staunch "*friends*"—an individual who had assisted him in the carrying out of many of his plans—Sir Thomas Cameron.

This individual bore a striking resemblance to Rochester, for whom, at a distance, he had frequently been mistaken.

A substantial meal having been ordered, Voldeck was summoned to Rochester's presence.

"How fares the girl?" he asked.

"Fairly well," was the reply.

"Ha! She has recovered?"

"To some extent. But I can tell you, your lordship, that on this occasion, at any rate, you have brought to this castle one who will not conform to your wishes."

"Indeed!" replied Rochester; "you shall find, Voldeck, that I will tame her as I have tamed others."

"Well, then," was Voldeck's reply, "let me assure you that you will have to use force."

"That will not trouble his lordship," laughed Sir Thomas; "he has me to assist him."

"Where is she now?" asked Rochester.

"In the room you said she was to be placed."

"Good. When I have had my meal I will ascend to her. In the meantime, you will go to her and prepare her for my visit."

The meal being finished, Rochester ascended to the room in which poor Olivia had been placed.

Mistress Voldeck was in the apartment, but at a sign from Rochester she withdrew.

Rochester then closed the door.

"Now, my dear Mistress Olivia," he said, "I have come to ask you for your love."

"My Lord," interrupted Olivia, sternly, "do not address me in terms of endearment."

"But I *shall* address you in whatever terms I may think proper!" said Rochester.

No doubt he thought that it would, in the first place, be better to try the effect of threatening language.

But it had not the slightest effect on Olivia.

Rochester, advancing towards her, stood for a few moments surveying her with great interest.

His keen eyes were fixed full upon her face, but Olivia Preston quailed not.

Her fine, but now somewhat wasted figure was drawn to its fullest height.

She displayed great firmness, as if she had quite made up her mind as to the course she was about to pursue.

Her beautiful face was deathly pale, and her swollen eyes showed how many, many hours had been passed in weeping.

Poor girl! she had many things to weep about.

But now, as she stood, returning with great firmness the look Rochester gave her, her eyes were perfectly dry.

"Olivia Preston," said Rochester, folding his arms proudly across his chest, "let me first tell you that I was born to be obeyed; that I have been obeyed all my life; that *you* are not the first person who has taken my fancy, and whom, for as long as I thought proper, I have kept here; and those I have kept here I have compelled to do exactly as I have thought proper, and you, I swear, will be no exception to the rule. You shall obey me."

"My lord," interrupted Olivia, "you but waste your breath. Ay, and you waste the time which I have heard is so very valuable to the king and the country. To the *country*? Great heaven! The time of a man of *your* stamp valuable to the country?"

"Listen to me, girl," he said, in fierce tones, "take my advice, and keep your tongue, which I see is inclined to wag dangerously, for other purposes. I repeat, Olivia Preston, that I will compel you to obey me."

"I repeat, Lord Rochester," cried Olivia, "that you will never, never compel me to do anything a maiden should not do."

"No more," thundered Rochester, "no more, girl, unless you wish me to lose my temper. You are mine! You are here—in my power!"

"No!"

"I say you are, and here you will remain until I tire of you, when you will be at liberty to go as soon as it suits your convenience."

"Villain!" cried Olivia with flashing eyes.

Rochester glared fiercely at her for a few moments, and seemed about to rush upon her.

"Ha, indeed!" sneered Olivia; "really, my lord, the persons on whom you bestow your favour ought to prostrate themselves before you in very admiration of your superior motives. But I, at any rate, cannot find words in which to express my intense disgust of you."

"Olivia Preston," cried Rochester, seizing her by the wrist, "let me tell you that you can never escape from my power!"

"I will leave you," continued Rochester, "to ponder over this—whether it would not be far better that you should reign here as mistress, with a large body of servants, the command of any amount of money, petted and fêted, than become the wife of a paltry apprentice, with no hopes in the future."

"I require no time to ponder over the matter," replied Olivia. "I can give you my decision now. I had much rather be the wife of a 'paltry apprentice,' than the slave of a profligate lord such as you."

Rochester bit his lips; the thrust was a keen one, and he felt it.

"Ah!" he said, "others have said something to the same effect, but they have quickly changed their opinions."

"Mine will never change; for you snatched me from a house wherein for many long weeks I had been face to face with death in its most agonizing form. If I had feared death, think you that I should have stayed in that house? I

had many friends who, far away from the plague-stricken city, would have received me with open arms. If I feared not death then, should I fear it now?"

"I do not understand to what all this leads," replied Rochester.

"Then your lordship must be dull indeed. It means this—that rather than conform with your wishes, I will die by my own hand!"

Rochester started.

He looked full into Olivia's face, and he there read that the words the girl uttered were no idle ones.

"And," he said, "if a certain Clifford Hansard were told that you perished by your own hand, what would he say?"

"He would say, 'Brave girl! thou wert indeed worthy of the deep affection I had for thee. But you—you, Lord Rochester, what can you know of Clifford Hansard?"

Rochester saw that he had inserted the right nail and driven it home.

"I know all about him," he replied. "People have thought he was dead——"

"Not all—nay, not all. I never thought so. I have all along felt that one day he would return to me."

"Do not deceive yourself; he will never return. He is too securely caged."

"Caged?"

"Ay, caged!"

"Great heaven! Would you tell me that he is in prison?"

"I will tell you nothing beyond the fact that he is caged."

"I will not believe you."

"Your disbelief does not alter the fact that Clifford Hansard is in the hands of his foes," answered Rochester. "But I will give you till to-morrow morning to ponder over what I have said. You will do well to accept of my terms; but if you do not, force will be used. You are in my power, and you cannot get out of it."

"Ah," cried poor Olivia, who fully recognised the truth of those words—"ah, that heaven would raise me up a friend—a friend who would hasten to my aid."

"No friend could pass these walls, Mistress Preston, without my permission."

With these words Rochester left the apartment.

In Olivia he had met with quite a

different person to what he expected, and he was more savage at the discovery of this fact than he cared to show Olivia.

Sir Thomas Cameron saw by his look that he had met with a rebuff.

Rochester gave him a brief outline of what had taken place, whereat Sir Thomas expressed his desire to see the girl.

"You shall see her in the morning," replied Rochester. "I expect Blood will soon make his appearance. I made inquiries about him yesterday and to-day, but was unable to learn anything of him."

"He may bring with him a few friends of the White Circle"

"He may, certainly."

"Has he the pass?"

"Yes."

Our readers know that this was not correct, for that pass was now in the hands of Blake.

"Well," said Sir Thomas, "let us pass away an hour with the cards."

"I am at your service."

The two adjourned to the card-room, and did not move from it until the hour of eleven had struck.

Rochester then said—

"I am about to retire, Cameron. Your room has been prepared."

"Good," was the reply. "I will retire ere many minutes have passed."

Rochester went at once to his room.

The master having retired, the servants commenced to retire also.

Before the hour of midnight the whole castle, with the exception of the guard-room, was buried in profound silence and darkness.

But Sir Thomas Cameron had not retired to his room.

He had waited in the card-room to enjoy the fire, his pipe, and the liquors upon the table.

But, by-and-bye, drowsiness stole over him.

His head dropped forward on his arms on the table, and he slept as soundly as if he had been lying on a bed of down.

Anon the lamp flickered and went out, the fire got lower and lower, and presently nothing was left of it but some smouldering embers.

Twelve o'clock struck, and barely had

the sonorous strokes died away ere a horseman rode up to the walls of the castle.

He was at once observed by one of the sentries.

"What want ye?" asked the man.

"Admittance," replied the horseman, who was none other than Blake.

"Your name?"

"Is Lord Verney."

"You cannot obtain admittance here unless you bear the proper pass."

"I *do* bear it—behold."

And Blake produced the pass.

"Well," said the sentry, "wait where you are, and I will summon Stephen."

The man Stephen quickly made his appearance, a lantern in one hand, and a loaded pistol in the other.

Looking through the bars of the little wicket set in the door, he said—

"Are you alone?"

"I am."

"I will admit you then."

The gate thereupon opened, and Blake, having passed through, dismounted, and handed over the pass.

Stephen at once handed the lantern and the pistol to the sentry.

"Take the pistol," he said, "and point it full at this man's heart, and if you hear me cry ''Tis false!' shoot him dead!"

Blake trembled as this fearful order was given, for he thought the man might consider the pass false.

But the fellow was not likely to do so.

Only too well was he acquainted with that pass.

"It is all right, your lordship," he said, as he returned the pass; "but you see we are bound to be careful in these days."

"To be sure. But I see that the castle is in darkness. Has his lordship retired?"

"He has; but there is, no doubt, a room at your disposal."

"As his lordship has retired, I wish to retire also, and without causing any disturbance."

"Well, your lordship, my man shall conduct you to the apartments on the second flight. I have no doubt you have been there before?"

"*Many* times."

Calling one of his attendants, Stephen gave him instructions, and the man, procuring a lantern, told "his lordship" to follow him.

The critical time had now arrived.

How was he to proceed?

In what room was he to find Olivia?

And when he had found her, how was he to escape from the castle?

The man with the lantern conducted him through two or three long corridors, and during the journey Blake looked eagerly into his face, as if to ascertain what sort of man he was.

"Was he likely to accept a bribe?" he asked himself.

The man's face wore a hang-dog expression, and it required no second glance to see that he was well able to take his share of liquor.

Money was scarce; the wages of these men were miserably poor. Would the sight of a handful of gold tempt this man to betray the secrets which he had taken a most solemn oath to preserve?

Well, he would try certainly.

But there was this to be considered; suppose the man refused to accept the bribe?

What would follow?

He would, doubtless, alarm the household and Blake would be arrested, his identity would be discovered, and death would follow.

But he was prepared to risk much for the possession of Olivia.

"One moment, my man," whispered Blake, placing his hand on the man's arm, "I want to ask you something."

The man, considerably startled, paused and looked up.

"What would you say," said Blake, "if you could place these bright guineas in your pocket?"

And he produced a handful of the golden pieces.

"I should say 'thank you,'" grunted the man.

"No doubt. Well, look you, my friend, you may easily earn this amount."

"In what way?"

"By answering my questions."

"I will answer any questions, so long as my answers will not betray his lordship's secrets."

"They will not. Take the money."

The man hesitated.

At last, however, he took the guineas and placed them in his wallet.

"Now proceed, my lord," he said.

"In what room is Olivia Preston?"

The man slowly shook his head.

"I've never heard the name before," he said.

"Well, the young girl his lordship brought here."

"Ah, I see! But that is a secret of his lordship, and so I cannot answer it."

"Five more gold pieces shall be yours if you answer me."

"Well, well," replied the man, putting forth his hand, "I will tell you."

"And for this sum you will answer my other questions?"

"To be sure."

The money being handed over, the man said—

"The girl is on the third floor ascending by the grand staircase. But what do you want to know this for?"

"I am much interested in the girl. I have heard a deal of talk about her beauty, and when I meet his lordship in the morning, I want to say that I have seen her. I shall of course say that I saw her in London."

"Ah! Well, if that is so, your lordship," replied the man, "you certainly will not see her."

"And why?"

"Because Mistress Voldeck the housekeeper is sleeping with her."

"Indeed!"

"Yes; I have heard it whispered that that order was given because Lord Rochester feared the girl would take her own life if she was not watched."

"Ah! Well I can try whether I can gain access to her chamber."

"Oh, you can try, sure enough. But I need hardly warn your lordship that if you are observed prowling about, your life is almost certain to pay the forfeit."

"That I must risk. On the third floor, you say, ascending by the grand staircase."

"Ay, and you cannot possibly mistake the room, because the door is screened by a pair of green curtains embroidered with silver."

"And, now, is there no means of leaving the castle unseen, supposing that I wished to do such a thing."

The man opened wide his eyes in astonishment, and an expression of fear rested for a moment on his face.

"The fact of it is," he said, "you

intend to attempt to carry off the girl."

"Such is really my intention," replied Blake, "and you must assist me. You have taken my gold, and your services are mine."

"But suppose I refuse to assist you?"

"I will inform Lord Rochester, that wishing to try your honesty, I pretended to tamper with you."

"By my faith!" gasped the man, "you are indeed a cunning villain."

He, however, saw that he was in Blake's power.

Not the slightest suspicion had he that Blake was any other than what he represented himself to be.

"There is one thing," thought the man, "if I show him the way out of the castle, he can say nothing about me. I will, however, see whether I can get any more money out of him. If I can it will be safer for me to quit this place for ever."

"Come," said Blake, "will you, or will you not assist me?"

"I will show you the way to a subterranean vault by which you can, unobserved, leave the castle. It runs beneath what was, at one time, the moat, and terminates in Lorne Wood."

"The very thing!" whispered Blake, exultingly.

"But," continued the man, "I should take my departure from the castle at the same time, and, therefore, should require of you an additional twenty guineas."

"I have no such sum left."

"Well, what sum have you, your lordship?"

Blake counted.

He had ten guineas.

"That will do," said the man; "I will take that sum since you have no more."

Blake reflected.

Could he do as the man asked? No, he thought.

But a sudden idea flashed through his mind.

The man had said he would leave the castle at the same time!

"Good!" thought Blake, "he shall have the money—*for a time—for a time!*

He placed the money in the man's hand.

"There," he said, "you have now sufficient to keep yourself in comfort for some time to come."

"Well, now," said the man, "listen to what I say. When you *descend* the grand staircase turn to the right and pass through the room exactly in front of you, which is the *card*-room. You will not forget that?"

"Nay, nay; but—quick, for time presses!"

"Having passed through the card-room, turn to the left, and descend a flight of steps. At the bottom I shall be awaiting you."

"Ay, ay. But why cannot you accompany me?"

"I have to go to the major-domo's room and procure the key of the secret door at the further end of the vault, and that is far more risky than what you are about to do."

"Well, I will do as you say; but, remember, deceive me and, if I lose *my* life in doing so, I will slay you."

"Do not fear. I will not betray you. Now take this lantern, and I will get another. But remember *this*, your lordship, if you wake the housekeeper, Mistress Voldeck, *you are lost.* And, in that case, you will not betray *me?*"

"I will not, I promise that."

The pair then separated, Blake concealing the rays of the lantern with his cloak, and ascending the staircase.

He quickly reached the third flight, and at once recognised the door of Olivia's room by the description given him.

He placed his hand on the handle and gently turned it.

The door yielded, and the next moment he was within the room.

On the inside the apartment was screened by a pair of heavy curtains, and standing between these, Blake took a survey of the chamber.

He was able to do this without uncovering his lantern owing to the fact that a small night taper was burning upon one of the tables.

But he was not able to see the occupants of the bed, because that also was surrounded with heavy curtains.

He listened and caught the sound of two persons breathing.

After a few moments' reflection, he decided on the way he was to act.

He stealthily drew from its sheath a long dagger.

Then he glided into the room, his footsteps being completely deadened by the carpet.

Advancing to the bed, he gently drew aside the curtain.

His eager eyes fell upon two sleeping figures—the first was Mistress Voldeck, and the other Olivia.

Blake contemplated Olivia's beautiful face for some moments, and he then drew slightly back.

Another second and the murderous blade was raised on high.

Exerting all his strength, the monster brought down the dagger, and it was buried deep in the housekeeper's heart.

A series of wild gasps escaped her lips, and then all was over.

As the blow was delivered, Olivia started up.

She was about to utter a fearful shriek, when Blake raised his hand.

"Hold!" he whispered in an assumed voice, "hold! as you value your life and your liberty. *I am here to rescue you by instructions received from Clifford Hansard.*"

The utterance of that dear name effectually sealed her lips.

Eagerly she looked into the bearded face bending so closely to her, as if wondering whether she should recognise anyone she knew.

But no. Still, that this man was there by instructions from Clifford, she felt quite sure.

Blake raised the lantern, and as its rays fell upon the bed, now fast becoming saturated with blood, Olivia fainted.

Blake hurriedly looked about the room.

His eyes fell upon an enormous rug, and picking it up he placed it at the end of the bed, then seizing Olivia in his arms, he dragged her out and wrapped her from head to foot in the rug.

Throwing the insensible figure over his shoulder, he proceeded to quit the room.

But remembering the dagger, he turned, and plucked it from the housekeeper's breast ere he left the chamber.

He descended the stairs very cautiously, and at last the bottom was reached.

The card-room was before him.

He pushed the door very gently, so that it should not creak, and was about to enter, when he was thunder-stricken to see a figure before him.

The fire had not quite gone out.

It threw sufficient light around the apartment to enable him to see that the figure seated in the chair was fast asleep.

"By heaven!" muttered Blake, "that man was mistaken, for this is the cunning villain, *Rochester!* Ah! yes. And on my life, he is in my power! He shall die! If I kill him there will be no necessity to *leave the parchment.*"

For some few moments he contemplated the figure.

He saw that there was no chance of delivering with his dagger what would prove a fatal blow, for the position of the sleeper was against it.

Blake thereupon sheathed his dagger, and drew his sword.

He raised the dreadful blade, and with all his force brought it down upon the head of the sleeper.

Sir Thomas Cameron—for he, as our readers know, it was—started up; but, bathed in blood, he sank into the seat again, and fell dead, with his face in almost the same position as it had been before the blow was delivered.

In that instant Blake saw that he had made a mistake.

He remained for a second or two petrified with astonishment.

However, he quickly recovered, for he knew the danger he was running by delay.

"'Tis his own fault he muttered as he sheathed his sword, " he had no business to be there! Then I *will* leave the parchment. Ha! ha! Clifford Hansard, thy death will follow this deed—*not* of *mine,* but of THINE!"

So saying, he placed his hand within his doublet and brought forth a sheet of dirty parchment on which were a few lines of writing, and taking Sir Thomas Cameron's dagger from its sheath, he passed it through the parchment, and then drove the blade into the table.

He now passed rapidly on.

Turning to the left as he had been directed, he descended the flight of stone steps, where he found the man awaiting him, lantern in hand.

The fellow's face bore evidences of the greatest agitation.

Directly he saw Blake he breathed a sigh of relief.

"Ha!" he said, "I thought it was all over with you."

"What made you think so?"

"Because you have been so long. Did you meet with anyone?"

"No."

"And you got the girl from the room without waking the housekeeper?"

"Certainly."

"Marvellous!" exclaimed the man. "Well, now that you have her all right it will be as well if we hurry through the subterranean passage with all speed, for if Mistress Voldeck should wake up and miss the girl she will rouse every inmate of the castle."

"Hurry along, then—hurry along," replied Blake.

"Proceed, your lordship," said the man, "and I will follow with the lantern."

"Nay," replied Blake; "do you go first, because then I shall not be so likely to miss my footing."

The man had no suspicion that his life was in danger, and so had no hesitation in leading the way.

This subterranean passage seemed to have no end.

The ground was uneven, and, in many parts, highly dangerous.

Moreover the atmosphere was stifling.

When quite five minutes had elapsed, Blake, now feeling Olivia's weight most severely, paused.

"How much further?" he asked.

"But a few minutes now," was the reply.

"You are sure you have the key?"

"Oh, yes; 'tis here safe enough."

And he held up the key.

"Proceed once more then," replied Blake.

The man again went on.

He had not taken half a dozen strides before his life came to an abrupt termination.

Once again that deadly blade was bared.

Forward it was thrust, and was buried in the man's back, and so deep that the heart was pierced.

The cry that left the man's lips was a fearful one; but it was not repeated.

In withdrawing the terrible weapon, Blake overbalanced himself, and dropped Olivia.

This, however, was not all; for, while taking the money from the man, the false beard and moustache fell off.

He picked them up, but before he could replace them, Olivia had recovered consciousness, and Blake found her horror-stricken eyes fixed upon his face.

"Blake Barrell!" she gasped.

"Ay, ay," replied Blake, uneasily, "it is. But I have delivered you from Rochester's clutches, Olivia. And in consideration of this, you will be mine."

"Never! Oh, heaven! breathes there such an unfortunate maiden as I? From the hands of one monster I fall into the power of another."

"Come," said Blake, looking uneasily back along the passage—"come, or all will be lost."

"I am already lost."

"Come, I tell you."

And dragging her to her feet, he seized her about the waist, and throwing her across his shoulder, once more proceeded.

The end of the long and dangerous passage was soon reached.

Blake had not forgotten the key, and to his joy, he found that there was not the slightest difficulty with it.

He at once opened the door.

Blake went forth, being careful to lock the door after him.

And now he looked on all sides of him.

He saw nothing but trees and bushes, and it was so profoundly dark, that if he had not carried a lantern, it is quite certain that he would have been unable to proceed.

Walking a little distance he looked back, thinking that he might see the castle walls.

But he could not.

He knew, however, that it must be a long distance behind.

The difficulty now was to find a path leading from the wood.

Standing Olivia down, he said—

"Remember this: I shall have to inquire my way, and if you make any appeal to the person of whom I may inquire, this dagger will find its way to your heart."

Sooner than remain in the clutches of Blake, Olivia would assuredly have preferred death.

"'I HAVE DONE NO HARM, YOUR LORDSRIP!' CRIED THE MAN."

But now that she was out of the castle, she trusted that something would occur which would free her from Blake.

On and on wandered Blake, trying to find a path.

But it was in vain.

The ground was so thick with leaves that it would have been impossible to discover a trace of a path.

Suddenly Blake paused and sniffed the air.

"Charcoal!" he muttered.

Still further on he went, and at last the hut of a charcoal-burner came into view.

Blake unceremoniously awoke the occupant, and when he came to the door, drew his sword.

The sight of this had the effect Blake desired.

It caused him to answer any questions with an appearance of good grace.

Blake learned that the nearest hostelry was the "Lorne Arms," distant some half a mile from the hut.

"I know not the path," said Blake, "and should not find my way out of the wood without assistance. Do you aid me, and here is a guinea for your trouble. But what is that standing yonder?"

"A pony, your worship."

"Do you think it possible that this lady can ride on it to the hostelry?"

"Ay, ay, your worship. She can do that well enough — that is, if she is strong enough to cling to the animal, for I have neither saddle or bridle."

"I will hold her," replied Blake.

So Olivia was lifted on the pony's back, and the party set off to the "Lorne Arms."

CHAPTER XV.

OF WHAT HAPPENED AT THE "LORNE ARMS"—OF THE ARRANGEMENT BETWEEN MARTHA WALTMAN AND CLIFFORD—OF HOW IT WAS BROUGHT TO A SUCCESSFUL TERMINATION—AND OF WHAT THE SOILED PARCHMENT CONTAINED.

WE will now return to Clifford.

Soon after Blake obtained admission to the castle, Clifford made inquiries respecting the hostelries in the immediate neighbourhood.

He learned that there were several within easy distance of the castle gates, but that the furthest, and the most out-of-the-way hostelry of the lot was called the "Lorne Arms."

Clifford for some time hesitated as to which he should go to, but at last he decided to go to the "Lorne Arms," for he considered that Blake would not throw himself into danger by putting up at an hostelry near the castle.

When Clifford reached the house, which was a very small one, and evidently did but a limited amount of business, it was just closing time.

The host, Martin Waltman, however, was only too glad to serve a customer, no matter what the hour.

In less than a quarter of an hour Clifford had told him and his daughter —a very fine girl of eighteen—the circumstances which had brought him from London.

He told them that it was just possible that the person he had been keeping in sight would put up at the hostelry.

But knowing the terrible temper and the great influence of Rochester, the host hesitated, though Clifford offered him a very fair sum for whatever trouble he or his daughter might be put to.

But suddenly he said—

"Ha! I have it. List to this, young sir. I will do all you ask—*more* if it should be required, if you will do me a favour: Do you know the 'Green Bowl' at Finsbury Fields?"

"I could easily find it."

"Well. I have, or I had, a brother there. I say I *had*, because not having heard from him since the outbreak of the fearful plague, he might be dead. Will you, at your earliest opportunity, make inquiries there, and let me know the result?"

"I will."

"Then enter, and we will do as you require. But what of the horse?"

"Leave him saddled and bridled."

Clifford was shown to a well-furnished

bedroom, a fire was lit, and there he waited.

Two hours passed away, and, at last, his patience was rewarded.

"Hold!" exclaimed a cracked voice. "Hold! here we are!"

Cautiously Clifford peeped through the window.

But the overhanging balcony prevented his seeing who had arrived.

He could hear, however, all that was said.

Oh, the thrill of joy which shot through his heart, when a voice which he instantly recognised as the voice of Blake Barrell, said—

"Return, then, and remember our arrangement. Attempt to break it, and you are a dead man!"

The charcoal burner protested that he would be very careful to keep his mouth shut, and he with his pony departed.

"He and that girl are mysteries," mutterd the charcoal burner. "He is forcing her away from somewhere. Good. Well, I will sell the secret to the *highest bidder*. Ha, ha."

The host, who was in bed, hastily slipped on his clothes, knocked up his daughter, and then, taking a lantern in his hand, descended the stairs.

But when he reached the door, and before he opened it, he heard Olivia's voice.

At once he turned back to the stairs.

"Martha, Martha," he whispered, "the girl is here."

"Ay, ay," was the whispered reply.

The host now opened the door.

"What is the name of this hostelry?" demanded Blake, in haughty tones.

"The 'Lorne Arms,'" was the reply. "Are you a traveller?"

"Ay; and I have with me a friend—a lady. Lead us at once to your best rooms."

"Pardon me, is the lady your wife?"

"No; I said a friend."

"Then had I not better summon my daughter to take charge of her?"

"No, I can take charge of her myself. Listen to me, my man—I am Lord Verney."

"Never heard the name before," replied the host.

"Then hear it *now*, fool."

"Listen to me, your lordship," said the host—"that is, if you *are* a lord—and you certainly speak like an uncombed one—if you do not keep a civil tongue in your head, I will close the door in your face. I am not in the habit of being bullied. Now, if you can be civil, enter."

Blake took Olivia by the arm, but the poor girl faltered at the threshold, and seemed about to drop, whereupon Blake hissed through his clenched teeth—

"Beware! The slightest thing might lead to our detection; and though your life would be spared, inasmuch as Rochester would take you back to his castle, my life would be lost."

Just as the pair entered, and the door was closed, Martha, the host's daughter, descended the stairs, taper in hand.

A little sigh of relief did Olivia breathe, as her eyes rested upon a woman's face.

Martha had been warned by Clifford, but nevertheless she fixed a searching look upon Olivia's face.

She instantly saw how terribly the poor girl was suffering.

"Sir—," she commenced.

But her father checked her with a wave of his hand.

"Our visitor," he said, "is a lord—a real live lord—and you must address him as such."

"Beware!" thundered Blake, placing his hand on the butt of one of his pistols—"beware how you sneer at me. It will take but little more to——"

"Calm yourself, your lordship," said Martha; "no one wishes to sneer at you. Pray let me take charge of the lady."

As she spoke she advanced towards Olivia.

But Blake waved her off.

"No," he said, "I will take charge of her. She does not leave my sight."

"Light the fire in the large front room," said the host.

Turning to Blake, he added—

"Pardon me, your lordship, the lady looks very ill."

"That may be so," was the surly reply.

"Do you not think it would be better if she were shown to a bedroom?"

"No!"

The host said no more, thinking that Blake might become suspicious.

When half way up the stairs, Blake

halted, and turning to the host, said—

"Have you any guests staying here?"

"No," was the reply.

"Not one?."

"Not one. This is not a house for travellers. It is too far removed from the high road."

Blake and Olivia were soon in the front room—the largest in the house—and a fire of logs was quickly roaring up the huge chimney.

On the host inquiring what refreshments he should provide, Blake told him to bring up a tray of the very best wines and eatables he had.

Martha lingered at the threshold of the door, her eyes fixed upon Olivia's pretty but sad face.

Sad! Sad is not the word for it; the suffering and misery depicted upon that face was enough to have brought tears to the eyes of anyone.

Olivia returned Martha's earnest, pitying gaze as well as she was able, but Blake's jealous eyes noticed it.

Turning abruptly to Martha, he peremptorily bade her begone.

Martha slowly took her departure, and Blake secured the door.

As the reader may have guessed, it had been Martha's intention to whisper a word of comfort in Olivia's ear—to assure her that a friend—a dear friend was near—but she had not obtained the opportunity.

She at once repaired to Clifford.

"Poor girl!" she said, as she sunk into a seat and burst into tears. "I never saw a young girl look so sad—so miserable. Oh, sir, she is not long for this world."

"Hush, hush! Talk not so, I conjure you," replied Clifford.

"I speak but the truth, sir. The one who is with her is a demon—a fiend in human form."

"There you speak the truth," replied Clifford; "but, thank heaven, she is safe out of the castle. There I could never have hoped to reach her. But here—oh, that I could lay the wretch dead at my feet; but if he recognised me, he would plunge his dagger into the girl's heart. Now, listen. Has your father such a thing as a drug?"

"A drug? Nay, I am certain he has not. You mean to drop into the wine?"

"Yes."

"It would now be too late, for I hear my father entering with what has been ordered. You must wait. From what you said, it is evident that this scoundrel has been awake for many hours. The wine and the fire will no doubt send him to sleep, then will come your opportunity."

Blake had refused to allow Olivia to leave his side until perfectly certain that there were no travellers in the house.

"You refuse to partake of any refreshment?" he said to Olivia.

"I require it not," replied Olivia, in low tones.

"Are you afraid that I have adopted Blood's plan, and drugged the wine?"

"I have not even thought of the matter. Ah, me! how very, very ill I feel."

"You would like to go to bed?"

To this Olivia made no reply.

"Look you," continued Blake, "if I order a bed to be placed at your disposal, will you swear to preserve silence as to all that has occurred?"

"I will."

"I like not the look of that girl. I can see that she regards me with suspicion. However, a bed shall be placed at your disposal, but I again say, beware!"

Already Blake had drunk nearly a bottle of wine, and when he rose he was somewhat unsteady on his legs.

This was not all the effect of the wine—the number of hours he had been awake, and the great fatigue he had undergone had had a great deal to do with it."

"Host!" he roared; "host!"

"Ay, ay," replied that worthy, at once opening the door.

"Let your daughter show this lady to a bedroom."

"Yes, my lord."

"And—but here she is. Girl."

"Well?" replied Martha.

"Conduct this lady to a bedroom, and provide her with some clothes, for which I am willing to pay the exorbitant sum I know you will demand. Whatever the lady may desire, provide her with; and here is a guinea to assist you in keeping your mouth shut."

And he flung a guinea on the table.

Martha darted upon it, and advancing to the fire, she deliberately flung it in.

"*That* for your guinea!" she cried, indignantly. "I can keep *my* mouth shut without a bribe."

"You will pardon her, your lordship," said the host. "You see she has been roused from her sleep."

Martha tenderly led Olivia from the room.

She had to half carry our poor heroine, for she could scarcely place one foot before the other.

"Oh, lady," whispered Martha, when out of Blake's hearing. "Cheer up. A dear, dear friend is close at hand——"

"Ha," returned Olivia; "what mean you, girl?"

"Your lover, Clifford Hansard, is within this house."

"Holy Mary! is this indeed possible?"

"It is. But come. Quick, or all will be lost."

"Oh, let me go to him; let me hold him within these arms ere death seizes me."

"No, no, lady," replied Martha. "You must not go to him now. Presently, presently, when he has settled with the villain who brought you here."

Half led, half carried, Olivia was taken to a bedroom.

"Turn the key in the door, lady," whispered Martha, "and wait."

* * * *

"Ha, ha!" chuckled Blake, "ho, ho! What will Rochester say to it? What will he say when he sees the body of that woman? And what will he say when he sees the body of Sir Thomas Cameron, his bosom friend? Ha! *that* will rouse him. He will read the *parchment*, and then he—no, he will not search the country. I know what he will do. There is evidence, plain evidence that these dark deeds were committed by Clifford Hansard. There is evidence *in his own handwriting* that he rescued the girl. Ha! I flatter myself that at last I have woven the hemp and placed the rope about his neck. As for myself, I must pretend still to be Rochester's slave—yes, I must take every care not to arouse his suspicion."

Opening another bottle of wine, and filling a goblet, he once more seated himself beside the fire, and prepared to enjoy the liquor, while gloating over the clever way he had obtained possession of Olivia, and the manner in which he had drawn the net about Clifford.

But gradually sleep stole upon him.

Several times he tried to rouse himself, but in vain, and at last he leaned quite back in the chair.

He was just dropping off into a sound sleep, when the door creaked.

The sound was hardly perceptible, yet he heard it.

"Who is it?" he growled, but without looking up. "Who is it, I say? Is it you, host?"

"No!" cried a voice of thunder, as a heavy hand descended upon his shoulder. "It is I, Clifford Hansard!"

A tremendous yell left Blake.

White as a sheet to the very lips, he turned.

Starting to his feet, he stepped back, and trembling as with the ague, he fixed his bleared eyes on Clifford's face.

There was not the slightest agitation visible on Clifford's features.

No, his face wore an air of stern determination.

"Clifford Hansard!" gasped Blake. "No, no; it *cannot* be."

"It is. I am changed since last you saw me, eh? for you did not see me distinctly on the stairs of Blood's house. Yes; I am changed, but you must recognise my voice. Villain! Atrocious ruffian! your last hour on earth has come. You thought to take that poor girl away—heaven knows where—but when you set out upon this journey you little thought that I was upon your track. You little thought that I would follow you step by step; but such has been the case. You have rescued Olivia Preston from the clutches of Rochester only to fall into my hands."

"It is false!" screamed Blake, snatching his dagger from its sheath. "If she is not mine, she shall never be yours! This blade will I plunge into her heart!"

And he took a few strides towards the door.

But Clifford barred his passage.

Drawing his sword, he said—

"Do you think, villain, that I will allow you to leave this room? No! You have a sword at your side—draw and defend yourself."

"I have no time to waste on a fool

like you. Out of my path, or I swear that I will send a ball through your brain!" cried Blake.

And as he spoke he took a pistol from his belt and pointed it full at Clifford's head.

Instantly Clifford dashed upon him.

Seizing the pistol by the muzzle, he wrenched it from his hand, and dealt him such a tremendous blow on the mouth that he was stretched upon the floor.

"Arise!" cried Clifford, "and if you have courage draw and defend yourself."

"If I refuse?" groaned Blake.

"If you refuse I will pierce your false, black heart!"

"I haven't strength to fight."

"What! you haven't strength to fight? Where did you find the strength to take that poor girl from the castle? Monster! Arise, I say, and defend yourself!"

"No, no; I—I—am unable to."

And the scoundrel vainly endeavoured to stanch the blood which was copiously flowing from his mouth.

"I cannot murder you," said Clifford, fixing a contemptuous look upon him; "but ere I quit this room I will take care to put you beyond the power of doing any mischief. Stand up!"

"No, no."

"Stand up, I say!" and Clifford, taking a pistol from his belt, cocked it.

The ominous sound at once had its effect on Blake, who jumped to his feet.

"Now," said Clifford, "throw your weapons over here."

"I refuse."

"Fool! are you weary of your life that you thus tempt me to take it? Throw your sword and pistols over here, I say."

Blake's trembling hands sought his arms, and one by one he threw them to where Clifford was standing.

"Host! host!" cried Clifford.

The host, as well as his daughter, who had been listening just outside, hastily entered.

"Host," said Clifford, pointing to Blake's cowering figure, "I think that the sight of this wretch satisfies you that all I have said is true."

"Ay, ay, my young master," replied the host, "more than satisfies me. He is indeed a rogue. What is your pleasure respecting him?"

"I know not what to say."

"Why not summon the two ostlers to *his lordship*, father?" sneered Martha, "and let them bring a halter. In Lorne Wood yonder plenty of trees will be found strong enough to bear his weight."

"Mercy, mercy!" screamed Blake, falling upon his knees. "Don't hang me! don't hang me!"

"Well, you *are* a miserable coward!" cried the host in disgust; "but I should advise you, sir," he added, addressing Clifford, "to accompany my daughter. She will take you to that poor girl. I will lock the door of this apartment, and you can presently consider what is best to be done with this villain."

So the arms, and, in fact, everything which Clifford thought might be used as a weapon, were removed from the room, and the door was securely locked.

With all speed Clifford repaired to Olivia.

Martha preceded him, and knocking upon the door, said—

"Open, lady, your lover is here."

At once Olivia threw back the door, and the next instant she was folded to our hero's breast.

"At last! at last!" she cried, rapturously. "At last. Oh, Clifford—my love—my love!—have we indeed come together at last?"

"Yes, my sweet Olivia," replied Clifford, straining her to his breast, "we have. But, oh! under what terrible circumstances."

"It is but for a short time, dear Clifford," said Olivia, in tones full of the most intense emotion, "for I feel that I am dying."

"Oh, say not that, sweet Olivia! Live—live for me. Oh, Olivia! after all that we have passed through, we deserve each other. But hark!"

At this moment sounds as the rattling of arms, and voices uttering loud words of command fell upon their ears.

Before Clifford had time to form any idea as to what it could mean, the host, pale, trembling, and greatly excited, rushed into the room.

"By the blessed saints, young sir!" he cried, "this is a fearful night's work for me. Hark!"

"Ay, ay," replied Clifford, "I hear a noise without the house. What is it?"

"Rochester and his men."

"Impossible!" cried Clifford, while Olivia, clasping her hands, shrank back in an attitude of deep despair.

* * * *

Ere we place before the reader the particulars of what followed, we will return to the castle.

Some quarter of an hour after Blake, with Olivia in his arms, had passed down the staircase leading to the subterranean passage, the major-domo of the establishment, becoming uneasy at the prolonged absence of his man, ordered a search to be instituted.

But the search party did not descend to the subterranean passage.

Of course, they did not think for an instant that anything could have called the man to that spot.

So they did not pass through the card-room.

Not finding the man, nor, indeed, any trace of him, the major-domo became alarmed. And first of all, the sentries were questioned.

No; they had seen nothing of him.

"Then there is no alternative," said the major-domo. "Lord Verney must be aroused."

Forthwith, with several men at his back, the major-domo ascended to the room in which he supposed "Lord Verney" would be.

He knocked at the door, gently at first, and then as loudly as possible.

But, of course, he received no reply.

So, taking a lantern, he opened the door, and stalked in.

He found that the bed had never even been disturbed.

So confounded was the man, that for some moments he could not speak.

"Wonderful!" he at last ejaculated.

"Perhaps he is in another room," suggested one of the men.

"Nay, nay," was the reply, "that cannot be; but still we will try."

Try, they did; every empty bedroom being entered.

But no "Lord Verney" did they find.

"I must at once to his lordship," said the major-domo, "and inform him of this most extraordinary circumstance. Great powers! how he will storm and rave!

I may at once reckon that I have lost my place.

To his lordship's room went the major-domo, his men still at his back.

He knocked several times before he got an answer.

At last Rochester's voice was heard.

"Enter!"

Into the magnificently furnished room walked the major-domo, his men still following him.

"In the name of all that is evil!" cried Rochester, starting up in the bed, "what means this? Is the castle invaded? Has the plague reached here?"

"No, no, your lordship," cried the major-domo, hastily; "but a most wonderful thing has happened."

"Ah, indeed!" sneered Rochester, has the moon dropped into the courtyard, or——"

"Pardon, your lordship, but this is a most serious matter."

"Well, well, out with it."

"Your lordship, at midnight your well-known pass was presented by Lord Verney, and——"

"*What!*" thundered Rochester; "a pass? *My* pass? Presented here by Lord Verney?"

"Yes."

"Fool!" roared Rochester, jumping clean out of the bed; *there is no such lord as Verney.*"

Truly, at this instant the major-domo presented a most pitiful sight.

In a half-stooping, stupid attitude, he stood looking blankly into the fierce face of Lord Rochester.

"I tell you!" thundered Rochester, "that there is no such name as Lord Verney. Describe the man who presented the pass—quick!"

The major-domo endeavoured to do what he was told, and, in the meantime, Rochester, assisted by one or two of the men, attired himself.

"And you have searched the apartments, and failed to discover either this impostor, or the man who showed him the room? By the saints! if aught has happened, thy life shall pay the forfeit! Come—quick! my arms—that sword will do. Buckle it on—quick! quick! Great powers! this is almost beyond belief. Let Sir Thomas Cameron be awakened. Lead the way to his room."

The room was quickly reached, and Rochester himself, with the hilt of his sword hammered upon the door.

No reply.

Rochester did not wait to knock a second time.

The door being unlocked, he pushed it open and entered, followed by the terror-stricken major-domo and his men.

"Awake, Sir Thomas!" cried Rochester. "Awake! a traitor is within the castle."

There was no reply, and yet Rochester's voice and the noise of the many feet, and the rattle of arms would have been quite sufficient to awaken the soundest sleeper.

Rochester advanced to the bed, and dashing the curtains aside, looked within.

No cry left his lips.

So thunder-stricken was he to behold the empty bed, that he could only stand still and look at it.

"Is the castle haunted?" he said, at last; "or what—here, varlet," he cried, wheeling suddenly round, and confronting the major-domo, "how do you account for *this* ?"

"I do protest, your lordship," replied the amazed major-domo, "that I know no more of this than your lordship."

After a few moments' reflection, during which the unlucky major-domo and his men regarded him with wondering looks, Rochester said—

"After all, Sir Thomas might have fallen off to sleep in the card-room. Let us—but stay! we will see that all is right in the girl's room. You knew that Mistress Voldeck slept with the girl ?"

"Ay, ay, your lordship; I know she did."

"Let us see that *they* have not mysteriously disappeared. Lead the way to the room."

This room was quickly reached, and Rochester himself thundered upon the loor.

But, of course, no answer was returned.

The major-domo's heart sank.

He wished that the flooring would open and swallow him up.

What was passing in Rochester's mind could e seen by the terrible expression on his ace, which was almost distorted by the furnace raging within his breast.

Only once more did he knock, and getting no reply, he pushed the door open.

Hastily the major-domo, lantern in hand, rushed forward.

A terrible cry left his and Rochester's lips, as the dreadful object upon the bed met their eyes,

"Dead!" gasped Rochester, "dead! stabbed to the heart! And the girl gone! She *has* foiled me, then, after all! Foiled me in my own castle! Ha! atrocious fool!" he yelled, raising his sword as if to plunge it into the heart of the cowering major-domo, "canst thou not see that this Lord Verney was a friend of this girl ?"

"Yes, yes, my lord!" faltered the man; but he had the pass—he had the pass, and I was bound to admit him. I but obeyed your instructions."

"I see it all!" exclaimed Rochester; "yes, I see it all! The person you admitted here was that girl's lover—he that I thought safe and sound in the cage at Blood's house. Yes, it was Clifford Hansard in disguise; and by heaven I will have an ample revenge for this. I will leave no stone unturned to trace him. Within a few hours he shall be in my hands. But you say the horse was left in the front of the castle."

"Ay, ay, my lord, 'tis now in the stable."

"Then he cannot have gone far. Listen—he bribed the man you sent with him to show him his room. And that man having received sufficient to warrant his accompanying him, he has done so, and, no doubt, they have left the castle by the subterranean passage."

"If that is so, your lordship," ventured one of the men, "you are certain to have them, for, as both are strangers, they would be lost in the wood."

"Ay, you are no doubt correct. You" he said to the man who had spoken, "proceed to the stables; let six horses be saddled and brought round to the end of the subterranean passage. Do you know the door in the wood ?"

"Ay, ay, your lordship."

"Let not a moment be lost! Now lead the way to the card-room," he said to the major-domo. "With Sir Thomas Cameron at my side, I do not fear but that I shall capture both ere long."

Stowed away in a box in his bedroom

the major-domo had a few hundred crowns, the result of many years' scraping, and every piece he was possessed of he would have willingly given had he been allowed to go behind, instead of being the first forward.

But Rochester was just behind him.

The lantern was raised high as the card-room was entered, and its rays fell upon what looked like the sleeping figure of Sir Thomas Cameron.

"Ha!" said Rochester, "as I expected. He has fallen asleep, and—holy Mary!" he shouted, as he pointed to Sir Thomas's back, which was completely covered with blood, "another terrible deed has been committed. Sir Thomas Cameron has been murdered!"

Completely overpowered now, Rochester sank into the nearest seat, and buried his face in his hands.

Neither the major-domo nor his men spoke one word.

They were far too terrified.

Their nerves were wound up to such a pitch, that had the slightest unusual noise been made they would have fled like rabbits before the ferret.

But in a few seconds the major-domo found his tongue, for he saw upon the table the dagger and the parchment.

"Look, my lord, look!" he said; "a parchment pinned by a dagger to the table!"

Rochester started up.

"Don't touch it!" he cried; "let me take it! let me take it!"

He placed his hand upon the hilt and found with what tremendous force the weapon had been driven into the table.

The first thing he looked at was the dagger.

The hilt was jewelled, and Rochester at once recognised it.

"This," he said, "is Sir Thomas's own dagger. 'Tis one I made him a present of long ago. 'Fore heaven! his own dagger used to pin this paper to the table! Now let us see—what says it?"

The major-domo held the lantern over the parchment, while Rochester, in loud tones, read these words—

"Foiled, my Lord Rochester, foiled! No cage, nor no prison can hold me! Foiled, I say, Rochester! What think you of it? I have mastered you in your own castle! Ha! what will the rabble of the Court say if this becomes known? First I foiled Blood, and now I foil you! Mine the girl is! Mine! base Rochester, I defy you!

"CLIFFORD HANSARD."

"It was Clifford Hansard!" shouted Rochester; it *was* him. I *knew* it was! He has foiled me in my own castle, murdered my dearest friend, and hurled defiance in my teeth! What ho! the key—the key of the subterranean passage!"

"But will you not take horse, your lordship?" asked the major-domo.

"Yes, fool, we will, but not if it so happens that we find them within the passage."

Off rushed the major-domo to get the key.

But, as our readers know, he was doomed to be once more startled and confounded, for of course the key had vanished.

He rushed back to Rochester and informed him of it.

"'Tis as I said," said Rochester "the man was bribed. The villain! let me but get hold of him and I swear that he shall swing from the highest turret. Remember, my men, a hundred guineas to whoever captures the villain! Now bring hammers and axes."

The first door closed of itself, but it was not a very strong one, and soon yielded to the blows of the axes wielded by the men.

Once more the major-domo had to go forward.

He, as well as Rochester, and every one of the others, had his weapons in readiness, but he was not called upon to use them.

Nothing whatever met their gaze until, presently, the major-domo, with a startled cry, recoiled from what seemed like a bundle of clothes upon the ground, and as he did so he dropped the lantern.

But Rochester darting upon it, picked it up, and held it over the figure.

One of the men turned the body over, and the face of the man who had shown "Lord Verney" to his room—a face distorted with agony, was revealed.

The sight of the unfortunate fellow's body had more effect on the men than the others had had.

Here was a body of one of their comrades.

That he had not met his death fairly was plain enough, because the wound was in the back.

"Search him," said Rochester, now absolutely appalled at the deeds which had been committed in such rapid succession.

The major-domo knelt down, and closely searched the body.

But he found nothing.

Blake had not only taken the money he had given the man, but also the other money the fellow happened to have about him, together with two or three paltry trinkets.

"It is thus evident, your lordship," ventured the major-domo, "that the man did not accept a bribe."

"Stand aside, fool!" roared Rochester. "Now you see, my men, what this villain, Clifford Hansard, has done; even slain one of your comrades—you will show him no mercy should we be lucky enough to capture him. Now on to the door."

Hammers and axes were again brought to bear, but it was a long time before this door showed signs of yielding.

It was a small one, but constructed of solid oak, and strengthened with bars and nails—in fact, it had been built for resistance many generations before Rochester reigned Lord of Lorne Castle.

Maddened at the delay, Rochester himself hammered away at the door until he was damp with perspiration.

At last the door yielded.

Forward rushed the major-domo, with Rochester close at his heels.

"Ho!" shouted Rochester, "where are the horses?"

"Here—here, your lordship," replied a voice, the owner of which could not be seen on account of the darkness.

"Where are your lanterns, fool?" shouted Rochester.

"We have links with us," was the reply, "but feared to light them, lest, if the persons we are about to search for should see them, they would take to flight."

"Ay, but light them now; and bring my horse here. Did you think of the pistols?"

"Yes, your lordship. Every holster contains a loaded pistol."

"Mount then, mount! and let the search be made. But I warn you—do not recklessly discharge your weapons, lest you hit the girl."

The links were lighted, and the search began.

Rochester directed the men to search every bush.

The bushes they could not get behind, he ordered them to thrash with heavy sticks.

But there was no result.

On and on they pushed, spreading themselves out in every direction.

Suddenly the major-domo, who had proceeded somewhat in advance of the others, uttered a loud cry.

"Here they are!—here they are!" he shouted!

Instantly Rochester plunged his spurs into his horse's flanks, and bounded forward, followed by his men.

"Where — where are they?" he cried.

"Ha!" replied the major-domo, "I thought I beheld a couple of persons."

"Forward, men!" shouted Rochester. "Let no one escape, or your lives shall answer for it."

At this instant a black figure darted from behind a tree, and was about to rush away; but it was quickly seized by one of the men, and then pounced upon by the others.

"A man, your lordship," they cried.

"Bring him this way," replied Rochester, in an excited tone.

The unfortunate wretch was dragged forward.

The flaming links were held before his face.

"Fools!" cried Rochester. "'Tis old Howland, the charcoal burner? Loose your hold!"

Instantly the man was released.

Panting violently, and nearly breathless, he threw himself on his knees before Rochester.

"I have done no harm, your lordship," he cried.

"What are you doing here? To what do you allude?"

"I thought that perhaps someone had done an injury to your lordship, and your lordship mistook me for that person."

"No matter what you thought. What I should like to know is this:

What are you doing in the wood at this hour?"

"May it please your lordship, I was but collecting——"

"Pah!" interrupted Rochester, with a haughty wave of his hand. "You were not collecting at this hour. Have you seen anyone pass this way?"

"I—I have."

"Two persons? A man and a woman?" asked Rochester, eagerly.

"I *may* have done so," repeated the man, who was as cunning as a fox.

"What do you mean by you *may* have done so, eh?"

"My memory is very bad," whined the man.

"So I am told," sneered Rochester. "But I perceive what you mean. Take these!"

"And he flung, almost in his face, a couple of guineas.

"Now can you remember?"

"Yes."

And thereupon the man gave the full particulars as to what had transpired between Blake and himself, and as to the hostelry they had put up at.

With a cry of joy away went Rochester and his men at full speed towards the "Lorne Arms."

We have learned of their arrival, and, once more, we return to those within the hostelry.

This discovery, on Rochester's part, meant a very great deal to the host.

Rochester, though the ground landlord of more than one hostelry within a bow shot of his castle, was not the owner of the "Lorne Arms;" but the host was only too well aware of the fact that the owner of his house was under Rochester's thumb, and Rochester's word would cause him to be quickly thrust from his holding.

"Alas!" said Clifford, "that I should have brought all this trouble upon you."

"There is no time to speak upon that matter now," replied the host. "Do you leave the young girl in my daughter's hands for a few moments, and she will see that she is made fit for the escape. For the attempt must be at once made."

"At what part of the premises are Rochester and his men?"

"In the front."

Clifford considered a moment.

He asked himself whether it was likely that Blake would give the alarm.

"No," he thought, "he would not do that. It is to his advantage to keep clear of Rochester."

Down the stairs went the host, followed by Clifford, and they proceeded to the door.

In the meantime, the noise made by Rochester and his men, had been fearful.

Just as the host reached the door, Rochester was about to order his men to bring the hammers and axes to bear upon it.

"What, ho!" shouted the host. "What want ye? We can't admit noisy travellers at this time of the night."

"Travellers!" cried Rochester. "If you open the door, knave, I will soon convince you that we are not travellers."

"Well then, if ye are not travellers, what are ye?"

"I am Lord Rochester, and I demand an entry into this house."

"You demand, your lordship? By what right do you make such a demand?"

Turning suddenly to Clifford, he said—

"The poor girl is now, no doubt, ready. Your horse is at the back saddled and bridled; now is your time. Go! and may heaven guard you!"

"You have, indeed, a true heart," said Clifford, with much emotion, as he wrung the host's hand. "I will not forget you."

"Go, young man, go, or all will be lost. Delay not another instant! While I parley here, you make your escape. My daughter will assist you. And remember—take my advice, and keep straight along the high road. Attempt to take to the fields, and a thousand to one you are lost."

"I will take your advice," replied Clifford.

Again he wrung the host's hand, and hastily thanked him.

But his words were lost in the thundering of the hammers and axes upon the door.

Clifford found Olivia and Martha at the foot of the stairs.

Our poor heroine was in a dreadful state of terror; but she kept up her courage as well as she was able, for she knew that Clifford's and her own safety depended upon her maintaining her composure.

"Hesitate not a moment, sir," said Martha, excitedly; "for if you do, you will surely be captured. I know not what that inhuman monster who brought this poor lady here, is doing; but he is making a tremendous noise. Perhaps he is trying to break out of the room. Come, sir, come."

Clifford, pressing a hasty kiss on Olivia's lips, took her in his arms, and followed Martha.

The back door was cautiously opened.

No one was there.

Martha hastily entered the stable, and dark, though it was, she placed the bit in the horse's mouth, and brought him forth.

Clifford set Olivia down and vaulted into the saddle.

Then Martha, having tenderly kissed Olivia—a kiss that was warmly returned, assisted our heroine to mount.

Quickly she was placed before Clifford, who then, with a hurried "God bless you," turned his horse's head.

At that moment Martha hastily seized the bridle.

Her intention was to prevent the animal from crossing the stones of the yard.

But it was too late.

Cross them the horse did, and the loud clatter caused by the iron hoofs instantly attracted Rochester's attention.

Pulling his horse round, he plunged his spurs into its flanks, and was quickly at the side of the house.

"By heaven!" he roared, as he caught sight of horse and riders. "Yonder they go! Away! after them. A thousand crowns to the man who brings him to the ground."

Away rushed the whole of the men on horseback and on foot.

No sooner had they left the spot, than a tremendous smash was heard.

The whole framework of the window above had been demolished.

Another moment, and a dark figure leapt over the balcony, clutched the woodwork for a moment, dropped, and then sped away into the darkness.

It was Blake Barrell.

Fortunately, the horse upon which Clifford was mounted was a powerful one.

Straight along the high road our hero went, with Rochester and his men in full cry.

Every now and then a shot was fired at the retreating horse and riders, but on account of the pace at which they were going, and the darkness, no accurate aim could be taken.

Neither their shots nor cries elicited any response for some time.

But presently Clifford was observed to stop.

"Ha!" roared Rochester, "something has happened. His horse is lame. Hurry, hurry!"

Bang!

The sharp crack of a pistol was heard, and, with a tremendous cry, the major-domo, riding at Rochester's side, fell mortally wounded from his horse.

Rochester and his men paused, but it was only for an instant.

"By heaven!" yelled the former, "if you capture him, my men, the reward shall be *five* thousand crowns."

Here was a reward indeed.

With another rush the men went on.

For another ten minutes the chase was kept up, but the pursuers seemed to get no nearer the pursued.

Rochester and his men had fired all their pistols, but without effect.

When rounding a somewhat sharp curve in the road, Clifford again stopped.

A bright flash lit up the gloomy spot, a sharp crack rang out, and Rochester's horse reared high up, uttered a pitiful neigh, and dropped dead.

Once more the pursuers stopped.

The horsemen dismounted, and assisted their discomfited master to rise.

"Run!" shouted Rochester—"run and get the major-domo's horse. But no—'tis now of no use. They will escape me."

"Your lordship," ventured one of the men, "there is no disguising the fact that that youth is well mounted. Also he appears to be a good shot. Behold! the shot struck your horse close by the left eye. A little higher, and we should have had to mourn your lordship."

"Mourn your lordship!" mimicked Rochester, "or rifle his pockets before he was dead, eh? Pah!"

"I trust your lordship is not hurt?"

"'Tis false. You trust nothing of the kind. Think you I do not know what is passing in your minds?" he asked, savagely. "Lift me up."

The men did so.

"Had we not better drag the body to the roadside, your lordship?" asked one.

"For what reason?"

"So that no passenger will fall over it."

Rochester's laugh rang out at this.

"Fool!" he roared, "think you that I care whether a passenger, or forty passengers fall over it? No; leave it where it is, and return with all speed."

"To the castle?"

"No; to the 'Lorne Arms.' I must have my revenge on someone, and since there is no one else, that someone must be the host of the 'Lorne Arms' and his daughter."

CHAPTER XVI.

OF WHAT TOOK PLACE AT LONG ACRE—OF THE SEDAN-CHAIR TO THE "SHIP TAVERN"—AND OF THE EXTRAORDINARY DARING OF CLIFFORD HANSARD.

OUR readers can easily imagine the sensation caused when our hero and poor Olivia arrived at Sir Richard Wemyss' residence.

It was just about noon when they arrived, and a deplorable sight they presented.

The horse, as well as Clifford and Olivia, were bespattered with mud and nearly dead.

Olivia was taken in hand by Lady Wemyss, and, oh, what joy pervaded her breast, when, presently, a young and beautiful face bent over her, and Lady Wemyss whispered—

"This is Clarissa Jardell, of whom, no doubt, your young lover has spoken."

Clifford had, indeed, told her all about the young girl—all about her and Sir Christopher.

He had told her that their fortunes seemed somehow bound up together, and such seemed to be the case.

Yes; Clarissa Jardell, the doctor, and Sir Christopher were now at the house of Sir Richard Wemyss.

The worthy doctor had been persuaded to take up his residence there with his daughter on account of Blood.

Our hero learned that the monster and his men were now as great a terror as the plague, which, by this time, was raging with appalling fury, and defied the skill of the most clever physicians.

Considering that Blood appeared to be always prowling about the city, and in the quarters where the plague was worst, Sir Christopher considered it certain that eventually he would fall a victim to the disease."

"The worst of it is," said Sir Christopher, gloomily, "if he dies, the secret as to the money dies with him."

"Such then," replied Clifford, "is not my opinion."

"What do you think?"

"I have no business to advise."

"On the contrary," interrupted Sir Christopher, "you have business to think and to suggest; for I have found your suggestions most valuable. Tell me what you think."

"I think that lady of whom you spoke knows quite as much as Blood."

"You mean Mistress Cameron?"

"Ay."

Sir Christopher shook his head.

"I don't think so," he said; "and the reason for my saying so is this: that his majesty is, and has been for a long time, short of money. If Mistress Cameron could get more, she would have done so —not only to keep his majesty favourably disposed towards her, but also to protect, to some extent, her abominable son."

"And Blood is really her son?"

"So the king told me."

"The king?"

"Ay; I had it from his majesty's own lips."

"Gracious heaven!" muttered Clifford, "what a king!—what a son!"

"You may well say that, my young friend."

"Is Mistress Cameron the reigning favourite?"

Sir Christopher smiled.

"There are a good many reigning favourites, I am afraid," he said.

"But I mean, does his majesty devote as much attention to Mistress Claribel Cameron as any other lady?"

"He *must* do, because Mistress Cameron seldom leaves her house, 'The Convent,' in Long Acre, and *never* comes to Court."

"Have you seen her?"

"Two or three times."

"Is she beautiful?"

"Marvellously so. To look at her, one can hardly think it possible she can be old enough to be Blood's mother."

"You do not think that she is well acquainted with the movements of this precious son of hers, and of the fact that he and Rochester are the heads of this White Circle conspiracy?"

"No, no," returned Sir Christopher. "She is a strange, mysterious woman; but I feel certain that she knows nothing, or very little of Blood's movements."

"Is his real name Blood or Cameron?"

"That I know not, Clifford. I have not heard anyone, not even the king, hint anything as to what his real name can be. But he is known only by the name of Blood."

"And that is the real name of Mistress Cameron?"

"Perhaps; but now let me tell you that yesterday I obtained an order from the king, and had the houses on each side of the chambers in Lincoln's Inn searched."

"Ah," exclaimed Clifford, "and the result?"

"Nothing was discovered. It is a mystery how the man could have taken away such a sum of money in so short a time, and unobserved; for that it was a vast sum there can be no doubt."

"Yes, yes," mused Clifford. "I feel certain that the sum was enormous. But you may yet be fortunate to discover, at least, a part of it."

Retiring to his bedroom, Clifford slept soundly for several hours.

When he awoke, he found a new costume awaiting him, and one of the servants informed him that Sir Richard desired to see him as quickly as he had attired himself.

With all speed, therefore, Clifford descended.

What was his joy when he saw, in a huge arm-chair, near the roaring fire, the figure of his beloved Olivia, and on each side of her Lady Wemyss and Clarissa.

After a most affectionate greeting, Clifford, turning to Sir Richard, who was gravely looking on, said—

"Oh, sir, how can I thank all of you for your great attention and kindness!"

"By saying nothing about it, my lad," cried Sir Richard, as he took and warmly wrung Clifford's hand. "Lads of your indomitable courage are not found every day; but when we find them it is our duty to make much of them. But come with me to my study."

Clifford accompanied Sir Richard to his study, and as he proceeded, it struck him that the baronet had news of grave importance to communicate to him.

He was right.

When in the study, Sir Richard closed the door, and turning to Clifford, he said—

"Rochester is in town."

"I expected as much," replied Clifford; "but I presume he knows not that I am here?"

Not that I am aware of. Now listen. Sir Christopher, who has been unable to get here, has sent me a long letter! Here it is, and it informs me that Rochester has brought against you a charge of murder—nay, he charges you with *three* murders!"

"*Three murders?* Impossible!"

"Not so; here is Sir Christopher's letter, which you are at liberty to read.

He, I say, charges you with having committed three murders, and he gives the names of two persons—one is Sir Thomas Cameron——"

"Heavens!" exclaimed Clifford, with a violent start, for he recognised the name, "Sir Thomas Cameron murdered! Then the murderer is Blake Barrell."

"One moment—one moment," cried Sir Richard; "the other is Rochester's housekeeper, one Mistress Voldeck. She was found by Rochester lying on her bed covered with blood. A dagger had been buried in her heart. The other killed was but a common serving man."

"Oh, Sir Richard!" cried Clifford, "of these horrible deeds I am entirely innocent."

"Ay, ay, my lad," replied Sir Richard,

"I am certain of it. But Olivia has given us some idea of the murder of this woman. It is of little account, however, because it seems that she was in such a state of mind at the time she was taken from the bedroom, that she had no time to look or think. Besides, it would not be well to drag her into the matter."

"Sir Christopher Cullum?" cried Clifford. "What thinks he of this matter?"

"The same as we do, my lad—that Blake Barrell is the murderer. But how such a thing is to be proved, I know not; for there were no witnesses—the scoundrel took care of that. But this is not all."

"Not all!" exclaimed Clifford. "Not all the charges he has brought against me?"

"No; this, in my opinion, is the gravest. It is most unaccountable. This is what Sir Christopher says— listen.

"'I have just seen a piece of parchment, bearing what appears to be the handwriting and the signature of Clifford Hansard. It breathes defiance to Rochester. That it is not the handwriting of our young friend, I am certain; but the resemblance is most marvellous. It is now in the possession of the king. It is my opinion, Sir Richard—and you will, no doubt, agree with me—Blake Barrell is not only the author of these terrible murders, but also the writer of that document which was found pinned by a dagger to a table; and all this he has done with a view of getting Clifford arrested and thrown into prison. The king is terribly enraged, and, at present, will not listen to what I would say.

"'Clifford must instantly leave your residence, for if the king should order his arrest pending inquiries, Rochester is bound to get to know that the young girl, Olivia, is with you; and though Rochester himself is not to be feared, he has Blood and his miscreants at his call.'"

Now, indeed, Clifford was beginning to see what a terrible enemy was Blake Barrell.

"It is my fate, I suppose," he said, in tones of deep emotion. "I have rescued Olivia Preston from destruction, only to be once more separated from her."

"The clouds are black, indeed, at present, my lad," said Sir Richard, laying his hand on Clifford's shoulder, and looking kindly into his face; "but hope on. Fear not, the black clouds will roll away, and sunshine will take their place. Remember that I am of Sir Christopher's opinion—that is, that it would be better for yourself and your affianced, Olivia Preston, that you at once depart."

"I thank you from the bottom of my heart," replied Clifford, warmly clasping the hand held towards him. "It wi'l, as you say, be best that I should go."

"It will," answered Sir Richard, sadly; "but fear not that you will be well looked after. Here is a heavy purse. That has been sent here by Sir Christopher, who begs you will accept it. It contains two hundred guineas. And here is another. That contains three hundred guineas. Take both, and as quickly as possible, place them in the hands of some honest person to whom you can go when in want of money. Now listen to this—

"Thinking that you would decide to go, I have written a letter to a person of my acquaintance, residing at the further end of Long Acre. Behold it. Read."

Clifford took the letter and read aloud—

"To Master Graystock,
        "Costumier,
            "Long Acre."

"Right," said Sir Richard, "and you will place it in his hands only. Leave this house secretly, and hurry off to Master Graystock. By the way, if it so pleases you, he is a man to be trusted with *any amount* of money."

"I will not forget that fact," replied Clifford. "And you advise me to be off at once?"

"Yes. You had better take an immediate farewell of Olivia. She will understand that the parting is but for a short time, and is for the best. My dear boy, I bid you a lieu for the present. If you should, unfortunately, get into any difficulty, remember that I am your firm friend. Remember also that letters to Sir Christopher Cullum, or to Doctor Jardell, will reach them if sent here."

In less than half-an-hour, Clifford Hansard had left the house.

"'ANY MESSAGE YOU MAY ENTRUST ME WITH, I WILL FAITHFULLY DELIVER,' CRIED DRINKWATER."

Olivia Preston understood how necessary it was that they should part; but in her present state, the blow fell upon the poor girl with dreadful effect.

Her sobs were heartrending, and not even the consoling words and tender caresses of the beautiful Lady Wemyss, or the equally lovely Clarissa, had the effect of checking her deep grief.

Clifford proceeded to Long Acre on foot, and knowing the necessity of concealing himself as well as he was able, for there was no telling when Blood, or his myrmidons, or Rochester, might suddenly make their appearance, he took the precaution of keeping well within the shadow of the houses.

The sights he beheld during that short journey were fearful.

The dead lay about in every direction, ready for removal.

Nearly every street was full of blackened wood ashes, the remains of the huge fires which, by command of the Lord Mayor, had been lit with the view of purifying the tainted air, but which had not the slightest effect upon it.

The only result was that the ashes, being moistened by the rain, turned into black, filthy mud.

Clifford met very few persons on his way.

Those he did meet seemed to shrink from him as if suspicious.

Now and then his footsteps, being heard by the few miserable wretches left within the plague-stricken houses, a window would be thrown open, a ghastly face thrust forth, and a voice would cry out—

"Hold! hold! kind sir. In heaven's name, find us help."

Or another would shout—

"Heaven save you, sir. From the plague we are perishing."

More than once Clifford heard the sweet, but plaintive voice of a child, who, having heard his footsteps, peered from the window, and was crying to him—

"Master! master! here is money! Do—do buy me some food!"

Clifford's kind, honest heart felt bursting, but he was compelled to turn a deaf ear to these dreadful cries.

As a contrast to some of these heartrending appeals, he saw, on the balcony of a house, near Long Acre, the figures of two men.

They had dragged on to the balcony a small table and a couple of chairs, and beside them stood at least a dozen bottles of spirits or wine, while on the table was a number of cards.

"Eat, drink, and be merry," they yelled; for to-morrow ye die!"

As Clifford passed they looked over the balcony at the risk of falling over, and breaking their necks, and shouted—

"A last game!—a last game! We have the plague, and must die! Ha, stranger, what are you? Whither are you bound? Join us—join us! Come, we have wine, and you shall share it with us!"

Again, beside the doorway of another house, a large and noble building, and one which Clifford well remembered to have visited when in the service of the locksmith, Clifford observed the kneeling figure of a woman.

He passed very near her, and was shocked to recognise the once beautiful mistress of the house.

Evidently the poor creature had caught the dreadful disease, and in loud impassionate tones, she was bemoaning the loss of her husband and children.

"All, all gone!" she shrieked, in tones which echoed again and again along the gloomy streets. "All gone! My husband and all my children."

With heartrending crys and sobs, and groans, she beat her breast, still calling for her husband and children.

Poor creature! her sorrows had turned her brain!

"Alas!" murmured Clifford, "she will soon be in heaven to join those she has lost! Poor creatures! This plague is dreadful! When—when will it end? Heaven only knows when!"

These last four words he uttered aloud, and a voice instantly replied to him—

"Ah!" it said, "when—when? Great powers! *when* indeed!"

Clifford turned, and saw in a doorway close at his side the figure of a man.

No sooner did the man look into Clifford's face, than a cry of wonder left his lips.

He started forward, and clutched Clifford by the hand.

For an instant our hero, fearing that the man had the plague, started back, endeavouring to wrench his hand free.

"Fear nothing, Clifford Hansard," said the man, sadly. "I have not the plague—not yet—not yet."

"Great heaven!" exclaimed Clifford, "do I really see before me Martin Waltman?"

"You do indeed, my young friend. It is Martin Waltman, once host of the 'Lorne Arms.'"

"Once host? Alas! has Rochester—"

"Rochester has wreaked his vengeance on me. You had not gone long ere he and his men came again to the house. They broke in, and a fight occurred, during which my poor daughter was shot!"

"Great heaven! Shot?"

"Yes."

"But who—who fired upon her?"

Martin Waltman shook his head.

"No one could tell that," he said, "for the fight took place in the darkness. It was, of course, Rochester's intention to wreak his vengeance on me. But when he found my daughter was shot, he withdrew his men. Then he ordered me to take the body of my daughter in my arms and come forth."

"I did so, and the monster then fired the house, which was soon reduced to a heap of ashes.

"A friend promised to see to my daughter, and I know the promise will be faithfully fulfilled. I hurried away in case Rochester should cause me to be arrested.

"And here I am, young man—here in London, friendless and penniless—for I have been to Finsbury, and found that my brother and his family have all died of the plague."

Clifford was shocked—completely overcome with this dreadful story.

He considered, and very rightly too, that this man's sufferings had arisen through the protection he had afforded him.

"Martin," he said, taking both hands of the unlucky host, "you shall not want a friend while I live. No, no; I swear you shall not. See here—this purse contains the sum of two hundred guineas; 'tis yours."

"No, no; I cannot think of taking it."

"You must—you must have it. Fear not, you shall always find a friend in me."

"One moment; you arrived in London safely?"

"I did."

"And the poor girl?"

"Is also safe, and in the hands of kind friends. But what of Blake Barrell?"

"He escaped from the house before Rochester and his men returned to it."

"Well, come with me; and when we are out of the streets I will tell you more."

The house of the costumier, Master Graystock, was soon found.

It was a small wooden building, standing far back from the road.

Clifford found it closed, and quite dark.

Upon his tapping gently on the rotten-looking door, a voice cried out—

"Who's there?"

"A customer."

"Eh? a customer? Well, master customer, I cannot serve you."

"My friend," whispered Clifford, through one of the cracks, "I bear a letter from Sir Richard Wemyss."

"Oh, indeed!" was the reply, and instantly the shop became illuminated with a bright light. "A letter, eh? Well, well, my friend, just push it through the crack."

Clifford did so, and the cautious old man, having carefully read it, proceeded to unlock the door.

"Enter," he said, "but—hillo! there are two of you. Who is this man?"

"This is a friend of mine," replied Clifford.

"Ah, very well. Enter both of you, and close the door. You see, my friends, in these times we have to be very careful. Those villains in the service of this Colonel Blood, Captain Drinkwater and John Jeevers, are here, there, and everywhere. They rob and murder incessantly. Lord! it's horrible business. What will become of the city and its people?"

"Heaven only knows," replied Clifford.

"You are right," said Master Graystock. "But now let us see. Sir Richard says that I am to furnish you with whatsoever disguise you may think proper to select. Good. As you see, I have plenty from which you can select."

"In the first place," said Clifford, "I wish to place in your hands a sum of money. Here is a purse containing three hundred guineas, and my friend's contains two hundred."

"I will take charge of your money, young sir; but bear this in mind: London is now so full of dastardly assassins, that there is never any telling when a man may meet with a terrible and violent death. Then there is the plague. At any moment a man may be overtaken. I make these remarks in case anything happens to me."

"Yes, yes; I fully understand you. Now take the money, and I will pay you for your trouble."

"Not so. The letter says that I am to look to Sir Richard for payment. Besides furnishing you with whatever costumes you may select, I am to do as much else as I can for you. From what Sir Richard says you have met with many misfortunes."

"I have indeed," replied Clifford; "and so has my friend here."

At that moment a loud knock came upon the door.

"Disappear behind yonder counter," whispered Master Graystock.

Clifford and his companion having concealed themselves behind a huge array of clothes, the costumier opened the door.

A young woman, closely muffled, appeared.

"Well," queried the costumier, "and what seek you?"

"Ah," replied the young woman, "then you know me not, Master Graystock. Have but a few days so changed me?"

"Holy Mary!" cried Master Graystock, "'tis Caroline Bury, Mistress Cameron's maid."

"Yes, 'tis indeed Caroline," was the reply, in sad tones. "And do you think me much changed?"

"Yes. But enter, my dear. How fares it at the convent?"

"There are only us two left."

"Only you two—your mistress and yourself?"

The maid nodded.

The costumier raised his hands in horror.

"The other servants then are dead?" he said.

"Yes," faltered the maid, "all are dead. But let me tell you my business. My mistress implores you to provide her with a sedan-chair and two attendants."

"Impossible!" exclaimed the costumier. "I could not get a man for love or money. And your mistress wishes to set out upon a journey?" he asked, in tones of astonishment. "In heaven's name, girl, where does she wish to go?"

"To the 'Ship Tavern.'"

Master Graystock fixed upon the girl's face a look of incredulity.

"Impossible!" he said.

"No," was the reply. "She wishes to go to the 'Ship Tavern.'"

"Has she ever been there before?"

"Never to my knowledge."

"Is she aware that the 'Ship Tavern,' at the side of the Tower of London, is the resort of the lowest of the low? Is she aware that she would not be safe there for a single instant?"

"She said but little about the place to me. But I do not think anything would happen to her. She is about to visit an individual who would take care she was safe."

"And who is that?"

"*Colonel Blood!*" whispered the girl.

"Colonel Blood! Heavens! Everyone seems to talk of that villain. Well, well, my dear, what is your mistress's business is no business of mine."

"Mistress Cameron says that if you will get her a couple of trustworthy men, she will pay you a large sum."

"My dear girl," cried the costumier, "I tell you that it is impossible to procure the men; but stay—stay! Now I come to think of it, I fancy that I know where to find *one* man. He may find another, and, in that case, the difficulty will be removed. Return to your mistress, and say that I will try hard for the men."

"Good-bye, Master Graystock," said the girl, turning.

"Good-bye, my dear girl. Keep up your courage."

"Alas!" replied the poor girl, in bitter tones, "I fear my time on earth will soon expire. All my fellow-servants, my parents, my brothers, and sisters—all—all are swept away."

"Lord have mercy upon us!" cried the costumier, in fervent tones, as he opened the door. "These are, indeed, days of darkness."

When the girl had gone, he carefully closed the door.

As soon as he had done so, Clifford rushed forward.

"Sir," he exclaimed, "you can render me a great service.

"Indeed! How?"

"By letting me and my friend act as chair-bearers for Mistress Cameron."

The costumier was amazed.

"The request is a most extraordinary one," he said. "Why, may I ask, do you make it?"

Clifford told him of what had occurred between Blood and himself, and of the money which the ruffian had stolen from Sir Christopher Cullum.

"Then," said the costumier, "are you under the impression that this lady has something to do with the money?"

"No, not exactly; but knowing Blood's way of boasting, he might, in the course of conversation, let out something of the secret."

"Well, Master Clifford Hansard, your request is granted. But let me tell you this: your disguise must be perfection itself, for if Colonel Blood happened to recognise you—well, you may easily guess the result. You would *never* escape from the 'Ship Tavern.'"

"What disguise would you recommend us?" asked Clifford.

"Chair - bearers. The costume is simple, and will not inconvenience you in any way. Within your jerkins you can carry a couple of small pistols and a dagger. Thus, in the event of needing them, they will be ready to your hand. Blood does not know your friend here, perhaps?"

"Nay, he knows me not," said Waltman.

"Well, Master Hansard, come with me, and I will so alter your face that your dearest friend would not know you. While we retire, your companion can change his clothes."

Having procured the two costumes required, Master Graystock led Clifford into an inner room.

They were absent some quarter of an hour, and when Clifford reappeared, he was so completely altered, that Waltman uttered a cry of astonishment.

"What think you of it?" smiled the costumier.

"Marvellous," answered Waltman.

Clifford's face had been plastered with a mixed powder of some kind, which had then been wiped off, and his cheeks, upper lip, and chin dotted with a hard brush dipped in some black preparation, so that he looked like a man sadly in want of a shave.

His hair now appeared to be turning grey.

Attired as he now was in the "costume" generally adopted by chair men, linkmen, and the like, it was utterly impossible that anyone would recognise him.

Having provided Clifford and Waltman with lanterns, the costumier led them through a door in the back of the building, and an out-house was reached.

Here there were several sedan-chairs

The costumier pointed out one covered with a cloth.

"That," he said, "is the one Mistress Cameron has been in the habit of using."

Clifford took off the cloth, and there was revealed an elegant chair, cream coloured, and profusely ornamented with gold and silver.

The interior was beautifully decorated and cushioned.

Clifford and Waltman soon had it out, and into the street.

"Farewell, my young friend," said the costumier. "I trust you may be successful. But you will remember that whatever happens, you are to protect the lady."

"I will not forget that," replied Clifford.

"And also do not forget that you are to change your *voice*. Blood is as sharp and as cunning as a fox, and he might smell a rat in an instant if you happened to speak in your natural tones. '

With many thanks and a promise to return as soon as it was possible, the pair set off to the "Convent."

It was the first time Clifford had ever been there, and, consequently, he was unable to see what a great change had occurred even on the exterior of the house.

The grounds presented a most deplorable appearance.

No one, to look at the surroundings, would have thought that a single soul resided there.

On every door was painted the fatal red cross, and the words—

Lord have mercy upon us!

For a long time the Convent had remained untouched, but suddenly the destroying angel had swooped upon it, and all its inmates, with the exception of Mistress Cameron and her maid, were carried away in less than *two* days.

Blood soon found out that the plague had attacked the house, and though he had business of importance to transact with its mistress, he did not go there.

The king's visits were not by any means frequent, but his love for the lady compelled him to pay attention to her at times.

Up the avenue went Clifford and Waltman. Their footsteps were heard before they reached the door, which, when it was gained, they found open, and the maid beside it.

"Thank goodness you have come," she said, "for my mistress is most anxious to set out upon her journey, dangerous though it be."

"We have come as quickly as possible," said Clifford. "Men are scarce in these days, mistress."

"Ay," replied the maid, "and so are women. Wait, and I will inform my mistress of your arrival."

But Mistress Cameron had also heard the arrival of the sedan-chair, and was descending the stairs, quite ready to depart.

She was attired in a heavy cloak, lined with costly fur.

A fur hood concealed her head, but not her face—beautiful as a poet's dream—but sad beyond description.

Her eyes were somewhat hollow, and the dark rings around them showed plainly that she had recently been weeping.

She was weak, too, for when the maid held out her arm, she gladly rested upon it.

"I shall not be long, Caroline," she said. "You will wait up for me?"

"Oh, madam, I could not rest in my bed were you absent."

"You should go with me, Caroline; but 'twould not be safe to leave the house entirely deserted; and, besides, Master Rushton might come at any moment."

"If he happens to come I am not to say whither you have gone?"

"No, no. On your life, no!"

Clifford opened the door of the chair, and respectfully stood aside, while Caroline escorted her mistress to it.

For an instant Mistress Cameron fixed her eyes upon Clifford's face.

"Have you ever borne me before?" she asked.

"Nay, lady," answered Clifford; "nor has my comrade here. Nearly all in our line of business have been carried off by the plague."

"Ah, yes," sighed Mistress Cameron. "The plague spares neither the rich nor the poor. But if you serve me faithfully, my men, I will well repay you. The streets are full of desperate men."

"We will carry you safely, lady; and we will defend you from any attack with our lives."

"I thank you. My destination is the 'Ship Tavern' at the Tower. Dost know it?"

"Right well, lady."

Mistress Cameron entered the chair, and the journey was commenced.

It was a terrible journey—a journey which Clifford never forgot so long as he lived.

There was hardly a shop or private house in any of the thoroughfares through which they passed that did not bear, either on its door or shutters, the fatal cross.

The owners of some houses and shops having packed up what goods they could, and fled into the country, the *looters* were hard at work taking what remained.

The doors and shutters of other houses had been nailed up.

Mistress Cameron saw a little of the terrible sights which were passed.

So horror-stricken was she, that burying her face in her hands, she remained in that position until the "Ship Tavern" was reached.

This noted old hostelry—the scene of many incidents recorded in history—was the resort of men connected with the sea.

Sailors of all nationalities congregated there; and, as a matter of course, where they were to be found, so were also the "land-sharks," the villains who hung round the drunkards, and "saw them to their homes"—in other words, took them to some dark spot, and robbed, and, perhaps, murdered them.

The "Ship" was also one of the "resting" places of Colonel Blood and his followers.

The first floor, consisting of one very large room, and two smaller ones, was expressly set apart for him.

The large room, which Blood used as his "reception" room, was very handsomely furnished.

He transacted a great deal of business with France, and his messengers between that country and this were smugglers.

The two smaller rooms communicated with the larger by folding doors.

One was a bed-room, and the other Blood was pleased to call his "cabinet."

The sedan-chair was set down before the principal door of the tavern, and it at once became the object of attention.

A crowd of ugly, desperate-looking wretches surrounded it, and their whisperings and pointings caused Clifford great uneasiness.

Suddenly a man pushed his way through the crowd.

In him Clifford recognised Captain Drinkwater.

Though he felt inclined to send a ball through the ruffian's heart, he was well aware of the fact that, on this occasion, at any rate, he must gain his confidence.

"Hi!" said Clifford, seizing him by the shoulder, and whispering into his ear. "Hi! the lady in this chair is Mistress Cameron."

"Lord!" gasped Drinkwater, "never!"

"Such is the case. Look!"

The captain did look, and Mistress Cameron happening to glance up as he poked his bloated face within the chair, he had a full view of her features.

"Sarvan't, ma'am," said Drinkwater, snatching off his greasy hat—"sarvant, ma'am. I trust you are quite well, ma'am?"

"She wishes to see the colonel," whispered Clifford.

"Ma'am," said Drinkwater, "I have the honour to be one of the noble colonel's body guard."

"His body guard?" repeated Mistress Cameron in astonishment.

"That is so, ma'am," replied the captain; "and any message you may entrust me with, I will faithfully deliver."

"The colonel is within the tavern, then?" asked Mistress Cameron, eagerly.

"He is, ma'am."

"Is he alone?"

"*Quite* alone."

"Whom does he expect?"

"Haven't the least idea, ma'am."

By this time the crowd had considerably increased, a fact which Mistress Cameron noticed with much uneasiness.

"My chairman will convey a message to Colonel Blood," she said, "if you will be kind enough to stay here, and see that I am not interfered with."

Drinkwater bowed.

"I will see that no harm happens to you, ma'am. Away!" he yelled, suddenly turning upon those behind him. "Away, lest Colonel Blood, whom this lady has come to see, suddenly makes known his presence by plunging his sword through your vile bodies. Now then, you chairman, come forward."

Clifford came forward.

Drinkwater wished very much to hear what the lady said; but though he craned his neck forward, he caught not one word.

Mistress Cameron whispered in Clifford's ear.

"Good, madam," replied Clifford, "I will do exactly as you say."

"Here," whispered Drinkwater, clutching his arm, "you will find a door on the landing closed. Place your mouth to the keyhole, and say '*The Black Priory*,' and the door will open. Then go up a few more steps, and the colonel's room will be reached."

Clifford nodded, and elbowing his way through the motley crew assembled around the threshold, he ascended the stairs.

Reaching the landing he did as Drinkwater had directed; the door instantly flew back, Clifford passed through, and the door again closed.

It was evident that if anyone, who had no business there, happened to get possession of the password and passed through, they would not get out again very easily.

The door of the reception room was ajar.

Upon it Clifford knocked, and a well-remembered voice said, in surly tones—

"Enter!"

Clifford pushed open the door, and once more stood before Colonel Blood.

Attired in a splendid costume, the wretch was sitting at a large table, busy in the perusal of a number of documents.

No sooner did his eyes rest upon Clifford's strange figure, than a muttered exclamation escaped his lips.

Leaning back in his chair, he surveyed our hero from head to foot.

"What do *you* want?" he cried. "How came you with the password?"

Two loaded pistols were within our hero's jerkin.

He had only to plunge his hand within it to bring one forth.

And, from his position, was it likely that he could miss his man?

No.

But he must hold his hand on this occasion; he knew that only too well.

And yet, the temptation to lay this monster dead at his feet was almost irresistible.

"May it please you," said Clifford, "the password was given to me by a man below—one of your own men."

"Describe the man; but first—what are you? A chairbearer?"

"I am."

"Well, go on; describe the man."

Clifford did so.

"And," he continued, "the man is outside seeing that no harm comes to the lady we have brought from Long Acre in a chair."

"Holy Mary!" exclaimed Blood, starting from his seat. "A lady from Long Acre."

"The lady's name is Mistress Cameron."

"By the thunder of Job, this *is* news indeed!" muttered Blood; or, rather, I suppose she *brings* news. What can have caused her to stir from her plague-stricken house? Well, my man," he said aloud, as he threw a guinea across the table, "I will at once see the lady. Conduct her up the stairs, and when you have shown her into this room, close the door, descend, and remain without the hostelry until you are called. And look you, the man who gave you the password is to remain below. Understand?"

"Perfectly."

And down went Clifford, the door on the landing—the machinery of which was manipulated by Blood—opening as soon as he reached it.

When Clifford had given Drinkwater his directions, which were not at all relished, he opened the chair door, and having told Mistress Cameron what the Colonel had said, she got out, a movement which instantly caused considerable commotion among the loafers, some of whom pressed forward.

But they failed to see the face of the beautiful woman, for Mistress Cameron drew her hood over it in such a manner, that only her eyes were visible.

Drinkwater cleared the way, and Clifford escorted the lady.

Quickly she ascended the stairs, and when once more Clifford uttered the password, the door opened, and the pair passed through.

In a few moments Mistress Cameron was within the reception room.

"Now close the door, my man," said Blood; "and when you get on the other side of the door on the landing, shout 'right.'"

Clifford nodded.

He got to the door on the landing, but he did not pass through it.

Craning his neck forward, he shouted "Right," and the door closed with a bang.

Like a flash of lightning Clifford was through a door at the end of the landing, and within a few yards of the one leading to the "reception" room.

It was a bed-chamber.

Getting beneath the bed he listened attentively.

"My dear madame," said Blood, when the door on the landing had closed, "what on earth can have caused you to pay me this visit?"

"Listen, Cecil, I wish to transact what business I have with you as speedily as possible. This is, indeed, a most horrible place. What on earth causes you to have quarters——"

"Hold!" cried Blood. "Remember our arrangements — our agreements. You were to go your way. I was to go mine."

"Yes, yes; I remember."

"Dismiss from your mind all thoughts as to the character of this house, which is quite as good as a few others I could name, and of which you know. Now tell me what has brought you here."

"Cecil, I am in want of money."

"My dear madame, you may not think it, but it is a fact that everybody is in want of money. *The king himself is in want of it.*

This direct shot was not lost upon Mistress Cameron.

She looked up into Blood's face, and she well knew the meaning of the glance he directed upon her.

"Ah!" she sighed, "no one knows better than myself how stands the king's private treasury."

"To be sure—to be sure," chuckled Blood. "Has his most gracious majesty been worrying you?"

"Not exactly worrying, but he has again and again urged upon me the necessity of procuring him some ready money."

"Confound his impudence!" cried Blood; "but your reply?"

"I have said I would try."

"He knew where you would eventually go to get it."

"I fancy so."

"What sum does he want?"

"Ten thousand pounds."

Blood uttered a cry of astonishment.

"He must be mad," he said.

"No; he seems sane enough."

"Do you know what he wants this money for?"

Mistress Cameron shook her head.

"What security does he offer?" asked Blood.

"His royal bond," replied Mistress Cameron.

"Not worth *that*," cried Blood, snapping his fingers. "I cannot let you have the money—nay, I have it not."

"Listen to me, Cecil. The advancing of this money means this: your own safety."

"Ha! What mean you?"

"I mean this—from what the king has said to me, I fancy that unless the sum I have mentioned is at once advanced, you will once more find yourself in Newgate."

"Oh, indeed, that is the arrangement, is it? You mean this: the *lending* of the sum of ten thousand pounds is *giving* it away, and that by giving it to his gracious majesty, I purchase my safety. But do you really think it possible that I am in possession of this sum?"

"You may not have it about you, of course; but you can easily get it."

"Where?"

"*At Lincoln's-inn-Fields.*"

Blood paused a few moments before he gave a reply to this.

At last he said—

"Yes, there is a huge sum of money in that neighbourhood, my property; but it would necessitate a great amount of trouble to get it."

"Then you *will* let me have the money?" cried Mistress Cameron, excitedly, as she started up. "Oh, thanks, Cecil, thanks — a thousand thanks."

"Yes," replied Blood, "I will let you have the money, because my safety is an important matter."

"You will not have so very much trouble; for did you not tell me that you had only to enter a vault, and then——"

"Not so," interrupted Blood. "I told you that I shall, first of all, have to enter the office of Master Prior, the attorney, pass through his strong room, and thence get into the vault which holds those bags of money. Then there is the task of conveying them to the horses I should have to take. But I will get the money, and have a firmer hold over the king."

"When — when?" asked Mistress Cameron, eagerly.

"You may expect me at the 'Convent' some time after midnight."

Clifford waited to hear no more.

The precious secret was in his possession.

He looked round the room for the ready means of escape.

He saw that there was a small window at the further end, partially concealed by curtains.

Creeping up to it, he drew the curtains aside, pushed back the catch, and opened the window.

Looking out he saw that a small wooden balcony was before it.

He did not pause to consider whether it was strong enough to hold his weight; but he quickly found that it was a construction intended more for ornament than use, for as soon as he stood upon it, it swayed dangerously.

Gently closing the window he looked below.

He found that he was at the back of the house.

He could not see anyone below.

Very carefully he got over the balcony, hung for a few seconds, and then dropped.

He had been observed, for no sooner did he reach the ground, than a dark figure darted upon him, and seized him by the shoulders.

Almost at the same instant another figure dashed to the spot, and a heavy blow stretched Clifford's captor at his feet.

"Only just in time," whispered Waltman, for he it was, as he clutched Clifford, and drew him swiftly from the spot; "and I certainly should not have seen you but for the fact that I had become uneasy, and was walking up and down the front and back. Come—quick —the man evidently did not see your face, neither did he see mine."

This was quite true.

The sedan-chair was quickly reached, and the pair sat upon the handles, for all the world as if nothing had occurred.

In a few seconds the man, whom Waltman had knocked down, came swiftly round to the front.

He was evidently a bully after Drinkwater's stamp; an individual who thought a very great deal of himself.

He saw the two chair-bearers; but he paid not the slightest attention to them.

He was soon heard telling his story, but that it was not believed was evident by the loud shouts with which it was greeted.

"What have you learned?" asked Waltman. Did you manage to overhear any part of their conversation?"

"Ay, I did. I have heard all—all! Sir Christopher Cullum's money shall be in my possession within two hours! You will assist me?"

"Ay, with all my heart. But there is a very large sum?"

"Enormous, I fancy."

"In what part of London is it?"

"Lincoln's Inn."

"And if you succeed in recovering it, where will you place it?"

"You shall see. But hist—she comes!"

The interview between Blood and Mistress Cameron had terminated, and from the commotion round the entrance to the hostelry, it was evident that the lady was coming out.

On all sides the men eagerly pressed forward in order to get a view of the lady; but they failed, for, as before, Mistress Cameron had concealed her features with her hood.

"Stand back!" roared Drinkwater, pushing the men from before him, and receiving for his pains more than one ugly blow. "Stand back! Out of it! Room—room for a lady! Stand back, fools!"

And Drinkwater drew his sword.

"Colonel Blood is approaching!" he shouted. "Stand aside, I tell you!"

Eventually Mistress Cameron was escorted to the chair.

"Home," she whispered; "and as speedily as possible."

Having reached the house in Long Acre, Mistress Cameron said—

"You have well performed your duty, my men. If you will wait here but a short time, I will reward you well."

"Pardon us," said Clifford; "but would your ladyship be pleased to hand over whatever you may think proper to give us to Master Graystock? We have other duties to attend to, your ladyship, and are anxious to get away."

"Be it so," answered Mistress Cameron. "Without fail the money shall be lodged with Master Graystock."

Once more Clifford and Waltman proceeded.

Having got out of sight, Clifford said—

"Now let us make for the back streets, and as quickly as possible."

"But the chair?"

"We will take that with us," replied Clifford; and I hope that the next thing it will carry will be gold. Ah, if I am only successful, I shall not only recover at least a portion of Sir Christopher's property, but I shall deal a stunning blow at that villain—Colonel Blood!"

CHAPTER XVII.

SHOWS HOW CLIFFORD OBTAINED AN ENTRY INTO THE VAULT—OF HOW HE CARRIED OFF THE BAGS OF GOLD — AND OF WHAT EXTRAORDINARY THING HAPPENED TO COLONEL BLOOD.

SWIFTLY through the gloomy and deserted streets went Clifford and his friend.

They proceeded as noiselessly as possible, so as not to attract attention.

Yet they were seen by many a miserable wretch, cooped up in the Red Cross marked houses, and doomed to die of the plague or starvation.

Time after time a window was silently opened, a ghastly face was thrust forth, asking for help.

Both Clifford and Waltman were compelled to move on. They knew they could give no help, and that they had a dangerous task to perform in securing the money left in the vaults by Blood.

In one or two of the narrow, miserable turnings they passed through mothers thrust their children to the window—poor little mites, hollow-eyed and wasted, and for their sakes, pleaded.

Alas! all appeals had to be ignored. Clifford would willingly have helped the poor wretches; but he had not the power, and he knew, as also did Waltman, the fearful danger of attempting to do so.

Hardly a dozen persons did they meet on the journey to Lincoln's Inn.

Two or three of these, as soon as they saw the chair, the windows of which were closed, took to their heels, and ran like the wind.

It was evident they were under the impression that the chair held some person attacked with the plague.

On the west side of Lincoln's Inn they came upon three men with a plague cart.

Each man had a lantern.

The light from them threw a strange, weird glow on their repulsive faces.

Clifford shuddered as he recognised in one of them the mercenary wretch, Mollbury.

They were bending over the bodies of two unfortunate wretches who had died of the plague.

"What are they doing?" whispered Waltman.

"They are robbing the bodies of whatsoever articles of value they may have on them."

"The wretches!" exclaimed Waltman.

"It is a strange thing," said Clifford, " but, nevertheless, a fact, that those villains who continually mix up with, and despoil those who have died of this horrible disease, seem to escape it. But their time will come——their time will come."

Lincoln's Inn was reached at last.

Clifford thought it likely that they would have some difficulty in passing the gates; but no, the gates were open, and there was not a soul to interfere with them.

But as soon as the centre of the square was reached, two watchmen made their appearance.

"Hold!" said one, thrusting a lantern almost into Clifford's face. "Hold! Who are you, and whom have you there?"

"You can see what we are if you are not blind," replied Clifford.

"Silence, thou saucy knave!" cried the watchman, furiously. "I want to know who is within that chair. Tell me, or we will pull the door open."

"You will do so to your cost!" cried Clifford. "We are on our way to the office of Master Prior."

The watchman was evidently astonished.

"Why," he said, "I understood that Master Prior had died of the plague!"

"My friend, there is a great deal of misunderstanding in existence nowadays," said Clifford.

He feared lest the man should persist in opening the door; for, in that case, it was almost a certainty that they would be turned back.

But, after a brief consultation with his comrade, the fellow said—

"Pass on."

And once again, and at increased speed, Clifford and Waltman proceeded.

The well-remembered spot was reached at last.

On the left side were a number of builder's utensils, covered with a large tarpaulin.

Some kind of work had been commenced; but when it was to be finished, heaven only knew.

"See," whispered Clifford, "let us take this tarpaulin off, and cover the chair with it. Thus, if the watchmen come, they will fancy that we have left by this gate."

"Where does that lead to?"

"Chancery Lane."

"I observe that it is barred."

"You are right. But when we are ready, we will quickly unfasten it."

Waltman felt that they were about to transact some risky business! but he was a man of great courage.

"You are certain that you know the place?" he asked.

"Thoroughly well," replied Clifford.

"I suppose you will force the lock?"

"No; the lock leading to the attorney's office I put on myself, and know well enough that it could not be forced without a considerable noise being made. We will not enter by the door, but by a window at the side—that is, if I am lucky enough to—— Ha! I have it," he cried, as he picked from among the building materials a large iron bar. "This is the very thing. Now, conceal your lantern beneath your cloak, and let us descend."

But a few steps were necessary to reach the office of Master Prior.

For many, many weeks it had been closed.

The watchman was perfectly correct when he said that he thought Master Prior had died of the plague.

It had not only seized the master, but every clerk connected with him.

At the bottom of the short flight of steps, Clifford nearly fell over something which lay on the ground.

Taking the lantern, he held it down, and was horrified to behold the lifeless body of a man.

It seemed certain that he had had something to do with the chambers, for he held a key in one of his hands.

"Touch him not," whispered Waltman, "if you value your life."

"Hold your lantern again," said Clifford, "and let us commence operations on the window bars.

Some little distance from the office door, which was barred and padlocked, was a small window.

It was secured with three thick iron bars, which appeared capable of resisting any ordinary force brought to bear on them.

But Clifford's iron bar proved a splendid lever.

Yet he could not have forced the bars out alone.

All his and Waltman's strength was necessary to move one of them.

The time it took too was great, and when the first bar was forced out, and fell with a thud to the ground, Clifford heard with dismay a neighbouring clock proclaiming the fact that three hours had passed since they had left the "Ship."

The second bar quickly followed the first, and then the third was forced from the already broken stonework.

"Now the most difficult task is over," said Clifford. "Hoist me up, Waltman, and then hand me the lantern."

"You do not want me to enter?"

"No, no; for you must take the money as I hand the bags to you."

Waltman handed Clifford up, and very quickly he was through the aperture, and the lantern was handed him.

"Be not alarmed," said Clifford, "if you hear the noise of a shot."

What an office it was in which Clifford now stood!

How changed since last he saw it.

When he had been in the habit of going to that office to attend to the locks, all had been life and bustle, for Master Prior was a popular and successful attorney.

Now the silence of the grave reigned.

On the tables lay piles of manuscripts and rolls of parchment, thickly coated with dust.

At the further end of the office was a large iron rack.

This held a number of lead boxes of various sizes.

Behind it was the door which led to the vault where Blood had deposited the money.

Approaching it, Clifford took out one of his pistols, placed it against the lock, and fired.

The report was tremendous.

The office was instantly filled with a blinding, suffocating, and foul-smelling cloud of dust.

But Clifford found, to his great joy, that the shot had shattered the lock, and the door was open.

He was soon within the vault.

His trembling hand raised the lantern, and its light fell upon the treasure.

A huge pile of bags lay before him.

Hastily he ran his eye over them, and was astonished to see that on each bag was marked the sum of five hundred guineas.

His astonishment at the apparent vastness of the sum was great.

But time was flying—Blood, perhaps, was already on the road—therefore, not a moment was to be lost.

Placing the lantern down he seized two of the bags, and hurried to the window.

"Waltman, Waltman," he whispered, "be ready!"

"Ay, ay!" returned Waltman. "Quick."

Down dropped the two bags, and Martin, seizing them, hurried to the chair.

Throwing the bags in, he brought out one of the cushions, ran with it to the window, and threw it down just as two more bags came through the aperture.

The idea of this was to deaden the sound of the fall of the gold, and it was entirely successful.

Again and again bags of gold were dropped out of the window, to be seized upon and carried to the chair.

Presently Waltman said—

"It is useless to attempt to place more within the chair, for we shall never be able to carry it."

No sooner had he mentioned this fact than Clifford got through the window, and clambered to the ground.

"We must hasten to dispose of what we have," he said. "Quick! let us drop the curtains of the chair, and unfasten the bars of the gate."

"But in heaven's name," returned Waltman, "where are you about to take this money?"

"Have I not told you of my unhappy master?"

"Ha! the locksmith?"

"Yes; his house is opposite. We can throw the gold in the smithy there, then return for the remainder of the wealth, and afterwards, at our leisure, we can think as to what is best to be done."

"Yes, yes," replied Waltman, whose face, however, showed what a state of anxiety he was in, "the idea is a good one if it can be carried out."

"It must be carried out," cried Clifford—"ay, at any risk! I have made up my mind to obtain possession of all the money."

Rushing to the gate he unfastened the bars, pulled open the massive barrier, and looked up and down the lane.

Not a soul was visible.

Like everywhere else the silence of the dead seemed to reign; but as he listened, he heard in the distance, the melancholy cry of the plague cart attendants—

"Bring out your dead! Bring out your dead!"

"Come," said Clifford, returning to Waltman, "the road is clear. Hoist and away."

Waltman seized the handles, and away they went with the load of gold.

The weight was enormous, and the pair fairly staggered with it to the late locksmith's residence.

Reaching the smithy, Clifford lifted the lid of the bin, which had been used for logs, and the bags were hurled into the aperture.

This done, they returned, and once more proceeded with their task.

Every bag having been secured, Clifford once more got through the aperture.

"The task is completed," he said, "and a large number of Blood's villainous plans will be upset, for now he has not the money to carry them out. Also, when the king finds that the money he required is not forthcoming, he will again order his arrest."

"Pray heaven it may be so!" replied Waltman, "for a greater monster never lived. But you promised to show me the chamber wherein the murder of the man Lucas occurred."

"I did."

"And the room in which this money, for so many years, had been concealed."

"The false ceiling. True. I should much like to see it myself."

"Then you have never seen it?"

"Never."

"Think you there will be time? Blood may come at any moment."

"I think we have time for that. It will take us but a few moments. But first let us cover the chair with the tarpaulin, so that it will escape observation."

The chair was accordingly pushed close in with the building materials, and completely covered with the tarpaulin.

Clifford now took the lantern, and telling Waltman to keep close to him, proceeded up the stairs of the house in which the murder of the man Lucas had taken place.

We must here leave them awhile.

Some considerable time had elapsed, and the two watchmen began to think it high time that the chair-bearers should have returned.

"Hardman," said the individual who had, on the stopping of the chair, acted as spokesman, "they cannot have passed us unobserved?"

"No, no, Davies," replied the other, "that would be impossible. But I'll tell thee what, the old gentleman (meaning the attorney) might have invited them to enter his office, and have served them with refreshments."

"No, no," growled Davies; "I'll not believe it. And I'll tell you what it is, I am more suspicious than ever of those two men. We were fools not to have had a look inside the chair."

"Well, well, let us go round to his office, and satisfy ourselves."

"Ay, we will. But first pick up and hand me yonder lantern. It is so dark that I can scarcely see my hand before me."

Dark indeed it was; moreover, a black fog was slowly descending, and this was accompanied by the finest of rain, thus making everything appear more gloomy, forbidding, and miserable than ever.

Lantern in one hand, and a short bludgeon in the other, Davies strode forward, his comrade at his side.

The office was quickly reached, and the first thing Davies did was to look for the sedan-chair.

He could see nothing of it.

"Verily one would be inclined to think that chair, men and all, had suddenly vanished through the ground," he exclaimed.

"I think I can tell you how it is," chuckled Hardman, as he pointed to the Chancery Lane gates, "they have gone that way."

"Ay, ay, it may be so," replied Davies. "But we will have another search, and then we'll have a look in the office."

Look about again they did.

They made the most minute inspection everywhere; but it never struck them that the chair might be beneath the tarpaulin.

The second search proving fruitless, Davies taking a pistol from his belt, proceeded to the office door.

It was, of course, locked.

"What do you make of this?" he whispered. "Look at this door. Observe the dust about the lock, and here on the step. What does that prove?"

"Don't know," replied Hardman, moodily.

"Fool! does it not show that the door has not been opened for a long time?"

"Ay; so it would appear."

"It proves that neither the attorney nor the chair-bearers have entered the building by it—ah! what is this? Why here is a bar of iron. With all our watchfulness a robbery has been committed! For, see this loosened stonework! It shows that the place has been entered, and there is the place the thieves got through!"

And holding up the lantern, he pointed to the window.

Hardman was too astounded to make any remark at this startling discovery.

"But wait one moment," said Davies, "they may be *within the office now.*"

Hardman shook his head.

"I don't think it," he said, "because if they were within the office the sedan-chair would be out here somewhere."

"Well; but look at this—it is pretty certain that there was no Master Prior in that chair, eh?"

"Seems like it."

"But there might have been two or three of the associates of Colonel Blood within it, eh?"

"Ah! so there might."

"Good. Well, now, hoist me up, and I'll get in."

"What?" cried Hardman, "get in there? Why if there is any robber within that office, you would, perhaps, be shot!"

"I must risk that. So lift."

Hardman, trembling somewhat at what he considered would be likely to follow, complied, and in a few seconds Davies was through the aperture.

Before he jumped down Hardman handed him the lantern, and the next moment Davies' voice was heard, challenging anyone who might happen to be in the office.

Eagerly Hardman listened, but he became so nervous, that at last he drew both his pistols, and, with one in each hand, stood ready to fire upon anyone who attempted to pass him.

So eagerly was he listening for his comrade's voice, that he seemed entirely to have forgotten his surroundings.

While he stood beneath the aperture a tall figure, masked, and wearing a long cloak and a huge slouched hat, stole softly towards him.

"Just in time," muttered the new-comer; just in time! Ha! Who can have revealed this secret? *Who but Mistress Cameron!* Ay, ay; no one knew it but her. Yes; she has revealed my secret to the king, and, by heaven! I will have revenge!"

At this moment Hardman placed his pistols on the ground, brought from his pocket a tinder box, and proceeded to strike a light.

Having lit a small taper, he had pressed it against a wall so as to afford him some kind of light, if only for a few minutes, when Blood—for he the cloaked figure was—once more crept forward.

The faint light of the taper showed him the iron bars on the ground.

Picking up one of them, he crept behind Hardman, and brought it down, with tremendous force, on the unlucky watchman's head.

It sent the poor fellow to the ground as swiftly as if a bullet had ploughed its way through his heart.

"I don't fancy he will ever speak again!" muttered Blood, as he took the taper from the wall, and bending, looked into Hardman's face. Who can he be?

I don't recognise his features. Still that is of no consequence. Now how many of them are in *there*, I wonder? I care not if there is a round dozen. I will enter!"

He essayed to reach the aperture by raising himself, but failed.

Thereupon he pulled Hardman beneath the aperture, and, standing upon him, jumped up and succeeded in clutching the sill.

By the exertion of all his strength, he at last succeeded in drawing himself right up, and managed to pass through the window.

He dropped to the floor, and the noise he made attracted the attention of Davies, who had been examining the vault from which Clifford had taken the bags.

Instantly he rushed into the office, holding the lantern over his head, so that its rays should penetrate to every corner.

"By heaven!" he roared, as his eyes fell upon the figure before him, "it is Colonel Blood *himself*."

He waited for no reply.

Raising his pistol, he pulled the trigger.

But no report followed.

The weapon had missed fire.

He attempted to snatch his other weapon from his belt, but it was too late.

Not one word had left Blood's lips, neither had he stirred from where he stood when the pistol was pointed at him.

But no sooner did he see that Davies' weapon had missed fire, than snatching a pistol from his belt, he discharged it.

His weapon did not miss.

Alas! no. The report was echoed by an ear-piercing scream of mortal agony as Davies, staggering back, fell dead.

In his fall he brought down the rack which was before the vault.

The deed boxes fell to the floor with a tremendous crash, and blocked up the entrance to the vault.

With frantic haste Blood threw them aside.

At length he had cleared a space, and seizing the lantern, he entered the vault.

A wild yell left his lips as the lantern rays revealed the startling fact that the vault was empty.

" ' HOW DO YOU KNOW WHOSE MONEY IT WAS?' YELLED BLOOD."

"By heaven, I am like a man in a dream!" he cried. "Not one bag left. Not one—not one. But what were those two men doing? Had they taken the gold, and then returned to see if there were any more? No, no! I see it plainly. Those two men must have been the watchmen. And they had seen something which had attracted their attention. Fool that I was in my haste to kill them. But it cannot be helped."

Around the vault he went, raving at the loss of his gold.

At last he rushed from the vault, and proceeded to make his exit from the office.

In such a state was he, that it took him some time to scramble out.

At last he was successful.

Dropping to the ground, he muttered—

"No time must be lost. I must consult Rochester. By all that is evil, I will have that money back—ay, every bag. Ha! what is *that?* As I live, it is a light."

By this time he was beneath the gateway.

Happening to glance upward, he noticed the faint glimmer of a light in one of the upper rooms.

It moved not.

Steadily it burned, and from its brightness, it seemed to him that it must be very near the window.

A few moments' reflection convinced him that that light was burning in the chamber whence he had originally taken the money.

A thrill of joy pervaded his whole body as he thought—

"What if, after all, I am mistaken? What if these men were not watchmen? What if they had been lured to take the bags from this vault, and replace them in the false ceiling until such time as the money could be conveniently carried away? I believe that that is the solution to the mystery."

Blood snatched another pistol from his belt, and dashed up the ricketty stairs.

* * * *

Clifford had conducted Waltman to the old chambers.

They had examined the bed and all its surroundings, the deed boxes, and the papers they saw lying about.

So interested had both of them become, that they totally forgot to give attention to the flight of time.

No sound reached them from below, and Clifford was showing Waltman the secret button, and explaining all the particulars to him, as they had been explained to himself by Sir Christopher Cullum, when loud footsteps were heard ascending the stairs.

"In the name of wonder!" cried Clifford, "who can that be?"

"By heaven!" exclaimed Waltman, "we are caught."

"No, no," whispered Clifford. "Come! Quick! on your life! Get beneath the bed. Quick! and have a pistol ready in your hand."

In a moment both were beneath the bed.

But though the hangings effectually concealed them from sight, Clifford would have a good view of whoever came into the room.

Presently Blood came with a rush into the apartment.

Uttering furious cries, Blood looked round the gloomy chamber.

His pistol was ready in his hand, and it would have fared ill with whoever crossed his path.

"I am right!" he almost yelled, as he fixed his flashing eyes on the lowered ceiling (for our readers will remember that Doctor Jeevers and Sir Christopher Cullum, after their examination of the secret ceiling, had left the trap down). "Yes, I am indeed right. They have taken the bags into the ceiling. Ha, ha! I have foiled them again. The money is still mine."

So saying, he dashed up the trap.

Instantly Clifford darted from beneath the bed, and rushing to the fireplace, placed his foot upon the button.

At once the trap began to move upward.

The noise it made attracted Blood's attention, and he turned swiftly.

Just as he turned, Waltman scrambled from beneath the bed, and without the slightest hesitation, Blood fired.

The shot fortunately missed Waltman, who, answering to Clifford's frantic motions, placed his foot on the button as Clifford took his off.

"Perdition to you," cried Blood. "Take your foot off the button, or your life shall pay the forfeit."

And throwing himself on to the rising flap, he vainly attempted to check it.

He was about to hurl himself over, when Clifford, raising his pistol, thundered—

"Back, Colonel Blood! Attempt to get over there, and I will put a ball through your dastardly heart!"

Blood fixed his eyes on Clifford's face, and he at once recognised the "chair-bearer" who had brought Mistress Cameron to the "Ship."

"Hound!" cried Blood, "by whose orders have you come hither?"

"By my *own* orders," interrupted Clifford. "I am Clifford Hansard. *You* have not foiled me again. It is *I* who have foiled *you* this time. Monster that you are, you have met a well-deserved doom."

As Clifford spoke, Blood once more tried to hurl himself over the trap, but it was useless.

Another second, and with a loud "click, click!" the trap fixed itself.

With the butts of his pistols, Blood hammered at the trap, and wildly he offered all the money he was possessed of to be liberated.

"You have ample time, Colonel Blood," said Clifford, "to reflect on the enormity of your many crimes. Remember that you are within a stone's throw of that house where you committed one of the most horrible crimes that ever darkened the soul of man."

"No, no," cried Blood. "'Twas not I. 'Twas Rochester who did the deed."

"No matter; the accessory is as guilty as the actual murderer. Think, Colonel Blood, of the dreadful sufferings of those whom you have had in your power. Think of what *my* sufferings were in the cage at your residence in Leicester Fields. Think of the man you murdered in these rooms—think of poor Henri Hadden, and of the many others who have fallen victims to your villainy. Think of all this, Colonel Blood, and try to ask pardon of that heaven you have so grievously offended."

Again and again Blood's frantic blows were rained upon the door.

They heard him going round and round the room as if seeking a weak part whereon he could make an attack.

But his hands met nothing but iron and steel, and ponderous beams of wood.

"Come," said Clifford, "let us leave the house at once."

"But," said Waltman, "he has his sword and dagger in his possession; he can use them to pick away the woodwork."

"You are right. But such a work would take him days before he could get his body through any portion; and, in the meantime, he would be exhausted."

Down the stairs went the pair.

Blood heard their retreating footsteps, and his cries became greater than ever.

The street door being reached, Clifford listened.

Not the slightest noise was now heard.

"Colonel Blood," cried Clifford, "you are a doomed man!"

"Is it your intention to take the remainder of the money to the locksmith's?" asked Waltman.

"Yes; we will place the whole of it in that house, but in a safer spot than that where it is now. But first, follow me."

Thereupon, Clifford walked swiftly through the square, and out of the other gates, Waltman following, and marvelling much at the extraordinary courage, determination and energy Clifford displayed.

Outside the gates they came upon a boy holding the bridles of two horses.

"As I thought," whispered Clifford, "these horses are Blood's."

Turning to the boy, he said—

"Look you, my lad, the gentleman who told you to mind those horses was wearing a mask and a long cloak, eh?"

"Yes, sir," replied the lad, "and he said that I was to bring the horses through the gate when he whistled; but I've not heard his whistle yet."

"No, he is engaged, and will be engaged longer than he expected. Here is a guinea, and you are to hold the horses until we fetch them."

"All right, sir," answered the delighted lad, as he pocketed the guinea."

"Once more we return," said Clifford; "we will take the money to Potter's Bar, secrete the whole of it in one of the vaults, and then return here."

"But what of the chair?"

"We will leave that at Potter's Bar. It can be taken away anon."

It was quite an hour ere they returned to the lad.

"Have you seen either of the watchmen, my boy?" asked Clifford.

"No, sir; haven't seen 'em for an hour-and-a-half or more."

"It is very strange," replied Clifford. "I cannot understand what can have become of them. However, we will not stay to see."

In another moment each was in the saddle.

The astonishment of the boy may easily be imagined, when, instead of entering the gateway, they turned and galloped off in an opposite direction.

CHAPTER XVIII.

IS OF WHAT PASSED BETWEEN SIR CHRISTOPHER CULLUM AND CLIFFORD—BY WHOM THEIR CONVERSATION WAS OVERHEARD—OF WHAT TRANSPIRED AT LONG ACRE—HOW COLONEL BLOOD WAS RELEASED—AND OF THE TERRIBLE REVENGE HE DETERMINED TO TAKE.

STRAIGHT to Whitehall rode Clifford and Waltman; but on presenting themselves at the gate, they were stopped by one of the guard.

Dismounting, Clifford said—

"I wish to see Sir Christopher Cullum."

"Very likely," replied the soldier, grimly; "we have a dozen here every day with the same, or a similar tale."

"I have important business to transact."

"That is what they all say. It is nothing new, and a pretty looking object you are to want to pass these gates. Pah! Take my advice, and be off."

"Since you will not allow me to enter the gates," persisted Clifford, "at least tell me the name of the captain on duty."

"The name of the captain on duty," cried a deep voice, "is Winter. And here he is."

"Captain Winter," said Clifford, "do you recognise my voice?"

"I fancy I recognise a voice I have heard before. Stand back, my man," he added to the soldier.

The man, having fallen back, Clifford approached.

"Captain Winter," he said, "I am Clifford Hansard."

"What?" cried the captain. "Impossible!"

"Nay, nay, 'tis not impossible," returned Clifford. "I am no other, and your not recognising me, proves how effectual is my disguise."

"You wish to see Sir Christopher Cullum, no doubt?"

"I do."

"I am afraid it will be impossible. However, I will inform him of your wish. The fact is, he is engaged with the king and his lords."

"Ah! is Rochester with them?"

"I fancy he is. But wait where you are a few moments."

Captain Winter returned in less than ten minutes.

"Sir Christopher Cullum," he said, "cannot see you in the palace. He directed me to tell you to hasten to the 'White Boy Tavern' at Charing Cross, to enter the principal room, and there await his coming. He will shortly join you."

"I sincerely thank you, Captain Winter, for the trouble you have taken."

"Don't mention it, my lad," replied the captain, warmly shaking Clifford's hand. "I shall be only too proud to assist you at any time. I am sorry to hear that you are in difficulties."

"Alas! yes."

"Serious rumours are afloat concerning you. It is said that you committed two or three terrible murders at Rochester's castle."

"But you, captain, could never believe me guilty of such terrible deeds!" said Clifford, in tones of deep emotion.

"No, my lad, no," replied Captain Winter, in emphatic tones. "But all this proves that you are surrounded by terrible enemies—the chiefs among them being Colonel Blood and Rochester."

"Colonel Blood——," said Clifford, eagerly, "I have——"

But he was not able to communicate to the gallant captain what had befallen Blood, for Winter was, at that moment, summoned away."

Clifford remounted, and he and Waltman rode off to Charing Cross.

The " White Boy," so called owing to the fact that it was kept by a tall, powerful African, was soon reached.

The pair alighted, and the horses having been handed over to the care of a miserable-looking ostler, they entered the tavern.

Amid a huge pile of barrels, his arms folded across his broad chest, sat the African giant, smoking an enormous pipe of Indian manufacture.

One miserable oil lamp, suspended from the ceiling, shed a strange light over the gloomy place, making everything look weird and forbidding.

As Clifford and Waltman entered, the host rose.

" What can I do for you, my masters ? " he asked.

" Serve us with a couple of bottles of your best," replied Clifford. " I suppose you have a room where a private interview can be held ? "

" Oh, yes," said the African, pointing to a door on his right; " you will find a room there, but I am sorry to say that it is not in very good condition. You see, gentlemen, things are changed now to what they were when my wife was alive."

His faltering voice attracted Clifford's attention.

" Have you suffered from the plague ? " he asked.

" Suffered ! Suffered ! Ah, yes. The cruel disease spares neither whites nor blacks. I have lost a wife and children ! "

" Children also ! "

" Ay. They were swept away in seven days. Ah ! I would that I could leave London. But enter ; a good fire is burning within the room, and—ha, I forgot to say, a young man is asleep there. I trust it will not be necessary to arouse him ? "

" Oh, no," replied Clifford.

" It is always best to be cautious," whispered Waltman. " Better have a look at the sleeping man ere you decide to stay there."

" You are right," replied Clifford.

A fine fire was burning on the hearth, and it afforded sufficient light to view the whole of the room, and to see the figure of a man at the further end.

He was lying at full length on a low bench, apparently fast asleep.

Clifford approached, and bent over him.

" He is attired in a blue blouse," he said, " and looks very much like a Frenchman. His moustache and beard are covered with mud. I should say he has been indulging in a wild debauch."

At this moment the host entered with a tray, on which where the bottles ordered.

Catching the last words Clifford uttered, he said—

" You are right. That man is the biggest drunkard in London, I should think. But he has been more drunk to-day than ever I saw him. He got into trouble with a number of apprentices, and I heard that they thrashed him soundly. If he is in your way, I will remove him."

" No," replied Clifford; " let him sleep off the effects of his carouse."

" It is my intention to tell him not to darken my door again," said the host.

" Is he a foreigner ? "

" If he is a foreigner, he speaks English remarkably well," replied the black host. " He is one of the vilest wretches I ever saw. If it were not for the fact that he has, on many occasions, brought me good customers, he would not be here now."

As these words were spoken, neither of the three observed the man suddenly raise his head, and then drop it again.

But such was what took place, and his wide open eyes showed that he was very much awake.

" A gentleman will shortly come here," said Clifford, " and you will please conduct him to us."

Half-an-hour passed, and then Sir Christopher made his appearance.

Apparently he was well known to the black, for, as Sir Christopher walked in, he started in surprise, and then bowed.

Sir Christopher nodded, and passing into the room, seized Clifford's hand, and shook it warmly.

" Once again we meet, my lad ! " he

said in joyous tones, "right glad am I to see thee ! But in this strange guise I should never have recognised the gallant Clifford Hansard."

At the mention of this name the man on the table once more raised his head, looked swiftly at the speakers, and then dropped it again.

"But," continued Sir Christopher, speaking rapidly, "I can see by your eyes that you have news for me, so out with it, my lad, for no doubt it is important."

"Very important news, Sir Christopher—news that will fill your very soul with joy."

"But who is your companion ? I do not remember him."

"Allow me to introduce him to you, Sir Christopher. This is Martin Waltman, the host of the 'Lorne Arms.'"

"Ha, I remember your story of the fight at the inn, and how you were protected."

"It was not finished then, Sir Christopher," said Clifford, sadly. "I will finish it now. After our escape his house was attacked, and his daughter shot."

"By whom ? "

"That he knows not. Still there is no doubt that the shot was fired by Rochester's orders."

"Ay, there can be no doubt of that. And yet, despite the fact that Rochester's crimes are continually cropping up, the king shuts his eyes to his villainies, and still allows the wretch to join his councils."

"Tell me, Sir Christopher—tell me how fares it with Olivia ? " exclaimed Clifford.

"She is but poorly," replied Sir Christopher.

He paused with a deep sigh.

"Go on, I beg," replied Clifford.

"I fear, my lad, that she is not long for this world."

"Oh, heaven ! " cried Clifford, wildly wringing his hands, "say not that, Sir Christopher—say not that ! "

"I say to you, Clifford, hope for the best. But I feel that it is my duty to tell you exactly how matters stand. At times she seems strange—so strange that even Doctor Jardell is puzzled. Occasionally she talks of the terrible scenes at the house in Chancery Lane ; then of what happened at Rochester's castle ; but though these matters, I fear, have, to a certain extent, affected her brain, there is one whom she has not forgotten, and that is yourself. She cannot hear the faintest footsteep but that she asks if her Clifford is coming. Yet you have not long been absent."

"Nay ; but I am afraid an hour seems a day to her."

"No doubt it may be so. But I repeat—hope for the best. You might, in your disguise, go—but no—no! That must not be. Clifford, my lad, you seem to me to be about the most unfortunate person with whom I have ever had to deal."

Once more Sir Christopher paused.

Instantly Clifford noticed his troubled look.

"Keep me not in suspense, Sir Christopher," he said ; "but let me know the truth."

"I will. It is better that you should know. There is a warrant out for your apprehension."

"Great heaven! Through Rochester's persuasion."

"Even so ; the king, however, signed the warrant with no willing hand. I did my best to prevent its being signed. But I failed. Rochester has it in his pocket at this very moment. I suppose he will arrange with the villainous Blood to capture you."

"No," cried Clifford ; "he will never —never arrange with that monster again. Listen now to my news. Sir Christopher Cullum, in that false ceiling whence those bags of money were stolen, is the murderer Blood ! "

"What ! " exclaimed Sir Christopher, starting back in astonishment.

"I repeat that, in that false ceiling, is the murderer Blood—caught like a rat in a trap. I have recovered the greater portion of the money which he stole from the chambers in Lincoln's Inn, and which belongs to you."

"Great powers ! " faltered Sir Christopher, who was now trembling with excitement, "this is news indeed ! And the money, Clifford—quick—where is the money ? "

Once more the head of the supposed drunken man was raised.

The fellow appeared to be trying to catch every word which fell from Clifford's lips.

But if it was his intention to hear where the money had been hidden, he failed, for Clifford placed his mouth to Sir Christopher's ear, and whispered the desired information.

"I am bewildered," cried Sir Christopher; "the place seems going round and round."

"Take a drink of wine, sir," said Waltman.

"And be seated," added Clifford, "while I tell you the story."

Without the least delay, he told his story, commencing with what occurred at the costumier's, and at the "Ship Tavern."

Sir Christopher eagerly questioned him as to what passed between Blood and Mistress Cameron, and he was not surprised to learn that the lady had attempted to borrow money of the Colonel for the king.

"In consequence of what you have done, Clifford," said Sir Christopher, the king will have to go without his loan. I am, indeed, glad of it, for it will, to a certain extent, prevent him from continuing his horrible debauches and reckless extravagance."

"You will not let him know that you have any money at your disposal?"

"Certainly not."

"But supposing that he learned you had the money?"

"I would not lend him a penny, Clifford. No; not a penny. But listen to me—we must continue this conversation at another time, for I have none to spare now. Ha! I know what is best to be done. I must smuggle you into the palace—disguised as you are. And when I have a little time, the conversation can be resumed.

"But do you not think it necessary, Clifford, that the house in Lincoln's Inn should be watched? Though Blood is so securely caged, his associates will continue to prowl about, and there is no telling when they may take it into their heads to search the place."

"I think it a most wise suggestion," said Waltman, "and I will watch the place for you."

"So be it," said Clifford; "you shall watch the house, and fear not, you shall be well provided for."

"Above all things have plenty of arms at your disposal," said Sir Christopher.

"We have two horses in the stable," remarked Clifford.

"Let them remain there for the present," replied Sir Christopher. "It would be better did Master Waltman go on foot, for by so doing he would not attract so much attention."

The three now seated themselves, and the necessary arrangements were made.

They then left the house.

Martin at once proceeded on his journey to Chancery Lane, while Clifford accompanied Sir Christopher to Whitehall.

Little did he dream what a terrible drama was to be enacted there, and what a share he would take in it!

Some few minutes after their departure, the man on the bench again raised his head and cautiously looked round, a cunning twinkle in his eyes.

He listened, but not hearing the host moving, he, with the stealthiness of a cat, got upon his feet.

Stepping forward a few paces, he peered through the door, and noticing that the host had resumed his usual position against the barrels, a chuckle of satisfaction left his lips.

On tip-toe he crept to the table on which were the bottles, and carefully examined them.

Two were empty, and one nearly full.

The latter he placed to his lips, and in a few seconds, there were *three* empty bottles on the table.

"Most excellent wine," he chuckled. "It's astonishing how nice a wine is that one don't pay for. Ha! so you intend to give me the cold shoulder, you black hound, do you?" he hissed, as he shook his clenched fist in the direction of the host. "But wait. I will be even with you. I will put Drinkwater on your track."

After a brief pause, during which he drained the other two bottles, he continued—

"A fine tale I've heard. Blood fairly caged. But that I am likely to get something for liberating him, I would let him stay there. And Clifford Hansard caged him. Well, if that isn't turning the tables, *my name is not John Jeevers.*

"But where have they taken all this

money? Ha! I lost that much. If I had overheard, why it would soon have been all in my possession."

Having had another look through the doorway, and observing that the huge host was apparently half asleep, he returned to the fire-place.

"This beard and moustache have become a nuisance," he muttered; "they're covered with mud and blood, and though I had to leave a good deposit on them, they must go."

With this he unfastened the beard and moustache, and flung them on the fire.

After a brief reflection he took one of the bottles off the table, and then falling on his hands and knees, proceeded to crawl through the doorway, and so on through the shop.

Having reached the entrance without attracting the black host's attention, and having taken care to see that no one was observing his movements, he suddenly rose to his feet, and with all his force, flung the bottle at the host's head.

Very fortunately it missed him, but striking one of the barrels within an inch of his head, it was smashed to pieces.

With a howl of astonishment and rage, the brawny host started up, and dashed through the doorway.

But John Jeevers had vanished.

Who could have thrown the bottle? the host wondered.

It never struck him to look within the room which Jeevers had quitted, until when reaching the doorway, he fancied he smelt burning hair.

Entering the room he saw the burning beard and moustache on the fire.

Then looking round, he found that the man in the blouse had gone.

"Ah, what a country is this," cried the host. "Disease raging on all sides, and almost every man sailing under false colours. They say that my people are savages. Pah! if they are, what, then, are many of those in this country of England?"

Swiftly across St. Martin's Fields went John Jeevers, and never stopped until he reached the first hedge.

Not a soul was in sight, and the gloominess and desolation of the place were depressing in the extreme.

"What is the first thing to be done?" mused Jeevers. "Why drink. I must have some brandy ere I can do anything, for my nerves are unsteady, and I am trembling all over. But I have no money—not a fraction. Oh, that I had overheard where that money had been taken to. If I had, and could have found Blake Barrell—ah! I wonder what has become of him? Shouldn't be surprised if he has been stricken down by the plague or killed in some fight.

"I wonder whether I shall ever take the disease? My old mother says no, because the rope will do the business. *Will* it? But I know what saves me from the plague—it is the drink. I must have some more, and I *will* have it. Many of the houses hereabouts are open all night, so I should have no trouble in getting the drink if I had the money. I'll go on and see what luck throws in my way."

Across the Fields he went, taking care to keep as near the hedges as possible.

He met no one until he arrived at the further end of the Fields, when he observed a dark figure rapidly advancing.

Drawing back he waited, and when the figure was almost upon him, he cried—

"Sir, sir! for the love of heaven give me help."

"Ah, give, give, give is the only cry I hear day and night," cried the traveller, in stern tones. "Keep back, as you value your life!"

And he laid his hand on his sword hilt.

"I have not the plague," whined Jeevers. "I do assure you, your worship, that I have it not."

"I believe no one," was the reply. "Stand back! I'll *give* if only to get rid of you. By my soul, London is filled with robbers and beggars. Here is a crown for thee—'tis all I have. Pick it up, and be off with you."

And he flung a crown at Jeevers' feet.

Jeevers thanked him warmly and picked up the coin, while the traveller continued his journey at increased speed.

"By heavens!" cried Jeevers, "that is all he has, he said. He spoke falsely. I saw his purse. It is full—full. Ay, and of something besides crown pieces. It shall be *mine!* I have only a dagger, it is true, but I have little to fear from him, for he is evidently not a strong man."

Cautiously he stole after the traveller, but so swiftly did the latter walk, that Jeevers occasionally had trouble to keep pace with him.

An opportunity to dash upon him soon occurred; but before Jeevers could take advantage of it, two or three persons crossed his path.

So intent was he upon getting possession of the purse, that this fact did not have the effect of causing him to abandon his intention.

Long Acre was reached, but no other chance occurred.

Suddenly the traveller vanished.

"By heaven!" exclaimed Jeevers, in astonishment, "he has entered the Convent. Ha, I may learn something which Blood would willingly purchase at a large price."

Increasing his pace to a run, he reached the Convent.

It was, as usual, buried in profound darkness.

Not a sign of life was anywhere visible.

The gate being open, Jeevers crept into the avenue.

In a few seconds he stood, or rather crouched, opposite the traveller, who was impatiently tapping on the door.

Some few minutes passed ere he was answered.

At last the ponderous door was thrown open, and a white figure appeared.

It was Mistress Cameron.

In her hand she carried a taper, and the light of this being thrown full upon her face, showed its ghastliness—the sunken, but eager eyes, and the trembling lips.

A sharp cry left her lips as she recognised the person on the threshold.

"*You!*" she gasped. "*You!* at this hour?"

"Ay, at this hour. You know well enough, Claribel, that Master Rushton is not given to picking his hours. But why are you here? Why not send your maid to admit me?"

"Maid!" said Mistress Cameron, with a deep sigh; "the poor girl is dead!"

"Dead! Did she die of the plague?"

"She did, and was taken hence but one hour ago."

"The Lord save us. But whom did you expect? For that you did expect someone is certain from the fact that you are fully dressed."

"I did expect someone. Anxiously have I been watching here for a long time past. I expected Colonel Blood."

"Then you have seen him recently?"

"I have."

"Where?"

"At the 'Ship' near the Tower."

"Odd's fish. What recklessness on your part, Claribel."

"Nay; it was on *your* part."

"Ah, you visited him respecting the money?"

"I did."

"And the result?" asked Master Rushton, eagerly.

"He promised to let me have the money. I expected he would have been here with it before this. But he has not come."

"Nay; of course he has not come. Blood told you he would let you have the money on my behalf only to get rid of you. From what Rochester tells me, I am certain that he would not lend you or anyone else any more money."

"You wrong him."

"Nay, nay; I do not. But let me know what transpired between you."

Mistress Cameron begged him to enter the house.

Master Rushton made a movement as if to comply, but remembering the recent death, he said he preferred to remain where he was.

Rapidly Mistress Cameron informed him as to what had occurred between her and the villain Blood.

When she had finished Master Rushton said—

"Now listen to what I say, Claribel. You are well aware of the fact that my love for you is great—that I would do much for you. For your sake, Claribel, I would let the murderous villain go free. But the populace is clamouring for his arrest, and arrested he must and *shall* be."

"Oh," cried Mistress Cameron, "you would not break your solemn pledge."

"Hish, hish! We may attract attention. Blow the taper out, soh, now we cannot be seen."

Up to this point Jeevers had heard nothing but the name "Master Rushton."

No sooner was the taper blown out, however, than he crept further forward, laying flat on the ground; and in that position was enabled to overhear much of what was said.

"Claribel," continued Master Rushton, "it is now time that you quitted this dwelling. If you will consent to leave it, I will put a pretty cottage at Oxford at your disposal."

"You were talking of Cecil," interrupted Mistress Cameron, in low, agitated tones.

"True. I said that he must be arrested; so he must, and lodged in Newgate. But I will take care that no harm shall there befall him on one condition."

"Name it."

"That you reveal to me the place where lie those bags of gold."

There was a pause of a few moments, during which nothing was heard but Mistress Claribel's rapid breathing.

At last she said—

"Oh, how can you ask me such a thing? I cannot—cannot reveal the secret."

"Then mark it well," said Master Rushton, impatiently. "Blood shall suffer for it."

He turned as if about to go, when Mistress Cameron laid her hand on his arm.

"One moment," she said. "If I told you—but, no, no, no; it cannot be."

"I will allow you time for reflection. I will give you twenty-four hours, and I am sure that in that time you will have thought whether it would not be as well to save Colonel Blood's life by revealing his secret."

So saying, Master Rushton turned and strode rapidly down the avenue.

Plain enough was it now to Mistress Cameron that Master Rushton loved her only for what he could obtain from her.

She started to the broad steps as if to recall him; but at that instant the fierce figure of the villain Blood seemed to stand before her, and sternly motion her to go back.

Uttering a low, bitter cry of despair, she fell insensible on the threshold.

In the meantime, Jeevers, still determined to have the stranger's purse, left his hiding-place, and stole after the traveller.

Seeing him turn to the right of the building, he turned to the left, ran along beside the wall, and waited.

For a few moments only.

On came the traveller at a sharp pace, and as soon as he reached the corner, Jeevers dashed upon him,

He seized him by the throat, and in the semi-darkness, Rushton caught the glitter of a dagger.

"Your purse," hissed Jeevers, "quick, your purse, or you are a dead man!"

And once more the bright blade flashed before the eyes of the startled traveller.

In a few seconds the purse was in the hand of Jeevers, who then released the stranger.

No sooner did Master Rushton find himself released than he turned and fled.

"And now for the brandy," chuckled Jeevers. "Master Rushton, eh? Who can he be? And what has he to do with the arrest of Colonel Blood? Well, we shall see what Blood says about it; but I shall, in the first place, ascertain how much the information which I am prepared to give is worth."

He quickly reached Holborn, where at an hostelry he refreshed himself.

No further pause did he make until he reached Chancery Lane.

Finding the gates closed, he went round the other way.

Proceeding through the square he quickly reached the gateway.

But he knew not which were the chambers mentioned by Clifford.

"Not a soul to be seen," he growled; and then shouted—

"Watch! watch!"

No answer was returned save the echo of his own voice, which sullenly traversed the long gloomy corridors.

Round the gateway he went, pushing at the doors, but none yielded.

Presently his foot kicked against something, and stooping, he found that it was a lantern.

After a great deal of fumbling, he produced a tinder-box, and managed to light the lantern.

Very carefully he again examined the doors, but from their appearance, one might have considered that they had been unopened for weeks.

Suddenly a deep sigh fell upon his ears.

Jeevers started back as if some ghastly spectre had suddenly appeared before him.

"Help!" cried a voice. "Oh, help, help!"

"Help!" replied Jeevers, holding the lantern in the direction of the sound. "Who cries for help?"

Cautiously forward he went, but suddenly he halted, for there, just by his feet, in a kneeling attitude, was the figure of a man.

It was the watchman Hardman.

He presented a terrible sight.

The rays of the lantern showed Jeevers a large gaping wound, from which the blood still slowly flowed.

The unfortunate man's face could not be seen on account of its being completely bathed in blood.

His sufferings must have been, and were still, fearful.

Jeevers had had a great deal of experience in matters of this kind, and he saw that the man had not much longer to live.

"Master! master!" moaned the watchman, "give me a drop of water or wine if you have it."

"My good man," replied Jeevers, "I haven't such a thing."

He paused, for the thought flashed through his mind that this man could probably give him a deal of information concerning old Driffield's chambers.

"I haven't wine," he continued; "but I have some brandy. Here," taking out the flask, and placing it to the man's lips, "drink, but not too much, lest it does thee harm instead of good."

The watchman took a small quantity, and, for a few moments, the effect was satisfactory.

"Who has ill-treated you?" asked Jeevers.

"Alas!" moaned the man, "I know not. Someone robbed the office belonging to Master Prior. My comrade entered the place to see——"

"Why, what are you then? A watchman?"

"Yes. My comrade entered, I say, and I waited without. Suddenly I received a fearful blow on the back of the head, and dropped insensible. How long I remained so I know not; but, tell me, sir, who are you?"

"I—why look you, I am a friend of a gentleman interested in this Master Prior. He learned that a robbery was to be committed, d'ye see? And he set off to prevent it. He detected the robbers at their work. In order to shut his mouth they knocked him down, and carried him to the chambers of one David Driffield. There they have locked him in. I learned all this, and I have come to release my friend. But I could not find the chambers, and through not being able to find them, I have been able to render you assistance."

"The chambers, once the property of old David Driffield," said the watchman; but his voice was scarcely above a whisper, "are there — there on your right. Hold the lantern up—higher. Ha, someone has closed the door. 'Tis generally open—oh, merciful heaven! I feel that I am dying."

"Nay, nay; talk not thus, my friend," cried Jeevers. "Keep up thy courage for but a short time. If I can obtain admission to these chambers, and liberate my friend, I will render you every assistance."

"You swear that?"

"I do."

"And you will enter the attorney's office, and find out what has become of my comrade, though there is hardly a doubt but that he has been murdered."

"I will do as you ask, my friend; but now can you suggest as to the way I can enter these chambers?"

"There may be a log of wood among the building materials yonder. If there is, you may be able to burst the door open, for the locks are none of the strongest."

It was with the greatest difficulty that the poor man spoke these words; and having spoken them, he lay flat on the ground, groaning dismally.

Jeevers searched among the building materials, and found a huge piece of wood which was used to hammer down the street stones.

So heavy was it though, that he had the greatest difficulty in pulling it from its place, and hoisting it in a horizontal position.

Having accomplished it at last, however, he delivered upon the door a mighty crash.

Instantly the door flew open, and Jeevers went headlong into the passage.

Quickly recovering himself, he picked up the lantern, and commenced to ascend the stairs.

Before he had got far the sound of a voice fell upon his ears.

He paused and listened.

"Help!" said the voice, the tones appearing to proceed from a great distance. "Help! help!"

"Ay, ay," chuckled Jeevers, "that's him sure enough. But his voice is fainter than it was when *last* I heard it. Ah, how he used to torture me about my old mother, and about my being a pauper—his slave—his dog—ay, his dog, who was only too thankful to wait on him hand and foot, and pick up the crumbs which fell from his table. Ah, that I had learned where that money was!

"I would have come here all the same, though; but not to liberate him. No, no; I would have tortured *him*; and I would have continued the torture too until he died.

"Not a crust, not even a drop of water would he have had from me. Ha! ha! I am rejoiced to know that he has lost a large amount of his money; but—but I wish I had it. Lord! what a fine figure I would cut in London."

After a short pause, during which Blood's voice was heard piteously calling for help, Jeevers continued the ascent.

The rooms were reached at last.

"Help is here," said Jeevers. "Who calls for help, eh?"

A howl of joy left Blood's lips—lips now parched with thirst, which he had thought there would be no chance of quenching.

"Help at last!" cried the ruffian. "I am saved!"

"Dont be too sure of that," replied Jeevers, entering the bedroom, and setting down the lantern. "Don't be too sure of that, my man. But first, where are you?"

"Here! *here!*" yelled Blood.

Jeevers laughed in his sleeve.

He seated himself beside the table, and leisurely took out the brandy flask.

"I'm here," continued Blood, using the butts of his pistols like a madman on the woodwork. "Here—in here."

"Well, if that is so," said Jeevers, "all I can say is, that it is a very strange kind of a place for a man to get into. I would not stay there any longer, if I were you. Why don't you come out of it?"

"I can't—I can't. I am fixed. Oh, I implore you, release me."

"Wait a moment. Don't be in too great a hurry," returned Jeevers. "I want to say just this——"

Jeevers had been speaking in an assumed voice, but at this instant he used his natural one, and Blood instantly recognised it.

"Ah," he cried, in tones of frantic joy, "it is John Jeevers. Speak! Tell me. Quick! It is Jeevers?"

"Yes; you are right enough," answered Jeevers. "And who are you?"

"By the thunder of Job, can't you recognise my voice? I am Colonel Blood. Don't delay a single instant. You know what firm friends we have ever been. At the fireplace you will see a steel button. If you place your foot——"

"Hold, hold!" interrupted Jeevers. "If you go on like that you will make me choke myself, for this brandy I have is so confoundedly strong."

"Brandy!" almost screamed Blood.

"Yes, brandy. Sorry I can't hand you up a little. Now colonel, listen to me, will you?"

"Oh, yes, yes. But be quick—be quick. I am half dead!"

"Well, colonel, I know all the circumstances by which you came here. Strange that—isn't it? But 'tis a fact. Clifford Hansard caged you."

"Yes, yes; he did. May my most blighting revenge be on him."

"Oh, with all my heart and soul, so far as that is concerned. But what will you give John Jeevers to let you out? That's the question."

"I'll give you every gold piece I possess."

"The money on you, do you mean? Or do you mean all the property that you possess?"

"If you'll only let me out, I'll at once satisfy you that your reward shall be a large one."

"No, no; I'd rather be satisfied *now*. Which do you mean, colonel?"

"I have a lot of money on me. How much I know not, for I cannot count it here in the dark."

"Is it twenty guineas?"

"More—much more."

"You'll give me twenty-five down, and owe me one hundred?"

"Willingly—most willingly. And you know, Jeevers, that I have always acted honestly by you."

"So you have, except when you *haven't*. Well, I'll let you out of the cage. Put my foot on the button, eh?"

"Ay, ay; just beneath the fire-dog. Press it hard, and *keep* pressing it."

"Ay, ay."

Jeevers found the button, and acted as desired, with the result that the ceiling began slowly to descend, much to the astonishment of Jeevers.

Blood could not wait until it had stopped.

As soon as he had sufficient room to pass, he rushed down the ladder-like trap, and jumped to the floor.

A most extraordinary object he looked.

During the short time he had been in that wondrously-constructed place, a most striking alteration had taken place in him.

His face was as white as death; his eyes seemed starting from their sockets; his lips, nostrils, and hands trembled violently, and his hair appeared to be standing on end.

The first thing he spied was the brandy flask.

He did not wait for an invitation, but seizing upon it, he placed the neck to his lips, and drained the bottle dry.

Then he dropped into the chair, and heaved a deep sigh.

"A nice object you look, colonel," said Jeevers, standing before him, and staring at him in the most insolent manner.

"Beware how you talk to me!" growled Blood. "I have my sword at my side."

"Oh, oh, that's it, is it? Presently you will make me regret having released you."

"Silence," growled Blood—"silence! See you not that I require time to compose myself? By the shade of the Evil One!" he hissed through his clenched teeth, "revenge — revenge. Oh, a speedy revenge!"

After a pause of a few seconds, during which he fixed his eyes on the floor, he looked up, saying—

"Clifford Hansard it was who stole the money."

"Whose money?"

"My money."

"I thought it was Sir Christopher Cullum's money."

Blood started from his seat, dashed upon Jeevers, and seizing him by the throat, yelled—

"How do *you* know whose money it was?"

"Loose your hold!" gasped Jeevers. "You will choke me. Loo—loose your hold."

"There," said Blood, flinging him from him with such violence that, losing his balance, he fell with a crash against the wall—"there! Now tell me how you know, or I'll kill you as sure as you're alive."

"I know all," groaned Jeevers. "I overheard Clifford Hansard, Sir Christopher Cullum, and another man, whom I know not, speaking about it at the 'White Boy.'"

"You did? And you heard where the money was hidden? But no—no; you did not hear that."

"What makes you say so?"

"I know you too well. If you had learned where the money was, and you had had the luck to get it, I should never have been released. But tell me what you *did* hear."

"I have a long story to tell you, colonel — a most interesting story certainly—but I must be paid to relate it."

"You shall be satisfied."

"I don't know that. You have not handed over the twenty-five guineas for releasing you yet."

Blood eagerly searched his pockets, and he found himself in possession of a good many guineas over and above the twenty-five, which sum he handed to Jeevers, but with very bad grace.

Money was precious to him now that his ill-gotten wealth was gone.

"Proceed now," he said, "and tell your story quickly; but if you lie to me, and I find it out, you can imagine what will follow."

And he placed his long sword before him.

"First of all," said Jeevers, "I want to ask a question — who is Master Rushton?"

At these words, Blood almost leapt from his seat.

For a few seconds he glared in such a manner at Jeevers as to cause that young ruffian to wonder whether it was his intention to spring upon him again.

At last he replied, in low tones—

"Master Rushton! Who is he? Why — why he is Master Rushton. Why do you ask that?"

"You will see in a moment," answered Jeevers. "Now listen attentively."

Thereupon Jeevers told him everything which had transpired since Clifford and Martin had entered the hostelry at Charing Cross, not omitting the robbery, nor the cowardice "Master Rushton" had displayed.

Blood did not once interrupt.

During the recital, he stared blankly at the floor.

When Jeevers had finished he looked up, saying abruptly—

"Give me the purse!"

"Nothing in it now," replied Jeevers; "nothing but a key."

"A what?"

"A silver key."

This seemed to excite Blood in no small degree.

"Give me the purse!" he cried. "Quick!"

Jeevers took it from his pocket, and flung it over to him.

With trembling hands Blood unfastened the purse, and brought out the key—a small glittering article of solid silver.

"By heaven and earth!" he cried, in exulting tones, "the possession of this is worth untold gold."

"Indeed. I see nothing in it; but, ah! perhaps you are acquainted with Master Rushton's house, and know where he keeps the box which this key will fit."

"No, no; listen to this, Jeevers—listen!"

And here he laid his hands on Jeevers's shoulders, and stared into his face. "I will have a speedy revenge!"

"On Clifford Hansard?"

"Yes, I will have my revenge on him, as well as on Sir Christopher Cullum; but that must wait. My revenge must first fall on Master Rushton. Now, can you keep a secret?"

"Ay, ay; If I am paid for it."

"Fool! you shall be paid! Master Rushton is none other than King Charles!"

Jeevers opened his bloodshot eyes in wonder, and uttered a long, low whistle of astonishment.

"Then," he said, "I'm done for sure enough; for he, no doubt, would know me again."

At once Blood saw that this was a chance not to be lost.

"You are right," he said; "he would recognise you again. You would be arrested and hung off-hand."

"Ay, and you will be arrested, colonel, as I have already said. You are to be flung into Newgate again, and no chance this time is to be given you to escape. Were I you, I would not be in Newgate for a fortune. Remember what the warders owe you for slaying one of their comrades."

"Peace!" thundered Blood, "there is but little chance of my again getting into Newgate."

"There is every chance of Clifford Hansard getting into Newgate," chuckled Jeevers, "for I heard Sir Christopher Cullum say that there was a warrant out against him, and that Lord Rochester had it in his pocket."

"Ah! if that is really so—but let me tell you, Jeevers, of how I propose to be revenged. But 'tis not safe to remain here. Let us leave this place, and go to Bartholomew Close. There, as you know, I have refreshments in plenty."

Jeevers agreed to this proposition with all his heart, and the pair at once descended the stairs, Jeevers carrying the lantern.

Reaching the gateway, he looked for the watchman.

There he lay flat on the ground.

"This is the man I spoke to you about," said Jeevers.

"Ay," replied Blood, calmly. "I have no doubt but that that fearful blow was delivered by Clifford Hansard. Raise his head, and see if he still lives."

Jeevers did so.

One glance was sufficient.

"He is dead!" he said.

"Yes," replied Blood, "he is dead sure enough. Well, well, leave him were he is. The plague cart will take him away."

So saying, the cold-blooded rascal led the way through the square.

He did not expect to find his horses where he had left them, but still curiosity led him that way.

With all speed the pair traversed the streets, and soon the house in Bartholomew Close was reached.

Not a soul had been left in charge of the place.

Blood opened the door, and bade Jeevers follow him to his private room.

Here, in very quick time, he had candles burning, and directing Jeevers to throw some logs on the hearth, and make a fire, he proceeded to bring out what refreshments he had.

Biscuits and edibles of a like character he had in plenty, as well as wines and spirits.

Jeevers quickly made a fire, and when it was roaring up the chimney, Blood bade him sit down, and eat and drink.

"Will you not have any, colonel?" asked Jeevers.

"No."

"Not good enough, eh?"

"I am already full."

"Oh."

"Full of revenge—revenge!" cried Blood, fiercely.

"Ay, I should think so. By all that's evil, colonel, to think that Clifford Hansard should, after all, completely have you in his power."

"Stay, stay! Your words fire my blood. Be silent. I must think—think. My revenge will be of such a character that all London will be paralyzed."

Jeevers went on eating and drinking, while Blood thought over the plan which was dimly floating in his mind.

For at least a quarter of an hour he sat without stirring—without so much as raising his head; but suddenly he jumped up, went to his secret cupboard, opened it, and brought out a bag.

This he placed before Jeevers on the table.

"There," he said, "what is that?"

"A bag of money."

"Correct. It holds five hundred guineas. This bag is like many of those stolen from me by Clifford Hansard!" groaned Blood.

"How many were there altogether, colonel?"

"I had many of them, but how many I can't say. At any rate, there were scores left."

"Scores?"

"Yes. Enough gold to fill a cart—enough gold to live like a prince, Jeevers—like a king for the remainder of one's life. All gone—gone!"

His voice died away in a deep, bitter moan, and once again he dropped into his seat.

But he was quickly on his feet again, and picking up the bag, at which Jeevers had been intently gazing, as if calculating how many wild debauches the sum in it would purchase him, he said, in hoarse tones —

"Jeevers, only fancy what that sum would bring you."

"Five hundred golden guineas! Lord! it is a large sum."

"You can earn it easily. Yes, yes, easily. You can earn all of this, Jeevers."

"Yes, yes," interrupted Jeevers, eagerly; "but tell me *how* I can earn it. Is it by running a knife into the heart of Clifford Hansard? Or do you want me to slay Sir Christopher Cullum?"

"No, no; nothing of that. Listen to me. You know well enough that it was my mother you saw in conversation with Master Rushton, the king himself."

"Why, of course."

"Well, you see that it was his intention to steal this money."

"No doubt of it."

"And if my mother does not reveal my secret within the twenty-four hours, I shall be sought for, and, if found, thrown into Newgate?"

Jeevers nodded.

"Not the least doubt about it," went on Blood. "The king cares no longer for Mistress Cameron, and my life he seeks, and will take it if he lives."

"But you have not told me how I am to earn this money."

"I am coming to it. *You must slay the king!*"

"ERE THE DAGGER COULD DESCEND, A FIGURE DASHED UPON JEEVERS."

Jeevers started up, a stupefied stare in his eyes.

Blood returned the look.

For some few seconds the ruffians continued to stare into each other's face.

But presently Jeevers dropped into his seat, and, shaking his head, said—

"No, no; that is almost too much. I might have slain Master Rushton, for I knew not that he was the king; but to slay the king when I know it *is* the king, would *never* do."

"But why?"

"Detection would surely follow; but perhaps you mean that I should wait until he once more appeared in his disguise in the streets, then spring upon him and slay him."

"No, no. I will not wait for that. So if you do not feel inclined to earn this money," said Blood, snatching up the bag, "then I will get someone who will. If Drinkwater were not so big, he could manage the affair."

"Wait, wait," interrupted Jeevers. "Don't put it back—don't put it back. Wait but a moment, I'll consider."

"Decide at once!" cried Blood; "for no time is to be lost."

"I will do it," replied Jeevers. "Yes, yes, I will do it. But—but where is the deed to be done?"

"At the palace."

"Whitehall?"

"Yes."

"It is impossible, Colonel," said Jeevers, shaking his head; "it is impossible!"

"And why?"

"How can I obtain admittance?"

"I can manage that; and this key will admit you by a secret door to his bedroom."

"How do you know that?"

"Rochester told me of it. He described the staircase, the door, and this key, and his description was so exact, that I recognised this key at once. There are only two of these keys known to be in existence. One is in possession of the chief gentleman of the bedchamber, and this is the other. It is certain that the king, having lost this, will borrow the other from the gentleman of the bedchamber; thus, as that person cannot obtain admittance that way, it is not likely that he will interrupt you. Do you understand?"

"Yes; I understand perfectly," replied Jeevers, moodily.

He was still hesitating, and what wonder was it? He had committed some fearful deeds in his time; but this one Blood was tempting him to undertake was about the most risky and the most terrible. He knew well enough that if he happened to be caught in the palace, and especially near the royal bedchamber, he would be hacked to pieces; not one spark of mercy would be shown him, for his villainous hang-dog face would show him to be an assassin.

While Jeevers hesitated, Blood closely scrutinised his features as if endeavouring to read what was passing in his mind.

At the same time though, he was considering whom else he could trust to commit the horrible deed in the event of Jeevers giving him a downright refusal.

He thought of many, and among the number Blake Barrell.

He was wondering what had become of him, whether he had met his death by the plague, the bullet, or the dagger.

Perhaps Jeevers thought that Blood was thinking of whom else he could employ, for abruptly rising, he said—

"No longer will I hesitate. I *will* do it."

"Right," cried Blood, giving him a hearty clap on the shoulder. "Right! I knew that you could not be such a coward as to refuse."

"But," said Jeevers, "I must have the money ere I proceed to carry out your design."

"Why, how can you carry all this huge sum about your person?"

"Well," commenced Jeevers, but Blood stopped him. "Look," he said, opening the mouth of the bag, "dip your hand in, and take out as many guineas as you can. That's it. Now see, I tie this up again, and place it in the corner thus, and there it can remain until you claim it. And now that that is settled, let us draw up the plan of vengeance; it must be done speedily."

The plan of the murder of King Charles was thereupon formed.

All having been settled, Blood handed Jeevers the key.

"Now," he said, "we will at once to Leicester Square, where I will provide you with an impenetrable disguise. And I must also disguise myself to get you admission."

"Why not use the secret passage?" asked Jeevers, who was not a very great believer in disguise.

"What passage?"

"That which is entered by the treasurer's room."

"You mean the way I went when we captured Clifford Hansard?"

"Yes."

"No use," replied Blood. "I only wish it were; for, in that case, all difficulty would be removed. You could reach the bedchamber from which we took Clifford Hansard. But then you could not pass thence without detection. But come now, we must start for Whitehall."

CHAPTER XIX.

OF THE CUNNING MANNER IN WHICH COLONEL BLOOD OBTAINED ADMISSION FOR JEEVERS INTO THE ROYAL PALACE—AND OF WHAT TERRIBLE EVENTS OCCURRED THEREIN.

THERE cannot be the least doubt but that Colonel Blood was possessed of many varied and most extraordinary talents.

Had he turned these to honest account, he would certainly have become a person of importance, and a person of wealth legitimately come by.

His brain was a wonderful one; for there was always some scheme floating in his mind, and he did not take long to be ready with a way to carry out any such which he thought was worth the undertaking.

"At one stroke!" he chuckled, "I shall revenge myself and Mistress Cameron, and throw the whole kingdom into a state of the wildest excitement, amid which I will endeavour to reap a rich harvest. *But* the actual author of the deed (Jeevers) must die within a few hours of the crime. I know his love for drink too well to trust to his tongue. Thus, rid of him, I alone shall be the possessor of the secret."

Reaching Leicester Fields, Blood first of all procured pens, ink, and paper; and after some little practising, he wrote, in the handwriting of Mistress Cameron, these words—

"SIR,—

"The bearer, a youth who can be trusted with all safety, has instructions from me to communicate to his majesty my decision concerning a matter of the utmost importance to his majesty.

"Your sincere friend,

"CLARIBEL CAMERON."

Having sealed this document with a seal, the property of his mother, he carefully tied it with silken thread, and addressed it to—

"SIR ARCHIBALD ACRINGTON."

Beyond question the handwriting of Mistress Cameron was beautifully imitated.

In less than an hour after this there issued from the Black Priory two figures, one a grey bearded old man, and the other a youth attired as page to a good family.

The first was Colonel Blood, and the second John Jeevers.

With all speed they took their way to the palace at Whitehall, but, on nearing it, Blood commenced to walk with slow and faltering footsteps.

His imitation of the gait of a very old man was remarkably good.

The palace being reached, they made straight for the principal entrance.

The whole palace appeared to be almost in darkness.

"Remember," whispered Blood, "if the king is not within the palace, you will wait for him. As soon as you get to the private staircase move not until you hear him above. If you have to wait long 'tis a thousand to one that those on duty will not miss you, or they will think you have become impatient and departed."

The principal entrance being reached, they were challenged by the sentries.

The inscription on the letter, and the

seal being scanned, they were allowed to pass into the hall.

There they were soon accosted by one of the gaudily attired servants, who peremptorily demanded their business; at the same time he eyed them with suspicion.

"Pardon, sir," whined Blood.

"Quick!" interrupted the servant, sternly, "your business."

"To—to deliver this note to Sir Archibald Acrington."

And Blood handed him the letter.

The man took it, turned it over and over, looked closely at the seal, then at the visitors, then again at the letter, and finally said—

"A nice time to bring a letter to Sir Archibald Acrington. From whom do you come?"

"We are not allowed to say."

"Hem! Are you to await an answer?"

"Yes, sir."

"Both of you?"

"Nay," replied Blood; "only this young man, sir. I brought him, because he knew not where the palace was."

"What! Did not know where the palace was? Is he a fool?"

"Nay, sir—a page."

"Well," continued the man, after a pause, and addressing himself to Blood, "since he has to wait, you can retire."

"To be sure, sir."

"You," said the man to Jeevers, "follow me. But I know not whether Sir Archibald will read this note. He is in bed, and will have to be awakened."

Blood having fixed, for a single instant, a significant look at Jeevers, turned and shuffled off.

Just before leaving the house at Leicester Fields, he had said to Jeevers—

"Remember, as soon as the deed is done, you will make all speed to join me. I shall be at the 'Ship Tavern.'"

The servant conducted Jeevers to a waiting-room, and told him not to move until he returned.

Now that Jeevers was well within the palace, the magnificence of everything about him filled him with a kind of awe.

He knew now that he must remain cool and self-possessed, for the slightest thing might betray him.

In that huge handsome room he remained for fully half-an-hour, the only sound which broke the stillness being the steady tramp of the guard.

At last the hall porter returned, accompanied by a youth clad in a dress which Jeevers remembered only too well, the same kind of costume which poor Henri Haddon had worn.

The youth was one of the king's special pages.

"Sir Archibald Acrington," said the servant, "has read the note. He says that you are to wait, for at present the king is engaged, and cannot be disturbed. Follow this page, and he will conduct you to where you are to wait."

Jeevers nodded, and the page at once going on, he followed.

Up the grand staircase they went, along several passages and corridors of enormous length, and, at last, the page halted before a gilt door, screened by a pair of very handsome silk curtains.

"You are to wait in here," he said; "but how long the king will be before he summonses you, I know not."

"This is a beautiful place," whispered Jeevers. "Pray, sir, what part of the palace is this?"

"This is the royal waiting room. Yet," continued the page, with a light laugh, "though this is such a beautiful chamber, the one immediately beneath it is a lumber room. Just beneath yonder ebony table is a trap concealing a hole communicating with this lumber room. But it is never used now. Enter."

So saying, he pushed open the door, and Jeevers found himself in a room which, though much smaller, was considerably more magnificent than any of the others.

"I suppose you will stay here with me?" queried Jeevers.

"Nay," replied the page; "I have duties elsewhere, and must now see about them. But do not be at all alarmed, for no one will interfere with you."

Left alone, Jeevers sat down for a few moments' reflection.

His thoughts were not by any means of the brightest.

The idea of being discovered ran through his mind; but this soon vanished.

He presently rose, and slowly went round the room.

To look at the pictures?

Certainly not.

He went round that beautiful room for two reasons : One was to see if there were any small, but costly articles, such as snuff boxes, &c., which he could conceal in his clothes; and the next was to find the door by which he was to ascend to the royal bedroom.

In this latter he had the greatest difficulty, for Blood had no accurate knowledge of it, and so was unable to give a faithful description of its exact position.

Somewhat listlessly he, at first, began the search, but as no door met his expectant eyes, he became nervous and uneasy, and great drops of perspiration stood out like beads on his forehead.

Most bitterly he thought of Blood for not furnishing him with more accurate details.

At last he stood before an enormous picture.

It reached from the floor almost to the ceiling.

On first entering the room he had noticed it, but had paid little attention to it.

Yet now that he stood right before it, he paid particular attention to it.

The subject was a splendidly attired courtier smiling at a lady, while, at the same time, he motioned with his right hand towards a door, as if to ask whether he should open it.

Eagerly Jeevers looked at this door, and he at once noticed that just below the handle was a small hole.

With trembling hands he brought out the silver key, and after listening intently, plunged it into the hole.

It entered and fitted perfectly.

Here then was the secret entrance to the king's bedchamber.

The door in the picture was the actual door leading to the secret staircase.

It was a most ingenious piece of workmanship, and King Charles thought a very great deal of it, for it was made and painted by his directions, though he got the original idea from France.

Congratulating himself on having made this discovery, Jeevers once more went round the apartment.

Half-an-hour elapsed, and then the door, by which he had entered, was thrown open.

Jeevers expected to see the page re-enter.

But no; the person who entered was King Charles himself.

A very different personage to what he was in the disguise of Master Rushton, he now stood confronting John Jeevers, who had thrown himself upon his knees.

"Rise," said Charles, "and on your life make no noise."

In such peculiar tones were these words uttered, that Jeevers fixed a curious look upon the monarch's face.

He at once saw that he was the worse for drink! Ay, very *much* the worse.

He was supposed to be in the council chamber for the purpose of consulting with his lords respecting the dread plague.

In a chamber beneath, which was connected with the council chamber by a small trap in the flooring, sat Sir Christopher Cullum and Doctor Jardell.

Jeevers rose, and Charles looked straight into his face, or, at least, as straight as he could under the circumstances.

As the monarch looked at him, Jeevers trembled.

He wondered whether Charles, or anyone else, had discovered that the letter was a fraud.

He was soon convinced that nothing had been discovered.

"You have come straight from Misstress Cameron, eh?" said Charles.

"I have, sire."

"Hem! And how fares she?"

"Fairly well, may it please you."

"Ah, fairly well. What are you? She never told me that she employed a page."

"Oh, yes, sire. I have been with Mistress Cameron for some months past."

"Ha! now listen. The reply I desire to send Mistress Cameron, is for no one but the lady herself. You understand that?"

"Most perfectly, sire."

"That's well. You can stay here until my letter is written."

So saying, he left the apartment as hurriedly as he had entered.

He was most anxious to return to his play, for he had latterly been fearfully unlucky, and had lost large sums; but now he felt that his coffers were as good as replenished, for what did this note from Mistress Cameron imply?

Why, that she was about to betray her son's secret as to the money.

"Though that will not prevent me carrying out my intentions," chuckled Charles, "for to Newgate that villain Blood shall go!"

As soon as Charles had gone, Jeevers went to the couch and lay down, intending to do so for a few moments, in case the king should return.

But while laying there his attention became fixed on the ebony table, of which the page had spoken.

"He said there was a trap beneath that table," thought Jeevers, "and that it led to a lumber room. I should, perhaps, be more safe in making my exit that way than by the way I came. I made sure, when the king fixed his eyes on me, that he had penetrated my disguise!"

For some time he lay upon the couch, pondering upon the fearful deed he was about to commit.

Jeevers thought that perhaps, after the deed, Blood would attempt to put him out of the way.

"Ah," he muttered, "he is cunning enough; but with the money which will be mine, I can easily conceal myself in some place where he will not find me."

It never struck him that, supposing he was caught, he had no positive proof that the terrible deed was designed by Colonel Blood.

Not a sound reached his ears save the distant echo of a soldier's tramp, or the dull sound of the closing of a door.

At length he got off the couch, knelt down, and examined the place beneath the table.

Pulling away a huge bear's skin he saw that the page's words were true, for there was the trap.

It was a very small affair, and square in shape.

After contemplating it for a few moments, and again listening for footsteps, Jeevers brought out his dagger, and proceeded to attempt to prize up the piece of polished oak flooring.

He failed, either owing to the fact that the point of his dagger was not strong enough, or because the trap was securely fastened below.

He concluded that the latter was the reason.

"That trap," he muttered, "is fastened safe enough, and no one can pass into the lumber room from this apartment."

Another half hour passed, but still deep silence reigned.

Once only he caught the sound of rapid words, and that he recognised as connected with the changing of the guard.

At last he heard footsteps above.

Instantly he was on his feet.

Was that the king? If so, he was considerably more than half intoxicated, for his footsteps were heavy and unsteady.

Jeevers crept to the secret door and listened.

One moment was sufficient. It was the king, for he recognised his voice and his peculiar chuckle, which did duty for a laugh.

To whom he was talking, if he was talking to anyone, of course he could form no idea.

Presently all was still again.

"I now understand," thought Jeevers. "It was his intention to sleep off the effects of what he has drunk before he sat down to write the letter. By heaven, the time has come! In ten minutes Charles II. will have ceased to exist, and the pockets of John Jeevers will be lined with gold."

Every moment now seemed an hour to him.

Presently Jeevers considered that sufficient time had elapsed, and that now he could venture to ascend.

Once again then the key was inserted in the tiny hole and turned, and the secret door was opened, but very slowly and cautiously.

Jeevers listened for a few seconds; then he stole just within the doorway, and again listened.

At this moment, had he turned his head, he would have seen something which would, no doubt, have caused him to cry out.

The trap door beneath the ebony table was raised to the distance of three or four inches, and a pair of glittering eyes peered through.

Those eyes belonged to no less a person than Clifford Hansard.

But the trap was instantly lowered, and just as Jeevers turned, he pulled the door to after him.

He was now on the first step of the secret staircase.

No sooner had he closed the door, however, than he thought of a most important matter.

He had left the silver key on the other side of the door.

Yet he could have opened it from the inside, but he considered that he had better not, in case one of the pages might enter the waiting-room.

The whole of the secret staircase was profoundly dark, but there was not much chance of making any great noise even if he slipped, for the stairs were most richly carpeted, and silken ropes ran along each wall.

But Jeevers was careful to feel his way as he proceeded.

He counted twelve steps, and then found himself on a narrow landing.

Was the door leading to the king's bed-chamber here?

He felt the walls. Apparently no door was there.

Down on his knees he went, and felt for more stairs.

He found them on the left, and at once commenced to ascend.

He counted six stairs more, and again he was on a small landing.

Looking before him he saw the faint gleam of a light, and he knew from the size of it that it was shining through a keyhole.

Erect now he stood for a few moments to listen.

A terrible object he looked with the glittering weapon clutched firmly in his right hand.

Hearing no sound, he peered through the keyhole.

There, on a magnificent bed, just opposite, fully dressed with the exception of his shoes, lay King Charles.

Apparently he was sound asleep, for while Jeevers looked, he stirred not, and his breathing was the somewhat difficult, uncertain breathing of the intoxicated.

Narrowly Jeevers watched him, and as he watched, his excitement became so great, that he could hear the rapid beating of his own heart.

Once more he turned from the door and listened.

Silence—deep silence—still reigned.

It was an awful moment for John Jeevers.

Another hasty look through the key-hole, and he placed his hand on the handle of the door and gently turned it.

Another second and the door was open, and not the least sound had been made.

Down on his knees went Jeevers, and crept into the splendid apartment after the manner of the deadly Indian who comes upon the object of his hate with the noiselessness of a snake.

Historians have recorded how on many occasions Charles came near losing his life by the hand of the assassin, but he never came so near losing it as on this occasion.

Jeevers got into the shadow of the heavy and richly-embroidered bed curtains, and made ready to strike the blow which would deprive England of a monarch, and cause consternation and horror throughout the whole world.

But suddenly his greedy eyes caught the glitter of a splendid diamond brooch which lay on a dressing table a little to the left.

He could not resist the temptation.

He crept towards it, and just as he reached the table, a face looked in the doorway. Another second, and a dark figure glided in, and like the lightning's flash, darted behind the curtains at the head of the bed.

Having secured the brooch, which he knew must be worth an enormous sum of money, about his person, Jeevers hastily turned and approached the bed.

An instant's glance at the sleeping monarch, and the long terrible blade was upraised over his heart.

Ere it could descend, a figure dashed upon Jeevers.

A sharp, but loud cry, a curse, a wild struggle, and then with a mighty crash, John Jeevers fell dead at the side of the royal bedstead—a dagger plunged to the hilt in his heart.

At the same moment Charles, with a fearful cry, leapt from his bed.

Seizing a silken cord which hung near him, he frantically pulled it.

" Help ! " he screamed—" help !

Here's murder, my lords! Ha, murder. By the saints, murder, my lords!"

Swiftly through an opposite door dashed several noble lords, together with a number of pages.

Most of the former had been partners of his majesty during the night, and were more or less intoxicated.

But when they beheld the horrible sight on the floor, they were quickly sobered, and each gave utterance to a genuine cry of horror and surprise.

Before a word could be spoken, another nobleman walked in.

It was Rochester.

Leisurely, with proud, and certainly more king-like tread than Charles himself, he strode into the royal bed-chamber.

Room was made for him, and, in a moment, he stood beside the trembling king, looking down upon the evil face of the would-be assassin.

"What is this, sire?" he asked, in cool, steady tones. "Eh? What can be the meaning of this terrible scare?"

"The meaning, eh? The meaning?" cried Charles, as he pointed his trembling finger at Jeevers. "Is any explanation required, eh? Look—an assassin, my lords! Holy Mary! I came near being finished had it not been for that courageous young man."

"How did he get here?" asked Rochester.

"Eh? How? Odd's fish! how the devil should I know? For the matter of that, my lord, how on earth did *this* one get here?" And the king pointed to Clifford.

"It is a matter for investigation, of course," said Rochester, fixing his eyes full upon the face of the individual standing so firm and erect over the body of John Jeevers. "Who are you, sirrah? What is your name?"

"Clifford Hansard!" was the bold reply.

"Clifford Hansard!" shouted Rochester, drawing slowly back.

"Clifford Hansard!" muttered the king, fixing his eyes upon our hero. "Can it be possible?"

"'Tis true," replied Clifford. "I am Clifford Hansard. How I came to be here, and have saved your life, sire, will be explained."

"Explained!" yelled Rochester, furiously. "By whom—by whom, sirrah?"

"By Sir Christopher Cullum."

"What does his words prove, your majesty?" said Rochester. "What! but that Sir Christopher is concerned in some plot to take your life."

"It is false!" interrupted a ringing voice, and Sir Christopher Cullum himself strode rapidly across the apartment—a look of stern indignation upon his handsome features.

Striding immediately before Rochester, he said—

"I repeat, my lord of Rochester, that the accusation you were about to make against me is a lying one. His majesty has no more loyal servant than myself. And to that his majesty will bear testimony."

"Yes, yes," answered Charles; "we never had reason to doubt the loyalty of Sir Christopher Cullum, and you were wrong to hint that he was concerned in anything against our person, Rochester. But odd's fish! Is this a time to haggle about such matters? Lord help us all!" he cried, "what scant attention you pay to the fact that, even at this very instant, I might have been lying on that bed with a dagger through my heart. There lies the wretch, the would-be assassin."

"But who is he?" once again Rochester interrupted.

"God's mercy on us!" cried Charles, "how should I know who he is?"

"Let me have a closer look at him," said Rochester, bending over the prostrate, repulsive - looking figure. "Ha! you see he was disguised. His hair—— ha! as I live, I recognise him."

"Eh? You do?" cried Charles. "Well, who is he?"

"His name is John Jeevers."

Clifford started violently, and so did Sir Christopher Cullum, for our hero knew not who the person was he had slain—in fact, it had never struck him that he was disguised.

But now Clifford bent down, and looked closely into his face.

"Yes," he said, "I also recognise him. His name is certainly John Jeevers, and he was one of the ruffians in the pay of Colonel Blood."

"Lord save us!" moaned the king, "Colonel Blood again."

"He was nothing of the kind—at least, not to my knowledge," said Rochester, hastily correcting himself. "Colonel Blood is bad enough, no doubt; but he is not so utterly abandoned as to plan an attempt on the king's life."

Clifford looked quickly up.

Contain himself any longer was out of the question.

"You, my Lord Rochester," he said, "are as bad, if not worse, than Blood."

"Sire!" thundered Rochester, "will you permit this, and in your presence?"

"Peace — peace — peace!" cried Charles.

"Sire, have I not proved that this youth, Clifford Hansard," continued Rochester, in furious tones, "is a murderer of the most determined type? And did not your majesty sign a warrant for his committal to Newgate? I have it here," he cried, in exultant tones, as he snatched the document from his pocket, "and he shall be at once arrested."

The king was bewildered.

Only just recovering from the fumes of the various intoxicants he had consumed—dazed by what had occurred, and horrified at the hideous sight before him—it was no wonder he trembled.

"Sire," said Sir Christopher, directing a most contemptuous glance at Rochester, "surely your majesty, in view of the fact that Clifford Hansard has saved you from a horrible death, will cancel the warrant?"

"Most assuredly we do," replied Charles, who at once remembered that the cancelling of a warrant cost him nothing. "Yes, yes; to be sure—to be sure. We never did believe that he committed the murders you accused him of, Rochester, and we cancel the warrant."

"Would it not be as well, sire, if I saw it properly destroyed?" asked Sir Christopher.

"No," said Rochester, angrily. "Since it has pleased his majesty to direct that the warrant be cancelled, he will see that it is destroyed."

"And now I hope ye have done haggling," cried Charles. "If such be the case, perhaps ye will attend to the matter which, to me at any rate, is the more important. Now," he said, turning to Clifford, "let us know how ye came to be within this palace? Of course, we know that you were appointed assistant to Sir Christopher Cullum."

"With your permission, sire," said Sir Christopher, "I will give you the explanation, and I feel assured that you will be perfectly satisfied with it."

"Well, well; go on."

"We had most important matters of a domestic nature to talk about, sire: and, as you know, I was so busy with State affairs that I had not any time to spare, I bade him accompany me to the palace, knowing that, in his present disguise, he would not be recognised."

"Odd's fish! you are right there," muttered the king.

"So he came with me," continued Sir Christopher; "but as I had to work in the room immediately beneath the council chamber in which your majesty was, I deemed it advisable that he should retire until a convenient opportunity occurred for us to continue our conversation. I, therefore, placed him in the chaplain's room. Of what occurred since I put him there, he alone can explain."

"Not feeling inclined to sleep," said Clifford, "I wandered about the apartment looking at the arms. While looking at some, I noticed a small door. Pushing it open, I saw that it led to a kind of passage. It was full of arms of all kinds. I took a lantern and entered.

"Seeing a ladder before me, I raised the lantern and looked upward. Then it was that I noticed a peculiar scraping noise, like someone trying to raise the trap with a dagger. Curiosity prompted me to ascend the ladder. I found that there was a kind of well sunk in the vaulted ceiling.

"I carefully felt it, and found that there was a door at the top. It was secured with a couple of bolts; and then, after listening and hearing no noise, I raised the flap just a little. I saw this would-be assassin looking through the secret door. When he had passed through, he closed it, but he had forgotten to take the key—a silver one—from the other side. So, after a short time, I followed him.

"Your majesty knows the rest."

"You have done well, Clifford Hansard," cried the king, warmly, "and we shall not forget you. I must have time to think about what has occurred. Sir Christopher shall communicate to you the result of our deliberations.

"In the meantime, we charge you all here present to utter no word as to what has occurred. The state of our kingdom is bad enough at present. The affair must be hushed up, my lords—hushed up. Had the villain been captured instead of slain, it would have been a different affair; but as it is, it must be hushed up. For the disposal of this body, Sir Christopher, I look to you."

"And the warrant, sire?"

"Eh? Ah! the warrant, yes. Where is Rochester, my lords?"

"Just this instant left the chamber," was the reply.

"Gone, eh? Ah, well, trouble not about the warrant, Sir Christopher—nor you, Master Hansard; it shall be destroyed."

Sir Christopher summoned two or three of the soldiers, and the body of John Jeevers was taken away, a grave was dug for him, and he was buried.

The king hurriedly made his way to Sir Archibald Acrington, made him acquainted with all the facts, and then gave him particular instructions what to do.

The result was that some little time after, when Sir Christopher made inquiries, not a single soul had seen Jeevers enter the palace.

Sir Christopher knew from this that the king had some private, as well as public, reason for hushing the matter up; but how did the assassin get possession of the silver key?

"At any rate, on this occasion," he said to Clifford, "we know that it is not Colonel Blood who was the author of the plot, for he is too securely caged."

"Ay," replied Clifford, "and I fancy that unless some wonderful miracle has occurred, he is still within his cage. And there he is likely to remain until the flesh rots from his bones, and his bones crumble into dust."

"He deserves his fate," replied Sir Christopher, gravely; "but you have to remember this, my dear Clifford, in Rochester you have as bitter an enemy as Blood. I noted the fierce look of hatred he frequently directed at you. I know this, that the greatest injury anyone can inflict upon Rochester, is to take from him a woman on whom he had set his heart—if heart he has—and that you have done; but, above all things, keep wary of Rochester and his emissaries!"

CHAPTER XX.

UNDER WHAT CIRCUMSTANCES A MARRIAGE CEREMONY TOOK PLACE AT PALL MALL—AND OF WHAT TOOK PLACE AT THE OLD TOWER STEPS.

THE day after the attempted assassination of the king saw Clifford once more attired in a becoming costume.

On this occasion it was a costume far more costly than any he had previously donned.

He was seated at Sir Christopher's table busily engaged with the copying of some documents, but, in reality, most anxiously awaiting Sir Christopher's appearance, that gentleman having left the palace some two or three hours previously, in order to explain to those at Pall Mall what had occurred, and to prepare them for Clifford's re-appearance.

It was about six in the evening, and Clifford was becoming anxious, when Sir Christopher entered.

Clifford instantly noticed that his face wore a most grave expression—so grave, indeed, that he was at once filled with the most direful apprehensions.

Starting up from his seat, and rushing towards Sir Christopher with outstretched hands, he asked—

"Sir Christopher, what has happened? In heaven's name, tell me!"

"Stay, stay, my dear lad!" interrupted Sir Christopher, in tones of deep affection, as he laid his hands on Clifford's shoulders, and looked into his eager face. "One moment, and I will tell you all. You know, my lad, it was but a short time ago that I urged upon you the necessity for being prepared for any news of an alarming nature so far as Olivia wa concerned.

"Hish! interrupt me not, my lad! The worst has not come to her you love! Doctor Jardell, as you know, is a clever man. There is hope!"

"Ah!" gasped Clifford, fervently clasping his hands. "Hope! hope! God be thanked! But from the seriousness of your face I thought——"

"My seriousness," said Sir Christopher, "arose from these facts—the doctors unanimously agree that if Olivia is to be restored to health, it is necessary that she leave the country."

"Leave the country!" exclaimed Clifford. "Alas! she has not a friend or relation abroad."

"Nay, nay. We know it; she has told us so. But the solution has been reached. It is this—that a marriage should at once take place between you, thus Olivia can leave the country, escorted by her husband. I shall lose, at any rate for a time, a dear friend—yourself."

A thrill of joy rang through Clifford's frame as he thought of the suggestion.

"With all my heart and soul do I agree," he said. "And Olivia, Sir Christopher, what says she?"

"She agrees, Clifford. She loves you most passionately, and only desires to be always as near you as possible."

"But where should we go, Sir Christopher?"

"To France. Sir Richard has an intimate relation in Calais, and you will bear a letter to him. I need not tell you, Clifford, that money matters will not be a source of worry to you, as it is my intention to place at your disposal exactly half of what you rescued at Chancery Lane."

"Oh, Sir Christopher," exclaimed Clifford, "such generosity——"

"Has only been deserved by you, Clifford. Say not another word. I am determined that you shall have half. It is only right and just; for had it not been for your indomitable courage, not a crown of that money would ever have been mine.

"I propose to place it in the hands of Master Richard Reiner, the well-known merchant of Eastcheap, in your name, and you can draw upon his agents in France."

"All you advise I will do," replied Clifford, "and I return you my heartfelt thanks. I shall leave the country with the hope that poor Olivia, under the influence of a different atmosphere, will soon entirely recover. But I shall not leave the country without feeling a bitter pang at parting with my friends —the best of whom is you, Sir Christopher."

"My dear Clifford," said Sir Christopher, as he shook Clifford warmly by the hands, "though many months must elapse ere Olivia can be restored to perfect health, we shall be in constant communication with each other; and, by-and-bye, if heaven is pleased to spare us, we shall meet again. Most devoutly do I hope that, if you are both spared to return to this country again, it will be when the terrible plague shall have completely departed.

*   *   *   *

"But now to speak of something else.

"On leaving Pall Mall one of Sir Richard's servants accosted me, and requested permission to speak. I told him to proceed, and thereupon informed me that Rochester had been several times seen in the neighbourhood. Evidently he has some object in view, but what I cannot imagine. I instructed the servant that if he should again see his lordship, he must find an opportunity to speak to him, and inform him that Olivia Preston was sick unto death. If he has still Olivia Preston in his mind, that will, beyond doubt, put an end to his thoughts in that direction, at any rate, for a time, and until you have left the country.

"And now, Clifford, let us depart. First, we will procure the necessary license and a clergyman, and then to Pall Mall to complete the business."

In two hours' time, there was assembled in the beautiful drawing-room at Sir Richard's residence, the following persons—

Sir Christopher Cullum, Clarissa, and Doctor Jardell; Clifford Hansard and Olivia Preston, the clergyman, the host and hostess, Sir Richard and Lady Wemyss; and in the background, several of the upper servants. Olivia— poor girl!—was most beautifully attired.

She looked lovely indeed, but her face was very pale and looked thin.

But a joyous smile lit up her face as she stood, her white thin hand in her lover's grasp.

They were never to be parted again. Oh, what rapture was there in that thought.

Amid a deep silence the clergyman, in impressive tones, commenced the marriage service.

The ceremony was soon concluded, and the young couple having received the warm congratulations of all present, Clifford, with Sir Christopher and Doctor Jardell, retired with Sir Richard to his study, where the necessary arrangements were to be concluded.

It was decided that the pair should sail in a merchant vessel, the property of the merchant, Richard Reiner, which was then lying off the Tower; and a letter was at once written, directing Master Reiner to make the necessary arrangements, and to request the captain to keep himself and his men on the alert.

It also requested the merchant to make his appearance at Pall Mall, with half-a-dozen of his most trusted and strongest men-servants.

This letter was despatched by a young page of the name of Crowley, of whom more anon.

It reached its destination in safety, and an hour afterwards, the banker and his servants made their appearance.

Master Reiner's astonishment may be imagined when he learned that he was required to take charge of so vast a sum of hard cash.

An hour afterwards a waggon was hired, and Sir Christopher Cullum, the merchant, and his servants went to Chancery Lane.

They found the money closely guarded by faithful Martin Waltman—so faithfully, indeed, that one of the servants came very near losing his life—the result of not answering when challenged by Martin.

Another hour saw the money safely deposited in Master Reiner's vaults.

Sir Christopher assured Waltman that in future he would take care of him.

Clifford gave him a note to the costumier, directing him to give up all the money in his possession to Martin, less the amount for the use of the disguises and the chair.

Of that sum Martin was to take one hundred to the villainous undertaker, Mollbury, and get a receipt, and the number of the grave at St. Andrew's where poor Master Preston and his wife were lying.

On the following night he was to act as one of the chair-bearers to Clifford and his wife.

It was arranged that they should go unaccompanied, so that they would not attract attention.

We will not describe the leave-taking.

It is sufficient for us to say that it was of a most affecting nature.

* * * *

The young page, Crowley, was a good-looking, but remarkably careless youth, of about sixteen or thereabouts.

The taking of a message all the way to Eastcheap was a source of the greatest joy to him; for not knowing the actual terrors of the plague, he made up his mind to enjoy himself.

But Sir Richard was a strict master, and knowing this only too well, the page made his way without stopping to the merchant's.

As we have seen the letter was safely delivered, but not before the page had made himself perfectly familiar with the contents, which was owing to the fact that Sir Richard had omitted to seal the letter.

It is a thousand to one that the page would never have taken the trouble to read the letter, but he felt sure that it must be something about the young couple who had been married, under such peculiar circumstances, in his master's house.

Having delivered the letter, he set about "enjoying himself."

But he soon found that he would have to abandon his intentions, for when he came to look about him, he found sufficient on all sides to horrify him.

He was appalled at what he beheld.

Wandering on, he at length reached the Tower of London.

It was the first time that he had beheld the grim-looking fortress in his life.

While attentively scanning it, a hand was laid upon his shoulder.

Swiftly turning, he found himself face to face with a man attired in a long cloak, having a broad beaver hat drawn over his brows, and a mask concealing his features.

The young page trembled in his shoes.

He thought himself in the power of one of the Alsatian bravos, about whom he had heard such terrible stories.

But such was not the case.

The person who thus laid his hand on his shoulder was no less a person than Lord Rochester.

"Well, my young friend," said Rochester, "and what do you in such a neighbourhood at such an hour?"

"I—I——" stammered the page.

"Don't be afraid, my young friend," laughed Rochester. "I am no bogie, I do assure you, and I shall neither eat, drink you, nor wilfully attack you. I asked you what you did in this neighbourhood, because, you see, I recognise you as one of Sir Richard Wemyss' pages. Eh, is not that so?"

"Oh, sir," exclaimed the page, "I beg that you will not inform my master that you saw me hereabouts."

"Fear it not," answered Rochester, with another laugh, "though I am a most particular friend of Sir Richard's, I should not think of getting one of his pages into trouble. I see you are a stranger to these parts."

"Oh, quite, your worship."

"Out for a holiday?"

"Nay, sir; I have been to Master Reiner's, the banker at Eastcheap, with a letter—a very important letter."

"Indeed!"

"He has not long ago left the house in Pall Mall, that is certain," thought Rochester; "and if I am careful, I may learn a deal as to what is taking place there."

Aloud he said—

"Let me tell you, my lad, that it is dangerous in the extreme to wander alone about such a neighbourhood as this. But, of course, you, like all youths of your age, are curious. Now, if you will promise not to say one word to Sir Richard, or anyone else, I will protect you round the Tower walls, and, on a future occasion, I will take you within the fortress."

The page thanked the masked stranger.

Rochester showed him round the hoary old walls, pointing out this and that, and answering the questions put to him by the unsuspecting page.

Not the slightest idea ever entered the youngster's head as to who his conductor might be.

The wearing of a mask was, as we have previously remarked, so common an occurrence, that the page had no cause for wondering why his conductor should wear such a thing.

"And now," said Rochester, "having shown you the Tower, come with me, and you shall partake of a glass of most excellent wine."

"No, sir," interrupted the page, "that I really must not do, though I sincerely thank you; but I must hurry home."

"You shall not stay more than a few minutes," said Rochester. "What! refuse a splendid cup of wine? Come, don't be so foolish, but follow me."

So saying, Rochester turned, and strode swiftly towards the "Ship."

Strange to say, on this occasion, there were very few loafers about.

Had there been, no doubt their appearance would have frightened the page, and he would have taken to his heels.

Rochester walked through the passage, up the stairs, and giving the signal, the door opened, and in a few moments, he, with the page at his side, stood before the door of Blood's room.

Knocking on the door in a somewhat peculiar fashion, he uttered four words in French.

Blood, who was at his table, started up as the knock was given, and recognising what was said, snatched a mask from the table, and assuming it, placed his hat upon his head.

Then dropping into his seat again, he said—

"Enter!"

Rochester walked in, the page at his heels.

"At last!" exclaimed Blood. "At last! Are you aware how long it is since last we met?"

This question was asked in such fierce, stern tones, that Rochester opened his eyes in wonder.

Giving utterance to his well-known laugh, he sank into a seat.

"Business anon," he said. "Behold a young friend of mine."

"Friend, eh?"

"Ay. Come here, master page, and show yourself. One of Sir Richard Wemyss' servants."

At these words Blood almost leapt from his seat.

The fierce look in his cunning eyes disappeared as if by magic, and smiling graciously, he said—

"Anyone in the service of my very dear friend, Sir Richard Wemyss, is more than welcome. Come hither my lad, and let me shake thee by the hand."

The page, considerably astonished, and somewhat uneasy at the way he was addressed, advanced and shook Blood by the hand.

Had he known whose hand that was, he would have flown through the door as if Satan himself were at his heels.

"He has no time to stay," said Rochester, directing a significant look at Blood; "he will drink just one small cup of wine, and then he must return."

While Blood was pouring out the wine, Rochester took a piece of paper from his pocket and spread it out, saying—

"Oh, here is a letter from our French friend. I suppose you neither read nor speak French, master page?"

"No, your worship."

"Listen to what he says," continued Rochester, and thereupon, while pretending to read the letter in French, he informed Blood that now was the time to get full particulars of what was transpiring at Pall Mall.

Most readily did Blood understand.

"Ah," he said, "and a very nice letter, too; but put it aside now while we have a word or two with master page. Good wine, eh?"

"Most excellent," was the reply.

"Have another, and——"

"Oh, no, sir; thank you."

"Pooh! that wine will never hurt you, my lad. Do have another. You will not often have the chance to taste such excellent wine, I warrant you."

The page certainly found the wine very palatable, and he did not require much urging to accept another.

Little by little Blood and Rochester wormed out everything the page knew.

He told them what the letter contained, but, very fortunately, nothing was said in it in reference to the money.

Having learned what they wanted to, Rochester gave the page a guinea, escorted him to the door of the hostelry, and bade him hasten to Pall Mall, and, above all, mention not one word as to where he had been.

"Now," cried Rochester, "what think you of the whole proceedings?"

"Most remarkable!" exclaimed Blood. "I cannot understand it."

"And they are about to slip through our fingers for ever!"

"That they shall not do, I swear!"

"But just one moment. Blood, what think you is the reason of this visit?"

"I don't know, except it is to keep an appointment."

"No!" cried Rochester. "I have come for some money. It is most urgently needed."

"Listen to me, my lord!" thundered Blood, bringing his fist, with a mighty crash, upon the table. "Had you kept the appointment sooner, you would have learned what had occurred to me; how I was shut up in those chambers in Lincoln's Inn and robbed of all my wealth."

"What! Shut up? Who shut you up?"

"Clifford Hansard!"

"By heaven! is it possible?"

Blood told him all that had occurred; but he said nothing of the plot in the attempt to work out which Jeevers had lost his life.

Rochester listened intently to his recital, and when he had finished, he said—

"Yes; it is evident that the king is determined to place you where he will always be able to find you. But if your plot had been successful——"

"What plot?"

"Colonel Blood, do not pretend ignorance of what has occurred at Whitehall Palace. You know, quite as well as I do, that your last plot—unquestionably the biggest plot you ever conceived—has failed."

"Yes, yes," said Blood, moodily, "I will not pretend ignorance of it—to you who are so penetrating and suspicious—and I know that it failed, and that Jeevers was slain."

"A most fortunate circumstance for you, Blood!"

"Why?"

"Because had he been taken red-handed, he would have made a confession, and your arrest and death by torture would have followed."

Blood scowled, and shifted uneasily in his chair.

After a few seconds' pause, he said—

"The man who slew John Jeevers—the man who prevented the carrying out of that splendid plot was Sir Christopher Cullum."

Again Rochester's sardonic laugh rang out.

"Sir Christopher Cullum," he said, contemptuously, "nothing of the sort. Rumours of all sorts have been flying about the palace; but this is the first time anyone suggested that the slayer of the assassin was Sir Christopher Cullum. The one who slew John Jeevers was Clifford Hansard!"

With such frantic haste did Blood leap to his feet, that the table was almost overturned.

"What!" he roared, "Clifford Hansard! If this is true, I will have his life."

"It is true; but sit down, my excitable friend. Drink a glass of wine, and I will tell you the story."

Blood obeyed.

"I will tell you what it is," said Blood, in hoarse, deep tones, when Rochester had concluded, "we must set our hearts upon one thing: Sir Christopher Cullum and Clifford Hansard must be removed."

"That is your everlasting cry, Colonel. Had I been in your place, it would have been done long ago. Now it is almost too late—with regard to one of them, at any rate."

"Why?"

"Why! What does the page say? This newly-wedded couple are about to take an immediate leave of the country; but they shall be intercepted. Have you a bag here?"

"I have—behold!"

And opening a drawer in the table, Blood brought out a bag bearing the dreaded White Circle, and placed it before Rochester.

"Good!" said his lordship; "that will be for Clifford Hansard. If we are careful we shall have him this time; but bear this in mind: the girl is, on no account, to be injured. She shall yet become my abject slave."

"As, I trust, Clarissa Jardell will yet be mine," said Blood.

"You can depend upon my aid when the proper time arrives," returned Rochester, gnashing his teeth; "for I am determined to revenge myself on Sir Christopher Cullum for his contemptuous and defiant speech to me in the presence of the king. And remember this, Blood: Clifford Hansard, when captured, is not to be confined in one of your houses; he is to be slain at once."

"Do not fear," replied Blood, fiercely, as his hand wandered to his dagger. "He shall not escape my vengeance this time."

* * * *

It had been intended that the vessel which was to convey our hero and his beautiful, but ailing wife to the shores of France, should have sailed early in the evening of the following day; but owing to the fact that the captain—a tall, burly mariner, named Seth Collins—had important family matters to attend to on shore, the departure had to be delayed until the hour of ten.

The vessel, the "Ocean Wave," a small, smart-looking craft, lay at some little distance off the Tower, and the banker's orders were to the effect that a boat, fully manned, was to be kept at the ship's side, ready to push off to the Tower steps the instant the signal (three blasts from a whistle furnished by the captain himself) should be given.

The night came on, and a terrible night it was in good truth.

For hours a fine rain had been falling; but soon after night a fog began to descend upon the unhappy city.

Gradually it became denser and denser, until at last nothing could be seen a few feet ahead. Yet some of the streets were most brilliantly illuminated.

Many of the inhabitants, still believing that the burning of huge bonfires would have the effect of purifying the nauseous atmosphere, had lit them here and there in the middle of the streets.

It was just about half-past nine when the sedan-chair containing Clifford and Olivia, halted before St. Paul's Cathedral for a first rest.

So far all had been well.